TAKEN BY THE KRINAR

ANNA ZAIRES

 Mozaika Publications ♠

Copyright © 2019 Anna Zaires and Dima Zales
www.annazaires.com

Published by Mozaika Publications, an imprint of Mozaika LLC.
www.mozaikallc.com

Cover by Najla Qamber Designs
www.najlaqamberdesigns.com

eISBN: 978-1-63142-488-5
Print ISBN: 978-1-63142-489-2

THE KRINAR CAPTIVE

CHAPTER ONE

I don't want to die. I don't want to die. Please, please, please, I don't want to die.

The words kept repeating in her mind, a hopeless prayer that would never be heard. Her fingers slipped another inch on the rough wooden board, her nails breaking as she tried to maintain her grip.

Emily Ross was hanging by her fingernails—literally—off a broken old bridge. Hundreds of feet below, water rushed over the rocks, the mountain stream full from recent rains.

Those rains were partially responsible for her current predicament. If the wood on the bridge had been dry, she might not have slipped, twisting her foot in the process. And she certainly wouldn't have fallen onto the rail that had broken under her weight.

It was only a last-minute desperate grab that had prevented Emily from plummeting to her death below. As she was falling, her right hand had caught a small protrusion on the side of the bridge, leaving her dangling in the air hundreds of feet above the hard rocks.

I don't want to die. I don't want to die. Please, please, please, I don't want to die.

It wasn't fair. It wasn't supposed to happen this way. This was her vacation, her regain-sanity time. How could she die now? She hadn't even begun living yet.

Images of the last two years slid through Emily's brain, like the PowerPoint presentations she'd spent so many hours making. Every late night, every weekend spent in the office—it had all been for nothing. She'd lost her job during the layoffs, and now she was about to lose her life.

No, no!

Emily's legs flailed, her nails digging deeper into the wood. Her other arm reached up, stretching toward the bridge. This wouldn't happen to her. She wouldn't let it. She had worked too hard to let a stupid jungle bridge defeat her.

Blood ran down her arm as the rough wood tore the skin off her fingers, but she ignored the pain. Her only hope of survival lay in trying to grab onto the side of the bridge with her other hand, so she could pull herself up. There was no one around to rescue her, no one to save her if she didn't save herself.

The possibility that she might die alone in the rainforest had not occurred to Emily when she'd embarked on this trip. She was used to hiking, used to camping. And even after the hell of the past two years, she was still in good shape, strong and fit from running and playing sports all through high school and college. Costa Rica was considered a safe destination, with a low crime rate and tourist-friendly population. It was

4

inexpensive too—an important factor for her rapidly dwindling savings account.

She'd booked this trip *before*. Before the market had fallen again, before another round of layoffs that had cost thousands of Wall Street workers their jobs. Before Emily went to work on Monday, bleary-eyed from working all weekend, only to leave the office the same day with all her possessions in a small cardboard box.

Before her four-year relationship had fallen apart.

Her first vacation in two years, and she was going to die.

No, don't think that way. It won't happen.

But Emily knew she was lying to herself. She could feel her fingers slipping farther, her right arm and shoulder burning from the strain of supporting the weight of her entire body. Her left hand was inches away from reaching the side of the bridge, but those inches could've easily been miles. She couldn't get a strong enough grip to lift herself up with one arm.

Do it, Emily! Don't think, just do it!

Gathering all her strength, she swung her legs in the air, using the momentum to bring her body higher for a fraction of a second. Her left hand grabbed onto the protruding board, clutched at it... and the fragile piece of wood snapped, startling her into a terrified scream.

Emily's last thought before her body hit the rocks was the hope that her death would be instant.

———

The smell of jungle vegetation, rich and pungent, teased Zaron's nostrils. He inhaled deeply, letting the humid air fill his lungs. It was clean here, in this tiny corner of Earth, almost as unpolluted as on his home planet.

He needed this now. Needed the fresh air, the isolation. For the past six months, he'd tried to run from his thoughts, to exist only in the moment, but he'd failed. Even blood and sex were not enough for him anymore. He could distract himself while fucking, but the pain always came back afterwards, as strong as ever.

Finally, it had gotten to be too much. The dirt, the crowds, the stink of humanity. When he wasn't lost in a fog of ecstasy, he was disgusted, his senses overwhelmed from spending so much time in human cities. It was better here, where he could breathe without inhaling poison, where he could smell life instead of chemicals. In a few years, everything would be different, and he might try living in a human city again, but not yet.

Not until they were fully settled here.

That was Zaron's job: to oversee the settlements. He had been doing research on Earth fauna and flora for decades, and when the Council requested his assistance with the upcoming colonization, he hadn't hesitated. Anything was better than being home, where memories of Larita's presence were everywhere.

There were no memories here. For all of its similarities to Krina, this planet was strange and exotic. Seven billion *Homo sapiens* on Earth—an unthinkable number—and they were multiplying at a dizzying pace. With their short lifespans and the resulting lack of long-term thinking, they were consuming their planet's resources with utter disregard for the future. In some ways, they reminded him of *Schistocerca gregaria*—a species of locusts he'd studied several years ago.

Of course, humans were more intelligent than insects. A few individuals, like Einstein, were even Krinar-like in some aspects of their thinking. It wasn't particularly surprising to Zaron; he had always thought this might be the intent of the Elders' grand experiment.

Walking through the Costa Rican forest, he found himself thinking about the task at hand. This part of the planet was promising; it was easy to picture edible plants from Krina thriving here. He had done extensive tests on the soil, and he had some ideas on how to make it even more hospitable to Krinar flora.

All around him, the forest was lush and green, filled with the fragrance of blooming heliconias and the sounds of rustling leaves and native birds. In the distance, he could hear the cry of an *Alouatta palliata*, a howler monkey native to Costa Rica, and something else.

Frowning, Zaron listened closer, but the sound didn't repeat.

Curious, he headed in that direction, his hunting instincts on alert. For a second, the sound had reminded him of a woman's scream.

Moving through the thick jungle vegetation with ease, Zaron put on a burst of speed, leaping over a small creek and the bushes that stood in his way. Out here, away from human eyes, he could move like a Krinar without worrying about exposure. Within a couple of minutes, he was close enough to pick up the scent. Sharp and coppery, it made his mouth water and his cock stir.

It was blood.

Human blood.

Reaching his destination, Zaron stopped, staring at the sight in front of him.

In front of him was a river, a mountain stream swollen from recent rains. And on the large black rocks in the middle, beneath an old wooden bridge spanning the gorge, was a body.

A broken, twisted body of a human girl.

CHAPTER TWO

*S*wearing under his breath, Zaron jumped into the river. Had he been human, the powerful current would've instantly carried him away. As it was, he had to use all of his strength to swim across the foaming water. Several times his kicking legs struck underwater rocks, but he ignored the pain. Bruises were nothing to those of his kind; by the time he reached the boulders ahead, the injuries would already be healed.

Finally, he was there, clambering up onto the slippery rocks and crouching beside the girl lying there. She was alive; he could hear her weak, erratic heartbeat and the gurgling sounds of her breathing.

She was alive, but judging by her injuries, she wouldn't be much longer.

Her lower body was twisted at a strange angle, and her slender limbs were broken in several places, with bone fragments protruding from torn, pale flesh. Half of her face was covered with blood, the dark red liquid oozing sullenly from a deep gash in the side of her skull. Her short-sleeved shirt hid most of the damage to her torso, but Zaron suspected she was hemorrhaging internally, her ribcage likely shattered by her fall.

His stomach tightening with a mixture of pity and strange despair, Zaron stared at the broken human. She was young and, from what he could see, quite pretty. Long pale blond hair, clear skin, a slim, shapely build... If she hadn't been on the verge of death, he might've been attracted to her.

But she was as good as dead. At best, she had a few more minutes to live. With such extensive injuries, it was surprising that her heart was beating at all. Humans were fragile creatures, easily hurt and slow to heal. He doubted human doctors would be able to fix her, even if they managed to get here in time. Krinar medicine could save her, of course, but Zaron didn't have anything on him, and the girl was unlikely to survive the trip to his house.

Lifting his hand, he lightly touched the uninjured side of her face, running his fingers along her jawline. Her skin was soft and smooth, like that of a baby. A sharp pang of regret pierced his chest; under different circumstances, he would've very much enjoyed her.

Suddenly, a small broken sound escaped her throat, startling Zaron. And then, much to his shock, her eyes opened.

Framed by thick brown lashes, they were a bright blue-green and strikingly beautiful.

For a moment, she seemed disoriented, those sea-colored eyes clouded with pain, but then her gaze sharpened, focusing on his face.

She knew she was about to die. Zaron could see it on her

face. She knew, and she was fighting it with every cell of her being.

Her mouth moved, her lips opening in a wordless plea, and he knew what he had to do.

Reaching for the girl, Zaron gently picked her up, cradling her against his chest.

It was almost certain she would not survive the trip, but he couldn't let her go like this.

Nobody who clung to life so fiercely should have to die without a fight.

———

The trip seemed to take forever, though Zaron ran as fast as he could, taking care not to jostle the girl too much. The hardest part had been the river; battling the current with one hand while holding the girl above the water with another had been challenging even for him.

She was unconscious again. He could hear the harsh rattling in her lungs, and he knew she wouldn't last much longer. Her face was deathly pale, her skin cold and clammy from the river.

Finally, they were there.

Carrying her into his dwelling, Zaron carefully laid her on his bed. A sharp voice command and one of the walls opened, allowing *jansha*—a small, tubular healing device—to float toward him. Grabbing it from mid-air, Zaron placed it on the bed before starting to undress the girl. She wasn't wearing much—just a T-shirt and cut-off jeans—and he made short work of her clothing, his chest tightening at the sight of protruding bones and torn flesh.

Picking up the device, he ran it over her nude body, letting it diagnose her injuries. As he had suspected, they were extensive. Aside from damage to her internal organs, she had a spinal cord injury. Even if she had managed to survive, she would've been paralyzed from the waist down.

There were other injuries as well. Broken bones, a gash on her skull, scrapes and bruises—those all seemed to be from her accident. However, there were signs of an earlier trauma as well. At some point, she'd broken her wrist, and there was scar tissue on her leg from some other mishap. She'd also been subjected to primitive human dental care, with some of her teeth hollowed out and patched up with non-organic filling.

Zaron hesitated only for a moment before enabling jansha's complete healing mode. If he had more time and her injuries weren't so severe, he could've calibrated the device to focus on specific wounds. But as it was, a full-body procedure was her best chance at survival.

The device vibrated for a second, releasing the healing nanocytes, and Zaron watched as the girl's damaged flesh began to knit together, each of her cells regenerating from within.

CHAPTER THREE

*S*lowly waking up, Emily became aware of the fact that she felt good.

Really, truly good.

She was neither hot nor cold, and the blanket covering her was of just the right weight and thickness. The mattress underneath her was incredibly comfortable as well; it was as though she was sleeping on something custom-made for her body. She was also surprisingly relaxed. The ever-present tension in the back of her neck was absent for the first time in months.

A smile of contentment curved her lips, and Emily snuggled deeper under the covers. This had to be the best night of sleep she'd had in ages. She could hardly believe it had occurred at a cheap little inn in a remote area of Costa Rica.

It had to be the fresh air and exercise, she decided, still reluctant to open her eyes. All that hiking must've worn her out. *Hiking…* Something buzzed at the back of her brain, something disturbing—

The fall off the bridge! Gasping, Emily jackknifed into a sitting position, her eyes flying open.

She wasn't at the inn.

She also wasn't dead.

For a second, those two facts seemed irreconcilable. If she had dreamed the entire horrible event, shouldn't she have woken up at the last place she remembered going to sleep? And if it hadn't been a dream, where was she? Why wasn't she dead, or at least badly injured?

Her heart racing, Emily took in her surroundings, clutching the blanket protectively to her chest. She could feel the soft material brushing against her body—her *naked* body—and the realization that she wasn't wearing any clothes increased her panic a thousandfold.

Where the hell was she?

It wasn't a hospital, she was sure of that.

She was sitting on a large round bed that had the weirdest mattress texture she'd ever come across. Neither traditional spring nor memory foam, it seemed to be shaping itself to her body. The impression was so strong she could practically feel the thing moving underneath her.

Other than the bed, the room was completely empty. Emily couldn't even discern the source of light that bathed everything in a soft glow. The walls, floor, and ceiling were cream-colored, as were the sheets on the strange bed.

There were also no windows or doors.

What the fuck?

Feeling like she was hyperventilating, Emily tried to take

deep, calming breaths. There had to be an explanation for this —a rational explanation. She just had to figure out what it was.

Moving cautiously, she scooted to the edge of the bed and swung her feet down to the floor. The fact that she could move so easily, with no pain or soreness, was disconcerting. If she hadn't imagined falling off that bridge, shouldn't she have at least a couple of broken bones? The alternative—that it had all been a vivid dream—didn't make much sense in light of her current location.

Standing up, Emily pulled the blanket off the bed and wrapped it around herself, trying not to give in to the panic that fluttered at the edge of her mind, when part of the wall in front of her dissolved.

It literally *dissolved*, letting a man enter the room.

Tall and powerfully built, he stepped through the opening as casually as one would walk through a doorway, his large body moving with fluid, athletic ease.

"Hello, Emily," he said softly, his dark eyes trained on her. "I didn't expect you to be awake so soon."

CHAPTER FOUR

*S*truck speechless, all Emily could do was stare.

The man in front of her was stunning.

Not attractive. Not good-looking. Not even handsome.

Absolutely stunning.

His glossy black hair was longish on top and so thick it added inches to his already-impressive height. His face was sharply masculine and boasted the most perfect features Emily had ever seen. High cheekbones, a strong jaw, full lips—it was as though some sculptor had decided to make a template for a Greek god. Even his bronzed skin appeared flawless, as if on a picture that had been airbrushed.

He looked foreign, exotic… and drop-dead gorgeous. Emily had no idea what race or ethnicity he was, but she had never seen anyone so beautiful. She hadn't even known men like him existed.

And he knew her name.

As soon as that fact registered, her heartbeat spiked again

and the reality of her situation hit home. It didn't matter what the man looked like; what Emily needed to know was where she was and what had happened to her.

"Who are you?" she asked, clutching the blanket tighter to herself. "What is this place? How do you know my name?"

His gaze was dark and unreadable. "Your driver's license was in your wallet," he said softly, his deep voice sending a shiver down her spine. "It contained some information about you, Emily Ross from New York City."

Emily blinked. "Right, okay. And you happened to have my wallet because...?"

"Because it was in the pocket of your shorts," he said, advancing farther into the room. The wall behind him re-solidified, the entrance disappearing as though it had never been there in the first place.

Emily felt the fine hair on the back of her neck rising. "What the hell is this place? Where am I?" She could hear the hysterical edge in her voice, and she forced herself to take a deep breath. In a slightly calmer tone, she asked, "What happened to me?"

"Have a seat, Emily." The man motioned in the direction of the bed. "You still need to rest. Your body has been through a serious trauma."

Emily took a step back, ignoring his suggestion. "Are you saying that I did fall off the bridge?" She felt like she was in an episode of *The Twilight Zone*. "Is this a hospital? Are you a doctor?"

His sensuous lips curved in a faint smile. "Not exactly, but you can think of me as such."

"Is this some kind of research facility?"

"No." The man looked vaguely amused. "It's nothing like that."

"Well, what is it like?" Emily demanded in frustration. "Who are you?"

"You can call me Zaron." Walking over to the bed, he sat down on it, stretching out his long muscular legs. For the first time, Emily registered the fact that he was dressed casually, in a pair of blue jeans and a white sleeveless shirt that exposed bronzed, thickly muscled arms. On his feet, he wore a pair of gray sandals, and his only accessory was a strange-looking watch on his left wrist. If he was a doctor, he certainly wasn't dressed as such.

"Zaron?" she repeated, frowning. "Is that your first or last name?"

He just continued looking at her, his dark gaze inscrutable, and Emily swallowed, realizing that he had no intention of answering her. "Okay, Zaron," she said slowly, emphasizing his strange name, "what happened to me? Why am I here?"

"You fell off the bridge, Emily." His voice was calm, his perfect face expressionless. "I found you and brought you here."

"Right, uh-huh." She gave him a disbelieving stare. "And how is it that I am perfectly fine?"

"Are you hungry?"

"What?" Emily blinked, startled by the change of topic.

"I asked if you're hungry," he repeated patiently, watching her with those dark, exotically beautiful eyes. "You didn't eat anything for two days while you were healing. Would you like some food?" There was something in his gaze that reminded her of her cat George—an odd intensity that made her feel like a mouse about to be played with.

All of a sudden, the comparison seemed very apt—and extremely threatening. "What I would like is something to wear," Emily said evenly, acutely aware of the fact that she was butt-naked under the blanket and locked in a room with a strange man.

A very large, very muscular man.

Who had likely stripped her naked earlier.

Her palms began to sweat, and her heart rate accelerated further. For the first time, the full extent of her vulnerability dawned on Emily. The man sitting on the bed wasn't only gorgeous; he was also big. Much bigger—and undoubtedly much stronger—than Emily herself. At five-foot-seven, she was above average in height, but Zaron was at least a full head taller, with steely muscle packed on every inch of his broad-shouldered frame.

If he decided to hurt her, there wasn't a single thing she could do to stop him.

Some of what she was feeling must've shown on her face because he rose to his feet, his powerful body uncoiling in a strangely graceful motion. "Of course," he said softly. "I will bring you some clothes right away."

And as Emily watched in shock, the wall dissolved again, letting him step out through the opening, and then immediately re-solidified, locking her in.

———

As soon as the wall closed behind him, Zaron drew in a deep breath, his hands tightening into fists. He could feel the heavy pounding of his heart, and his entire body was taut, his cock hard and swollen with need. He was grateful she'd kept her eyes trained on his face as he exited the room; if she had looked down, her natural female wariness would've morphed into outright fear—and with good reason.

The strength of his physical reaction to her was disturbing. Even now, Zaron could smell the faint sweetness of her scent, and his hands itched to touch her again, to feel the softness of her creamy skin under his fingers. It had taken all of his willpower to leave, to step away from her instead of doing what his body demanded and burying himself deep inside her silken flesh.

He hadn't wanted a woman this much in years.

Eight years, to be exact.

The realization was like a punch to the gut. For a moment, the memories threatened to consume Zaron again, to drag him down into the black pit of despair. It was only through sheer willpower that he was able to turn his thoughts back to the human girl—a much safer subject to dwell on.

For the past two days, he'd taken care of her every need, ensuring that she would be clean and comfortable as she healed. He'd bathed her, washed her hair, and kept watch over her as she slept. At this point, he was more intimately acquainted with her body than with that of most women he'd fucked, yet he was still a stranger to her.

A stranger who could barely contain his lust for her.

He wasn't sure when his desire to help the girl had turned into this deep, uncontrollable hunger. In the beginning, all he had seen was a broken creature to be fixed—a fragile human who clung to life with surprising determination. He had wanted to heal her injuries, to stop her suffering, and sex had been the last thing on his mind.

At some point over the last two days, however, that had changed. As her body mended, he'd begun to notice the fullness of her breasts, the softness of her lips, the sensuous dimples at the base of her spine... Although slender, her figure was deliciously feminine, and after a while, all he had been able to think about was touching her, tasting her... fucking her.

It was insane. Though beautiful, the girl was far from his usual type. During his time on Earth, Zaron had discovered that he liked tall, sleek brunettes who reminded him of Krinar women, not delicate-looking blondes with unmistakably human coloring. No Krinar had hair so light or eyes of that strange bluish shade, but on her—on Emily—that combination seemed oddly appealing, reminding him of the illustrations of angels he'd seen in human books. As far as her species went, his little guest was more than pretty.

She was downright exquisite.

At least his cock seemed convinced of that fact.

Taking another deep breath, Zaron forced his hands to unclench, determined to regain his equilibrium. He had no idea why he wanted this human girl so badly, but patience was key here. Patience and self-control. He didn't want to scare her. She was already confused and anxious from waking up in a strange place, in a condition that no human could easily comprehend. He would have to be careful with her, to reveal the truth to her gradually so she wouldn't panic.

He didn't want her to be afraid of him when she came to his bed.

And she would come to him. That much Zaron was certain of. A quick background check on his guest had revealed that she was unmarried with no kids, living alone in a small studio in the Manhattan borough of New York City. She was unclaimed, and Zaron wanted her more than he had wanted any woman since Larita.

He wanted her, and he intended to have her.

All he needed was a little patience.

CHAPTER FIVE

*E*mily waited for Zaron to return, her foot tapping impatiently on the floor.

After he left, she'd gone to that same wall and touched it, trying to figure out how it worked. Surely there had to be a sliding mechanism of some sort, and the wall only *looked* like it was dissolving.

To her disappointment, she hadn't found anything, although she did learn that the wall had a strange texture. It felt warm under her fingertips—warm and smooth, almost like a living thing. She had entertained herself for a minute by stroking it, but then she got tired of that activity and sat down on the bed to wait for the strange not-exactly-doctor to return.

For the first time in her adult life, Emily had no idea what to do. She was always the calm, resourceful one—the one who could tackle any problem in an orderly, analytical manner and arrive at a workable solution. This situation, however, was not something she'd ever encountered. She had no idea where she was or how she'd gotten there, or even how she was alive. Everything about this felt surreal, from the exotically beautiful man with his foreign-sounding name to the room that reminded her of something out of science fiction.

Could this be some secret government research facility after all? Zaron had denied it, but then again, what incentive would he have to tell the truth? This whole place—whatever it was— might be classified, and he could potentially get in trouble for telling her anything.

The fact that she was entertaining conspiracy theories about secret government labs amused Emily on some level. She had always been a rational, common-sense person, not someone given to flights of fancy. Even as a child, she'd never believed in Santa Claus or things that go bump in the night; those possibilities had never seemed logical to her—any more than secret government labs in Costa Rica seemed now.

But what was the alternative? The question gnawed at Emily, adding to her impatience. She couldn't think of anything that would explain her current situation—other than her mind making up the entire event. Could that be it? Was it possible she'd hit her head and was lying in a hospital with a brain injury?

Before she could pursue that train of thought, the wall opened again and Zaron entered the room, moving with the same strange, flowing grace she'd noticed before.

"Here you go," he said, handing her a pale pink dress and a pair of white sandals. "You can get dressed if you wish."

"Um, thanks," Emily said uncertainly, taking the items from him. "Is there a restroom I could use?"

"Of course." He crossed the room, heading to the opposite wall. "Come, let me show you."

Emily followed him, wondering where the restroom could be hiding. As she got close to the wall, it dissolved again, creating an entryway into a small room. Zaron stepped in, motioning for her to join him.

"That's the toilet," he said, pointing toward a white cylindrical object in the corner when she came into the room. "You just sit on it, and it'll take care of you. Then you can refresh yourself near that other corner." He gestured toward a small sink-like protrusion. "If you need a shower later, I can show you how to operate it as well."

Emily felt her face grow warm. "Okay, thanks. I should be able to take it from here. Can you please step out again? I just need a minute."

The corners of his mouth lifted in a small smile. "Sure," he said, and with one smooth motion, he was gone, leaving Emily alone again.

As soon as the wall closed, she dropped the blanket on the floor and pulled on the dress the man had provided. It was a sundress with thin straps. To Emily's surprise, it fit her perfectly, gently hugging every curve of her body. Even her breasts felt comfortably supported by the thin yet sturdy lining in the bodice. The material was again something unusual. The texture was that of fleece, but with the lightweight feel of cotton. The sandals also fit her well; it was as though they'd been custom-made for her feet. There was no underwear, but Emily decided not to quibble about that for now. Just having some clothes was already a big improvement.

Next, she turned her attention to the strange toilet. It was an upright hollow cylinder with rounded edges. There was no water inside, nor was there any visible flushing mechanism attached. Zaron had said she was just supposed to sit on it.

Emily hesitated for a minute, thinking it over, then hiked up the skirt of the dress and plopped down on the cylinder with a mental shrug.

A girl had to pee when she had to pee.

When she was done, she felt a warm breeze moving over her exposed flesh. Her skin tingled for a second, and Emily gasped, jumping off the cylinder. The tingling immediately faded. When she peeked back at the cylinder, she saw that it was spotless, as perfectly clean as it had been in the beginning. At the same time, she realized that she also felt clean and dry, even though she hadn't used any toilet paper—another thing that was missing in this strange bathroom.

Frowning in confusion, Emily walked over to the sink-like object in the other corner. There were no faucets or buttons, so she just waved her hands at it, hoping it had motion sensors. Almost immediately, a warm stream of liquid came out, covering her hands with a pleasantly scented substance that vaguely resembled soap. Before Emily could rub her palms together, the substance evaporated, leaving her hands clean and dry.

A fancy hand sanitizer. Nice.

All pressing matters taken care of, Emily walked over to the wall where the entryway had been. At her approach, the entryway appeared again, as though it had sensed her coming.

"Right, okay," she muttered, stepping through the opening before it had a chance to close again. As soon as she entered the bedroom, the doorway to the bathroom disappeared.

Emily stared at it for a few seconds, then shook her head. She needed to talk to Zaron and get some answers soon. This was ridiculous.

Spotting a movement out of the corner of her eye, she

turned and saw that the entryway leading out of the room had appeared again. Zaron was standing on the other side of it.

"Come," he said, motioning for her to step through the opening. "I'd like you to join me for lunch."

"Okay, sure." Emily cautiously stepped out, this time looking at the sides of the wall to see if she could figure out the way it operated. To her disappointment, there was no visible mechanism here either. The edges of the opening were smooth and polished, with no grooves or ridges to indicate any kind of sliding doors.

As soon as she was on the other side, the wall re-formed again, solidifying right in front of Emily's eyes.

Unbelievable.

Turning toward Zaron, Emily glared at him in frustration. "How does this thing work?" she demanded, tapping at the wall. "What kind of material is that?"

Zaron looked at her calmly. "I could tell you its name, but it wouldn't mean anything to you. As to how it works, I'm not a designer, and I wouldn't be able to give you a good explanation."

Not a designer? What did he mean by that? "Well, what are you then?"

A hint of a smile appeared on his gorgeous lips. "I'm what you would call a biologist, with an extra specialization in edaphology. I study all manner of living creatures as well as the soil that nourishes them."

Emily blinked. "I see." So he *was* a researcher of some kind. "And is this your lab?"

"No." He shook his head. "This is my temporary home."

Home? Emily looked around the room with disbelief. Like the bedroom she'd just left, everything around her was decorated in shades of ivory and cream, with a soft light coming from some indeterminate source. There were no windows or doors, and the furniture was again minimal. Other than a long white plank in the middle that resembled a flat bench and some blooming plants in the corners, the room was essentially empty.

Frowning, Emily took a step toward the bench-like plank. She was pretty sure her eyes were deceiving her because— "Is that thing hovering in the air?" she asked incredulously, kneeling down to peer underneath the plank. "Is it held up by some kind of magnets?"

"Of course not," Zaron said, walking over to stand next to her. "It's utilizing force-field technology."

Still kneeling on all fours, Emily looked up at him. Looming over her, he looked even bigger—and powerfully male. An unwelcome tendril of fear slid down her spine again. "Force-field technology?" she repeated slowly, feeling like she'd fallen down a sci-fi rabbit hole. "What are you talking about?"

He watched her with a cool, dark gaze. "Why don't we eat something and I'll explain," he suggested gently. His tone was soft, but Emily could hear the steel underneath. He had no intention of answering her questions right now.

"All right," she said warily, starting to rise to her feet. "I just —" And then she almost gasped because his hand was on her elbow, helping her get up. His touch was light, solicitous, but there was something possessive in his grip, in the way his fingers lingered on her arm for an extra couple of seconds before letting go.

Her heart jumping into her throat, Emily took a step back, staring at him. As illogical as it was, she felt branded by his touch, her skin tingling where he had touched her. He was looking at her too, his eyes gleaming with some strange emotion. For the first time, Emily noticed that his irises were not dark brown as she'd initially thought—they were black.

Feeling completely off-balance, Emily did what she had always done during difficult times in her life.

She put on her cheerful mask.

"Okay," she said brightly. "Let's eat and chat."

————

Amused by the girl's sudden enthusiasm for the meal, Zaron led her to the kitchen.

He was glad he'd had the opportunity to touch her in a casual, non-sexual manner. It was important to get her accustomed to his touch. In many ways, seducing Emily would be like domesticating a wild creature. He needed to approach her slowly and gain her trust. She needed to believe he wouldn't hurt her; otherwise, she would panic at the first hint of sexual intent on his part.

The good thing was that she was aware of him. It was the primitive female awareness of a healthy, attractive male. She might've been startled by his touch, but she had also been subtly aroused. It had been there in the slight dilation of her pupils and the rapid increase of her heartbeat. Her feminine scent had strengthened, too. If Zaron had touched the delicate folds between her thighs, he would've undoubtedly found her warm and slick, her body instinctively preparing itself for the mating act.

His people had discovered their sexual compatibility with *Homo sapiens* a long time ago. Although their species' DNA was different enough that no interbreeding was possible, the efforts of the Elders had ensured that humans would be quite similar to the Krinar in terms of their outward appearance and body structure. Nobody knew why the Elders had chosen to do it that way, but the end result was a species that many Krinar found quite desirable as bed partners—especially given the aphrodisiac qualities of human blood.

And this particular human was more desirable than most, Zaron thought, watching as Emily stared in wide-eyed shock at the table and chairs in the kitchen. Like the couch in the living room, they were held in place by a force field of sorts, giving the impression that they were hovering in the air. To a typical twenty-first-century human, such technology had to seem rather magical—although most humans were now enlightened enough not to attribute everything to the supernatural.

Zaron was still debating how much he should tell the girl. Over the past two days, while he'd been taking care of her, he had thought about the possibility of revealing nothing—of pretending to be human. He had even considered taking her back to the bridge and leaving her there before she regained consciousness. Let her attribute her survival to a miracle or her fall to a dream, whatever was easier for her mind to accept. He had hesitated, however, his growing lust for her battling with his desire to avoid a potentially tricky situation—and then she had woken up, a couple of hours earlier than he'd expected.

Now he had a wary, confused human on his hands—a human who was regarding him with a frustrated look in her clear aquamarine eyes.

"Let me guess," she said, waving toward the table. "More force-field technology?"

Zaron's amusement deepened at the thinly veiled sarcasm in the girl's question. "Yes, exactly," he said, walking over to sit down on one of the floating chairs. The intelligent material immediately adjusted itself to his body, assessing his posture in order to provide the most comfortable sitting experience possible.

"You want me to sit on that?" Her voice rose. "On a board that floats in thin air?"

"You won't fall, I promise," Zaron said, stifling his urge to smile as the girl approached the table with all the enthusiasm of someone about to be tried for murder. "It's quite nice, in fact."

"Uh-huh," she muttered, cautiously lowering herself onto the seat. Then her eyes widened. She must've felt the chair moving as it adjusted to her. Within seconds, she was sitting with her back fully supported, looking quite shocked.

This time Zaron couldn't suppress a chuckle. He hadn't expected to be enjoying this part, but he was. Introducing this little human to his world might be pleasurable in more ways than one, he thought, watching as she twisted around trying to see the back of her chair. Of course, the intelligent chair twisted with her, the back disappearing just as Emily tried to study it.

When she turned back to face him, the look on her face was indescribable. "Seriously, what is this stuff?" she demanded, her hands gripping the edge of the table. "Where am I?"

Zaron laughed softly. "You're in my house, Emily," he said, patiently repeating the information he'd already given her. "And this *stuff* is my furniture."

"What kind of furniture does that? The thing *moved*. It disappeared on me."

"Yes, it did," Zaron agreed. "It's designed to shape itself to your body in order to provide the most comfort. When you turned around, it was no longer comfortable for you, so it adjusted itself."

"Right, of course." Squeezing her eyes shut, she rubbed her temples with a pained expression on her face.

Immediately concerned, Zaron reached across the table and pressed the back of his hand to her forehead. "Are you feeling okay?" Humans were unbelievably frail, their bodies weak and prone to all kinds of maladies that were utterly alien to his people. Headaches, for instance. Zaron had never suffered from one except for a few brief moments after a head injury, but he knew it was a common affliction among Emily's species.

At his touch, she jerked back, her eyes flying open. "Of course," she said with that same false brightness. "I'm just peachy." When Zaron continued looking at her doubtfully, she added, "No, seriously, I'm fine. I'm pretty sure I fell a couple of hundred feet, but I'm totally fine."

Zaron chose to ignore the last part of her statement. "All right," he said, leaning back. "But if you do have a headache, let me know. I can fix it for you."

She drew in a slow, deep breath, drawing his gaze to the soft swell of her breasts. "Fix it how?" she asked, and Zaron forced himself to refocus on her face.

Now wasn't the time to give in to this attraction.

"Did you heal me before?" she persisted when Zaron didn't respond right away. "How is it that I'm perfectly okay after falling that far?" Her eyes widened as though some thought had occurred to her. "Wait a minute, what day is it? Was I in a coma or something?"

"No, you weren't in a coma," Zaron said, understanding her concern. "Today is Thursday, June 6th."

"So I was out for two days."

Zaron nodded. "Yes, precisely." He was getting hungry, and

he was certain the girl had to be, too. Explanations could wait. Switching to Krinar, he swiftly ordered a salad for them.

Emily frowned at him. "What did you just say?"

"I requested some food for us," Zaron explained. "I'm afraid my house is not programmed to respond to commands in English."

"Uh-huh." She was looking at him like he was insane. "But your house is programmed to respond to commands in whatever language that was?"

"The language in question is Krinar," Zaron said, finally reaching a decision. He could continue keeping the girl in the dark, but that wasn't really necessary. Given how much she had seen already, he wouldn't be able to let her go anyway—and she would learn the truth soon enough.

"Krinar?" She looked confused as she repeated the word with a faint American accent. "What part of the world is that?"

"Krinar is the language spoken on Krina," Zaron said softly, watching Emily's face. "My home planet."

CHAPTER SIX

$\mathcal{E}$mily stared at the gorgeous man in front of her, unable to believe her ears. "Wait... *what?* Did you just say your home *planet?*"

He nodded, his face calm. "Yes, Emily. I know it goes against what your society accepts as the truth right now. If you choose not to believe me, that's fine. You wanted to understand why you're alive and why my house seems strange to you, and I'm providing you with an explanation. If it's not one you want to hear, you're more than welcome to believe something else."

Emily swallowed, her heart starting to beat faster. He didn't look like he was joking. He was watching her with those dark eyes, and there was no trace of laughter on his face.

He was either insane, or she had fallen down that rabbit hole after all.

"Are you seriously telling me you're an alien?"

"From your perspective, I suppose I am," he said thoughtfully. "I prefer the term *Krinar*, however."

"An alien? As in, an extraterrestrial being?" Emily could not believe those words were coming out of her mouth. This had to be an unusually vivid dream. It simply had to be. That was the only reasonable explanation for this whole chain of events. She must have dreamed everything—including the fall off the bridge—and was currently lying asleep in her hotel room.

"Yes," he answered patiently. "I'm from Krina, not Earth, so that makes me an extraterrestrial as far as you're concerned."

Okay, it was official. Emily was dreaming. How else could she be sitting on a floating chair across a floating table from a man who was too beautiful to be real?

Or too beautiful to be human, a small voice whispered at the back of her mind, sending a chill down her spine.

"Okay," she said slowly, "let's suppose for a second it's true. If you're from a different planet, then how did you get here and how can you possibly look human?" Let the dream man answer *that*, she thought. There had to be limits to her mind's ability to make up rational-sounding explanations during sleep. At any moment, Emily would wake up and wonder how she could've possibly dreamed something so strange.

To her dismay, her question seemed to amuse the man. "As you can probably guess, I arrived on a ship," he said, his sensuous lips curving in a slight smile. "A spaceship, if you will. As to how I look human, that's the wrong question, Emily. I don't look human." He paused, watching her intently. "It's you who resembles a Krinar."

Emily opened her mouth to ask what he meant by that, but at that moment, the wall to her right opened, and a bowl filled with something colorful floated out. Reaching the table, it landed in front of Emily. A second bowl immediately followed, landing on the table in front of Zaron.

Emily stared at the table, fighting the urge to rub her eyes. *A dream*, she told herself. *It's just a dream.*

The bowls were filled with what appeared to be a salad—an unusual mixture of fruits and vegetables covered with a light green dressing. In the middle of each bowl, there was a strange utensil that resembled miniature tongs.

Cautiously picking up the utensil, Emily poked a piece of tomato with it. "That doesn't look very alien," she said, giving Zaron a dubious look.

"It's not. These are all Earth plants at this point—like this *Citrus sinensis*." Lifting a piece of orange with his own utensil, he put the fruit into his mouth and began to eat with obvious enjoyment.

Emily stared at him. "Right, okay. So you can eat our food?"

He swallowed and nodded. "Sure. Some of it is quite good, actually," he said, then resumed eating with gusto.

Still holding the utensil, Emily watched him for a few seconds. She felt like the rabbit hole was expanding all around her, sucking her in even deeper. Why wasn't she waking up? In general, was it normal for someone in a dream to know that they were in a dream and yet be unable to wake up?

Not knowing what else to do, she began eating the salad. The crisp flavors exploded on her tongue, the combination of zesty vegetables and sweet fruits unusual but delicious. The dressing was both tangy and rich. Emily couldn't remember ever eating anything quite like that before. She liked salads, and this was one of the best she'd ever had.

This dream was far, far too realistic.

Swallowing the bite she'd been chewing, Emily put down her utensil. "I'm not dreaming, am I?" she asked quietly, looking at Zaron.

"Did you think you were?" He cocked his head to the side. "Is that why you've been so calm? I was wondering about that. Everything I know about your kind suggests that your reaction should've been far more extreme."

Emily felt like having that "far more extreme" reaction right now.

Slowly rising to her feet, she stepped away from the table, staring at Zaron. She could hear the rapid thudding of her own heartbeat, and her breathing was fast and shallow. It felt like there was not enough air in the room.

If this was truly happening—if her mind was not playing a cruel trick on her—there was no way to explain what she'd seen without venturing into the realm of the improbable.

"Can you prove it?" Her voice was low and shaky. "Can you prove to me that you're from another planet?"

He leaned back in his chair, a half-smile playing on his lips. "How would you like me to prove it to you, Emily? Isn't it enough that you're alive and well when you should've died from your injuries? Do you know of any human medicine that can heal severe wounds like that?"

Emily moistened her lips. "How badly was I hurt?" The words came out in a barely audible whisper. She pictured the bridge and the big rocks below, and her stomach twisted. For the first time, the fact that she was alive truly dawned on her.

She was alive… when by all rights she should've been dead.

"You had multiple bone fractures, as well as severe damage to your internal organs," Zaron said, pushing a thick lock of hair off his forehead. "Your spine was broken as well."

Feeling like a steel band was squeezing her ribcage, Emily fought to draw in air. She remembered it now—that brief, awful moment when her body slammed into the rocks. She remembered wishing for instant death and experiencing agony instead.

Her eyes burning, she lifted her arms, studying them as if she'd never seen them before. Her skin was smooth and pale, completely unblemished. There was no trace of injury of any kind, not even a bruise or a scrape.

She was alive.

She. Was. Alive.

As that realization sank in, Emily began to shake. She could've died. She should've died. She had been certain that she would die.

And if it hadn't been for the man sitting at the table, she would have.

Lifting her eyes, she saw him gazing at her with that same coolly amused expression. "You saved me…" Her voice was thin with shock. "You saved my life."

He nodded, rising smoothly to his feet. "Yes," he said, approaching her with predatory grace. "I did." Stopping less than a foot away from her, he raised his hand and lightly brushed the back of his fingers against the side of her jaw.

Emily drew in a startled breath, stunned by the unexpectedly proprietary caress. His nearness was overwhelming, adding to her inner turmoil. Her skin tingled from his touch, and she felt hot chills going down her spine, her entire body trembling from shock.

The man who had just touched her—the man who had saved her life—was claiming to be from another planet.

Her heart pounding heavily, Emily took a step back. "Why did you save me?" she whispered, staring up at him. "What do you want from me?"

"You don't have to be afraid, Emily." His voice was gentle,

soothing, but she again got that disquieting impression of a big cat toying with its prey. "I won't harm you."

She swallowed thickly, taking another step back. She wasn't sure if she believed him—if she believed any of it. How could there be humanoid aliens? The idea was right up there with Bigfoot and mermaids. A secret government lab facility was a far more plausible scenario, except it couldn't explain how Emily could've healed so quickly from her fall. That kind of medical technology would not have remained secret for long.

She had no choice but to allow for the possibility that he was telling the truth, and if that was the case, then she was in the presence of an actual, real-life extraterrestrial.

An extraterrestrial who had saved her life.

A being from another planet who was watching her like a hungry lion watches a gazelle.

CHAPTER SEVEN

*Z*aron watched as Emily slowly backed away from him, her eyes huge in her pale face. He could see the fine trembling in her limbs, and the urge to pull her to him, to hold her, was so strong he could barely control it. The brief caress earlier had only whetted his appetite.

He wanted her. He wanted to touch her, to feel the satiny texture of her skin. He wanted to tear off her clothes and spread her thighs wide, holding her open as he thrust into her. He wanted to cradle her against him and fuck her like a savage... and then slice his teeth across the tender skin of her throat and taste the hot, coppery richness of her blood.

His mouth watered at the thought.

"Why did you say I look like a Krinar?" Her hesitant question interrupted his musings, penetrating the haze of lust that seemed to envelop his brain in her presence. She had stopped on the other side of the room and was watching him warily. She felt safer with some space between them, he realized; she didn't know how easy it would be for him to clear that distance with a single leap. "As opposed to you looking human, I mean?" she clarified.

Taking a steadying breath, Zaron forced himself to remain still and give her the space she needed. It was natural for her to be frightened and overwhelmed; after all, humans didn't know about the Krinar yet.

"Because we are the original intelligent species," he said, answering her question. "Your kind was created in our image, not the other way around."

The girl's tongue flicked over her lips in a nervous gesture that sent a bolt of heat straight to Zaron's groin. "In your image? What are you talking about?"

"I'm talking about the fact that we created your species... all the species on this planet, really." Zaron paused, letting that sink in. "If it hadn't been for us, there wouldn't be life on Earth."

Her eyes widened, an expression of disbelief stealing across her face. "What? Are you saying you *made* us? Like in a lab or something?"

"No, not in a lab," Zaron said. He was about to launch into a lengthy scientific explanation but caught himself in time. "What we did was plant some DNA here a couple of billion years ago," he said instead. "Then we nudged your evolution along, helping a Krinar-like species emerge over time." This was a gross oversimplification, but he didn't think Emily needed all the evolutionary subtleties at this point.

As it was, Emily's mouth opened and closed without making a sound. Zaron could practically see the workings of her agile brain inside that pretty little skull. She didn't know if she could trust him or not, and her initial inclination was to reject anything that didn't fit into her existing worldview. But she couldn't deny what she'd seen today.

"A couple of *billion* years ago?" she asked, staring at him. "You're telling me that your civilization is that old?"

Zaron nodded. "Yes, we've been around for a very long time. Our planet is much older than yours."

Emily drew in a shuddering breath. "I see." Raising her hands, she rubbed her temples again, as though suffering from a headache.

Zaron's eyes narrowed. He didn't like the idea of her being in pain—not if he could help it. It was a strange thing, but on some level he felt as though she belonged to him and her well-being was his responsibility. Crossing the room in a few strides, he stopped in front of her. "Emily... Do you need me to get you some medicine?"

Lowering her hands to her sides, she looked up at him, her thickly lashed eyes more green than blue in this light. "No, thank you. I'm perfectly fine. It's just a lot to take in."

"Of course." Zaron again felt the urge to pull her into his arms—this time to soothe her. Unfortunately, she was not yet ready for that kind of intimacy, and any move he made in that direction was more likely to scare her than reduce her anxiety. He settled for giving her a reassuring smile. "I understand."

"I'm still in Costa Rica, right?" she asked, her delicate eyebrows coming together as if the idea had just occurred to her. "I'm not somewhere on your ship, am I?"

"No, you're not—and yes, we are in Costa Rica. We're only about a dozen miles away from that bridge. Like I told you, this is my home for now."

Her forehead smoothed out, and a small smile appeared on her lips. "Oh, I see." She appeared relieved, and Zaron suppressed a smile of his own, knowing her question was likely inspired by her culture's stereotype of alien abductions.

Watching the girl, Zaron realized that he hadn't felt this lighthearted in years. He'd never spent much time with a human before, and he hadn't expected to find it so enjoyable. From her driver's license, he knew that Emily was twenty-four —little more than an adolescent compared to his own six-hundred-plus years. However, she seemed more mature than a Krinar of the same age, likely because her species generally reached full adulthood by that time.

It suddenly struck him that for the past hour, he hadn't thought about Larita once. A sharp stab of agony accompanied that realization, and he immediately pushed the thought away. He liked the way he felt around this human girl, and he intended to hold on to that feeling.

Emily cleared her throat, drawing his attention back to her. "Zaron," she said quietly, holding his gaze, "I haven't thanked you yet for healing me. I remember that fall, and I know I should've died"—she swallowed, her voice growing thick—"and I can't even begin to thank you for doing whatever it was that you did—"

"It's okay, Emily," Zaron interrupted, sensing that she was on the verge of tears. "I'm just glad you're alive."

She swallowed again, then gave him a wry, tremulous smile. "Sorry, I didn't mean to get all emotional on you. I guess even aliens get squeamish when a girl is about to cry, huh?"

"You have no idea," Zaron said dryly. He hated seeing a woman's tears; they made him feel helpless. Whenever Larita cried, he'd bend over backwards to fix whatever was bothering her. Emily didn't seem prone to crying, and he liked that. The human girl's angelic prettiness hid a core of strength that he couldn't help but admire.

Emily's smile widened, lighting up her entire face. "Well, in that case, I won't cry. I'll simply say thank you, and that's that."

Zaron laughed. "Good, that's the way—"

A soft vibration on his wrist startled him, cutting him off mid-sentence. Glancing down at the computing device he wore on his arm, Zaron saw an urgent message waiting for him. "Excuse me," he said, giving Emily an apologetic look. "I'll be right back."

Before she could respond, he swiftly walked toward his study.

A meeting request from the Council always needed to be addressed promptly.

———

Her heart racing, Emily watched Zaron disappear into the other room. For a second there, she'd felt the beginnings of a genuine connection—a connection that was both exciting and disconcerting.

He made her nervous, yet she felt drawn to him. When they were talking, she'd found herself wondering what it would be like to trace the straight lines of his eyebrows with her fingertips and feel the texture of his thick, glossy hair. With him standing so near, she had been hyperaware of his large, muscular body—of the purely masculine perfection of him.

It was ridiculous. He was gorgeous, yes, but by his own admission, he wasn't human. He was Krinar, an alien from a multi-billion-year-old civilization.

A civilization that had supposedly created life on Earth.

Squeezing her eyes shut, Emily reflexively rubbed her temples again. When she'd told Zaron that it was a lot to take in, she hadn't been kidding. Her brain felt like it was about to explode, her thoughts whirling around in circles. She didn't have a full-blown headache, but there was a definite band of tension around her forehead.

Sighing, Emily opened her eyes and walked back to the table, sitting down on one of the hovering chairs. When the object moved around her, shaping itself to her body, she purposefully relaxed into the motion, letting it do its thing. She was growing used to some of Zaron's technology—at least the most basic, domestic kind.

Just how advanced were they? she wondered, some of the tension draining out of her as the chair began a soothing vibration to relax her muscles. Clearly, Zaron had been able to come to Earth, so they must've mastered interstellar travel. Faster-than-light travel, perhaps? According to current scientific theories, such a thing was impossible, but so was healing wounds of the kind Emily must've sustained during her fall. Krinar medicine was so far ahead of anything Emily had heard of that she couldn't even imagine what else they could do. Teleportation, perhaps? There were so many possibilities for cool technology her head was spinning.

Emily had always had an interest in science, often reading articles about the latest discoveries and watching nature shows on television. Sometimes she even wished she'd chosen biology or astrophysics as a field of study. But she hadn't. She'd gone into finance instead, lured by the promise of big money on Wall Street. After growing up in foster homes, Emily craved financial security and stability, and banking had seemed like the perfect way to achieve that quickly. To succeed in most scientific fields, one needed a graduate degree—a Ph.D. or at least a Master's. But to become an investment banking analyst, four years at a prestigious college, a couple of summer internships, and a willingness to work eighty-plus hours a week were more than sufficient. At the age of twenty-four, Emily had been well on her way to achieving her goal of financial security, with her savings account healthy and growing—at least until the stock market took its most recent dive.

Now her savings had been cut in half, and she had lost the job that had consumed her life for the past two years. Emily waited for the familiar bitterness to wash over her, but all she felt was a mild twinge of disappointment. For the first time since the layoffs, she wasn't worried about her future. She had far more important things on her mind—like the fact that an alien had saved her life.

The sheer insanity of that thought almost made her laugh out loud. For a moment, she again had that dizzying Alice-in-Wonderland sensation, but then she took a few calming breaths and got a grip on herself. She needed to be able to think without freaking out because if Zaron's claims were true, the implications were simply staggering.

There was another intelligent species out there—a species far more advanced than humans. A species that had supposedly indirectly created humans. What did they want? Why was Zaron here, living in a Costa Rican jungle? Why had he bothered saving Emily's life?

Also, why did no one know about the Krinar? If Zaron's people were the real creators of mankind, shouldn't humans have learned about them a long time ago?

A cold sensation spread through Emily's body as she drew in

a shaky breath, then another and another. Her chest was beginning to feel tight again.

There was only one answer to that question.

No one knew about the Krinar because they didn't want to reveal their existence to humans.

Yet Zaron had risked exposure by letting Emily see his home, by telling her what he was and where he'd come from. He didn't seem concerned that she could go to the media with that knowledge, or that he'd potentially compromised what had to be thousands of years of secrecy on the part of his species.

Slowly rising to her feet, Emily stared at the ivory wall, her hands mindlessly gripping the table.

Was Zaron telling her all this because he wasn't going to let her go?

CHAPTER EIGHT

*E*ntering his study, Zaron activated the meeting mode on his computer and closed his eyes for a second. When he opened them, he was standing inside a large white chamber—the Council gathering place on Krina. He wasn't there physically, of course, but the simulation was real enough that he could see, feel, touch, and smell everything, almost as if he was there in person.

There were only three Councilors waiting for him there: Korum, Arus, and Saret. Not a formal meeting then, Zaron realized; that would've required all fifteen Council members to be present. Inclining his head in a gesture of respect, he waited to see why he had been summoned.

The three men standing in front of him were among the most influential on Krina, each of them having been on the Council longer than Zaron had been alive. The Council—the formal ruling body of Krina—was answerable only to the Elders, the nine oldest Krinar in existence. And since the Elders

47

rarely interfered with anything, that meant the Council enjoyed almost unlimited power when it came to passing laws and upholding order in their society.

Up until two years ago, Zaron had only occasionally met some of the Councilors in social situations. But since the Council had become interested in his research, he'd gotten to know most of its members.

"It's good to see you, Zaron," Arus said, taking a step forward. "Thank you for responding so quickly. We're about to depart and wanted to catch up with you for a minute to see if you've made more progress on selecting the sites." His expression was pleasant and mildly interested, designed to make one feel at ease. With a background in societal studies, Arus was the consummate politician, well-liked and respected by nearly everyone—Zaron included. It was Arus who had approached him two years ago about heading up the settlement efforts, dragging Zaron out of the bleak depression that had consumed him since Larita's death.

"I did," Zaron answered. "I believe the most promising location is that of the Guanacaste region of Costa Rica." A flick of his wrist brought up a detailed three-dimensional map of Earth, and he zoomed in on the place he was referring to. "The climate is very comparable to some areas of Krina, and I should be able to alter the soil enough to make it hospitable to many of our edible plants."

"What about the other nine Centers?" It was Korum who spoke this time, his unusual amber-colored eyes watching Zaron with cool, piercing intelligence. Of the three Council members present, he was by far the most intimidating, with a reputation for ruthlessness that went far beyond the usual ambition. He was also the driving force behind the upcoming invasion.

"I have seven of the sites selected," Zaron told him. "The remaining two will be finalized in the next few weeks. They should be in the United States, so we have a presence there. I've narrowed it down to Florida, Arizona, and New Mexico, but each of those places needs to be explored in greater detail before we make our final choice."

"Very good." Arus gave him an approving smile. "That is quite a bit of progress. I suspect that in the first few months, we'll spend most of our time on the ships anyway, until the human population has had a chance to get accustomed to our presence."

"Are you expecting a lot of unrest?" Zaron inquired, trying to picture how everything would unfold. Given Emily's reaction to his revelations, he suspected many humans would have a difficult time dealing with something so far outside their accepted structure of beliefs.

"Hopefully, not too much," Saret responded, speaking for the first time. Considered the top mind expert on Krina, he was quiet and generally laid-back, tending to fade into the background next to the more forceful personalities on the Council. "I expect some will be quite upset when we arrive, but hopefully, once we explain everything—"

"They'll adjust." Korum sounded impatient. "They'll have no choice in the matter. Besides, from what I've observed, their species is quite adaptable."

Arus frowned at Korum, then turned back toward Zaron. "Thank you for the update. This is exactly what we were hoping to hear. Is there anything else we should be aware of at this time?"

"No," Zaron said, though for some strange reason, he thought of Emily. The Council would not be interested in something as trivial as a human girl staying in his house, so there was no point in informing them about that.

"In that case, we'll see you on Earth," Arus said, and the room blurred around Zaron, causing him to close his eyes.

When he opened them, the virtual environment of the meeting was gone, and he was standing in his own study.

––––––––

By the time Zaron came back, Emily was a nervous wreck. She'd gone back to the room that she assumed functioned as the living room—the one with the long, floating plank that turned into the most comfortable couch imaginable when she sat down on it. She'd sat there for a few minutes, thinking about her situation, and then she got up to search for an exit, too wound up to remain still. Running her hands over the walls, she tried to find something, anything, that would indicate the presence of a door, but the walls were frustratingly smooth and warm under her fingers.

Abandoning that futile task, Emily began to pace.

As far as she could tell, if Zaron wanted to keep the existence of his people a secret, then he had only three options when it came to Emily. He could let her go and trust her to keep quiet; he could tamper with her memories (assuming they had that kind of technology); or he could do something that would prevent her from telling anyone—such as take her away to his planet when he left. Theoretically, he could also kill her, but that wouldn't make much sense, since he had gone to all this trouble to save her life.

She very much hoped he was leaning toward the "trust her" option.

"Sorry about that." Zaron's deep voice broke into Emily's thoughts, causing her to whirl around in surprise. Despite his size, her savior was incredibly light on his feet. He was already a few feet away, and she hadn't even heard him enter.

"Oh, that's no problem." Emily gave him an overly bright smile to hide her nervousness. "I'm sure you have many important things to do, and I'm probably distracting you from them. If you don't mind, I'll just be on my way..." Her voice trailed off as Zaron's expression darkened.

"You're not distracting me." He came toward her, walking without making a sound. For the first time, it struck her that there was something not quite human in the way he moved, something that made her think of a carnivore stalking its prey. "You still need to recover, Emily, and it's my pleasure to have you as a guest."

"Oh no, I feel perfectly fine," she protested, her pulse jumping at the realization that he was *not* leaning toward the "trust" option. "Whatever medicine you used on me was amazing, and I'm as healthy as I've ever been—"

"Emily..." Zaron paused a couple of feet away from her, his dark eyes locked on her face. "Please, don't get stressed. Your body has been through a severe trauma, and you need time to heal fully."

"How much time?"

"A couple of weeks."

"A couple of weeks?" Emily stared at him, her unease abating only slightly. "I can't stay in Costa Rica that long. I have to go back home; my plane tickets are for Saturday."

Zaron regarded her silently. "I'll get you new tickets," he said after a moment. "It shouldn't be a problem."

"Really?" Emily blinked. "You can buy me plane tickets?" What was he going to do, purchase them online with a credit card? Did aliens have credit cards? She pictured him applying for a Mastercard from his spaceship and bit the inside of her cheek to keep from bursting into semi-hysterical laughter.

"Of course." He looked puzzled by her question. "Human wealth is not something we lack. I can buy you anything you want, Emily."

The urge to laugh disappeared without a trace. "That's very generous of you," she said, trying to remain calm, "but I would feel terrible asking you to spend your money on me like that." She attempted a smile again. "Why don't I just call the airline and have them change my flight date? If you think I'm not in good enough shape to travel, I could probably stay here a couple of extra days. I would just need to make the appropriate arrangements—"

"Emily…" He let out a very human-like sigh. "As you've probably guessed, I can't let you do that."

Her heart climbed into her throat. "I wouldn't tell anyone about you—I swear, I wouldn't." Emily knew she was babbling, but she couldn't help herself. "You saved my life, and I wouldn't betray you. Besides, who would believe me? Nobody believes in aliens—"

"It doesn't matter," he said, cutting short her rambling appeal. "They wouldn't have to take your word for it. All they'd need to do is compare your old dental records to your current ones."

"My dental records?"

"Your body has undergone the full healing procedure,"

Zaron said. "It means that *all* of your injuries were healed, including the ones inflicted by your primitive dentistry. Your teeth now bear no traces of cavities or fillings, and regrowing live tissue of that kind is not something your science is capable of yet."

Her panic increasing, Emily ran her tongue over her teeth in an effort to verify what he was telling her. Her mouth did feel subtly different, but she didn't know if she was just imagining things.

"Do you have a mirror?" she asked, trying to slow her frantic breathing. What else had his procedure done to her? Was she now different in some way?

He smiled in response and said something in his own language. The words sounded slightly guttural to her ears.

"Here," he said, pointing toward the wall to her right. "Take a look."

The wall had become a giant mirror—a transformation that barely fazed Emily at this point. Walking over to the mirror, she opened her mouth wide, trying to see her back teeth, where her childhood love of sweets had resulted in a few cavities.

There was no trace of those cavities or fillings. Her teeth were as white and perfect as if she'd had new ones put in.

Zaron hadn't lied. His procedure had left an indelible trace —evidence that something had been done to Emily that modern science could not explain.

Closing her mouth, Emily turned back toward Zaron, who was watching her actions with some amusement. "Is there anything else?" she asked evenly. "Am I changed in other ways?"

His lips curved in a slight smile. "No, Emily. Unless you count missing a few scars as being changed."

Pulling up the skirt of her dress a couple of inches, she

peeked at her left thigh. One of her foster brothers had pushed her into a garbage bin when she was twelve, causing her to cut open her leg on broken glass. The resulting scar had made her teenage self so self-conscious she'd foregone wearing shorts for five years. It was only as an adult that Emily had begun to accept it as a part of her body... and now that scar was gone.

Completely gone. Erased by alien technology.

Stunned, Emily raised her eyes to meet Zaron's gaze across the room. "It's not there anymore. This and my fillings—they're gone."

He nodded. "They are."

"So what are you planning to do with me now?" She did her best to rein in her panic. "Are you going to take me to your planet?"

"No, of course not." He looked amused again. "I told you, you will only need to stay here for a couple of weeks. Seventeen days, to be exact."

"Why? What's going to change in seventeen days?" Emily would still have her perfect teeth and scarless body. If he didn't trust her now, why did he think he could trust her then?

"In seventeen days, it won't matter if you go public with your story," he said, crossing the room to stand next to her. "It won't even matter if your newspapers believe you." He paused for a second, looking down at her, then said gently, "You see, Emily, by then my people will have arrived."

CHAPTER NINE

*Z*aron watched as Emily's pupils dilated and her face turned even paler. "What?" she whispered. "What do you mean, your people will have arrived?"

"We're getting ready to formally meet your species." Zaron leaned against the mirrored wall. "In seventeen days, we'll make contact with your leaders—and at that point, you can return to your regular life if you wish."

"You're going to reveal yourselves to us?"

"Yes," Zaron confirmed. "So you see, you have nothing to worry about. You can just stay here as my guest and recuperate for a little while."

She drew in a deep breath. "Right, as your guest. Until your people arrive. Until everyone learns that aliens exist. Got it." She sounded like she was in shock, and Zaron wanted to pull her to him and rock her back and forth, soothing her anxiety— and then carry her off to bed and thoroughly fuck her. The curious mixture of protectiveness and lust she awakened in him was different from anything he'd experienced before. Even with Larita—

No. He stopped that line of thought before it went any further. It was ridiculous to compare his feelings for his mate to the primitive physical attraction he was experiencing for this human. The two had nothing in common. He might as well try to replace Larita with a house pet, like some humans tried to do with their loved ones.

To be fair, though, Emily would make a very fuckable house pet, he thought dryly, his gaze dropping to the delicious fullness of her breasts underneath the light fabric of her dress.

"Why now?" Her voice jerked him out of a daydream in which he was pulling down the top of her dress and cupping those soft white mounds in his hands. Dragging his eyes back to her face, he saw that some of her shock had faded. "Why are you choosing to reveal yourselves to us now?"

"Because it's time," Zaron answered. "Because we think you're ready." And because the Council was concerned about the devastating impact humans were having on their planet, but that was not something he intended to tell Emily at this point.

She stared at him. "I see. So you're just going to show up in your spaceships and say, 'Hello, here we are?'"

His lips twitched in a brief smile. "Yes, pretty much." There was going to be more to it than that, but she didn't need to know that yet, either.

"Okay, well, if that's the case, then I understand your dilemma about the timing," she said slowly, "and I am extremely grateful for everything you've done for me. But I have a problem too. I can't be your guest for that long because I have obligations back home." She took a breath. "I have a job interview next week. A very important interview that I absolutely can't miss. I also have a cat that my friend is watching for me, and she'll be very worried if I don't come back on Saturday."

"Your cat?" Zaron frowned in confusion. He had studied the *Felis catus* species recently, and they rarely exhibited that kind of deep attachment to humans.

"No, of course not." Emily gave him an exasperated look. "My friend."

Zaron couldn't help grinning at that. "Ah, that makes more sense."

An answering smile flashed across Emily's face. "Yes, it does, doesn't it?" Sobering up, she said, "But seriously, you have nothing to worry about with me. I'm not going to say a word to anyone about what happened—and I'll avoid doctors and dentists like the plague for the next seventeen days, just in case they decide to examine me for signs of alien procedures."

Zaron sighed. He could already see that convincing Emily to enjoy her extended vacation wouldn't be as easy as he'd hoped. She was right: it likely wouldn't do any harm to let her return to her life at this point. However, until the Krinar officially made contact, he was bound by the non-disclosure mandate set by the Elders, and the mandate stated that he was not allowed to do anything that could expose his species to humans before the ships' arrival.

There was also another factor—one Zaron was reluctant to admit even to himself. He didn't want to let Emily go before tasting her... before satisfying the hunger that burned within him.

No. It wasn't that, he told himself. He was merely adhering to the mandate, like any law-abiding Krinar should.

"I'm sorry, Emily," he said. "I understand you might not

intend to reveal anything, but I have to follow the rules. I'm afraid I must insist that you stay here for a little while."

Her soft mouth tightened. "Right. For two and a half weeks… without letting anyone know where I am or what happened to me."

Zaron exhaled, starting to feel frustrated. "You can email your friend if you wish." It should be easy enough to control what the email said, particularly if he accessed her email account and sent the message himself.

"That would be good, but I still have that interview—and that's an interview I can't miss or reschedule," Emily said. "It's with the biggest hedge fund in New York, and it's my dream job. I've been preparing for it for two months, ever since I got laid off. At Evers Capital, they don't accept excuses, and they won't give me another shot if I screw up. Bill Evers—the head of the fund—is known for putting work first and everything else second. He was once in a car crash that put him in a coma, and the first day he came out of it, he had his wheelchair taken to the office." There was a note of admiration in her voice, which annoyed Zaron for some reason.

His temper began to simmer. "Listen to me, Emily, you need to understand one thing here," he said, straightening away from the wall. "You are only alive because I found you and brought you here. If it were not for me, you would be heading home in a body bag right now—"

She blanched, all color draining from her face.

"—so you might want to think about that the next time you worry about missing an interview." He paused, still feeling inexplicably angry with her. When he spoke again, his words came out harsher than he intended. "You are my guest, and you will remain as such until the mandate is no longer in effect."

"I see." Her tone was calm, but there was a suspicious glimmer in her eyes as she stared at him. "So for the next seventeen days, I am your captive."

Zaron's eyes narrowed. "Call it whatever you wish."

Before he could say or do anything he would later regret, he turned away from her and swiftly walked toward his study.

————

When he was gone, Emily leaned against the mirrored wall, wrapping her arms protectively around herself. She didn't know what had caused Zaron's anger, but she knew it wasn't smart to provoke him in her situation. She should've just accepted his "hospitality," such as it was, instead of arguing about it.

It wasn't as bad as it could be, she told herself, ignoring the churning in her stomach. He was only detaining her for a couple of weeks, not taking her off the planet as she'd initially feared. In a way, he was right: it was silly to worry about a lost job opportunity when she had almost died two days ago. When Emily had been dangling off that bridge, her career had been the last thing on her mind. She was grateful that Zaron had chosen to save her... even if everything inside her raged at the idea of being held prisoner, of being deprived of freedom for as long as he deemed necessary.

If there was one thing Emily hated, it was being confined. Before entering the foster care system, she had lived with her father's sister—a socially awkward woman who'd had no idea how to deal with a four-year-old who'd just lost her parents. Whenever Emily misbehaved, her aunt would lock her in her room as punishment, sometimes for several days at a time.

Wendy Ross was never abusive, strictly speaking—she would bring Emily meals and give her toys to play with—but Emily still hated being locked up. Even now, the mere thought of being held somewhere against her will was enough to make her feel like a caged animal: trapped and furious.

No, don't dwell on that. The last thing she needed was for her weird indoor phobia to kick in. Drawing in a calming breath, Emily walked over to the couch-plank and sat down, letting the alien furniture cradle her body and take away her tension. If she didn't focus on the fact that she was being held captive, then her situation could actually be viewed as an amazing opportunity—a chance to get to know an intelligent being from another species.

A species that all humans would meet soon.

The magnitude of what Zaron had just told her was almost beyond belief. Emily's brain was buzzing with a million questions. Why did Zaron's people decide that humans were ready for first contact? What would happen when they showed up? She couldn't imagine that everyone would welcome them with open arms, even if the Krinar had peaceful intentions. What were their intentions, anyway? A simple meet-and-greet or was there something more? And how would the planet react to their arrival? To the revelation that humans were not alone, that they had been created by an ancient extraterrestrial race?

A very gorgeous, very humanoid race.

To her shock, Emily realized that she was seriously attracted to Zaron. She had been so overwhelmed by everything he'd told her that it had somehow slipped by her, the sheer physical impact he had on her senses. Even now, just thinking about him, she could feel her skin heating up and warm moisture gathering between her thighs. The pull she felt toward him was unlike anything she had experienced before, and it was as strong as it was disturbing.

Zaron looked like a human man—*okay, way better than a human man*—but he was not human. If his kind had truly evolved on a different planet, there had to be some pretty significant differences between their species, and at this point, Emily could only speculate as to what those differences might be. It made no sense for her to be sexually attracted to him, but her body didn't care about that. As far as her hormones were concerned, Zaron was the most delicious thing they'd ever come in contact with.

Great. That's all she needed now: a bad case of Stockholm Syndrome, and for an alien, no less. Emily mentally groaned, burying her face in her hands. If his civilization really was as advanced and ancient as he'd said, then there was a strong possibility that he saw her as little more than a smart monkey—as something to be studied and observed. He'd even said he was a biologist, she remembered with a sinking feeling in her stomach.

No, lusting after him was stupid. They were from different species, and even if they weren't, this kind of situation did not exactly lend itself to a relationship. If Zaron hadn't lied, in seventeen days she would leave and probably never see him again.

All she needed to do until then was hang on to her sanity.

CHAPTER TEN

*H*is jaw tense with anger, Zaron entered his office and sat down. Pulling up a three-dimensional image of the local landscape, he superimposed a map of a prospective Center on it and started running the calculations. He had a lot of work to do prior to the Council's arrival, but all he could think about was his ungrateful human guest.

He had saved her life. *Saved. Her. Life.* Without him, Emily would be a rotting corpse. And she was balking at having to stay in his house for an extra couple of weeks? He gritted his teeth, leaning forward in his chair. Was the idea of being with him so repugnant to her? Or was she just anxious to get back so she could work with that insane hedge fund leader she seemed to worship?

Zaron's anger deepened at the thought. Issuing a curt order to his computing device, he accessed Bill Evers's records, quickly scanning all available information about the human, from newspaper articles to his residential address. What he saw was not reassuring. The object of Emily's admiration was only in his mid-thirties and had risen far in their society during his short lifespan. He was also decent-looking for a human, with regular bone structure, a lean body of average height, and sandy brown hair.

Was that why Emily was so determined to get a job at this fund? Zaron wondered savagely. Did she want this human as a potential mate? If so, she was shit out of luck. He had no intention of letting another male near her—at least not until he had a chance to sate himself with her delicious, curvy little body.

And therein lay the reason for his anger, he realized, staring blankly at the three-dimensional map in front of him. No matter how hard Zaron tried to be an enlightened, rational scientist, he was a Krinar male first and foremost, and he was feeling territorial toward Emily. He wanted her, and he didn't want anyone else to have her—or for her to even think about another man. Her unabashed admiration for Evers had infuriated him because it had brought up the specter of another male in her life—someone she seemed to respect quite a bit.

It wasn't logical, but there it was. Zaron was feeling possessive toward Emily... as possessive as he'd once felt about Larita.

No. Everything inside him instantly rejected that conclusion. This was different. The pretty human might've triggered his primitive Krinar instincts, but it was only because Zaron felt like he had a right to her.

Yes, that was it, he decided. He saved her, and now he felt like she belonged to him—like she was his already. It didn't make a lot of sense, but he didn't care.

If he was to preserve his sanity, he needed to have her. Soon.

CHAPTER ELEVEN

"*W*hat are you doing?"

At the sound of the familiar deep voice, Emily jumped and whirled around, trying not to look guilty. "Just examining the texture of these walls," she said brightly.

"Uh-huh." Zaron didn't look like he believed her. And then she knew he didn't believe her because he said gently, "Emily, they won't open for you, no matter how much you search for the mechanism. This house is intelligent, and it's programmed to respond to me, not you."

Emily's mouth tightened. "Right, of course." She'd suspected as much. For the past hour, she'd diligently searched every nook and cranny of the living room and kitchen area for a way out, and as far as she could tell, there was none.

Unless Zaron did whatever it was that he did to make the walls open, she was stuck.

He crossed the room and stopped next to her. "Why do you insist on making this so difficult?" he murmured. His fingers brushed across her cheek, sending a warm shiver through her. "This doesn't need to be a bad experience for you, angel. On the contrary, it can be quite pleasant..." His big hand cupped her cheek, his thumb softly rubbing her lower lip. "Very pleasant, in fact."

Shocked, Emily stared at him, her heart beating like a drum. There was no mistaking his meaning—or the hunger in his gaze. Had he somehow read her mind earlier? Was he capable of mind reading? "Um..." Her brain seemed to have turned to mush, leaving her unable to string together a coherent sentence. "Um, what are you... what do you...?"

"You don't have to be afraid, Emily," he said softly, stepping closer. "I won't hurt you." And as she stood there in stunned disbelief, he lowered his head, capturing her mouth with his.

His lips were velvet soft, his breath warm and faintly sweet. He didn't seem to be in a rush to deepen the kiss; it was as if he was just tasting her, learning the contour and texture of her lips. At the same time, he knew exactly what he was doing. There was no hesitation in his actions, no fumbling uncertainty. He kissed her as if he'd done it a million times, his fingers sliding into her hair and holding her with a gentle, yet inescapable grip.

At first, Emily was too astonished to respond, but as he continued kissing her with that unerring expertise, a warm, melting languor began to permeate her body, originating at her core. Her hands unconsciously rose to his chest, her palms pressing against the hard wall of muscle, and she swayed toward him, her knees growing weak.

Sensing her response, he deepened the kiss, his tongue parting her lips and delving into the warm recesses of her mouth. Still holding her head with one hand, he pressed his other palm to the small of her back, pulling her flush against his powerful body. She could feel the hard, thick ridge of his erection against her stomach, and she moaned, her sex clenching with a sudden intense ache.

A low growl rumbled deep within his chest, and the hand in her hair moved down to grasp the thin strap of her dress. Before Emily could register his intent, she heard a ripping sound, and then his palm was on her breast, his large, strong fingers cupping the soft weight with startling possessiveness, his thumb rasping across her peaked nipple and setting it afire.

Somewhere at the back of Emily's mind, alarm bells started ringing, penetrating the fog of desire. "Wait, stop," she gasped, turning her head to avoid his kiss. "Zaron... please, stop!"

His body tensed and his grip on her breast tightened, his fingers squeezing her flesh almost to the point of pain. For one terrifying second, Emily thought he wouldn't listen to her, but then he let go of her and stepped back, giving her some much-needed space.

Trembling all over, Emily tried to cover her naked breasts with the torn material of her dress. How could she have done this? How could she have let a strange man—no, a strange *extraterrestrial*—almost have sex with her? Had she somehow lost all reason and common sense?

The dress wouldn't stay up on its own, and she finally gave up. Holding the ragged material tightly against her chest, she lifted her eyes to meet Zaron's gaze, feeling wildly off-balance.

He was watching her with unconcealed lust, his eyes pitch black and glittering. There was a large bulge in his shorts, and his muscular body was practically vibrating with tension. He looked like it took all of his self-control not to pounce on her.

Emily's alien captor wanted her.

This was not good. Not good at all.

Emily took a step back, her panic intensifying.

Zaron's nostrils flared as he observed her instinctive retreat. "I won't force you," he said evenly. "You don't have to be afraid of me."

"Right, of course." Emily forced herself to stop backing away. "Look, Zaron…" She inhaled. "I am not sure what you have in mind for us, but this is a bad idea—"

"Why?" His burning black gaze held her. "You want me. Or did I just imagine your response?"

Emily swallowed. "No, you didn't imagine it," she admitted, her face heating up. "But that doesn't mean I want to have sex with you. I hardly know you and—and you're not even human."

His mouth quirked with sudden amusement. "Are you afraid I have tentacles or a third arm? I can assure you, I have all the same parts as a human male."

"I know that," Emily said quickly, though she'd known no such thing. He *appeared* human, but that didn't necessarily mean his equipment functioned the same way. Regardless, she wasn't about to admit her doubts to him now.

"So then what's the problem?" he murmured, closing the distance between them again. "You will enjoy the experience, I promise you that." His hand reached for hers, his large palm covering the tightly clenched fist that was holding up her dress. She could feel the warmth emanating from his body, smell his clean masculine scent, and her nipples hardened again, her breathing quickening as a melting sensation spread through her body. Unconsciously, her grip on the dress loosened… and suddenly, the soft material was falling, leaving her bare from the waist up.

Zaron's eyes seemed to darken further, and before Emily

could react, she felt his big hands cupping her buttocks, lifting her up with startling ease until her breasts were at his eye level. With a soft growl, he bent his head and captured one rosy nipple with his mouth, sucking on it with a strong pull. Emily gasped, her hands clutching at the heavy muscles of his shoulders as her toes curled from the sharp, unexpected pleasure. The wet heat of his mouth and the pressure of his tongue intensified the throbbing ache between her thighs, and she moaned, mindlessly rubbing against him to relieve the tension building within her.

"Yes, angel, that's it," he whispered, his hot breath washing over her as he lowered her slowly, letting her feel the hard contours of his body as his mouth moved up to taste the sensitive area where her neck and shoulder joined. She shuddered helplessly, overtaken by the sensations, and felt his fingers slipping between her legs as he held her suspended off the ground with one hand. His thumb circled around her clit, slowly, maddeningly, each circle tightening the coil of tension deep within her core. One long finger pushed inside her wet channel, and she heard him groan as her body clenched around his finger, her inner walls grasping eagerly at the intruder. She could feel her skin growing hot, and then his thumb was directly on her clit, massaging it with a circular, rhythmic motion. Emily cried out, her hips jerking from the intense lash of sensation, and felt her body splintering into a million pieces.

Before she could recover, the room tilted around her. Disoriented, she grabbed at Zaron's shirt—and realized he was lowering her to the floor, his hand withdrawing from her sex. Her back met the cool, hard surface, and the shock of it jolted her out of her sensual daze.

What was she doing? An alarm sounded in Emily's brain as

Zaron flipped up the skirt of her dress, baring her lower half. His knees were wedged between her legs, holding them open. Something hard and smooth brushed against her inner thigh, and she knew with sudden clarity that this was it, that in another moment he would be inside her.

She wasn't ready for this. As Zaron's mouth descended on her again, Emily pushed at him with all her strength and twisted her head to the side. "Stop. Zaron, please, stop!"

He froze over her, his breathing heavy and ragged, and Emily stilled, desperately hoping he would keep his word about not forcing her. She could feel the throbbing heat of his erection at her entrance, and a shudder of trepidation mixed with arousal ran through her. Slowly turning her head back, she met his gaze, trying not to panic at the violent hunger reflected there.

"I don't want to do this," she whispered, her hands pushing futilely at his chest. She could feel the hard muscles under her fingers, and the knowledge that she would never be able to fight him off made her stomach roil. "Zaron, please... let me go."

CHAPTER TWELVE

She wanted him to stop.

He was a second away from burying himself in her tight, slick warmth, and Emily wanted him to stop.

For a second, Zaron wasn't sure if he would be able to comply. She was lying spread beneath him, her soft, sleek body flushed with arousal and her heated scent enflaming his senses. Her deliciously round breasts were bared to his gaze, the nipples sticking up like ripe berries, and her pulse throbbed in the side of her neck, reminding him of the liquid ecstasy running through her veins. He could feel her slim thighs quivering with tension on the sides of his hips. One thrust, and he would have her. One thrust, and he would be deep inside her, satisfying the need raging through him. His cock was painfully hard, aching for her, and his body warred with his mind as he fought grimly for control.

It was only the fear in her eyes that enabled him to win that battle. She might desire him physically, but if he proceeded right now, it would be little better than rape.

His jaw tightly clenched, Zaron forced himself to roll off her. Rising to his feet, he turned away, rearranging his clothes to hide his engorged cock. He didn't look at her. He couldn't— not if he wanted to keep his word.

He heard her get up. Her movements were unsteady, her breathing coming faster than usual. He didn't know if it was from arousal or apprehension, but it didn't matter. Schooling his features into an impassive mask, Zaron turned back toward her, willing his erection to subside.

Emily was watching him warily, holding up the dress so it covered her chest. Her blond hair was tangled, streaming down her back in a cloud of pale waves, and her lips were swollen and reddened from the pressure of his mouth. With her skin glowing pink from her orgasm, she looked mouthwateringly fuckable.

Downright edible, in fact.

It took all of his self-control to say calmly, "I'm sorry if I frightened you, Emily. That was not my intention."

"What was your intention then?" Her voice was as steady as his, though her grip on the dress betrayed her nervousness. "What do you want from me, Zaron? Is this some kind of kinky thing for you, having sex with a woman you're keeping imprisoned in your house? A woman who's not even of your own species? Is this why you saved me?"

As she spoke, Zaron's lust slowly transformed into anger. The fact that there was some truth to what she was saying only added to his fury. "Why, yes," he said in a silky tone. "That's exactly right, angel. I saved you so I could fuck you. Would you rather I left you to die on those rocks instead?"

She held his gaze defiantly, but a faint, almost imperceptible tremor ran over her skin, making him regret his harsh words. "No," she said, her lips barely moving. "I am obviously grateful to be alive. Is that the payment you expect from me? Sex?"

Suddenly disgusted with himself, Zaron shook his head. "No." Frustrated, he ran his hand through his hair. The little human had him tied up in knots. "That's not what I meant." Knowing that anything else he said would only make the situation worse, he walked over to the wall, causing the entryway to Emily's room to appear.

"Why don't you rest for a bit?" he suggested, gesturing toward the opening. "I have some work to do right now, and you can catch a little nap before dinner." He knew that humans needed a lot of sleep, and it was possible that she was tired already.

She nodded, almost imperceptibly, and walked past him into the room, taking care not to look at him. She was still holding the torn dress protectively in front of her chest, and her delicate scent teased his nostrils as she passed by.

"I'll get you some new clothes," Zaron said in a strained voice, and walked to his office before he could grab her again. Taking out his fabricator, he created a few more dresses for her, using the time to picture himself submerged in a vat filled with ice-cold water—an image he hoped would be able to help his self-control.

When he was certain he wouldn't jump her, he went to her room.

Emily was sitting on the bed, her slender legs crossed. She had somehow managed to tie the torn straps of the dress together, and it was staying up on its own now.

"Here you go," Zaron said, opening one of the walls to reveal a closet. "This will be yours for the duration. You can just walk up to it, and it'll open for you." He placed the dresses in the closet and turned around to face her.

"Thank you," she said quietly, watching him with her unusual sea-colored eyes. "Do you by any chance have books that I could read? Maybe some magazines?"

Zaron thought about it for a moment, then issued a terse command in Krinar, causing the house to send a thin tablet floating in his direction from the other room. Snatching it out of the air, he spoke a few instructions in Krinar to allow Emily to control it with English language and then handed it to Emily. "This should give you access to any book you want," he explained. "Just tell it what you want to read, and you should be able to get it."

"Really?" She glanced up as she took the tablet from him. "Is this like an e-reader?"

He smiled. "Something like that." It was as good of a comparison as any, though the device he'd handed her was far more advanced. "You can also watch TV on it, if you'd like. Just tell it what you want to see, and it'll display the video for you."

"I just talk to it and it works?"

"Yes." He knew that some human technology worked like that now too, so the concept wouldn't be foreign to her. For Krinar, verbal commands and gestures were the old-fashioned way of doing things, but Zaron still preferred it for some reason. The alternative was to embed a computing device within his body, enabling him to use his mind to control technology. It was something he intended to do at some point, but hadn't gotten around to yet.

"Okay, then how about showing me *Avatar*?" she said,

looking down at the device. She spoke slowly and loudly, as though addressing a deaf person. "Please show me *Avatar*."

"It understood you the first time," Zaron said, watching with amusement as Emily's eyes widened at the three-dimensional image that appeared in the room. "You should be able to watch it now if you wish."

"Holy shit," she gasped, jumping up as the image expanded, taking up most of the space near the wall. "This is amazing!"

"Enjoy," Zaron said, smiling at her enthusiasm. "I'll see you in a couple of hours."

He was pretty sure she didn't notice as he left the room, all her attention focused on the spectacle unfolding in front of her. He would have to introduce her to a simulation soon, he thought, and grinned, picturing her reaction to *that*.

CHAPTER THIRTEEN

There was watching, and then there was watching with Krinar technology. Emily had seen *Avatar* twice in a movie theater, each time in IMAX 3D, but today she felt like she was experiencing it for the first time. The imagery was so real, so vivid, it was as though she was there on Pandora, watching the action unfolding all around her.

The next couple of hours flew by with Emily fully absorbed in the movie. It was a relief to let her mind focus on something other than her insane situation—though she quickly realized that a movie about humanoid aliens might not have been the wisest choice for that.

When the movie ended, she visited the strange restroom again, marveling at how her every need was anticipated, the technology working so intuitively it was almost as if the house was reading her mind. She managed to get water to come out of the sink-like protrusion and washed her face with it, then looked around for something to moisturize her skin.

Immediately, she felt a warm, soft breeze on her face. When the breeze stopped, she discovered that her skin was no longer feeling dry and tight; in fact, it was so smooth it was as though she'd been to a spa. She wished she had a mirror, and as soon as she began to search for one, one of the bathroom walls shimmered in front of her eyes, transforming itself into a glistening, mirror-like surface. It was truly spooky.

Stepping closer to the mirror, Emily studied the image that was reflected there. It was both familiar and different. When she had glanced at herself before, Emily had been too overwhelmed to actually focus on her reflection, so now she took a closer look.

It seemed as if Zaron's healing procedure had done more than fix her teeth and scars. It had also taken away the subtle signs of stress and sleep deprivation that had etched themselves into her skin over the past two years. Gone were the dark circles that had framed her eyes, the faint lines of tension around her mouth. She looked healthy and well rested for the first time in months.

She also looked like she'd been thoroughly kissed.

Swallowing, Emily turned away from the mirror and headed back to the room. She didn't want to think about that, but she could no longer keep the images out of her mind. What had occurred earlier had been raw, sexual... and deeply disturbing.

Her extraterrestrial captor wanted her. There was no longer any doubt of that. If she hadn't stopped him, he would've taken her right then and there, on the floor. Her breathing quickened at the memory of his powerful body over her, the hard pressure of his legs forcing her thighs apart, the wet heat of his mouth on her nipples...

Groaning, Emily plopped down on the bed and buried her head in the soft blanket.

She'd never engaged in casual sex—not even in college, where the hookup culture was prevalent. She'd always been too cautious, too careful. Too cognizant of the possible consequences. For her, that kind of intimacy required trust, and she wasn't someone who trusted easily. With her ex-boyfriend Jason, they'd been friends for a year before they'd started dating, and even then, they'd been together for a full month before she'd finally gone to bed with him.

Yet she had almost fucked a stranger—an inhuman stranger —on the floor of his futuristic house after knowing him for less than a day. He hadn't even worn protection, Emily remembered with a cold shudder. Could he have made her pregnant or given her some disease? Thinking about it, she decided that the latter possibility was unlikely, given the advanced state of their medical technology, but she was less sure about the former. Emily had stopped taking the pill after breaking up with Jason four months ago, so pregnancy was now a real concern for her.

What would happen the next time Zaron tried to seduce her? And he would try, she was certain of that. Would she be able to stop him? Would she *want* to stop him? She had never before been so attracted to a man, had never felt that desperate, all-consuming need. Sex had always been something Emily enjoyed, but what she'd experienced today was nothing like the tepid encounters she'd had with Jason. It was more of a conflagration that had nearly burned her alive.

And she had seen the same kind of uncontrollable hunger in his eyes. One way or another, he was going to have her.

Emily wasn't sure if the knowledge excited or terrified her.

CHAPTER FOURTEEN

For dinner, Zaron ordered a wide variety of dishes designed to appeal to Emily's palate. The only foods missing were animal products of any kind. He'd tried meat twice during his time on Earth, but he couldn't get used to the unpleasant taste and texture. He had no idea how humans in the developed nations had become so carnivorous in the past few decades; it was certainly not something anyone on Krina had anticipated. To this day, it amazed him that Emily's species thought it normal to eat meat every day—even three times a day, in some extreme cases.

When everything was ready, he went to get Emily.

He found her lying on her stomach, reading something on the tablet. She'd changed into a white dress, and her small feet were bare, her pink toes flexing rhythmically against the blanket as she hummed something to herself.

"Emily." He said her name softly, not wanting to startle her, but she still jumped, quickly turning over and sitting up to look at him. "Dinner is ready."

"Okay, great." Bending down, she pulled on her sandals and got up. "I'm looking forward to it." Her tone was upbeat, but Zaron noticed that she was trying not to look at him. She was determined to maintain a distance between them, he realized with dark amusement.

They sat down at the table, which was already loaded with dishes. "Wow, this meal is more like a feast," she said in amazement, putting a few bites of everything onto her plate. "Do you normally eat like this?"

"No," Zaron admitted, reaching for a *Cucurbita pepo* stuffed with roasted *Pleurotus ostreatus*—or, as Emily likely thought of it, zucchini with oyster mushrooms. "I ordered this for you. I wanted to make sure you enjoy the meal."

She looked surprised, but then a quick, radiant smile flashed across her face. "Thank you. You didn't have to go to all this trouble, though. I'm about as far from a picky eater as it gets."

"Oh?"

She nodded. "I'll eat anything. Just give me food and I'm there."

"Why? Did you ever go hungry?" Zaron inquired curiously. According to her driver's license, she lived in the United States, one of the more affluent human nations.

She shrugged, looking uncomfortable. "A few times. One of the foster homes where I lived had a very strict food rationing policy. They had twelve kids living with them, and they were always running out of funds."

"Foster homes?" Zaron tried to remember if he'd ever heard of that particular human institution. It seemed to imply that she had lived away from her family—something he hadn't come across in the basic background check he'd run on her in the beginning.

She nodded but didn't explain. Instead, she asked, "How is it that you speak English so well? I assume it's not your native language."

"You're right, it's not." Her attempt to change the topic was beyond transparent, but Zaron decided to allow it and made a mental note to research foster homes later. "I have a little implant that acts as a translating device."

"An implant? Like in your brain?"

Zaron smiled. "Exactly."

"That's incredible." She appeared excited now. "Do you speak other languages too?"

"Yes, I do."

"Which ones?"

"All of them."

She gasped, her mouth falling open. "Every single language out there?"

"Yes," Zaron confirmed, enjoying her reaction. "Every language that currently exists and a few that have died out."

She blew out her breath. "Holy shit…" Shaking her head in amazement, she began to eat.

For the next few minutes, there was only companionable silence as they demolished the dishes sitting on the table. Zaron noticed that Emily took a second serving of a salad made of *Beta vulgaris* bulbs and dried *Vitis vinifera* berries. No, a salad made of beets and raisins, he mentally corrected himself. He often had trouble taking off his scientist hat, but it was better to use common names for edible plants.

"That was amazing," Emily said, pushing her empty plate away. "It looks like your people like to eat well."

"We do." Zaron gave her a slow smile. "We tend to enjoy all aspects of life to the fullest, and gratifying the senses is a big part of that."

A faint flush brightened her pale cheeks. "I see."

Zaron's smile faded as his body reacted to the sight. He could tell the girl was thinking about what had taken place earlier; he could hear her rapid heartbeat and see the pulse throbbing visibly in the side of her neck. The skin in that tender area looked soft, inviting to the touch, and the urge to slice his teeth across it and taste the richness of her blood was so strong that Zaron almost reached for her.

As though sensing his hunger, Emily shifted in her seat, moving back from the table. Her hand tightened on the utensil she was holding, and Zaron forced his tense muscles to relax. He didn't know why it was so difficult to restrain himself in her presence, but he had no intention of losing control and leaping on her like some savage. It had not even been a full day since she'd woken up, and she was undoubtedly overwhelmed by everything. He needed to give her more time.

"Zaron," she said quietly, her eyes glued to his face, "can you tell me more about yourself? What exactly are you doing here on Earth? What are your people like?"

Zaron considered how to best answer her questions. The official post-arrival disclosure protocol was still being worked out, but he knew that the Council didn't intend to reveal much to the general human public, so he needed to be careful.

"I already told you we're here to formally meet your species for the first time," he said. "As far as what we're like, that's like asking you what humans are like. It's not easy to list all of your own attributes."

"But how are you different from me?" she persisted. "What exactly makes a Krinar not human?"

Zaron sighed. This was going to be tricky. "Well, for one thing, the Krinar live longer," he said, focusing on the most innocuous tidbit first. "Much longer, in fact."

"Oh? How much longer?"

"I'm six hundred and nine years old," Zaron said, watching as her jaw dropped in shock. "So much, much longer."

"Six hundred years old," she whispered, her gaze moving up and down his body. "How is it that you look so young?"

"We don't age," Zaron explained, leaning back in his seat. "Not like humans do. After we reach full maturity, we don't change much throughout our lives."

Her eyes were wide with shock. "Are you immortal?"

"No, not immortal, but we don't die of old age. Have you ever heard of negligible senescence?"

She frowned, appearing to think about it. "The term sounds familiar. I feel like I read it somewhere recently."

"Maybe you have," Zaron said. "There's some research being done into that now among your scientists. Essentially, a negligibly senescent organism doesn't exhibit reduced reproductive capability or functional decline with age. There are several Earth species like that, so it's not a Krinar-specific phenomenon. There's the planarian flatworm, for instance—"

"Oh, that's right," she breathed, her eyes roaming over him again. "I remember reading about this now. The article speculated that tortoises may be like that—that they don't age as they get older."

Zaron nodded. "Yes, precisely. The Krinar are like that, too."

She took a deep breath and met his gaze. "If that's the case, you can't be very similar to us genetically, right?"

"No, we're not similar to you genetically at all," Zaron said, smiling. The girl was quick to catch on. "As far as DNA is concerned, you have more in common with a dolphin than with me."

She gave him an incredulous look. "If that's true, why do you want to have sex with me? And how exactly does something like that work?"

Zaron laughed softly. "It works quite well, I assure you." Leaning forward, he reached across the table to take her slender hand. "I can't make you pregnant, angel, but I can give you more pleasure than you've ever experienced in your life." He slowly ran his thumb across the center of her palm, pressing lightly on the spots where he could feel tension. Women—human or Krinar—were highly susceptible to the pleasure of simple touch; it was something he'd learned centuries ago. The physical bond always began with basic skin-to-skin contact, and a smart man ensured there would be plenty of that.

To his satisfaction, Emily's skin pinkened with arousal, her hand twitching in his grasp. Zaron could hear her breathing quickening, and his own body reacted with sharp intensity, his cock hardening in an instant. Not wanting to test his self-restraint too much, he released her hand, letting her pull it out of his reach.

"Why do you call me 'angel?'" she asked in an unsteady voice. "Do you have such a concept on your planet?"

"No." Zaron inhaled deeply, drawing in her warm scent. "That's a uniquely human invention. But your coloring does remind me of some angel drawings I've seen here on Earth."

An unexpected smile danced across her lips. "Are you a fan of religious art? I must say, I wouldn't have expected that from an alien."

"I appreciate beauty in all forms," Zaron replied, studying her delicate features. "And I have to say, humans have managed to create some incredibly beautiful things during their short existence."

"What about the Krinar? Do your people have art, philosophy, music?"

"Yes to all three." He smiled at her. "Some of us dedicate our entire lives to creative pursuits, while others merely dabble in them. But either way, such contributions are highly valued—an artist is just as important in our society as a designer or a scientist."

Her eyes lit up with curiosity. "Valued how? Are they compensated financially? In general, how does your economy operate? What do you use as currency? Do you have something like a stock market?"

Zaron grinned at the barrage of questions. "We do, but it's not nearly as important," he said, addressing her last question. "Most businesses are privately funded, and if the project is big enough, the government gets involved. Wealth is not necessarily something we strive for; it comes with success in our chosen fields, as top experts are well compensated—both in the private sector and by the government."

"So you don't have capitalism?"

"Not in the same way you do." He paused, trying to think how to best explain it to her. "Because we are so long-lived—and because our population is significantly smaller, numbering in the millions instead of billions—our society functions very differently from yours. In some ways, it's simpler; in others, it's more complex. All of modern-day Krina is one cohesive socio-economic unit, with all that it implies."

She appeared fascinated. "So the entire planet is like one country?"

"More or less. We have one ruling body—the Council—and they make decisions to benefit us as a whole, as opposed to appeasing one specific region or faction."

"Well, that's certainly different," she mused. "Our politicians are nothing like that. How are the members of the Council chosen? Are they elected?"

"No." Zaron shook his head. "Those who are on the Council are there because they earned it in some way—because their contributions to society were greater than most."

She nodded, as though it made sense to her. "So you have the smartest, highest-achieving individuals running your planet? That seems like it would be an improvement over the way we do things."

"It works for us," he said, and was about to delve into the concept of social standing when his wrist computer vibrated softly, reminding him of a virtual meeting he had coming up. He was supposed to convene with a defense expert and several designers to determine the best layout for the ten Centers. Annoyed at the interruption, Zaron considered canceling the meeting, but he didn't want to risk a delay.

Reluctantly, he rose to his feet. "I'm sorry, but I have to go. You should rest and get some sleep. I have some work to do this evening."

"Of course, I understand." Getting up as well, she gave him a quick smile, and Zaron realized she was relieved for the dinner to be ending in such manner. She had probably been concerned that he would try to seduce her again, he thought with sudden irritation—and he likely would have, if it hadn't been for this meeting.

"Well, good night then," she said and, with a little wave, headed toward her own room. He heard her light footsteps and the sound of her kicking off her shoes, and then he went into his office, doing his best to focus on something other than the girl he wanted to fuck senseless.

————

Alone in her room, Emily lay down on the comfortable bed and closed her eyes, trying to clear her mind enough to fall asleep.

She'd used the futuristic bathroom again, even taking a shower there—which was an experience in itself, with the water coming at her from all directions at a perfect pressure and temperature. A variety of soaps, shampoos, and deliciously scented lotions had been applied to her skin and hair without her having to lift a finger, and warm jets of air had dried her off afterwards. By the time she was done, every part of her had been luxuriously clean, and even her mouth had felt fresh, as though she had just brushed her teeth.

Now, however, her brain refused to relax, her head buzzing with everything she'd learned today. In just a few short hours, her world had been turned upside down, and she couldn't stop dwelling on the incredible implications of what Zaron had told her.

Earth was about to make contact with an alien race—a race that had technology and medicine far beyond anything modern science could imagine. A race that had essentially created human beings.

If Zaron was telling the truth, in seventeen days nothing would ever be the same again. Would the Krinar cure cancer? Could they end poverty and hunger? Put a stop to war? It seemed as if Zaron's civilization had moved past such issues. Did that mean that humanity now would too? What did his people intend to say when they appeared? How were they going to reveal themselves to the public, and what would be the fallout once they did? She pictured the screaming headlines, the hysteria from end-of-the-world fanatics…

When she finally fell asleep, her dreams were a strange mix of erotic images, scenes from *Independence Day*, hungry lions with coal-black eyes, and three-dimensional Excel spreadsheets filled with bowls of exotic fruit.

CHAPTER FIFTEEN

*T*he next morning, Emily woke up with a much clearer head. To her surprise, she'd slept well, much better than could be expected under the circumstances. Apparently, her subconscious mind wasn't particularly bothered by the thought that aliens existed—or that she was being temporarily detained by one against her will.

Getting up, she put on the clothes Zaron had provided and used the facilities. Then she approached the wall, aware of an uneasy sensation in her stomach. Knocking on the wall, she waited, her fingers nervously twisting the soft material of her dress.

The wall in front of her dissolved, creating the entryway into the living room area. Zaron was standing on the other side.

"Good morning," he said softly, looking at her. "I hope you got good sleep?"

"I did, thanks." Emily did her best not to stare, but it was impossible. She had somehow managed to forget how gorgeous her captor was… and how her body reacted to him. Already, she could feel her heartbeat speeding up, her core clenching with sudden need. She had never wanted a man like that before—so instantly, so strongly. There was nothing rational or reasonable about the heat surging through her veins; it was animal lust, pure and simple. Her mind told her that he was not human, that she still knew nothing about him or his people, but her body didn't care.

He was dressed in a white T-shirt and a pair of khaki shorts —a plain outfit that somehow only emphasized his dark masculine beauty. His thick hair was slightly disheveled, and his broad shoulders strained the thin fabric of the shirt, his muscles clearly defined underneath his clothing.

Swallowing, Emily stepped through the opening, trying to ignore her racing pulse.

"Would you like some breakfast?" Zaron offered, his black eyes gleaming with subtle amusement. Emily had no doubt that he was aware of her physical response to him and was enjoying it tremendously.

"Um, yeah, sure." Emily took a deep breath. "First, though, can you please tell me where my things are? You said you have my wallet, right?" She'd realized this morning that she hadn't seen her wallet or phone since she'd woken up here—a realization that had made her feel even more like a prisoner.

Zaron nodded and said something in his language. A second later, one of the walls opened, and a stack of her belongings floated out. Grabbing them from the air, he handed them to her. "Here you go. The clothes were damaged, but I still kept them for you. The money inside your wallet got a little wet, but

I think it should be all right. This little piece of technology, though"—he pointed at her smartphone—"didn't survive its swim in the river."

Holding her clothes with one hand, Emily took her phone in the other and tried to turn it on. The screen remained blank, and she could feel the residual moisture in the protective case. Zaron was right: the phone was dead. Of course, if it had been functional, she doubted he would've given it back to her so easily.

She checked the wallet next. To her relief, her driver's license, credit cards, and cash were all there, although still a bit damp.

"I didn't steal anything, if that's what you're worried about," Zaron said wryly as she finished flipping through the folds.

"I didn't think you did." Emily looked up at him. "I just wanted to make sure I didn't lose anything during my fall. Thank you for returning this to me."

"Of course. Like I told you, you are my guest."

"A guest who can't leave," Emily said, holding his gaze.

His eyes narrowed slightly, but he didn't respond to her statement. "For breakfast, how about a fruit salad with macadamia-raspberry dressing?" he asked instead.

"Sounds good." Putting down her things on the floating couch, Emily followed Zaron into the kitchen. Perching on one of the floating planks at the table, she listened as he gave the house their food order—or at least that's what she assumed he was doing when he spoke in Krinar.

Shifting in her seat, Emily took a slow breath, then another, trying to keep calm. She could feel the first stirrings of that caged, claustrophobic feeling she got from being indoors too much—a feeling that was exacerbated by the knowledge that this time, she really was locked up, that her freedom was under someone else's control. Logically, she understood that her imprisonment was only temporary, but logic had nothing to do with the suffocating tightness in her chest.

Emily knew from experience that the tightness would only get worse. The last time she'd been forced to be indoors longer than a day was four years ago during a bad winter storm in Chicago. Nearly four feet of snow had fallen in a span of thirty-two hours, and it had been impossible to open the front door for almost three days. Emily, who had been sharing a small townhouse in Evanston with four roommates, had gotten so claustrophobic that she'd ended up climbing out of her first-floor bedroom window into a pile of snow—anything to get rid of the choking sensation of being stuck in a closed space for a prolonged period of time.

Ever since she'd woken up at Zaron's house yesterday, she hadn't been outside at all.

No, don't think about that. Breathe, and don't think about that.

"What's wrong?" Zaron frowned, apparently sensing her growing discomfort. "Are you feeling ill?" Sitting down across from her, he gave her a questioning stare.

Emily bit her lip. She hated admitting to weakness, but she couldn't remain indoors for the next two-plus weeks. She simply couldn't.

"I have a thing," she said after a moment. "I get weird if I stay inside too much. It's a claustrophobia of sorts. I can handle small spaces, but not if I stay there for long."

His eyebrows rose in surprise. "You were fine yesterday."

She nodded. "I can usually go about a day without it getting bad, but then I need to get some fresh air or I start going crazy. When I'm at work, I always volunteer to run errands—you know, getting coffee, dropping stuff off at the post office, picking up lunch for my team—anything I can do to leave the building for a few minutes. It's not usually a big deal, but I just can't be cooped up for long."

Zaron leaned back, regarding Emily beneath half-closed eyelids. "I see. Do you need to go outside right now, or can you wait until after breakfast?"

A wave of relief flooded her, chasing away some of the suffocating tightness in her chest. "I can wait," she said, giving him a genuine smile. "It's not too bad yet." She felt almost lightheaded with joy.

He wasn't going to keep her locked up in the house after all.

While they were speaking, their breakfast had landed on the table.

"We can go for a swim," Zaron said, reaching for a bowl of fruit and nuts in some exotic-looking sauce. "There's a nice lake near here."

"A swim? That would be great," Emily said, falling ravenously on the fruit. The salad was delicious, but she could barely taste it in her eagerness to be outside. Aside from alleviating her claustrophobia, going out would also give her a chance to look for an escape route.

If Zaron thought she would meekly accept losing the job opportunity of a lifetime, he had another thing coming. Emily had worked too hard to let her career be derailed so easily.

One way or another, she needed to get back home.

———

After breakfast, Zaron fabricated a swimsuit for Emily and some swimming shorts for himself. Adhering to the non-disclosure mandate meant that everything he wore had to at least *look* like human clothing, so he found the bikini design for Emily on human Internet.

Entering Emily's room, Zaron gave her the two pieces of cloth, then stepped out to let her change. He didn't mind the upcoming outing, but her condition puzzled him. As soon as he'd seen her this morning, he'd sensed a strange tension in her, and her anxiety had only seemed to get worse as the morning progressed. By the time they sat down to eat breakfast, Emily had looked like she'd wanted to crawl out of her skin. He didn't think she'd been faking it, either; unless she was a world-class actress, her discomfort had been real.

A knock interrupted Zaron's thoughts. He gave a quick command, and the wall to Emily's room opened, creating a doorway for her.

She stood there wearing the same dress as before, only with the blue straps of her bikini peeking out from underneath. At the sight of his semi-naked body, a pink flush spread over her face and neck, giving her pale skin a delicate glow.

"Ready to go?" Zaron asked, suppressing a smile at the way she tried to keep her eyes above his neck. He'd just changed into his own swimwear, and he hadn't bothered putting on a shirt. Her feminine reaction to his body pleased him; the stronger the attraction, the easier it would be to coax her into his bed.

Emily nodded and followed him toward the far wall of the living room. When they approached, the intelligent material parted, creating an opening leading to the outside.

Stepping out, Zaron inhaled deeply, enjoying the heat of the sun on his exposed skin. It was already mid-morning, and the air was warm and humid, filled with the scent of bromeliads and the sounds of various living creatures. This region of Earth reminded him of home—the primary reason why he'd chosen this location for the main Krinar colony.

Turning, he saw Emily standing a few feet away from him, staring at the house behind them. "Not what you expected, is it?" he asked, seeing the expression on her face.

Unlike most Krinar or human dwellings, his temporary home was not a building at all. It was a high-tech cave located deep inside a small mountain. With the outside opening sealed, it was completely invisible behind a thick wall of greenery. Unless someone already knew it was there, it was impossible to find—either from the air or on foot.

"No," Emily replied, turning to face him. "It's not what I expected at all. Is this because you're trying to stay hidden?"

"Yes. I don't want some plane or helicopter to spot a strange structure in your jungle and decide to investigate."

Emily gave him a thoughtful look but didn't ask any more questions as they walked through the forest toward the lake. Now that she was outside, Zaron could sense her anxiety easing, the pinched look on her face disappearing. For the first time since he'd known her, the human girl appeared relaxed and happy, her soft lips curving in a smile as she watched a *Sceloporus malachiticus*—a spiny green lizard—scooting off a nearby rock.

"You seem quite comfortable here for someone who lives in New York City," he remarked, noticing the ease with which she navigated the green jungle. She seemed to respect nature without being afraid of it, stepping carefully yet confidently through the thick grass. He was about to warn her about the painful sting of the *Paraponera clava*, but she avoided the bullet ant colony before he had the chance.

"I *am* comfortable here," Emily said, flashing him a quick smile. "I grew up in semi-rural Georgia, actually, and only moved to New York for work. I was a very outdoorsy kid, climbing trees and catching bugs all day long. If I had my way, I would've lived in a treehouse."

Zaron grinned, picturing a tiny Emily running through the woods. If she looked angelic now, he could only imagine what she must've been like as a child, with those large bright eyes and sunny hair.

"What about you?" she asked as they entered a small clearing. "What was it like for you as a child? Did you get to play outdoors a lot? I imagine your cities are very high-tech…"

"They are," Zaron said. "But they're different from your cities. We tend to build around the natural environment, instead of over it. In fact, our settlements look more like this jungle than one of your towns."

"Really?" She gave him a surprised look. "So no skyscrapers, no roads, no cars?"

"No." He shook his head. "Nothing of the sort. We do have some larger buildings for public events, but there aren't many of them. We don't like to cluster together like humans do, so our homes tend to be spread out—and we don't need roads because we either walk or use flying transport."

Zaron could see that Emily was about to ask him more questions, but at that moment they reached their destination.

About two miles across and three miles wide, the lake was a sizable body of water, fed by several different mountain streams—streams that were more like rivers at this time of year. Set deep within the forest, the lake was surrounded by walls of dense green vegetation and attracted all sorts of wildlife—a perfect spot for a biologist. Zaron frequently came here, both to enjoy the water and to study the local fauna.

"Watch out for that manchineel tree," he told Emily, taking her arm to steer her away from the plant as they descended to the water. "The *Hippomane mancinella* is highly poisonous, and I didn't bring any medical equipment with me." The milky white sap of the tree contained strong toxins; just standing under its leaves during rain could cause human skin to blister.

"Oh, thanks," she murmured, glancing up at him before turning her attention to the water. "I'll be sure to avoid it from now on." Her voice sounded slightly choked, and Zaron realized he was still holding her upper arm. His hand was startlingly dark against her ivory skin, his fingers almost encircling her slender arm.

For a moment, the temptation to pull her closer was unbearable. The air between them seemed to sizzle, the atmosphere rife with sexual awareness. She wanted him; he could smell the desire on her, hear her rapid heartbeat. Why was she resisting the inevitable? Surely Emily had to know that she would be his, that he wouldn't let her go without first sinking deep into her soft, tender flesh.

"Is the lake safe for swimming?" Her voice was higher-pitched than usual, her words coming faster. She could sense the direction of his thoughts, he realized, and was doing her best to distract him from his growing hunger. "Is there anything dangerous there?"

"No," Zaron said, reluctantly releasing her arm. "You have nothing to worry about." As much as he wanted to press the issue, she was still too anxious. He would have her soon, he promised himself. Soon, but not quite yet.

Turning away from Emily, Zaron took off his sandals and walked down the narrow strip of rocky shore toward the water.

A dip in the cool lake sounded more appealing—and necessary—by the second.

CHAPTER SIXTEEN

*H*ardly able to breathe, Emily watched Zaron as he walked into the water, the sun reflecting off his thick, glossy hair. Her heart pounded furiously in her chest, and she felt too warm, her skin tingling from the residual sensation of his touch.

She had known he had a good physique, of course; his clothes had done little to hide his powerful muscles. But knowing and seeing were two very different things—as Emily had discovered when she came out of her room and saw him standing there, dressed in nothing but a pair of light gray swimming shorts.

Her alien captor was devastatingly, inhumanly beautiful. Smooth, darkly bronzed skin, unmarred by even a hint of imperfection, covered every inch of his rippled torso. Wide shoulders, a lean waist, and narrow hips formed a striking V-shape, and there was no fat anywhere on his muscled body. From the smattering of dark hair on his chest to the clearly defined eight-pack on his flat abdomen, he was an unbelievably gorgeous male animal.

Walking next to him through the dense forest, Emily had barely been able to keep her eyes off his body, and the second he touched her again, she'd felt like she'd been set on fire. His strong fingers had held her arm with an iron grip, ostensibly to protect her from the poisonous tree, and her body had surged with desire, warm moisture inundating her sex.

Why was she still resisting? a small, insidious voice whispered in her mind. Would it be so bad to throw caution to the wind and enjoy herself for once? How often did one get an opportunity to fuck a man that hot? And what did it matter if there was no future for them, if he was from a different species and she would never see him again once she went home? Thousands of women hooked up with strangers during their travels. Emily's choice of partner might be more exotic, but ultimately, that's all it would be: a short vacation fling with a man who was literally out of this world.

No. Shaking her head, Emily shimmied out of her dress, pushing away the dangerous thoughts. She had to focus on getting her life and career back on track, and an affair with an extraterrestrial—an extraterrestrial who was holding her captive, no less—was the last thing she needed.

Kicking off her shoes, she walked toward the water, grateful that Zaron seemed to be swimming away from the shore and not paying attention to her. She had no idea how many more seduction attempts she could withstand before giving in, and she had a strong suspicion that being mostly naked together was not conducive to maintaining the appropriate distance.

Just a quick swim, Emily promised herself, enjoying the cool water lapping at her skin. Just a quick swim to clear her head, and then she could start figuring out how to get herself out of this predicament.

The bottom of the lake was as rocky as the shore, hurting her bare feet, but she didn't have to walk for long before it was deep enough to swim. Leisurely moving through the water, she saw Zaron swimming in the distance.

Very far in the distance.

Her pulse accelerated with sudden excitement. He was so far away she could barely see his dark head in the water. In fact, he was almost in the middle of the lake. She must've been standing there, staring at the water, much longer than she'd thought.

This was her opportunity, her chance to escape before the seventeen days were up. Emily was in good running shape, and she had a rough idea of where they were, having seen something that looked like this lake on a map she'd studied for her hiking excursion. She couldn't be more than ten, fifteen miles away from one of the towns. If she got enough of a head start on Zaron, there was a strong possibility she might make it to civilization before he could catch her—and she would be back home in time for her interview.

Keeping an eye on the dark head in the distance, she exited the water and nonchalantly walked toward her sandals, doing her best to pretend she was simply warming up. Pulling on her shoes and dress, she cast one last look in Zaron's direction—verifying he was still in the middle of the lake—and sprinted toward the woods.

———

Swimming through the calm water, Zaron enjoyed the relaxing exercise, his muscles moving and stretching with every slow, deliberate stroke. Cognizant of Emily's presence nearby, he did his best to slow his pace to that of a human, but he was not entirely sure he succeeded. Even after six months on Earth, he found it difficult to move as *Homo sapiens* did—another reason for his decision to leave human cities in favor of more remote regions.

Glancing toward the shore, he saw Emily coming out of the lake. With his sharp Krinar eyesight, he could see everything, right down to the droplets of water glistening on her pale skin. His breath caught in his throat, his cock hardening at the sight. Zaron had purposefully resisted looking at her earlier, unsure of his self-control, and now he could see that he had been right to avoid temptation. Clad in only a small blue bikini, his human guest was a symphony of long, shapely legs and feminine curves, her breasts full and upright and her small waist flaring out to a firm, heart-shaped bottom. With her blond hair twisted carelessly on top of her head, she looked like a ray of sunlight, her skin oddly luminous from the distance.

Unable to tear his eyes away, Zaron watched hungrily as she bent down and slipped on her sandals, then pulled on her dress. Her movements were casual, almost lazy. Deceptively casual, he realized, noticing the tension in her shoulders. Straightening, she briefly looked in his direction, her eyes squinting against the bright light... and then she bolted.

She was running away from him.

Driven purely by instinct, Zaron dove under, cutting through the water with ferocious speed. Sharp, irrational anger churned in his veins, adding to his visceral urge to hunt down fleeing prey. How dare she run? He had saved her life, and she was *his*—his to fuck, his to keep for as long as he wished.

It took him less than two minutes to cross the distance to

the shore. Surging out of the water, he caught a trace of her scent disappearing into the woods. She hadn't gotten far, but even if she had, it wouldn't have mattered. No human could ever outrun a Krinar.

His jaw set in a grim line, Zaron began the chase.

CHAPTER SEVENTEEN

*R*unning through the forest, Emily felt her breathing settle into a steady rhythm—one that she knew would enable her to keep the pace for the next few miles. To her relief, the strappy sandals Zaron had given her sat snugly on her feet, without even a hint of the rubbing discomfort one normally expected with such footwear.

Though the last two years had been tough, with her job consuming nearly all of her waking hours, Emily had usually managed to sneak in a five-mile run every couple of days. It didn't compare to the rigorous fitness regimen she'd had in college, but it was better than turning into a complete couch potato—and she was extremely grateful for those runs now. She could feel her muscles warming up and stretching, her lungs working easily, and she knew she would be able to keep this up for at least an hour. By then, Zaron should be far behind her, assuming he even bothered to come after her once he reached the shore.

If all went well, she would not see him again.

The thought was strangely upsetting, so she pushed it out of her mind. There was no going back now. For better or for worse, she had escaped, and now she needed to make sure she found civilization quickly.

Just one foot in front of the other, Emily. One foot in front of the other.

Focusing on the familiar runner's refrain, she leapt over a fallen log… and ran smack into an impossibly hard body.

The impact knocked the breath out of her. Reeling back, she tripped over the log and would've fallen if strong hands hadn't caught her at that moment. In a flash, Emily found herself stretched on the ground on her back, her arms pinned above her head, with six-feet-plus of dripping-wet, muscular male sprawled on top of her.

Zaron. He had somehow caught up with her.

He was breathing hard, and she could see a muscle pulsing in his tightly clenched jaw. His thick dark hair was plastered against his skull, his black eyes glittering like coals.

He looked savage—and utterly furious.

"Where the fuck do you think you're going?" His voice was a feral growl, his fingers like a steel vise around her wrists. "You can't run from me."

Her lungs finally started to function, and Emily greedily sucked in air, trying to gather her wits. How had Zaron gotten here so quickly from the middle of the lake? Even the best Olympic swimmers couldn't have covered that distance in such a short time. "What… how did you…?" She couldn't seem to get more than a few words out through the thunderous pounding of blood in her ears. She could feel every inch of his hard, half-naked body, the moisture from his skin seeping into her dress, and her flesh reacted instantly, her nipples pebbling into taut, erect buds.

"How did I what?" He lowered his head until his face was only a few inches from her own, his gaze burning into her. Water dripped from his hair onto her forehead, the droplets startlingly cold on her overheated skin. "How did I catch you?"

Emily managed to nod.

"I can always catch you." His voice softened to a hoarse whisper, and a hotter, darker gleam appeared in his eyes. "There's no place on this planet or beyond where I couldn't find you, angel… if I were so inclined."

Her heart skipped a beat, then began to gallop madly in her chest. She could feel a growing hardness against her leg, and an answering heat flooded her body even as deepening awareness of her own vulnerability made her stomach tighten. "Let go," she whispered, straining against his hold. It was like being pinned down by a mountain, and the sense of helplessness was both frightening and maddening. "Zaron, let me go…"

He stared at her, his jaw muscle flexing, and the blazing hunger on his face sent a surge of alarmed excitement through her. She could sense him battling for control—and she knew the exact moment when he lost the battle.

With a tortured groan, he lowered his head and captured her mouth with his.

There was nothing sweet and tender about this kiss; it was a raw, carnal claiming. Zaron's lips and tongue were everywhere, consuming her, stealing away her breath, her will to resist. His right hand effortlessly held both of her wrists above her head, and his left slid down her body, fisting in her skirt and pulling it up. Wherever his fingers brushed against her skin, her flesh was left burning, aching for his touch.

Overwhelmed, Emily arched against him, uncertain if she wanted to get closer or throw him off, and felt his knee parting her naked thighs as he grabbed her bikini bottoms and ripped them off. Only the wet material of his shorts separated them now, the heavy pressure of his erection pushing against her exposed sex.

Suddenly, her hands were free. Gasping, Emily grabbed at Zaron's shoulders, her fingers digging into his skin as he began a rocking motion with his hips, each move rubbing the hard length of his cock on her clit and sending waves of heat throughout her body. He was still kissing her with deep, drugging kisses that clouded her mind, and somewhere low within her belly, a familiar tension began to build as he pulled off her bikini top and closed his hand around her breast, firmly massaging the soft weight under the thin fabric of her dress.

Her head swimming, Emily moaned into his mouth, unable to focus on anything but the dizzying pleasure surging through her. All her fears, all her doubts evaporated, burned away in the searing heat of his embrace. Her fingers slid into his thick hair, holding him closer, and her hips began to move in an answering rhythm.

Zaron groaned again, and she dimly registered another ripping sound. He'd torn off his shorts, she realized vaguely, feeling the smooth head of his cock brushing against her inner thigh. The tension inside her intensified, her core throbbing with molten need, and she lifted her hips toward him, unconsciously begging for more.

At her move, Zaron stiffened and raised his head to stare down at her, holding himself propped up on one elbow. His breathing was harsh and fast, his lips shiny from their kisses. "Do you want this?" he whispered, his voice hoarse with lust.

He nudged his hips forward, the tip of his shaft pressing into the soft notch between her legs. "Do you want this, Emily?"

His eyes bore into her, demanding an answer, and she nodded helplessly, unable to do anything else. She'd never known such aching want, a desire so intense it bordered on agony. She wouldn't be able to bear it if he stopped now, and her usual voice of caution remained silent as he grasped her thigh with one strong hand, opening her legs wider, and began to push in.

Despite her arousal, the initial penetration wasn't easy. He was thick and long, much bigger than any man she'd been with, and as he advanced deeper into her yielding flesh, a cry escaped her lips at the stinging, stretching pressure. Tensing, Emily gripped his arms and felt a shudder run through his body as her inner muscles tightened around his hard length in a futile attempt to repel the invasion.

At her pained cry, Zaron stopped, his large body shaking with the effort of holding himself still, and Emily saw that his black eyes were glazed with hunger. Yet when he lowered his head, brushing his lips against her cheek, the gesture held startling tenderness. "Are you all right?" he murmured, his warm breath washing over her left ear and sending shivers of pleasure down her body.

Closing her eyes, Emily wound her arms around his neck and wrapped her legs around his hips. The discomfort was already passing, and the earlier fever was returning. "Yes," she whispered, arching up to take him even deeper, and shuddered in helpless delight as the movement intensified the sensations emanating from her core.

Zaron shuddered too, the last bit of his control disappearing, and began thrusting heavily, driving into her with punishing force. Gasping, Emily clung to him, feeling like a sliver tossed about in a storm. Her world narrowed, all her senses focused on him. His skin was slick with water and sweat, his muscles bunching and flexing underneath her fingertips. She could feel his thick shaft moving deep inside her, smell his warm, musky scent, and the tension within her spiraled higher, centering on the bundle of nerves at the apex of her sex. Her skin prickled with gooseflesh, her heartbeat skyrocketing... and then she was suddenly there, a gasping cry escaping her throat as her body exploded in the most powerful orgasm of her life.

He rode her through it, his thrusts hard and relentless, giving her no time to recover, and to her shock, she felt another climax approaching, her sensitized flesh requiring minimal stimulation this time. Sensing it, he picked up the pace, grinding his groin against her clit with every thrust, and Emily screamed as another violent orgasm ripped through her, leaving her shattered and breathless in its wake.

The convulsive clenching of her sex seemed to trigger Zaron's own release, and she felt him tense, a rough sound rumbling in his chest as he stilled, grinding his pelvis harder against her. Emily could feel his cock pulsing deep inside her, his seed spurting out in warm jets, and she clutched at his sides, stunned by the intensity of the experience.

For a few moments, they lay unmoving, their bodies glued together by sweat as their breathing slowly returned to normal. Zaron was heavy on top of her, and for the first time, Emily became aware that she was lying on the hard ground, with small rocks and twigs digging into the bare skin of her back. Shifting slightly, she tried to get more comfortable, and Zaron lifted himself on his elbows again, relieving her of the bulk of his weight. His softening sex was still lodged inside her, and the intimacy of their position made Emily's cheeks flame as she met his gaze.

"You're not going anywhere, angel," he said quietly. There was something different in the way he looked at her now, something dark and possessive that hadn't been there before. "Not until I let you go. Do you understand me?"

Emily's mouth tightened, but she gave a short nod. Now was not the time to argue—not with him still buried deep within her flesh, not while she was reeling from the devastating pleasure. Later she would try to regroup, to figure out a way to escape, but for now she had to pacify him, to play the part of a meek captive. She couldn't bear it if he decided to keep her locked up after today's incident.

"Good." Lowering his head, Zaron kissed her briefly, his lips brushing against hers, and carefully withdrew from her swollen channel. Rising to his feet, he pulled her up.

Emily had lost her bikini, but her dress had somehow managed to survive, and it now fell into place, covering her naked bottom. Zaron's shorts, however, lay torn on the ground. He didn't seem concerned about that, appearing as comfortable naked as he'd been clothed. She could see his balls swinging heavily between his legs, his sex glistening with their combined moisture, and her mouth went dry at the knowledge that she'd had him inside her—that she'd actually had sex with this man.

With this *alien*, a small inner voice corrected her, and Emily swallowed, not wanting to examine that fact too closely. Her legs felt like jello, but she took a shaky step back, wanting to put some distance between them. Zaron didn't let her, however, his hand tightening around her arm. Before she could object, she found herself lifted up off the ground and ensconced comfortably in his arms.

"We're going home," he said, glancing down at her as he headed toward the woods, carrying her as effortlessly as if she weighed nothing. "I think that was enough fresh air for today."

———

The return trip took less time, as Zaron maintained a brisk pace, navigating the familiar woods with ease. Emily protested being carried, saying that she could walk just fine on her own, but he refused to put her down, needing to feel her clasped securely against his chest. She hadn't succeeded in escaping and she never would, but he was still reluctant to let go of her, a strange feeling gripping him every time he thought of her attempted run.

Despite his initial anger, Zaron understood why she'd done it. The human girl was used to her independence, to being in charge of her own life. It undoubtedly rankled her to be forced to remain his guest. He understood and even sympathized with her dilemma to some extent. However, that didn't change his irrational, primitive conviction that Emily belonged to him, that somehow she was *his*.

Having sex with her had only strengthened the feeling. His body was temporarily sated, but he was already craving more of the addicting pleasure, hungering to fuck her over and over again. The fact that he had restrained himself from taking her blood didn't help. He hadn't wanted to get carried away out in the open, but now he couldn't stop thinking about the liquid aphrodisiac that ran through her veins—and about what it would be like to be deep inside her when he sliced his teeth across her throat and tasted her blood for the first time.

"You're stronger than a human, aren't you?" Emily's

question brought him out of his thoughts, causing him to glance down at her. She had her arms around his neck, hanging on as if afraid he would drop her. "You've been carrying me for half a mile, and you're not even winded," she explained, gazing up at him.

Zaron hesitated for a moment, then decided that he could reveal that much. Humans would discover that fact about the Krinar early on. "Yes," he confirmed, stepping over a small *Lippia alba* shrub. "We're stronger than your kind. And faster—which is how I was able to catch you."

Her throat worked as she swallowed. "How much stronger and faster?"

"Enough that none of your athletes would be a challenge," he told her, not wanting to go into specifics. He could crush every bone in the human body with hardly any effort, but Emily didn't need to know that. The last thing he wanted was for her to fear him. He would never physically harm her, but she might not believe him—particularly if she knew about his species' predatory origins and predilection toward violence.

She frowned at his response, but before she could pepper him with more questions, they arrived at his dwelling.

Approaching the entryway, Zaron stepped through the opening, carrying Emily inside like a prize of war. It wasn't until the wall securely sealed itself behind him that he finally let her go, lowering her to her feet. He knew he was probably acting like a barbarian, but he didn't care. If she didn't want to be his guest, then she would be his captive, with all that it implied. He had no qualms about keeping her prisoner—not after she had betrayed his trust by trying to run.

As soon as he released her, she backed away from him, her chin raised defiantly. "I'd like to take a shower," she said, giving him an even look. However, Zaron detected a small tremor in her hands. Emily was more distressed than she appeared to be. Was she regretting what happened between them? Or was she still trying to keep him at arm's length, to pretend that nothing had changed?

Either way, Zaron wasn't about to allow it. She had let him into her body, and she was his now. There would be no going back for her.

"Of course," he said. "You need a shower—and so do I."

Without waiting for her response, he stepped toward her. Grasping her skirt, he pulled the dress off over her head in one smooth motion, leaving her standing there fully naked.

Then he picked her up again and carried her into her room, heading straight for the bathroom.

CHAPTER EIGHTEEN

*C*radling Emily against his chest, Zaron stepped inside the tall circular stall and gave a quick command for the water to start.

"You can put me down, you know," she said dryly as the water began pouring over their bodies. "I can stand on my own two feet—and there's obviously nowhere to run here."

A smile tugged at the corner of Zaron's mouth. He was definitely acting like a barbarian. "All right. If you wish." Placing her carefully on the slick floor, he let the intelligent shower apply cleansing liquids to her hair and skin while he received the same treatment.

He had no idea why it was so difficult for him to keep his hands off Emily, but he could hardly bear not to touch her. It wasn't a purely physical need, either, though his body was again beginning to stir at her nearness. No, this compulsion went deeper, he realized with an inner chill. He wanted to keep her close, to feel her next to him at all times… to hold her and possess her.

Like he had wanted Larita.

This time, the slicing pain in his chest was too sharp to ignore, and Zaron turned away from Emily, not wanting her to see the agony on his face. He couldn't possibly want a human in the same way he'd wanted his mate. Larita had been his entire life for more than forty years, and the fact that he could even think of her in the same sentence as Emily felt like a betrayal of her memory.

And yet… he couldn't recall when he'd last felt so alive. For the first time since Larita's death, dark thoughts didn't consume Zaron's every waking moment, his rage and grief easing in Emily's presence. He'd smiled and laughed more in the past couple of days than in all of last year, and sex with Emily had been as intense and satisfying as what he'd once experienced with his mate.

It didn't make sense, but he couldn't deny it any longer.

For the first time in years, Zaron felt like his old self, and Emily was the reason for that.

Turning back toward her, he watched as she leaned into the water spray, her eyes closed and her wet hair streaming down her slender back. With her profile facing him, he noticed her small, straight nose and the pure lines of her chin and jaw. Her mouth looked soft and lush, swollen from their earlier encounter, and as his gaze drifted down her body, his cock thickened and hardened, responding to the sensual sight before him.

He didn't know why this particular human girl had this kind of effect on him, but he wasn't going to waste time worrying about it, he decided as heat built under his skin. He had his little captive for another sixteen days, and he intended to enjoy every single one of them.

Stepping toward Emily, he pulled her against his aroused body and captured her startled gasp with his mouth.

She tasted sweet, her breath slightly minty from the cleaning. Her lips clung to him, responding to his kiss, and her fingers clutched at the muscled flesh of his arms, her fragile nails digging into his skin. He could feel her naked breasts pushing against his chest, her nipples like hard little pebbles, and his balls tightened as fresh blood surged to his groin. Groaning, Zaron backed her against the wall of the stall, his hand slipping down her body to the soft, tempting opening between her legs.

She was already wet, ready for him, and Zaron felt his hunger intensify as she bucked against his fingers, a low moan escaping her throat. Pressing his thumb against her clit, he pushed his middle finger into her small, slippery channel, searching for the sensitive spot on her inner wall. "Yes, that's it," he murmured, lifting his head to gaze down at her flushed face. "Come for me, angel…" He could feel the soft, spongy area with the pad of his finger, and as he pressed on it lightly, her sheath contracted around him, squeezing his finger so tightly his dick jumped in response.

Emily was panting now, her pupils dilated as she gazed up at him, and he increased the pressure on that soft internal spot, his thumb simultaneously circling her clit. She cried out, her body jerking against him, and he felt her orgasm begin, her inner walls undulating around his finger in a sinuous, rippling motion.

Unable to wait any longer, Zaron removed his finger and gripped the back of her thighs, lifting her off the floor and opening her legs. Without further preliminaries, he aligned the head of his shaft with her entrance and pushed inside.

As before, the feel of her was heady, intoxicating. She was incredibly tight around his cock, her soft flesh squeezing him, embracing him as he advanced deeper. He could smell the sweet musk of her arousal, hear the rapid beating of her heart, and his eyes fell to her neck, drawn by the pulse throbbing underneath her pale, nearly translucent skin. An ancient, animalistic hunger rose within him, a predatory craving that no amount of genetic manipulation had been able to suppress, and he slowly lowered his head, brushing his lips against the delicate column of her throat. She moaned, her neck arching back, and the craving became unbearable. Using his left hand to hold her up, Zaron gripped Emily's hair with his right hand, forcing her to keep still. Then, in one sharp motion, he sliced the sharp edges of his upper teeth across her skin and pressed his mouth to the resulting wound.

Blood, hot and coppery, spurted onto his tongue, the flavor rich and uniquely satisfying. Emily cried out at the sudden pain, tensing in his arms, but then he felt the drugging effect of his saliva take effect on her. Her body melted against him, her sex clenching and pulsing around his cock, and he knew she was overcome by the same wave of pleasure that was sweeping over him. Ecstasy, fierce and effervescent, zinged through Zaron's nerve endings, enhancing his every sense until he felt like he would burst from the overwhelming sensations. Everything was brighter, hotter, more intense, and he felt all rational thought slip away as his body took over, the taste of her blood amplifying his lust to an unbearable degree.

He wasn't sure how long he fucked her up against that shower wall, or at what point he managed to carry her to bed. All he knew was that they both came over and over again, in a violent orgasmic frenzy that knew no end.

It wasn't until Emily passed out in his arms that Zaron found the will to stop, his body sated yet clamoring for more.

CHAPTER NINETEEN

Gradually regaining consciousness, Emily became aware of a puzzling array of aches and pains. Every muscle in her body felt sore, as though she'd done some major exercise. When she opened her eyes and shifted slightly on the bed, she realized that the discomfort ran deeper, her sex feeling swollen and tender from overuse.

She was also naked underneath the blanket.

Her heartbeat increasing, Emily frantically sifted through her memories, trying to make sense of it all. She remembered the outing to the lake, followed by her failed attempt to escape —an attempt that had ended in the most unbelievable sex of her life. She also vividly recalled showering with Zaron and the way he had reached for her again, overwhelming her senses and stealing away her will to resist before she'd had a chance to regroup from their first encounter.

At that point, however, things seemed to get fuzzy in her mind. All she could remember was a jumble of never-before-experienced sensations and a pleasure so intense it bordered on agony.

Holy shit. She'd had sex with an alien. An alien who was keeping her imprisoned in his house. Emily couldn't even begin to process the implications of something like that, so she shoved that thought aside for later analysis.

Frowning, she sat up, staring around the room. She was alone again, with no sign of Zaron. What had happened yesterday? Why did she feel this way?

Slowly climbing out of bed, Emily made her way to the bathroom, suppressing a moan at the deep internal ache between her thighs. She'd never felt this sore after sex, not even after her first time. Looking down, she noticed faint marks and bruises on her skin. Was sex with a male of Zaron's species different after all? A shudder ran through her at the thought, even as her core warmed at the remembered sensations.

No, don't think about it now. Forcing her mind off that topic, Emily took care of her basic needs and washed her hands. Just as she was about to step into the shower, she heard someone enter the room.

Turning, she stared at the man who had become her lover. She felt oddly conscious of her nakedness. She had never been particularly shy with her boyfriends, but somehow this was different. Neither Jason nor Tom had ever looked at her the way Zaron was looking at her now: with a deeply possessive hunger that made her sex throb in response. It was a look that made her viscerally aware of her body, of her femininity.

"You're already up," he murmured, his eyes gleaming as he came toward her. Dressed in a light blue T-shirt and a pair of snug-fitting jeans that hugged his powerful thighs, he was as stunning as usual, devastating her senses with his presence.

She'd actually had sex with this gorgeous creature.

"Yes, I woke up a little while ago," Emily managed to reply, her voice slightly hoarse. Clearing her throat, she tried to focus on the mundane. "What time is it?"

"Just after nine in the morning," Zaron said, a small frown appearing on his face as his gaze ran over her body, lingering on the finger-shaped marks on her thighs. In the next second, he was in front of her, his hands gripping her upper arms as he turned her this way and that, thoroughly inspecting every inch of her skin.

"Hey!" Emily tried to twist away. "What are you doing?" She'd been doing her best to pretend that this was just a regular morning-after so they could avoid any unnecessary awkwardness, but Zaron seemed determined to ruin her efforts.

Ignoring her ineffectual struggles, he released her arms and crouched in front of her, lightly running his hands down her thighs. When he rose to his feet again, the anger on his face almost made her flinch.

"I hurt you," he said, his voice filled with self-loathing, and she realized that he was upset with himself, not her. "Fuck, Emily, I didn't realize I'd marked you like this. I knew humans were fragile, but I didn't think—" He stopped himself from continuing, his chest rising as he took a calming breath. When he spoke again, his tone was marginally softer. "Are you in pain, angel?" he asked, his eyes holding her captive.

Emily felt a hot flush crawl along her hairline. "I'm a bit sore," she admitted reluctantly. She didn't want him to think of her as a fragile human. She had always prided herself on being strong and fit; even as a child, she'd enjoyed sports and other physically challenging activities, preferring games of tag to playing with dolls. She wasn't some frail maiden who needed to be treated with kid gloves. "It's not a big deal," she added, seeing the expression on Zaron's face. "Nothing that a hot shower wouldn't fix."

His mouth tightened, but he didn't say anything. Turning, he left the room, moving so quickly that Emily blinked in surprise.

Shrugging at his inexplicable behavior, she stepped into the shower.

Before the water had a chance to start, Zaron reappeared, carrying a small silvery object shaped like a tube. "Hold still, please," he instructed, kneeling in front of her.

Bemused, Emily stared as he moved the object over her body, focusing on the areas with visible bruising. There was a red light coming from the little device, a light that felt pleasantly warm on her damaged skin. To her amazement, the marks faded almost immediately, disappearing without a trace.

"Wow," she breathed, bending her right knee and wiggling her foot. The muscle aches from earlier were gone as well. "Zaron, is this how your healing technology always works?"

He nodded, looking up at her. "Yes. It uses nanocytes, if you are familiar with that concept."

"Nanocytes? As in, mature nanotechnology?" Emily had read about it while researching a tech startup, and from what she understood, the possibilities of such technology were pretty much limitless. Nanomachines were unbelievably tiny robots that could be programmed to function in a variety of different ways—something that modern science could only theorize about at this point. "Wait a minute... Are you putting these nanocytes into my body?"

"Yes, precisely." He seemed pleased that she'd grasped it so quickly. "That's what heals your injuries," he explained, moving the object toward her pelvis. Before she realized his intentions, he placed his hand between her legs and shined the light directly at her sore opening. There was a brief tingling sensation, and then the internal tenderness was gone.

"Now you can shower," Zaron said with satisfaction, rising to his feet. Bending his head, he brushed his lips against her mouth in a quick, proprietary kiss, then stepped back. "In fact, you better shower before I get carried away again," he said huskily and left the room, the wall closing behind him.

Emily showered on auto-pilot, her thoughts jumping in a dozen different directions. She was both fascinated and horrified by the idea of tiny alien machines running around in her body. Was that how he'd healed her before? It made sense. Just as a surgeon could sew together a wound, a nano-sized machine could theoretically fix damage on a cellular level. No, not theoretically, she corrected herself. It could actually do so. The fact that she felt perfectly normal was proof of that.

Stepping out of the shower, Emily let the air currents dry her off, then headed back into the bedroom to get dressed. It was only when she was pulling on her sandals that she realized something.

She still didn't know what had necessitated the healing in the first place. Her memory of last night was as fuzzy as if she'd been drugged.

CHAPTER TWENTY

"*Z*aron... What exactly happened last night?"

Munching on a plate of fruit salad across the kitchen table, Emily gave him an inquiring look. With the pale yellow dress she was wearing today, her eyes were more green than blue, reminding Zaron of *burit*—a moss-like plant on his home planet.

Finishing his own breakfast, he considered her question, wondering how to best answer it. While he didn't know what the official post-arrival protocol would entail, he suspected the Council would not be eager to reveal the vampiric tendencies of his race right away.

"What do you mean?" he asked, deciding to pretend ignorance for now. Giving Emily a slow smile, he reached across the table and picked up her hand, gently rubbing the inside of her palm with his thumb. "You know what happened, angel. Or would you like a reminder?"

She licked a drop of fruit juice off her lips, staring at him, and his body tightened at the memory of how those lips had felt and tasted. "I remember that we had sex, of course," she said, pulling her hand out of his grasp. "What I don't remember is the rest of the day after the shower, or how I ended up that sore. Did you give me something? Like a drug of some kind?"

"No, of course not," Zaron said, amused by the idea. It wasn't a drug that had made her memory of their encounter hazy; it was a naturally occurring substance in Krinar saliva, a leftover from the days when his kind hunted the *lonar*—a primate species whose blood had provided them with key nutrients. Schooling his features into an impassive expression, he asked silkily, "You don't remember all the orgasms I gave you?"

Emily's cheeks turned pink, but her gaze didn't waver from his face. "No, I don't. Are you telling me we had sex all day and night?"

Zaron nodded, suppressing a smile at the incredulous note in her voice. "Pretty much," he confirmed. "You finally fell asleep around three in the morning."

"Three in the *morning*?" She gaped at him. "But it was not even noon when we went to the lake!"

"I guess my people have more stamina when it comes to sex," Zaron said, watching her reaction. "We don't get tired as easily as humans."

The color in Emily's face intensified. "If that's true, then I don't think we're particularly compatible," she said tightly. "You'd be better off with another Krinar."

"But I don't want another Krinar." Zaron reached for her hand again. Capturing her fingers, he leaned forward. "I want *you*."

And it was true. He didn't simply want sex—he wanted

Emily. Last night had been one of the most incredible experiences of his life, and he couldn't wait to have her again. He could see that she still had reservations about being with him, but he had no intention of letting her back away from him.

He had her for another fifteen days, and he planned to spend a good portion of that time buried deep inside her sweet little body.

Emily frowned, trying to tug her hand away. "Look, Zaron, just because we had sex once—okay, several times"—she conceded at the ironic look on his face—"doesn't mean that this is going to be an ongoing thing. You're keeping me here against my will, and even if you weren't, this is just not a good idea. We're too different. For all I know, with that kind of appetite, you have an entire harem of women back home—"

"I don't," Zaron interrupted, his chest squeezing painfully. Releasing her hand, he leaned back, gripped by the familiar icy bleakness. "You have nothing to worry about in that regard, I can assure you." The words came out unintentionally bitter, and he saw Emily's eyes widen in surprise.

"You don't have anybody waiting for you back home?"

"Not in the sense you mean," Zaron replied, more calmly this time. "My parents and grandparents are on Krina, but I don't have a 'girlfriend,' as you would call it."

"Why not?" Emily asked, tilting her head to the side. Her gaze roamed quizzically over his features. "Surely you have no problems attracting women. Unless the ones on your planet have different tastes?"

Zaron stared at her, a strange temptation gnawing at him. "No," he said slowly. "They don't." Even by Krinar standards, he was considered an attractive male; he knew that without false modesty. Larita had always joked that his parents had made him too pretty, frequently teasing him about being better-looking than her.

"Then what is it?" Emily persisted, her eyes gleaming with curiosity. "You said you're six hundred years old. Shouldn't you have a wife and kids by now?"

"I had a wife," Zaron said abruptly, giving in to the temptation. "She died eight years ago." As soon as the words came out of his mouth, he wanted to take them back, but it was too late. The curiosity on Emily's face disappeared, replaced by shock and that which he hated most: pity.

To his relief, she didn't start mouthing platitudes. Instead, she asked softly, "Were you together for long?"

"Forty-four of your Earth years." Just three years short of the Celebration of Forty-Seven—the formal event that would've publicized their union and made it permanent in the eyes of the Krinar society.

"I see," Emily murmured, studying him. "May I ask what happened?"

"It was an accident." Zaron's mouth twisted. "Just a stupid, careless accident. Larita was what you would call an astronaut, an explorer of the geology of deep space. When she died, she was on a routine project in a nearby solar system, taking samples from a methane lake on a planet that somewhat resembles your Saturn's moon Titan—right down to the lack of oxygen in the atmosphere." He paused, swallowing the hard knot that had formed in his throat. "There was an unexpected volcanic eruption in a nearby area, and Larita's oxygen tank got damaged by the flying debris. She would've been fine—except some of the oxygen leaked out, combining with the methane in the atmosphere."

He could see the color leaving Emily's cheeks as she realized where he was heading. "Yes," he said flatly. "You can probably guess what happened next. Methane is highly flammable when oxygen is present, and with the volcano spewing hot magma, the lake around her became a fiery hell. Neither she nor her two colleagues survived."

He stopped then, unable to say more as he relived the horror of hearing that the woman he'd loved more than life itself was gone, her body incinerated by an inferno on a far-off world. He hadn't believed the news at first, had tried to deny it for as long as he could. It wasn't until the remnants of Larita's suit had been recovered that he'd accepted the truth: that his mate would never return from her routine expedition.

A warm, gentle pressure on his hand brought him out of the dark recollections. Glancing down, Zaron was surprised to find Emily's slender fingers wrapped around his palm. She had reached across the table of her own initiative, gripping his hand in a gesture of silent support. Lifting his gaze back to her face, he saw that her eyes were glittering with unspilled moisture.

"I'm sorry," she whispered achingly, and something about the look of genuine sympathy on her face tugged at his insides, chasing away some of the cold, heavy feeling in his stomach. "I'm truly sorry, Zaron. I can't imagine what it must've felt like, to lose someone you loved for so long."

He drew in a deep breath, letting himself be soothed by the soft timbre of her voice and the feel of her delicate hand squeezing his palm. He didn't know why he had confided in this human. It wasn't like him at all. Zaron never voluntarily talked about Larita's death; even after eight years, the memories were too fresh, too painful, and he wasn't the type of person to burden others with his problems. Yet for some reason, he'd wanted to tell Emily, to see if she would understand.

She was still looking at him, as if debating something. Then, apparently reaching a decision, she began to speak.

"My parents died when I was four," she said quietly, and Zaron froze, a chill skittering down his spine. "It was a car accident. They were passing a slow-moving truck on a highway, going about eighty miles an hour, when one of their tires blew. The car flipped several times before coming to a halt on the side of the road. My dad was killed instantly, and my mom passed away in the hospital a few hours later." Her fingers tightened convulsively around his palm as she added hoarsely, "I was home with a babysitter at the time, you see, and my parents were rushing to get back to me because the movie ended later than they'd expected."

"Emily…" Zaron didn't know what to say. In many ways, her loss had been infinitely greater. He had been an adult, and as much as he'd loved Larita, he hadn't depended on her the way a child depends on her parents. "I'm so sorry," he finally said, his heart aching for the human girl. "Who raised you after that? Was it these foster homes you mentioned before?"

She nodded. "Yes. Well, and my aunt Wendy, I guess—my father's sister. She took me in right after their death. Neither of my parents were from a large family, so she was the only close relative. I lived with her for eighteen months before she realized she was ill-equipped to deal with a traumatized child and put me in the foster system."

"She gave you to some strangers to raise?" Anger churned in Zaron's gut as he remembered Emily saying that there hadn't been enough food at one of these foster homes. How could her aunt have done this? What kind of monster gave away her own flesh and blood? Krinar orphans were extremely rare in modern times, but if such a misfortune did occur, any relative, no matter how distant, would gladly take on the responsibility of caring for the child; anything else would be unthinkable.

A faint smile appeared on Emily's lips. "Yes. It wasn't too bad, actually. I preferred it that way. Aunt Wendy wasn't... great with kids. It was a relief to be out of her house."

Zaron's blood ran cold. "Did she hurt you?" He leaned forward, covering her wrist with his other hand. He'd seen these types of stories on the human news, and the idea that Emily could've been abused... "Did she do something to you?"

"No." Emily shook her head. "Nothing like what you're imagining. She would occasionally punish me by locking me in my room, but she never did anything else to me. Neither did anyone else at any of the homes I stayed in. I was very lucky. Some of my foster parents were indifferent, but usually they were decent people who truly wanted to help—and who needed the extra money the government paid them for our upkeep."

"Wait a minute," Zaron said slowly, latching on to her throwaway comment. "Your aunt locked you in your room? Is that why you don't like being indoors?"

Emily bit her lip, looking uncomfortable all of a sudden. "Yes, probably." She pulled her hand out of his grasp, leaving him strangely empty without her touch. "It's not a big deal. Like I told you, I just need to go outside on a regular basis." Holding his gaze, she added quietly, "I don't do well in captivity—but then again, I don't know many people who do."

Zaron felt an unwelcome pang of guilt, followed by an irrational spike of anger. Slowly, he rose to his feet, his hands gripping the edge of the table. "I already explained why I have to detain you for a little while," he said, carefully enunciating each word. "You're the one who insists on making this into an ordeal. All you have to do is stay with me for the next fifteen days. Why is that so hard for you?"

She got up as well, her eyes narrowing. "Because I have a life out there." Her sharp tone matched his. "Because I can't stay here, having sex all day and night, while the career I worked so hard to build gets completely derailed. I'm not an animal that you can rescue and keep as a pet, Zaron—I'm a human being—and your so-called fear of exposure is nothing more than an excuse to deprive me of my freedom. You know as well as I do that I could run around Times Square screaming about aliens at the top of my lungs, and nobody would believe me—"

"Whether they do or not is irrelevant," Zaron interrupted, stepping around the table. With her eyes flashing with fury, Emily looked so adorable that he felt his own anger fading, chased away by a familiar surge of lust. There was some truth to her words, but he refused to dwell on that now. Stopping in front of her, he clasped her face in his large hands and stared down into her stormy gaze. "I will not risk breaking the mandate at this point. Not even for you, angel."

Her slender hands came up, her fingers curling around his wrists. "Zaron, please," she whispered, and he could hear her breathing hitch as he pressed his growing erection against her belly. "This is not a good idea—"

"On the contrary..." He bent his head, his lips hovering inches from hers. "I think it's an excellent idea." Cradling her face between his palms, he kissed her, reveling in the way her soft lips clung to him. It was as if she couldn't get enough of him either. Talking about Larita and learning about Emily's past left Zaron feeling unsettled, strangely vulnerable and hungry for something he couldn't define, even to himself. For a moment, he was tempted to take the girl again, but he controlled himself. As much as he wanted to stay in bed with Emily all day, there was work to be done—and he had to make allowances for the fact that his guest was, indeed, human.

Lifting his head, Zaron reluctantly lowered his hands and took a step back, ignoring the urgings of his throbbing cock. "I have something I need to take care of," he said huskily, staring at her flushed face. "But I'll be back in a few hours, and we'll go for a walk, I promise. Are you going to be okay on your own for a bit?"

"Um, yeah, sure." Emily blinked, the glow of desire slowly fading from her cheeks. "I'll be fine."

"Good," Zaron murmured. "Then I will see you soon."

Before he could get tempted again, he walked out of the room, heading for another virtual meeting in his office. There was a lot that needed to get accomplished in the next few days.

The main ships would be arriving shortly, and Zaron needed to make sure everything was ready.

CHAPTER TWENTY-ONE

*A*fter Zaron left, Emily went back into her bedroom. To her relief, the wall entrances between the rooms now worked for her, opening and closing at her approach. Zaron must've adjusted the door settings at some point, giving her greater freedom to roam around the house. The outside wall didn't budge, of course, but she hadn't expected it to. Like it or not, she was stuck here for the next two weeks—with a gorgeous, insatiable alien who expected her to warm his bed for the duration.

Sighing, Emily sat down on the bed. She couldn't pretend, even to herself, that she was anything but willing. She'd never had sex like that before, had never even dreamed that such ecstasy was possible. With Jason, they'd had fun in bed, but it had never gone beyond mild enjoyment for Emily. Still, her ex had at least known how to bring her to orgasm. With Tom, her boyfriend in high school, she'd never been able to come at all, their encounters ranging from painfully awkward to somewhat pleasant. But with Zaron, it was an experience unlike any other —at least as far as she could recall.

Why was last night so vague in her memory? The thought bothered Emily to no small degree. Zaron had deflected her question this morning, and she realized now that she was still completely in the dark. Was it possible that he was manipulating her mind somehow? Maybe with the help of the nanocytes he'd used to heal her?

The idea was so frightening that cold sweat broke out all over her body. Could Zaron do something like that? And more importantly, *would* he? He clearly had no qualms about keeping her captive for two-plus weeks, but taking away her freedom of thought was a different matter entirely. It would imply a complete and utter disregard for her as a person, and Emily didn't want to believe that of him. Sure, he could be incredibly domineering, riding roughshod over her objections to their affair, but he didn't treat her like she was less than human. On the contrary, she got the impression that he didn't often speak about his wife's death, yet he had opened up to Emily, trusting her with a subject that clearly pained him.

Forty-four years. He had been with his wife for forty-four years. The incredible longevity of the Krinar was still shocking to Emily. The only humans she knew who had been with their spouses that long were well into their sixties—and Zaron was clearly a man in his prime. If she'd met him on the street, she would've guessed him to be in his late twenties, never dreaming that he was old enough to have lived through the Renaissance.

She also wouldn't have guessed that he'd had such tragedy in his past. Emily's chest ached at the thought of what he must've gone through, losing his beloved partner of forty-plus years. Could that be why she was so drawn to him? Because she'd sensed that he was like her in that way: a survivor, someone who had also known suffering and loss? The fact that she'd felt so comfortable talking about her parents to Zaron seemed to indicate that. She rarely broached the subject with anyone who was not already a good friend, yet it had been the most natural thing in the world to share that experience with Zaron. In a weird way, she felt closer to him after three days than to Jason after three years.

If he were human, it would be easy to love him.

The thought came out of nowhere, shocking Emily with its stark clarity. Getting up, she began to pace, a cold pit of despair growing in her chest. As much as she wanted to deny it, she knew she'd hit upon the crux of the matter. This was why she tried to resist this attraction, why she felt so uneasy at the impact Zaron had on her senses. It wasn't because she was being smart and cautious.

It was because she was afraid.

Afraid to fall for a man with whom she could never have a future—a man who could leave her in pieces if she let him.

The pull she felt toward Zaron was more than sexual. She knew that now. Everything about him intrigued Emily, and it wasn't simply the fact that he came from another world and could tell her things no human knew. No, as fascinating as she found his alienness, the knowledge she craved was both simpler and more complex. She wanted to know his innermost thoughts and feelings, to delve into his memories. She wanted to see him smile and laugh, to banish the shadows she'd glimpsed in him today. And even though she resented being kept prisoner, she couldn't truly hate him for that—not when he had saved her life.

She was already falling for him, and there were still fifteen days left on her captivity clock.

No. Emily sat down on the bed again. This was insane. She couldn't—wouldn't—get attached to Zaron. That way lay a world of hurt. She needed to formulate a plan of escape, and she needed to do it now.

By Emily's calculations, it was already Saturday, which meant that she had missed her morning flight home. At some point this evening, Amber would come by to bring back Emily's cat and catch up, and she would get worried when she couldn't reach Emily. And Emily's interview with Evers Capital—the interview that could influence the entire course of her career—was this upcoming Thursday.

Frustrated, Emily reached for her damaged phone, picking it up off the floating plank next to her bed. She'd put it there after Zaron had returned it to her, though she didn't know why she'd bothered keeping it. The thing was completely dead after its swim in the river. Removing the still-damp protective case, Emily shook the phone, then tried to turn it on again. Unsurprisingly, the screen remained dark.

Setting the phone down, Emily began to pace again, too wound up to sit still. One way or another, she needed to figure out a way to leave before her fifteen days were up.

Her career and peace of mind depended on it.

CHAPTER TWENTY-TWO

*W*hen most of the remaining logistics were decided on, Zaron dismissed his team for the day. Only one member, Ellet, remained in the virtual meeting room at his request. A biologist like him, she'd chosen to specialize in *Homo sapiens* in recent decades and was considered a rising star in the Krinar scientific community. She was also someone Zaron thought of as a friend, even though he'd only known her for the past twelve years.

When they were finally alone in the room, Ellet walked over and sat down on the float next to Zaron, crossing her long legs in an unconsciously sensual gesture. A classic beauty, she was rumored to have been involved with Councilor Korum in recent months. Some of Ellet's detractors even said that Korum was the reason she'd gotten a spot on the settlement preparation team—a highly coveted position among human biology experts. Zaron didn't know if that was true and didn't care. For all of her ambition, Ellet was one of the nicest individuals he knew, and he genuinely liked and respected her.

"So how is life?" she asked, watching him with her large hazel eyes. "Do you like the jungle better than the cities?"

"I do, actually," Zaron said with a smile. Ellet had been the one to advise him to build his home near their future colony, and he was grateful for her suggestion. Even before Emily's arrival, he had found a measure of peace in the forest, his senses resting from the overwhelming noise and crowds of human settlements. "What about you? Are you still enjoying Rio de Janeiro?"

"I am." She grinned, her teeth flashing white. "It's warm, and I blend in well. Whenever I go somewhere in public, humans ask me if I'm related to Gisele. Apparently, she's a local supermodel."

Zaron laughed. "Good for you. Sounds like you have indeed found your niche."

"Yes, for now. I can't wait for the Centers to be built, though. I don't think I'll ever get used to the human appliances. Can you imagine having to manually put clothes into the washer?" She shuddered dramatically. "My apartment is so primitive it might as well be a cave. I wish I could build a normal house here, like you did, but it's too risky in a big city—too many humans, too much chance of exposure..."

"Right, of course," Zaron said slowly, wondering how to best broach the topic he wanted to discuss. "Speaking of exposure, I may have done something a bit... unusual."

Ellet arched her dark eyebrows. "Such as?"

"I brought a human into my house."

She blinked. "A human? Why? You don't usually study them, right?"

"No, I don't." Zaron tended to focus on other animal and plant species. "I didn't bring her in to study. I took her because she was dying, and I wanted to save her."

"She?" Ellet asked delicately. "Are we talking about a young woman here? Perhaps a pretty young woman?"

"Perhaps," Zaron conceded, a smile tugging at the edge of his mouth. Emily was more than pretty, but his colleague didn't need to know that.

"Okay, I think I'm beginning to get the picture," Ellet said, her eyes gleaming with amusement. If she was shocked by his admission, she hid it well. "I assume you did manage to save her. What do you plan to do with her? Does she know what you are?"

Zaron nodded. "She does. I'm keeping her with me for the next two weeks, until we go public."

"I see." Ellet regarded him curiously. "And have you already taken her blood?"

"Yes, once." Heat rippled over his skin at the memory. "And I want to do it again. Ellet, there's something I want to ask you about that…"

"You want to know about blood addiction," she said, her expression turning more serious. "That's why you're telling me about this, isn't it? I'm guessing you've done some research yourself?"

"I have, and there isn't a lot of data on this." Zaron raked his fingers through his hair. As a scientist, he hated not having all the facts. "I know it's not advisable to take blood from the same human with any significant frequency, but most of the information on the network seems anecdotal at best. Have you looked into this? What are the true limitations?"

"Well," Ellet said slowly, "I have looked into this somewhat.

Like you said, most of the evidence is anecdotal, and we're just starting to run simulations, so there is no definitive answer. What we do know is that humans get addicted to the experience overall, while we get addicted to the blood of a specific human. I would be careful if I were you. Let at least a couple of days go by between each session—maybe even a few days. With humans, there's so much variability... You don't want to get addicted, trust me—nor do you want her to become addicted to you."

"Yes, of course." Zaron had known about this phenomenon for a while, and he'd been careful to avoid taking blood from the same human more than once. It wasn't difficult; there was no shortage of willing sex partners in large cities. When he'd lived in Los Angeles and Miami, he'd enjoyed a different woman every night, easily picking them up in bars and clubs. For some reason, though, the thought of being with anyone but Emily turned his stomach now. "I'll be careful."

"Good," Ellet said, getting up. "If there's anything else you need from me, please don't hesitate to ask. I'll be in Costa Rica at some point in the next couple of weeks, so maybe we'll be able to meet up in person."

"That would be great." Zaron rose to his feet. "You are more than welcome to stop by and enjoy some home comforts here."

"Thank you." Ellet smiled at him. "I might take you up on your invitation. Maybe you could even introduce me to this human girl of yours. She sounds quite special."

"She is," Zaron said, smiling back. "I'm sure she would enjoy meeting you as well." With that, he exited the virtual environment, reality shifting and distorting in front of his eyes.

When his vision settled, he was back in his office, the bulk of his work finished for the day.

CHAPTER TWENTY-THREE

*B*y the time Zaron came back, Emily was ready to climb walls. Her claustrophobia was back in full force, her throat tight as she paced in circles around her room. Aside from her worry about the interview, what bothered her the most was the blurriness in her memory. The missing hours weren't a total blank—she had vague recollections of intensely pleasurable sensations—and that concerned her even more.

It was exactly as if she'd been drunk or drugged.

"What happened yesterday?" she demanded as soon as Zaron stepped into her room. Her tone was overly sharp, but she didn't care. She had to get some answers before she went insane. "What did you do to me to make me forget?"

"Emily..." Her captor's dark gaze was inscrutable as he stopped next to her. "Don't go there, angel. I can't tell you what you want to know without violating the mandate."

Her heart lurched. "So you did do something?"

"It's not what you're thinking." He clasped her shoulders,

stopping her from backing away. "What happened was a natural outcome of our coupling and nothing for you to be concerned about. You weren't harmed in any way."

Emily's pulse was pounding in her temples. Her dress was sleeveless, and his palms were strong and hot on her bare skin —as hot as the vague sensations that were all that was left of her memories. "Not harmed?" she said caustically, her body's uncontrolled reaction to his touch adding to her anxiety. "Scrambling my brains to the point that I lose a day and a half doesn't constitute harm in your book?"

Zaron's nostrils flared. "You enjoyed yourself during that time too."

"Did I? And how do I know that when I can't remember?"

"You can trust me," he said, his eyes narrowing. "Or I can show you—and this time, you'll remember everything."

"No, don't." Emily twisted out of his grasp and took a step back. Her breathing was fast and shallow, her claustrophobia intensifying with each moment. She needed to leave the confines of these walls before she lost her remaining shreds of sanity. "Please. You said you'd take me outside."

Comprehension filled his gaze. "Yes, of course. Come. We'll go for a walk."

Wrapping his fingers around her wrist, he led her outside through a dissolving wall—a technological wonder that no longer fazed Emily. Actually, at this moment, a spaceship could've materialized in front of her, and she wouldn't have blinked.

All that mattered was getting outside.

The moment Emily felt the warm breeze on her skin, the tight band around her throat began to loosen. Sucking in a lungful of fresh air, she closed her eyes and tilted her head back, letting the sun dance across her face. With Zaron holding her arm, she wasn't free here any more than she was inside his cave, but it felt different.

She felt different.

"Better?" Zaron asked when she opened her eyes, and Emily nodded. The suffocating sensation was gone, and with it, some of her anger and fear. She was also thinking more clearly. If Zaron hadn't lied about her memory loss being a "natural" result of their coupling, then she could see only one solution to the problem.

They couldn't have sex again.

Zaron wouldn't like that, but he'd have to accept it—at least until she found a way to return home.

———

By the time they'd been walking for several minutes, Emily's stark pallor faded, the pinched look leaving her face. If Zaron had needed any further confirmation that she wasn't faking her claustrophobia, he'd just gotten it.

His captive/guest genuinely couldn't tolerate being indoors for long.

"Have you ever tried seeing a doctor about this?" Zaron asked when they entered a sunlit meadow. At their approach, a pair of *Ateles geoffroyi*—Costa Rican spider monkeys—darted away from a fallen log, scrambling up the tree trunks. Emily jumped, clearly startled, but then a wide smile broke across her face and she ran up to the trees to watch the monkeys jumping across the branches. Zaron followed, smiling at her unabashed enjoyment.

"I love Costa Rica," she said, turning back to face him when the monkeys were gone. "The nature here is absolutely fascinating."

"It is, isn't it?" Zaron felt oddly pleased that she shared some of his interests. "Earth has some truly amazing creatures."

"Is that why you're here?" Emily asked. "Because you're interested in the Earth fauna?"

His smile faded. "In part, yes." He didn't want to think about his main reason for coming to Earth, but it was too late. Images of Larita as he saw her last slid through his mind, bringing with them the sharp sting of grief. They'd argued the day before her departure over something stupid, like where they should vacation next year, but on the morning Larita was supposed to leave for her expedition, they'd made up. Only she'd been in a rush, and they'd had to settle for a quickie. It was one of Zaron's greatest regrets: that he hadn't woken up earlier that morning and held his mate longer, that he hadn't tried to imprint every detail about her on his mind. It had only been eight years since Larita's death, yet he sometimes found himself unable to recall the exact hue of her hazel eyes or the precise taste of her lips. With every day that passed, his mate slipped further away from him, and it hurt, even as he tried to run from the memories, to distance himself from everything that reminded him of what he'd lost.

"Oh, I see," Emily said quietly, and he realized she understood. Her turquoise gaze held sympathy and a certain gentle warmth. Maybe it was because she'd known loss too, but he didn't mind this from her. He knew very few Krinar who'd lived through any kind of real tragedy. There was no disease in their society, no aging. No death outside of the Arena challenges and freak accidents like the one that had befallen Larita. To his friends, family, and colleagues, Zaron's grief was something foreign, and they didn't know how to cope with it, how to approach him after Larita's death.

But this human girl knew. She knew and sympathized, and with her, Zaron didn't feel quite as alone.

"There are some waterfalls nearby," he said. "Would you like to see them?"

Emily smiled. "Yes, that would be great."

They walked toward the falls without speaking, and there was something comforting in that also. Over the years, he and Larita had become comfortable enough to just *be* together, to enjoy each other's company without needing to fill every moment with chatter. It was odd that he felt similarly comfortable with Emily after knowing her for only a few days, but he did. Something inside him seemed to simultaneously relax and come alive in her presence, as if he was waking up from a tense, unpleasant dream.

"So have you ever sought help for your condition?" he asked again, recalling how tense *she* had been earlier. "Perhaps talked to any of your mind experts?"

"Mind experts?" She gave him a quizzical look. "Oh, you mean therapists. No, not really. I have it under control for the most part—or at least I do when I can control when I go out." She gave him a pointed look.

It was a blatant attempt to guilt him, and it worked. Zaron didn't like the idea that he was the cause of Emily's discomfort, either physical or mental. This morning, when he'd seen the bruises his fingers had left on her pale skin, he'd felt like the worst kind of monster. Though he'd had sex with human women before, he'd never gotten carried away like that, had never lost control so completely. Emily was so delicate compared to him, so breakable, and he had hurt her. And now it appeared that by holding her captive, he was hurting her too, in a different way.

Fifteen more days, he told himself, pushing away the guilt. He'd make sure she went outside regularly, so her phobia wouldn't act up, and he'd do his best to be gentle with her. He could now admit to himself that Emily was right: the mandate was just an excuse to keep her a while longer. Neither the Elders nor the Council would care if humans learned of Krinar existence a few days early—not that any legitimate human newspaper would even print Emily's story without extensive proof.

Zaron was keeping her captive because he wanted her, and for no other reason. It was wrong of him, and selfish, but he didn't care. For the first time in years, he felt a real connection to someone, and he couldn't bear to let it slip away.

Not yet, at least.

Reaching over, Zaron took Emily's hand, ignoring the puzzled glance she gave him. Her fingers were small and slender in his grasp, her skin soft and warm. Her hand was stiff at first, but as they continued walking, Emily relaxed and her fingers curled around his palm. It wasn't much, but it was enough. It was what he needed at this moment: some kind of acknowledgement that she didn't hate him, that the strange bond between them wasn't one-sided.

Before long, they were at the falls. It was another mountain stream that had become a river as a result of the recent rains. In this specific spot, the ground dropped away sharply, forming a cliff, and the turbulent water streamed down in two sizable waterfalls. Water spray filled the air, and in a few spots where sunlight penetrated the thick canopy of the trees, Zaron could see the light being refracted in a beautiful phenomenon known as the rainbow.

"This is amazing," Emily breathed as soon as the falls came into view. Pulling her hand out of his grasp, she ran up to the edge of the river and spun in a circle, laughing as the water droplets fell on her head and shoulders. The tiny blond hairs around her face curled from the moisture, creating a halo of sorts. With the light-colored dress she was wearing, she looked impossibly angelic—and so sexy Zaron's body hardened in an instant.

Closing the distance between them with a few long strides, he pulled her against his aroused body and bent his head, muffling her startled gasp with his lips. She tasted warm and sweet, her lips parting under the pressure of his kiss, and he swept his tongue into her mouth, needing more of her unique flavor. His hands slid down her back and gripped her buttocks, pulling her closer, and he felt her nipples harden against his chest as her body softened and melted in his hold.

Then, abruptly, she was fighting him. Her body went stiff, her hands pushing at his shoulders as she tried to twist away. "Stop, please," she gasped, and Zaron instantly released her, afraid he'd hurt her again. The need to possess her was overwhelming, but he was determined to keep the promise he'd made to himself.

"What happened?" he asked, forcing himself to take a step back. Even to his own ears, his voice was rough, thick with desire. "Are you okay?"

Emily nodded, her chest falling and rising with rapid breathing. "Yes, I'm just..." She took a couple of steps back, putting more distance between them. "Zaron, we can't do this."

"What?" His eyebrows snapped together. "Why not?"

"Because I don't want to lose my mind," she said, raising her chin. "I don't know what happened yesterday, but if memory loss is a natural outcome of sex with you—"

"It's not." Zaron drew in a deep breath. "It doesn't have to be, at least. What happened yesterday doesn't have to happen every time—or at all, if you don't want it." As much as he hated the idea of not being able to taste Emily's blood again, he could abstain from it. It might even be a good idea, given the uncertain parameters of the addiction Ellet had warned him about. "We could just have regular sex, like at the lake yesterday," he said. "You remember everything about that, right?"

Emily blinked at him. "Yes, but—"

"Then there's no problem." Zaron stepped toward her, and before she could come up with another objection, he lifted her against him and slanted his mouth across her lips.

CHAPTER TWENTY-FOUR

*a*t dinner, Emily had to fight a blush every time she thought of their outing to the falls. As her captor had promised, she'd been fully aware of everything they'd done— and they'd done plenty. Even now, her sex felt swollen and her clit pulsed with the aftershocks of all the orgasms Zaron had given her. He'd taken her on the grass, up against a tree, and in the river beneath the waterfalls, with the chilly mountain current cooling off their overheated bodies. They'd been there for hours, and by the end, Emily had been so exhausted that Zaron had to carry her home.

Now, after a nap, she was feeling much more refreshed, but she knew Zaron would want more sex soon. It was there in the way he was watching her, his dark eyes following every bite of food that traveled to her mouth, in the sexual tension that simmered in the air even as they discussed innocuous topics like recent movies—some of which Zaron had seen—and Emily's cat George.

"I adopted him from a shelter when he was a kitten," she told Zaron as they were wrapping up the meal. "My friend Amber dragged me there when I first moved to the city. She wanted a puppy, and she convinced me to go with her. I was sure I didn't want a pet—I work insane hours and can barely take care of myself—but there was George, and I fell in love."

"With the cat?" Zaron looked confused.

Emily nodded. "He was a kitten at the time, but yes. He was just so sweet and little, and he cuddled up against me, purring… I'm guessing you guys don't have cats?"

"No. We don't keep pets in general."

"Really? Why not?"

Zaron shrugged. "It never occurred to us to domesticate animals. We like to observe them in their natural environments, not confined to our dwellings."

"I see. But you have no problem confining humans to your dwellings?" The moment the words came out of her mouth, Emily wanted to take them back, but it was too late. Zaron's jaw tightened, adversarial tension replacing the companionable atmosphere that had prevailed throughout the meal.

Rising to his feet in one sleek motion, he stepped around the floating table and reached down to pull Emily up off her seat. His hands were impossibly strong as he held her upper arms, his eyes pitch black. He was angry; she could sense it. Her breathing quickened, her pulse leaping with anxiety, but he just released her arms and stepped back.

"Would you like to email your friend?" His voice was even. "The one who's taking care of your cat?"

"Oh." Emily felt completely off-kilter. "Yes, of course." She'd planned to ask Zaron about that later this evening—another reason why she'd regretted antagonizing him—but he was a step ahead of her. "Yes, please."

"Okay, then." He murmured something in Krinar, and the wall opened to let another thin tablet float out. Zaron snatched it from mid-air and handed it to Emily. "Here you go. You can just say your message, and it will be sent to your friend via your Gmail."

Emily frowned, glancing down at the tablet before looking up at Zaron again. "But how do I know that it'll go through? Are you saying that you have access to my email account?"

"Of course." Zaron's gaze was unblinking. "You don't think your passwords and firewalls can protect you from our technology, do you?"

Emily's stomach flipped. "No, I guess not." Given what she'd seen so far, their computers had to be unimaginably advanced; hacking her email probably took Zaron less than a nanosecond. Hell, hacking the Pentagon would probably be child's play for the Krinar. Then an even more disturbing thought occurred to her.

Would *any* of Earth's military defenses hold if the Krinar were coming with anything but the friendliest of intentions?

"Zaron..." Emily's voice shook a little. "You said your people are just coming to say hello, right? They don't want anything else, do they?"

His beautiful face turned expressionless. "Such as?"

"I don't know." Now that the dark seeds of suspicion were in her mind, they were multiplying uncontrollably. "Resources? Land? Cheap labor? Whatever it is that people always want when they explore new places."

Zaron's hesitation was so brief she would've missed it if she hadn't been so attuned to him. "We don't intend your people any harm," he said, and Emily's insides turned cold as she realized he hadn't explicitly denied any of the possibilities she'd listed. Her imagination went wild, every alien invasion movie she'd ever seen flashing through her mind. Zaron had never really said why his people were coming, or rather, she hadn't truly pried. Between learning about the Krinar and nonstop sex with her captor, she'd been too overwhelmed to think about the bigger picture. When Zaron had first told her his people were arriving soon, it hadn't seemed illogical to her that the Krinar might want to introduce themselves to an intelligent species that looked exactly like them and that they'd supposedly created. Now that she was thinking about it, however, her unquestioning acceptance of his initial explanation seemed naïve.

If all the Krinar wanted was to reveal their existence to the human race, they could've sent a message. They didn't have to fly to Earth in person. In fact, something like an introductory video as a heads-up, followed by a visit from a small delegation —some of whom were maybe already on Earth, like Zaron— would've made more sense as a friendly overture. But Zaron had said "his people" were due to arrive. That sounded like it was more than a small delegation.

It sounded like an invasion.

No. She couldn't jump to conclusions like that. Zaron had saved her life, and, temporary captivity aside, he hadn't mistreated her. The least she could do was find out some more facts before assuming the worst.

"How far is your home planet?" she asked, trying to sound casual. "You never really told me where Krina is."

Zaron's expression didn't change, but she could sense him relaxing subtly. "It's far," he said. "In a different galaxy, in fact. I could give you the exact coordinates, but they wouldn't mean anything to you or any of your people."

Emily's breath caught in wonder. "A different galaxy? How is that even possible? You must travel faster than the speed of light."

"We do. It's not my area of expertise, but from what I understand, our ships' warp drive creates an enormous energy bubble that essentially bends space-time. Distance is more or less irrelevant; going to a neighboring solar system takes us about as much time as coming to Earth."

"I see." Their technology was even more advanced than she'd thought. Emily wondered if Zaron could hear the heavy thudding of her heart. He was stronger and faster than a normal man. Could his senses be more acute than a human's, too? There was so much she didn't know about Zaron and his people, and what she was discovering was far from reassuring. Striving to maintain her casual tone, she asked, "So how many of your people are coming to Earth this time?"

"Why don't you email your friend?" he said instead of answering. "I have some work to do tonight, and I want to make sure the email goes through without any issues."

"Of course." Pushing her disappointment away, Emily forced a bright smile to her lips. "So I just speak to the tablet, and it'll know what to do and where to send the email?"

"Yes, exactly. Go ahead." He folded his arms across his chest, and her heartbeat sped up further when she realized he wasn't going to give her any privacy for this.

"Okay," she said, hoping he couldn't detect how sweaty her palms had become. "How about this? 'Hey, Amber. So sorry I didn't email you before, but I got delayed here in Costa Rica. I'll explain more when I get home, but in the meanwhile, would you mind keeping George for a few more days? Thanks in advance!'"

"For two more weeks," Zaron corrected, and Emily saw the text—with his correction—briefly appear on the tablet screen in front of her. Then her Gmail flashed on the screen, showing the sent message, and the tablet went blank again.

"Good job," Zaron said, taking the tablet from her, and Emily watched as the object disappeared back into the wall. "Now if you don't mind, I have to jump into a virtual meeting. I'll see you in a couple of hours."

Bending down, he brushed his lips across hers in a brief kiss and disappeared through an opening in the wall, leaving Emily alone with her suspicions.

———

Zaron worked all evening. By the time he came out of his study, Emily was half-asleep. He made love to her for a couple of hours, exhausting her further, and it wasn't until the next afternoon, when they went on their walk, that she had a chance to interrogate him again. At that point, Zaron knew he had to tell her something, and he opted for the truth.

It might upset Emily and make the next two weeks less pleasant than they could've been, but he didn't want to lie to her.

"So how many of your people are coming?" she asked as they were walking toward the lake. "Is it a big delegation?"

Emily's tone was calm, almost disinterested, but Zaron wasn't fooled. His human guest was smart. Once she got over the shock of meeting him and learning about the Krinar, it didn't take her long to start questioning everything.

Sighing, he answered, "About fifty thousand. But, Emily—"

"Fifty thousand?" She stopped under an *Enterolobium cyclocarpum*, the guanacaste tree, all color leaching from her face as she gaped at him. "Fifty thousand of your people are coming to Earth in two weeks?"

"Yes. But we don't intend your people any harm, I promise."

"What do you intend then? You're not just coming to introduce yourselves, are you?"

"No, not exactly," Zaron admitted. "We're also going to be settling here."

"Settling?" Emily's voice rose. "Settling where?"

"In ten different locations around Earth," Zaron said, wondering how much he could disclose. He decided to err on the side of caution. "We're still choosing them right now."

"Oh my God." Emily took a step back, her hand pressed to her mouth. "You want to colonize our planet, steal it from—"

"Emily, stop." Zaron caught her in two long strides and gently pulled her hand down, away from her trembling lips. "It's not like that at all. Yes, we're going to establish some settlements here, but we're not stealing your planet. Your people will continue to live in their cities and govern themselves as they always have. Your lives won't change much. We're just going to be your neighbors, that's all."

"That's all?" In the shade of the guanacaste tree, Emily's eyes were almost completely green as she stared up at him, and he could feel the pulse beating rapidly in her slender wrist. "How stupid do you think I am? You're going to do to us what more advanced civilizations have always done to the natives, and—"

"No, we won't," Zaron said. He wasn't privy to the Council's longer-term plans for Earth, but he was fairly sure they didn't have any nefarious intentions for humans. What would be the point? In a way, humans were children of the Krinar, or at least their creations.

Stroking his thumb across the inside of Emily's wrist, he said, "If we wanted to hurt you or take your planet away from you, we could've done so at any point during your evolution. We didn't need to wait until you had nuclear weapons and satellites; we could've come when you were still in the Stone Age. That was practically yesterday for us. But we didn't do that because that's not what we're after."

Emily didn't look reassured. "Then what are you after? What do you want from us? Why do you want to settle here?"

"Well, for one thing, our solar system is older than yours." Zaron released Emily's wrist, noting with pleasure that she didn't immediately back away. "In another hundred million years or so, our sun is going to die, and if we're still there when it happens, we'll perish along with it. I know that's still fairly far in the future—probably an eternity for a species as young as yours—but it's something we have to be cognizant of. Coming here is a diversification strategy for us, a way to ensure our survival beyond the natural lifespan of our solar system."

"So because your planet is old, you want to take ours?"

Zaron sighed again. She wasn't listening. "Not take it, share it," he said patiently. "All we're talking about at this point are fifty thousand of us, a drop in the bucket compared to the human population of Earth."

"Maybe, but I'm guessing our missiles are like toy guns compared to whatever weapons you have." Her eyes held his in a silent challenge. "Aren't they?"

"Yes—but that's only a consideration if you decide to use those missiles against us," Zaron said. "Like I told you, we don't intend your people any harm."

Emily turned away and took a couple of steps toward a tall *Cyathea arborea*, then spun around to face him again. "So how do you plan to do this? I don't see our governments letting you settle here without a fight. You can't just expect to waltz in here and say, 'Hey, give us some land,' and have it magically happen."

"I'm sure the Council has considered that and has a plan for just such an eventuality," Zaron said. "I'm not on the Council, so—"

"What is your role, then? Why are you here? You said you're a biologist."

"I am, and a soil specialist as well." Zaron had hoped she wouldn't go there, but he didn't want to lie about this, either. "My role is to choose the appropriate locations for our settlements—sparsely populated areas with suitable climate and soil."

Emily stared at him. "I see."

She turned away again, and Zaron could sense the barriers she was putting up between them. Her slim back was rigid, her shoulders bunched with tension. She didn't believe him, didn't trust him, and he couldn't blame her. His people *were* invading her planet. The Krinar might've planted life here, but Earth had been home to humans for as long as her species had existed, and now the Krinar were planning to settle here. Had the situation been reversed, his people would've been livid—and there was every reason to think the humans would be too.

"Emily." Stepping toward her, Zaron gently grasped her arm and turned her to face him. "I'm sorry if this upset you, but I didn't want to lie to you."

She gazed up at him, her face still colorless. "Is there any way you could talk to your Council, try to convince them not to do this? You have a perfectly good planet for another hundred million years—you don't need ours."

"Emily..." He knew she understood the impossibility of her request; her tone was dull, resigned. Still, his chest felt heavy as he said, "I'm sorry, I can't. Everything's already been decided, and the ships are on their way."

Her lips quivered for a moment before flattening into a firm line. "Okay. I understand. Now, please, let go of me."

Zaron glanced down and realized he was still holding her, his fingers wrapped around her upper arm. A pulse of anger shot through him as he realized that she intended to treat him as an enemy, ignoring everything that had passed between them. "No," he said, gripping her other arm and pulling her closer. "I'm not letting go of you. This doesn't change anything, angel. You're mine for the next two weeks."

Emily's mouth opened—undoubtedly to protest his highhandedness—but he was already bending his head to kiss her.

She tasted soft and sweet, even as she tried to twist away, her hands rising up to push at his biceps. "Don't," she managed to gasp out before Zaron recaptured her lips, and his body hardened as he deepened the kiss and felt the heat rising off her skin. She was getting turned on, the scent of her arousal inflaming his senses, and her struggles were lessening with each moment.

She still wanted him, and Zaron intended to capitalize on that.

Continuing to kiss her, he lowered her to the ground, stretching her out on the hard blanket of leaves and grass. Clasping her wrists, he pinned her arms above her head with one hand, then slid his free hand down her body and pulled up the skirt of her dress, using his knees to part her legs. She was open to him now, her sex warm and slick as he delved into her folds, and his cock throbbed, aching to be inside her.

Tearing his mouth away, Zaron lifted his head and stared down at the human girl, remembering the first time he'd had her like this. She'd wanted him then too, but she'd been scared and he'd let her go.

He wasn't going to let her go now.

Emily's bright eyes were glazed as she stared up at him, her lips swollen and glistening from his kisses. Blond hair lay in a tangle of pale waves around her face, and a flush brightened her creamy cheeks as his fingers played with her clit. She was too far gone to stop him now, and the primitive, savage part of him reveled in that.

He wanted her exactly like this: dazed with pleasure and helpless to deny him.

"That's it, angel," he murmured, hearing her breathing quicken as he pushed two fingers into her tight channel and rolled his thumb across her clit. "Let go. Let go and come for me."

Her eyes drifted closed, and a soft, choked cry escaped her throat as her inner walls spasmed, clenching around his fingers. She was so wet now that his fingers glided in and out with no resistance, and he fucked her straight through the orgasm, his balls drawing closer to his body with each thrust of his fingers. If he hadn't spent half the night buried inside her body, he would've lost control by now, but as it was, Zaron could hang on—barely.

When she lay spent and panting underneath him, he tore open his jeans, finally freeing his aching cock. "Emily," he whispered hoarsely, pressing against her soft opening. "Look at me, angel."

Her eyelids rose, long lashes sweeping up slowly, and an odd warmth glowed in his chest as her eyes locked on his face. "This, here, has nothing to do with what's going on out there," he said, his voice low and thick. "You and I, we're not enemies, no matter what happens. Do you understand? For the next two weeks, you're here with me, and that's all that matters."

Emily didn't say anything, but her gaze was tormented, and Zaron knew it wouldn't be that easy. She would fight him. Maybe not at this moment, but she would fight him, just as her people would fight the Krinar when they arrived.

Anger surged through Zaron again, mixing with the burning lust, and he pushed deep into Emily's body, penetrating her all the way without slowing. She cried out—a pained cry, he registered vaguely—but he couldn't stop, driven by a hunger that seemed to come from some dark place inside him. She was slick and tight around him, her body clasping him with soft, wet heat, and he wanted her more than he'd ever wanted anyone, everything inside him centering on one need only: to take her, to possess her, to make her his.

Before long, she was meeting him thrust for thrust, her hips rising to take him in deeper. He could hear her gasping cries and moans, and the need to take her blood, to taste her that way too, was as potent as the lust boiling in his veins. He was already lowering his head when Ellet's warning blipped somewhere in the back of his mind, and instead of slicing his teeth across Emily's tender skin, he turned his head away and increased his pace, hammering into her with each stroke. Her cries were growing louder, more frantic, her wrists tensing in his grasp, and Zaron felt the ripples of her orgasm as she came, her inner muscles tightening around him. He wanted to hold on, to draw out the ecstasy of possessing her, but the convulsive clenching of her body sent him over the edge. A harsh groan tore from him as he thrust deep one last time, and then he was coming, his seed jetting into her in several long bursts.

Gasping for air, he rolled off Emily and gathered her against him, his thoughts scattered as he held her from the back. She was breathing heavily too, her slim body shaking and her skin damp with sweat. Closing his eyes, Zaron tightened his hold on her and buried his head in her hair, inhaling her sweet scent.

There was only one word circling through his brain, only one thought he could formulate.

Mine.

CHAPTER TWENTY-FIVE

Over the next several days, Emily had so much sex she felt like she was drowning in pleasure. Zaron was insatiable and had inhuman stamina, which meant that by the time he was done with her, she was exhausted and on the verge of passing out. If it hadn't been for his handy healing devices, she would've been constantly sore.

"God, are your people always like this?" she mumbled when he woke her up by sliding into her from the back, his thick cock invading her for the third time that night. "Don't you ever get tired?"

"Not of you," he breathed in her ear, his hand moving down her stomach to find the bundle of nerves at the apex of her sex. "Not of this. I could fuck you for an eternity."

Emily didn't know about an eternity, but he certainly took her every chance he got, and then some. She suspected that nonstop sex was Zaron's way of distracting her from his horrifying revelations, and most of the time, the strategy worked. When she was in his arms, she couldn't think, much less worry about the upcoming invasion of her planet. The moment he left her alone, however, her stomach would churn with anxiety, and their conversations at mealtimes were frequently tense and adversarial.

"There will be war—interplanetary war. Don't you understand that?" Emily burst out when Zaron tried to convince her at lunch that she had nothing to worry about. "Your people will come, and there will be war."

"No, there won't be," he said with calm certainty. "Some resistance, maybe, but not war."

"No? You think we're just going to roll over and—"

"Emily." He reached across the table to take her hand. "There won't be war because we won't let it come to that. You were right: all your weapons are like children's toys to us. Would there be war if the United States army came to a kindergarten? No. Your soldiers would just do what they wanted, and that's it. And it will be the same with us."

Emily gaped at him in horror. "Are you even listening to yourself? You think it's somehow better that your people will subjugate us without a fight?"

"Of course it is." Zaron patted her hand before resuming eating. "No war is always better than war."

For the rest of the meal, Emily refused to speak to him, doing her best to give him the cold shoulder, but when he took her for a walk afterwards, they again ended up having sex in the forest. Emily hated herself for that, for her inability to resist his touch, but her body kept betraying her. The moment Zaron touched her, she melted into a puddle of need, and her captor knew it and took ruthless advantage of the situation.

"Don't you realize how wrong this is?" she asked when she

lay in his arms that evening, her body humming with satiation but her thoughts full of self-loathing. "What you're doing to me is really messed up."

Zaron turned her over to face him, his black eyes unreadable in the dim light illuminating the room. "It's only wrong if you don't want me, but you do." His voice was low and deep, enveloping her in a warm, seductive cocoon. "You want me just as much as I want you, angel, so let's not pretend and make this anything other than what it is."

"And what is that?" Emily whispered, her chest tight. "How do *you* see this? Because from where I stand, you're keeping me captive and your people are about to invade my planet. And yet you're—" She stopped at the rapidly darkening expression on his face.

"I'm what?" His hand slid down her side. "Touching you?" His fingers squeezed her ass cheek as he pulled her closer to him. "Fucking you?"

Emily caught her breath as his erection pressed against her thigh, as hard as if it had been days, not minutes, since he'd been inside her. "Yes, exactly," she managed to say, pushing at his muscled chest. "I'm not a sex doll for you to—"

"You're what I want you to be." He lifted her leg and pushed into her, wringing a startled gasp from her throat. She was still sensitive and swollen from the previous time, and he felt enormous inside her, his cock stretching her tender inner walls. "My sex doll, my sex everything. I can't get enough of you, angel. And for now, I don't have to—because you're mine. Aren't you?"

He rolled his hips, hitting her G-spot, and Emily's body tightened, clenching around him on a surge of need. She tried to cling to her anger, to think past her growing arousal, but he was already kissing her, his big hands kneading her breasts as he set a hard, driving pace, and for the rest of the night, there was no more talk of right and wrong.

There was just Zaron and the dark heat blanketing them both.

———

On Thursday morning, two hours before her hedge fund interview was scheduled to take place, Emily woke up to find herself alone in her comfortable alien bed. The intelligent material had shaped itself to her body while she slept, and she felt it massaging her neck and shoulders—a feature Zaron had enabled after learning that Emily's back muscles were often tight from tension. She lay still for a few minutes, enjoying the bed's ministrations, and then she got up. Despite sleeping fairly late, she felt tired and listless, almost depressed.

On Tuesday, Zaron had allowed her to send an email to Evers Capital explaining that she'd gotten delayed in Costa Rica by two weeks and asking to reschedule her interview. By Wednesday evening, they still hadn't responded, and Emily knew that this was it: she'd blown her one chance to work with a hedge fund legend—not to mention, have a job in her field any time soon. With all the recent layoffs, Wall Street was drowning in analysts with her skill set, and everyone was competing for a rapidly shrinking pool of jobs.

If the upcoming Krinar invasion didn't end the world as Emily knew it, she'd be unemployed for much longer than she'd hoped.

The thought brought her back to her senses. It was silly to worry about a missed interview when her entire species was facing a threat as serious as the Krinar. Over the last few days, Emily had tried to find out more about Zaron's people, and what she'd learned wasn't reassuring.

She'd already known her captor was stronger and faster than a human man, but she'd ascribed some of that to his tall, athletic frame. His body was magnificent, his sleekly bronzed skin covering layers of lean, hard-packed muscle. Any man of his build would've been stronger than average, and Emily hadn't realized the full extent of Zaron's differences until their walk two days earlier, when she'd seen him lift a fallen tree with one hand and move it off their path.

He'd done it casually, as if the thick trunk was a tiny branch, and Emily had stopped, gaping at him in disbelief. By her estimation, that tree was at least a foot and a half in diameter.

"What's wrong?" he'd asked, but she'd just shaken her head, struck mute by shock. Walking over to the tree, she'd crouched and pushed at it with all her strength, hoping it was somehow lighter than it looked, but the trunk hadn't budged even a fraction of an inch. The tree was so heavy it was practically welded to the ground, yet Zaron had moved it with no more effort than Emily would exert to lift a two-pound weight.

Her captor had observed her efforts with obvious amusement, his beautiful lips curved in a smile, and Emily had felt a cold trickle of fear as she recalled how fast he'd caught her that time at the lake.

The Krinar didn't just have superior technology; they were more powerful in every way.

"How did you evolve to be so fast and strong?" she'd asked when they'd resumed walking, and he'd shrugged, stonewalling her. She'd noticed that while Zaron seemed hesitant to lie to her outright, he had no problem withholding information when it suited his purposes. There were certain topics he preferred to avoid, and Emily suspected it had to do with things he thought might scare her. Whenever she tried to ask him about the types of weapons his people possessed or what they were going to do once they settled on Earth, he directed the conversation elsewhere or distracted her with sex—and it seemed like the topic of Krinar evolution was one that was also off limits.

It was the same when she'd noticed that all her meals at Zaron's house consisted of fruits, vegetables, and other plant-based foods. At first, she'd thought it had to do with his profession—he loved plants and was always telling her interesting tidbits about Costa Rican flora—but then she'd begun to wonder if there was another reason for his diet.

"Why don't you eat any meat?" she'd asked, munching on a salad his house had prepared for their dinner. "Is that your personal dietary preference or a general trait of the Krinar?"

"The latter," Zaron had said. "Like humans, we're omnivorous, but we prefer plants. On Krina, many plants are rich in nutrients and dense in calories, so we've never needed to eat animals to survive."

"Oh, I see." That had surprised Emily. For some reason, she'd assumed that the Krinar had been hunters and gatherers at some point, similar to primitive humans. And then she'd realized why she'd made that assumption.

There was something predatory in the grace with which Zaron moved, something that kept reminding her of a feline hunter. She had the disquieting impression that if provoked, he could pounce in an instant. His gaze, too, was sharp and clear, often tracking her movements with the intensity of a cat stalking a butterfly.

"Are there a lot of large predators on your planet?" she'd

asked. Maybe the Krinar had been prey at some point in their early history and had to develop their speed and strength to survive—though that still didn't explain Zaron's unusual way of moving.

"A few," he'd answered without elaborating, and Emily had known he was stonewalling her again.

Whatever Zaron was hiding had to be worse than his people's colonization plans—and that made Emily very, very nervous.

Still, as she was showering, her thoughts kept returning to the interview she'd missed and the job that was now out of her reach. Every day, she kept an eye out for an opportunity to escape, but Zaron watched her carefully during their walks, and there was no way she could get out of his intelligent house. And now it was too late: Evers Capital would never hire her.

Sighing, Emily stepped out of the shower and let the Krinar technology dry her. Putting on one of the dresses Zaron had left for her, she headed back to the bedroom, where her drowned phone lay on the floating plank next to her bed.

Sitting down, Emily picked it up. It felt dry, but the screen was dark and unresponsive. Automatically, she pressed the button on the side and held it, watching the screen without much hope.

The screen lit up.

Emily jumped up, her heart hammering, and stared at the screen in disbelief. The familiar icons loaded with agonizing slowness, but the phone was unmistakably alive.

Emily's hand shook as she swiped across the screen to unlock the phone. She'd paid for a roaming package before embarking on the trip, but there was only one bar of reception showing—likely because they were inside a cave. Not that the number of bars mattered: the battery was nearly depleted. At best, she had only a few minutes before the phone died, and she had to make them count.

Whom could she call? Her friends back home? The Costa Rican police? Emily had prudently programmed a few emergency numbers into her phone before leaving the US, and she flipped through them now, her mind racing. She dismissed the idea of calling friends right away; there was no guarantee any of them would pick up, and it would take too long to explain her situation and ask them to send help. With the local police, there would be a language barrier. Emily knew basic Spanish, but there was no way she could convey everything and make herself understood.

The best option was the American embassy, she decided after a moment. Odds were high they'd dismiss her as a nutcase, but if she could get through to them somehow, her warning could make a real difference.

Holding her breath, Emily pressed the call button and held the phone up to her ear. One second, two, three, four... The silence seemed to stretch forever, but just as Emily became convinced the call wouldn't go through, she heard the long *beep* of connection.

"United States Embassy." The female voice was pleasant and calm. "How may I direct your call?"

Emily's knees went weak with relief. "Yes, hi. My name is Emily Ross, and I'm an American citizen." She spoke quickly, not knowing when the battery would die. "I'm being held captive in the Guanacaste region. I need you to listen to me carefully. The man holding me here has told me that there is a threat to our country. An invasion will happen in a matter of days. The people who are coming call themselves the Krinar, and they have weapons that are far more advanced than ours. You have to warn the President. I know this sounds crazy, but—"

The quiet hum of background noise against her ear turned to silence, and Emily realized it was over.

Her phone was completely dead.

Lowering the device, she stared at the dark screen in frustration. Had the operator heard anything Emily had said, and if she had, would she pass along the message or dismiss it as the ramblings of a drunk tourist? Emily had purposefully avoided the word "alien," but what she *had* said was not much better. Even to her own ears, she'd sounded like a lunatic.

Emily's palms were damp and her legs shaky as she put the phone back on the floating plank and sat down on the bed. She was still buzzing with adrenaline, and it took several minutes before she calmed down enough to reach for the tablet Zaron had given her. Whatever happened next was out of her hands. Either the operator would convey her message, or she wouldn't. Emily had to be content with the knowledge that she'd done the best she could.

Taking a deep breath, she told the tablet, *"Independence Day,* please," and scooted back on the bed. The intelligent furniture immediately curved around her, intuiting that she wanted back support for her movie-watching experience.

Emily's choice of entertainment was masochistic, but she didn't care.

Maybe if she saw humans kicking some alien ass on screen, she'd believe Earth stood a chance against the real thing.

CHAPTER TWENTY-SIX

*A*s the days flew by, Zaron began to dread the ships' arrival. It wasn't because his team wasn't ready—everything was in place on their end—but because every hour that ticked by brought him closer to the day when he'd have to let Emily go.

Once the Krinar made contact with the human leaders, he'd no longer be able to use the non-disclosure mandate as justification for keeping her.

Ever since Zaron had told Emily about his people's true intentions, she'd done her best to keep him at a distance—emotionally, at least. There was no more talk about her past, no more sharing of painful experiences. But little by little, Zaron learned more about her, and every new tidbit he uncovered intensified his fascination with the human girl—a fascination that was beginning to border on obsession.

She liked strawberries but hated blueberries, enjoyed sci-fi movies but preferred to read nonfiction books. Her mind was sharply analytical—she was at home with numbers and spreadsheets—but she needed nature and the outdoors to feel complete.

"Whenever I have some free time—which is pretty much never—I like to go to the park," she confided as they sat by the lake, for once talking without arguing. "It energizes me, helps me rest my brain and shake off all the cubicle cobwebs."

Zaron understood that; his enjoyment of the natural environment was a key reason for his choice of specialization. Even as a child, he'd been fascinated with living things, both plants and animals. However, something about what Emily had said bothered him. "Why do you have so little free time?" he asked, frowning. "Don't most humans work nine to five?"

"Not the investment banking humans," she said wryly. "My breed works eighty-hour weeks, and that's when our workload is light. On one project last year, I had to work a hundred and forty hours a week for three months straight."

Zaron did some quick mental math. If she was working a hundred and forty hours a week, then she had only four hours a day when she wasn't working—less than half the daily sleep requirement for humans. *He* could work that much because the Krinar needed significantly less sleep, but Emily's health could suffer from that kind of pace.

"You shouldn't have put in those hours," he said, unable to keep the censure out of his voice. "You could get sick if you don't get enough sleep."

Emily gave him a puzzled look, then shrugged. "Yeah, I guess. I didn't plan to do it forever, just until I could get a similar job with better hours—which the job at that hedge fund would've been, by the way."

Zaron felt an unwelcome pang of guilt at the reminder that

he'd cost her the job she'd wanted so desperately. It was only as he'd gotten to know Emily better that he'd understood why that interview had been such a big deal for her. The human girl was fiercely independent, and she'd achieved a great deal in her twenty-four years despite having a rough start in life. From Zaron's initial background check on her, he'd known that she'd graduated from Northwestern, one of the highest-ranked US colleges, and gotten a job with a major investment bank right after graduation. However, it wasn't until two days ago, when Zaron had read up on the institution of foster homes, that he'd realized how difficult Emily's path must've been without any family to support her.

"Who paid for your college?" he asked, his frown deepening as the question occurred to him. "Those institutions are expensive in your country, I believe."

Emily nodded. "They are. I got lucky: I ran track and cross country, so I was offered a scholarship that covered the majority of my tuition. For the rest, I used a combination of government grants, part-time jobs, and loans."

"Your aunt didn't help you?"

Emily's eyebrows rose. "Aunt Wendy? No. She passed away from a stroke when I was seventeen, and for several years before that, she'd lived off a disability pension. She couldn't have helped me even if she'd wanted to."

"I see." Zaron struggled to keep his tone level. He felt angry on her behalf, and he didn't know why. "So you have no one you can turn to."

Emily blinked. "That's not true. I have my friends and my cat and my boyfr—" She stopped mid-word, but it was too late.

Zaron's anger transformed into white-hot jealousy.

"Boyfriend?" Even to his own ears, his voice sounded

dangerously low. "You have a boyfriend?" Zaron had assumed Emily was single because she lived alone in a studio and was traveling by herself, but now he realized the folly of that assumption. As independent as Emily was, she could easily have a man waiting for her in New York—a man she hadn't mentioned until now.

To Zaron's relief, she shook her head. "No," she said, her voice tight. "I don't have one. Not anymore."

Zaron's jealousy blazed back to life. It was obvious that whoever this male was, he'd hurt Emily—which meant she'd cared for him.

She might even be in love with him still.

"Who is he?" The rage searing Zaron's chest was irrational, he knew, but he couldn't shake off the conviction that Emily belonged to him, that she was his and any man who touched her deserved to be ripped apart. Krinar males tended to be territorial and possessive about their mates, but Emily wasn't Zaron's mate. He had no reason to feel so strongly about a human girl who was with him only for the next few days. Still, no amount of rational reasoning could keep the fury out of Zaron's voice as he demanded, "What is his name?"

Emily gave him a wary look. "What does it matter? It's over. We broke up over four months ago."

Four months? Red specks edged Zaron's vision. A mere four months ago, some puny human had been touching Emily, kissing her… making love to her.

"Who is he? How long were you two together?" Zaron could hear the dark edge in his voice, and he knew Emily could too, because she rose to her feet and took a step to the side, staring at him like he was some kind of feral animal.

Zaron forced himself to take a deep breath. He might've felt like said animal, but he didn't want to scare Emily. Getting up in a slow, controlled motion, he stepped toward her and caught her hand, keeping his grip gentle. "Tell me, angel," he said in a softer tone. "Tell me about this former boyfriend of yours. What happened between you two?"

Emily looked uneasy. "You... you won't do anything to him, right?"

Fuck. She was perceptive. The ancient predator within Zaron had already been planning to track down this human male and end his existence. Now he couldn't—if only because it would upset Emily.

"Of course I won't do anything to him," Zaron said with a calmness he didn't feel. "Why would I?"

The question was directed as much at himself as at Emily, but it had the desired effect. She relaxed slightly, though wariness still lurked in her gaze. "I don't know," she said. "You just seemed... angry for a moment."

Zaron took another deep breath and pulled Emily toward him, molding her slender curves against his body. "I'm not," he assured her. And he wasn't—not anymore. The primitive urge rising within him now was quite different in nature.

Sliding his hands into Emily's silky hair, he bent his head and took her mouth in a deep, voracious kiss.

———

Zaron didn't get the answers to his questions until a couple of hours later, when Emily lay tired and replete in his arms. Before they got completely carried away, he'd brought her to a grassy meadow just beyond the rocky shore of the lake, and they rested there now, watching the water sparkle in the sun some fifty feet away.

"So tell me about this mystery ex-boyfriend of yours," Zaron said, keeping his tone light despite his persistent desire to tear the unknown man into pieces. "How did you two meet?"

"It was in college," Emily answered without lifting her head off his shoulder. She sounded relaxed and mildly drowsy, and Zaron knew he'd succeeded in getting her mind off his earlier behavior. "Jason and I were friends at first; then he asked me out. We were both Econ majors, had the same circle of friends, and were applying for the same kinds of jobs. It made a lot of sense for us to be together, so we started dating. It was casual at first, just two college kids hanging out, but then we both ended up getting jobs in investment banking after graduation and moving to New York City. To save money, we decided to live together, and so we did—until four months ago, when he told me he couldn't handle my hours and moved out."

She spoke calmly, as if the breakup didn't bother her in the least, but Zaron felt the tension creeping back into her slim frame.

"Why couldn't he handle your hours?" he asked, keeping his tone even. "Wasn't he in the same profession as you?"

"He was, but he got lucky. About a year after our graduation, before the market tanked, he got offered a job at a venture capital firm, and his hours improved. So yeah." Emily glanced up at Zaron. "That was it, the whole story. Very low drama."

Except it wasn't, not for her—Zaron could tell that much.

"How many years were you together with this Jason?" he asked, fighting the jealousy that still threatened to consume him. "When in college did you start dating?"

Emily sighed and sat up, straightening her dress—which

was now somewhat torn and stained with grass. "We dated for a little over four years," she said, pushing her tangled hair off her face. "Not a lifetime or anything."

"I see." Zaron grabbed his discarded jeans off the grass. Getting up, he pulled them on and bent down to pick up Emily.

"Zaron, put me down! I can walk," she protested as he swung her up into his arms, but he ignored her objections.

He needed to hold her so he could control the rage boiling within him—and keep his promise about not hunting down the human bastard who had hurt Emily.

CHAPTER TWENTY-SEVEN

$\mathcal{A}$s the day of Krinar arrival and Emily's promised liberation approached, Emily found herself increasingly anxious. She had no appetite, and her nights were restless, her sleep frequently interrupted by bad dreams. When she was a child, she used to have nightmares about her parents' car crash, but she'd grown out of that—or so she'd thought. In those dreams, she was always standing on the side of the road, watching as the car flipped over, and her stomach would fill with cold terror at the knowledge that she was alone, that everyone she loved was dead.

Emily told herself the nightmares had returned because she was worried about the invasion, but part of her knew the truth.

It was the upcoming separation from Zaron that made her relive the old pain of loss and abandonment.

"You know, you've got to be one of the strongest people I know," her friend Amber had told Emily after her breakup with

Jason. "I don't know how you do it. Aren't you ever scared of being alone? You act like it doesn't matter that your boyfriend of four years just walked away and—"

"Because it doesn't matter," Emily had interrupted. "I never relied on him for anything." And it was true. Though the breakup had hurt a lot more than Emily let on, she'd never opened up to Jason fully. They'd lived together and been regarded as a great couple by all their friends, but they'd remained separate individuals, never bonding on a deeper emotional level. Emily used to think she loved him—and maybe she had, in a very tepid and superficial way—but she'd never let him get truly close. It wasn't because she was brave, however—just the opposite.

She'd been too scared to let herself depend on Jason, to love him for real. That was the true reason for their breakup, not the disparity in work hours that Jason had used as an excuse. Something had always been missing in their relationship, and Emily now knew it had been her fault.

She'd been so afraid of being abandoned she'd kept Jason at a distance until he did exactly that.

But Zaron had somehow gotten through her shell. Emily didn't know if it was the extraordinary sexual chemistry between them, or the hint of vulnerability she'd glimpsed behind his self-assured, arrogant façade, but she felt closer to Zaron than she'd felt to anyone in her adult life. Her captor scared her at times, but she was also drawn to him, pulled in a way that superseded normal attraction and something as simple as liking and friendship.

When they were together, she felt like her world was illuminated with a warm light, all her senses buzzing with electric awareness. As much as Emily wanted to hate Zaron after learning about the invasion, she couldn't. They'd gotten too close before that revelation, had opened up to each other too much for her to despise him now. Besides, he'd saved her life, and as much as Emily resented her captivity and feared the future to come, she never forgot that she was only alive because of him.

"Why did you do it?" she asked during a walk one day. "Why did you go to all this trouble to save the life of a stranger? You had to know it would get messy, with the mandate and all."

Zaron's jaw stiffened, and his hand tightened around her own. "Because I had to," he said, and before Emily could pry further, he drew her to him and kissed her with such savage passion she forgot everything but her own name.

And that was the problem. Zaron's sexual expertise and mastery of her body were such that she was powerless to resist him. Whenever she tried to put up barriers between them, Zaron would storm through them with pathetic ease. She couldn't give him the cold shoulder because he would just drag her off to bed and pleasure her until she melted, and then, when all her defenses were down, he'd do something sweet, like have his house make one of Emily's favorite foods or take her on an extra-long walk in the forest. His domineering tendencies were balanced with kindness, his rough-edged sexuality mixed with gentle caring. He consumed her and treated her like spun glass at the same time, and Emily didn't know how to cope with that.

Still, if their connection had been based solely on sex, it would've been easier. But whenever they managed a conversation without arguing, Emily had the unsettling sensation that she'd found her intellectual soulmate. Zaron's scientific mindset, his dedication to his field, even his tendency to identify common plants and animals by their official genus and species—all of it resonated with Emily, fascinating her to no end. A walk through the forest with Zaron was better than an hour of Discovery Channel; he had an encyclopedia-like knowledge of everything that grew, crawled, walked, and flew in the rainforest, and would often sprinkle in little anecdotes about analogous plants and animals on Krina. He was careful not to say too much—that damnable mandate again—but what Emily did learn was incredible.

"A flying reptile that carries its eggs in a pouch and eats them when it gets hungry? You say these things are common on Krina?" she asked in amazement when Zaron described a creature called *eponu*. "How does it survive and reproduce?"

"It lays hundreds of eggs," he answered, smiling. "It only eats about eighty percent of them throughout the incubation period. When the rest hatch, they battle it out in the pouch until a few winners emerge and fly away to feed on insects and other small creatures—until it's time for those new eponu to reproduce. Once the females lay eggs, the males go back to hunting, and the females use the eggs for sustenance, thus starting the cycle all over again."

Emily showered him with more questions at that point, and he answered them, apparently deciding that it would do no harm for her to know about some of Krina's unusual creatures. He also told her a little bit about his childhood and how his family had encouraged his interest in nature from an early age.

"I come from a family of scientists," he said as a way of explanation. "My mother is a botanist, my father is a physicist, and three of my grandparents are biologists like me. I guess you could say exploring nature is in our blood." He said it offhandedly, like it was no big deal, and Emily had to battle a familiar surge of envy.

She would've given anything to have her parents around to encourage her in her life's ventures.

"What does your family think about you being here, on Earth, so far away from them?" she asked, trying not to sound as jealous as she felt.

If Emily's parents and grandparents had been alive, she would've never left them to go to a different galaxy.

To her surprise, Zaron's face tightened. "I don't know," he said, stopping next to a lush tree fern. His gaze was inscrutable, but there was a hard undertone in his voice. "I haven't spoken to them much in the last few years."

He didn't elaborate, but Emily could read between the lines. Zaron's estrangement from his loved ones had to do with his wife's death; she was almost certain of that. He must've found it difficult to be around his family after his tragic loss. Grief could be isolating—Emily knew that better than anyone. For several years after her parents' deaths, she'd had trouble making friends in school because other kids felt uncomfortable around the orphan. It was as if they were afraid that misfortune was contagious, that by being around her, they might let loss and pain into their own lives. Even some well-meaning teachers had made her feel like an outsider by being solicitous in all the wrong ways, and it was entirely possible that Zaron's family had done that too, treating him like a broken person to assuage their survivors' guilt.

Without a word, Emily reached out and squeezed his hand, and they walked the rest of the way in silence. Zaron hadn't spoken about his wife since that one time, but Emily knew he still grieved for her. She suspected that part of the reason why he made love to Emily so often was because sex was a distraction for him too—a way to cope with his grief and pain. It was nothing he said or did, but every once in a while, she'd catch a look of raw agony on his face, and she knew that at that moment, he was thinking of the wife he'd lost.

Thankfully, in recent days, those moments had become increasingly rare. In fact, most of the time, Zaron seemed focused on Emily to an almost obsessive degree. When they weren't in bed together, he was constantly questioning her about her life, wanting to know about everything from her favorite foods to her friends to her former boyfriends—though the latter subject did make him oddly tense, as though he was jealous. In general, he seemed possessive of her—far more possessive than Emily considered reasonable under the circumstances.

"Zaron, you do know I'm leaving in a few days, right?" she murmured as they lay in bed one evening, their legs tangled together after another steamy bout of sex. "I'm not yours, no matter what you make me say when I'm on the verge of orgasm. This—you and me—it's just temporary."

He pulled back to meet her gaze, and she saw that his jaw was set in a hard line. "I know." His tone was even, but she could hear the lethal edge behind the words. It reminded her of when he'd questioned her about Jason. For a brief moment during that conversation, she'd had the crazy thought that Zaron might harm her ex-boyfriend. It seemed ridiculous afterwards, but at the time, she'd been convinced that she'd sensed something dark and violent in the man who held her captive—something that had terrified her.

"You *are* letting me go, right?" Emily asked, doing her best to keep the sudden anxiety out of her voice. "When your people arrive, I can go home."

Zaron's expression was unchanging, his eyes completely black as he said, "Yes, of course." But then he reached for her, pulling her to him, and Emily forgot all about her unease.

CHAPTER TWENTY-EIGHT

The day before the ships' arrival, Emily woke up particularly depressed. Her nightmares that night had been so bad she'd woken up crying twice. Zaron had been worried that she was sick or in pain, but once she explained that it was just a bad dream, he'd given her exactly what she needed: the comfort of his powerful arms holding her in the dark.

It was that night that Emily faced the truth.

Her fear had come true. She'd fallen for a man from a different planet, a member of a species she still knew very little about.

The realization shook Emily to the core. She couldn't love Zaron; she simply couldn't. He was holding her against her will, and his people were planning to invade her planet. What kind of twisted person fell in love under those circumstances? Besides, he wasn't human. He might look like a man, but he was as different from Emily as she was from her cat. Even their lifespans weren't compatible. In a few years, Emily would begin aging, but he would remain the same. And then where would they be?

No, stop. Back up. It was ridiculous for Emily to think so long term. Tomorrow she would leave, and that would be it. His strange possessiveness aside, by now Zaron had likely had his fill of sex with her, and he'd move on to someone else, maybe a woman of his own species... someone who could replace the mate he'd lost.

Someone who wasn't Emily.

Emily's chest squeezed painfully, her eyes prickling with tears. *You don't love him,* she told herself. What she felt had to be an infatuation, a result of their forced proximity. They'd spent so much time together over the last two weeks that it was only natural for her to become attached. Besides, even if she was crazy enough to want to stay, there was no future for them, no chance to be together in any lasting way.

No. Determined not to give in to her illogical feelings, Emily got up and headed to the shower.

Once she got back to her normal life, her attachment to Zaron would fade with time.

She was certain of that.

CHAPTER TWENTY-NINE

"So where is she, your human girl?" Ellet asked, looking around Zaron's living room. She was in Costa Rica this week, and had taken Zaron up on his invitation to visit. "You still have her, right?"

"I do. She's showering right now," Zaron said, sitting down on a long floating plank. "She just woke up, so you'll have to wait a bit to meet her."

"Ah, you're letting her sleep in. Good." Ellet walked over to sit down next to him. Like him, she was dressed in human clothes—a pair of shorts, a tight T-shirt, and hiking boots—but to Zaron's eyes, she looked unmistakably Krinar, with all the sleek dark beauty of their race. Giving him a wide smile, she said, "I was a bit worried that you might be wearing her out. Humans need so much more rest than us, you know."

Zaron frowned. Ellet had just voiced his own concerns. Emily had been looking rather tired lately—not to mention, sleeping poorly. Was it because of the demands he placed on her human body? "I'm careful," he said, but even he could hear the doubt in his voice.

"I'm sure you are," Ellet said consolingly. "It's just that it's easy for our males to get carried away and forget how fragile human women can be." She paused, then asked delicately, "Did you do it again?"

"Drink her blood? No." Zaron raised his knee to hide his body's automatic reaction to the subject. "I promised her I wouldn't."

"Wouldn't what?" Emily asked, stepping into the room.

Cursing silently, Zaron got up and turned to face the wall to Emily's bedroom—a wall that had dissolved soundlessly a moment ago, letting Emily in. Out of habit, he'd been speaking to Ellet in English, and she'd been responding in kind. How much had Emily overheard? The human girl's face was pale, her hands clenched in the skirt of her dress, but that could be because she was startled to see Ellet.

"Emily, this is my friend and colleague Ellet," he said with a smile that betrayed nothing of his thoughts. "Ellet, this is Emily, my guest."

"Hello, Emily." Ellet rose gracefully to her feet and stepped toward Emily, extending her hand in a human greeting. "It's very nice to meet you."

Emily hesitated for a millisecond, then shook Ellet's hand. Zaron noticed that the human girl's grip was firm, the delicate muscles and tendons in her forearm flexing as she squeezed Ellet's hand. "Hello," she said, her lips curving in a bright smile—the same smile she'd often given Zaron when they'd first met. It was Emily's artificial smile, he now recognized, the one she used to hide her nervousness. "It's nice to meet you too."

"Ellet is a human biology expert," Zaron explained, watching as Emily stepped back. "Your species is her life's work."

"Is that why you came to Earth?" Emily asked. "To study us?"

"Yes—and to assist in the settlement process." Ellet shot him a quick glance. "Zaron told you about that, I presume?"

"Yes, he did." Emily gave her that overly bright smile again. "He told me everything."

"Oh, phew." Ellet swiped her hand across the top of her head in an exaggerated gesture of relief. "And here I was afraid I'd have to walk on eggshells around you. That's the correct English expression, right?"

Emily's smile turned a bit more genuine. Ellet was charming her, Zaron thought with amusement.

"That's right," she said to Ellet. "Though I'm sure you know that, since your English is absolutely perfect."

Ellet grinned. "Why, thank you. Aren't you sweet? No wonder Zaron here finds you irresistible."

Emily's creamy cheeks turned pink. "How long have you and Zaron known each other?" she asked, clearly eager to change the subject.

"Oh, not that long," Ellet said breezily. "Twelve or thirteen years, right, Zaron?"

Zaron nodded. "We met at what you humans would call a biology conference—a gathering of experts in the field of species studies. Now, Emily, you haven't had your breakfast yet. Ellet, would you care for something to eat as well?"

"Sure," the Krinar woman said with a wide grin. "I haven't had house-cooked food in a long time."

Zaron had the house prepare a wide variety of dishes, and the three of them sat down to eat breakfast. Almost right away, Emily started peppering Ellet with questions, asking her about everything from Ellet's role in the settlement project to life on Krina. Zaron did his best to steer the conversation to relatively safe topics, but Emily kept prying and Ellet seemed oblivious to Zaron's subtle signals.

"Oh, yes, women on Krina have all the same rights as men," she told Emily when the human girl asked about gender relations. "I mean, the men tend to be highly territorial and protective of their women, but there's nothing stopping us from getting the jobs we want or even participating in the Arena fights if we're so inclined—"

"Arena fights?" Emily asked, latching on to the one tidbit Zaron had hoped she'd miss.

"It's just an old tradition," Zaron cut in before Ellet could respond. "A sport of sorts, like mixed martial arts here."

Ellet glanced at him with eyebrows raised but didn't contradict him. The deadly Arena challenges had more in common with gladiator fights in Rome than modern human sports, but Zaron didn't want Emily to know that. To explain the ancient institution of the Arena, he'd have to go into the violent history of the Krinar and their predatory origins. If Emily knew that his people had once hunted weaker primates for blood and that her kind had originally been designed as a substitute for those primates, she'd worry about the invasion even more.

"What about humans?" Emily asked next. "Are there any living on Krina? I mean, you guys have been coming here for a while, so..." She let the sentence trail off.

"Oh, sure," Ellet said, picking up a piece of roasted *Ipomoea batatas*—sweet potato. "We have a number of humans living back home."

She didn't elaborate further, and Zaron realized that his colleague had caught on to the fact that it might not be wise for Emily to know too much. Tomorrow morning, he'd have to let her go, and she would be free to share her knowledge with the others. They had to make sure they didn't tell her anything the Council wouldn't want the human media to know.

"So what do my people do on your planet?" Emily persisted. "Are they there because you're studying them, or are they considered something like immigrants? In general, what kind of rights do they have?"

"There aren't many humans on Krina currently, so there are no formal laws in that regard," Zaron said before Ellet could answer. "Maybe that'll change now that we'll be in contact more."

The truth was that humans had no rights on Krina. Over the millennia that his people had been visiting Earth, hundreds of humans had been brought to Krina, and Zaron suspected that not all of them had come of their own free will. Most of the older Krinar saw nothing wrong with that; they'd been around when Emily's species had lived in caves, so to many of them, humans were just a few steps above animals. But the younger Krinar, those of Zaron's and Ellet's generation, held more nuanced views, and Zaron was no exception. To him, humans weren't all that different from the Krinar—at least not in the ways that mattered.

"Tell me about yourself," Ellet said to Emily. The human biology expert now seemed eager to change the subject as well. "Why did you come to Costa Rica, and how did you get hurt so badly?"

Emily smiled politely and explained that she'd been on vacation and went hiking in the rainforest without considering the recent rains. "It was stupid of me, I know," she said with a wry grimace. "I shouldn't have tried to cross that bridge—at least not when I saw that it was wet."

She continued, explaining how she'd hung there by her fingernails, and Zaron's gut clenched as he remembered Emily's broken body lying on those rocks. If he hadn't heard her scream, if he hadn't gotten there in time... The agony that shot through him at the thought was as sharp as when he'd learned of Larita's death. For a moment, he couldn't breathe, couldn't think beyond the knowledge that he'd almost lost Emily—lost her before having the chance to know her. Another few minutes, and her life would've been cut short, her bright mind extinguished in the shattered shell of her body.

"Damn right you shouldn't have tried to cross that bridge." The words ripped out of him, terse and harsh, startling the two women into silence. "What the hell were you thinking, hiking alone like that? You could've been stung or bitten; there are all sorts of venomous creatures here—not to mention, you were fair game for any criminal asshole who'd crossed your path. How were you planning to protect yourself? You could've been raped, robbed... killed. Have you no survival instinct, no common sense?" As he spoke, Zaron found himself on his feet, his hands crushing the edge of the table. "What kind of idiot goes on a trip like this solo? What the fuck were you thinking, Emily?"

The human girl was staring at him like he'd lost his mind, and so was Ellet. Zaron couldn't blame them; he could hear the barely controlled rage in his own voice, and he knew he was acting like a madman. But he couldn't help it. Ever since Emily had become important to him, he'd purposefully tried to avoid thinking about her accident—and it was precisely for this reason.

He couldn't handle the idea that the human who'd filled the dark, painful void inside him had come so close to dying.

For a few moments, there was nothing but tense silence. Then Ellet said, "I think I should probably get going. I have quite a bit of work to do today, and—"

"No, please, you don't have to leave." Emily jumped to her feet, her falsely bright smile appearing on her lips. "I'm sure you and Zaron have some work matters to discuss, and I just remembered something I've been meaning to do. It was a pleasure meeting you, Ellet. Now if you'll excuse me..."

Turning, she disappeared into the living room, her footsteps light as she crossed the room. Then there was silence again, and Zaron knew Emily had gone back to her room, extricating herself from an uncomfortable situation as speedily as she could.

"Well, okay, then," Ellet said, her eyes gleaming with amusement. "I think I should get going too..."

"No, I'm sorry." Fury was still a toxic pulse in his veins, but Zaron forced himself to sit down and relax his coiled muscles. "You don't have to leave. You haven't even finished your meal yet. I promise I'm going to behave."

"Are you sure?" Ellet asked dryly. "You don't want to yell at your human guest some more?"

"No." Zaron took a deep breath and slowly let it out. "Please, sit. Let's finish our meal, and I'll apologize to Emily afterwards."

"Okay, if you're sure. I wouldn't want to get in the middle of a lovers' quarrel."

"It's not a lovers' quarrel." Zaron almost bit out the words, but managed to soften his tone at the last moment. "Emily's accident brought back some unpleasant memories, that's all."

"Oh, I see." Ellet's eyes widened with understanding, all traces of amusement disappearing from her face. "Of course, Zaron. I'm sorry. It was thoughtless of me. After your mate and all..."

"What?" Zaron frowned. "No, this has nothing to do with Larita. It's just that—" He broke off, not knowing how to explain the strange tangle of feelings inside him. "On second thought, maybe it *is* because of Larita," he said, seizing the conveniently provided excuse. "I'm sorry I ruined your visit."

"Oh, no, I'm fine," Ellet said, and demonstratively dug into the remnants of roasted vegetables on her plate. "You have nothing to worry about," she mumbled around a mouthful. "Now, please, tell me about the plan for tomorrow. When are we presenting the finalized locations to the Council?"

The rest of the meal passed in conversation about work, and by the time Ellet got up to leave again, Zaron was feeling much calmer. "I'm sorry about that," he apologized to Ellet again, leading her out of the house. "I hope I didn't make things too awkward."

Ellet stopped under a *Pachira quinata*, a pochote tree, some dozen yards away from his cave and gave him a reassuring smile. "Of course you didn't. Not at all. But, Zaron..." She hesitated.

"What is it?"

"Have you considered making this girl your charl?"

Zaron's expression must've reflected the shock that froze him in place, so Ellet quickly pressed on. "I know it's none of my business, but it seems like this Emily might mean something to you. If she doesn't become your charl, she *will* die. Maybe not tomorrow or next week, but in a few short decades. Have you thought about that?"

Zaron hadn't—because that way lay dark temptations and broken promises. He'd been so focused on the present, on enjoying every moment he had left with Emily, that he'd chased away all thoughts of the future and the cold, painful emptiness that awaited him after her departure tomorrow. He would survive it, he'd told himself. The fact that a human made him feel so alive was a good sign. It meant that he was healing, that the grief that had consumed him for eight years was finally lessening. He hadn't let himself think beyond that, but here was Ellet, bringing up the fears and dreams he'd been trying to hold at bay.

In as level of a tone as he could manage, Zaron said, "I can't make her my charl. I promised her that this is only temporary, Ellet. I can't just keep her—"

"You can." Ellet's hazel gaze was unwavering. "You can do anything you want, and you know it."

Zaron felt her words like a puncture wound to his lungs. She was right. Who would stop him if he decided to keep Emily longer? The Council couldn't care less about the fate of one human girl, and the human law held no sway over him. He could keep her in his house—and in his bed—for as long as he wanted her.

"No," Zaron said hoarsely. It was a denial of his own twisted desire as much as Ellet's words. "I can't do that to her. Not when I promised that I'd let her go."

Ellet regarded him silently for a moment; then her lips tilted up in a smile. "I knew you were one of the good ones. This girl of yours is luckier than she knows." She turned away, as if to keep walking, then spun around to face him again. "Zaron..."

Her voice was soft. "Have you considered simply asking her to stay?"

Zaron stared at her. "You mean, permanently? As a charl?"

Ellet nodded.

"No," Zaron said slowly. "Not really." Did he want that? Was he ready for such a big step? It was one thing to keep Emily with him for an extra few weeks or months—maybe even a few years—but taking a charl was a lifelong commitment. More than that, it would mean acknowledging to himself how much Emily had come to mean to him—and letting himself be vulnerable again. More vulnerable than with Larita, because Emily was human, with all the weaknesses and frailties of her species. What if Zaron took her as a charl and then lost her, like he'd lost his wife? A human body was so fragile, so breakable...

He must've stood frozen in thought for some time because Ellet said gently, "All right. It's obviously up to you. I'm sure you know what you're doing."

"Yes." Zaron shook off the uncharacteristic paralysis. "I'll figure it out. Thanks for stopping by. It was good to see you."

"It was my pleasure." Ellet gave him a warm smile. "Take care, Zaron, and good luck."

She turned and disappeared into the trees, and Zaron went back into the house, his mind filled with possibilities and his chest aching with emotions he couldn't acknowledge.

CHAPTER THIRTY

*E*mily lay on her bed, her eyes burning as she stared at the ceiling. Could it possibly be true, what she'd overheard? Did Zaron's people actually drink blood?

Extraterrestrial vampires. It sounded ridiculous, like something out of a fifties sci-fi movie. If anyone had mentioned this to Emily a month ago, she'd have laughed her head off. But the Krinar were real, and their traits—biological immortality, superhuman speed, and extreme strength—were something people had ascribed to creatures of the night for centuries. Could it be? Could the Krinar have been the source of all those legends?

It had taken every ounce of willpower Emily possessed not to betray herself, to smile and shake Ellet's hand like everything was normal. To act like she was simply curious about humans living on Krina instead of wondering in horror about the possibility of blood farms on Zaron's planet.

Ellet had asked if Zaron had done it again—"it" being Zaron drinking Emily's blood. That meant that her captor had done it at least once before. Was it when she'd lost her memory? She didn't want to jump to conclusions, but it fit. At the time, he'd said that her mental fuzziness was a "natural" outcome of their coupling, that he hadn't drugged her in any way, yet he'd promised that it wouldn't happen again—which meant that something other than regular sex had taken place between them. That promise must've been what he'd been referring to with Ellet.

Getting up, Emily strode into the bathroom and splashed warm water on her face. She would've liked it to be cold, but the intelligent Krinar technology wasn't intelligent enough to read her mind. The sink insisted on giving her water of comfortable temperature, even though comfort wasn't what Emily was after. She needed to clear her mind and chase away the conflicting emotions crowding her chest.

She needed to think about what to do next.

Returning to her room, Emily sat down on the bed, staring at the wall through which Zaron would arrive. As far as she could see, she had two options: she could talk to Zaron about her suspicions, or she could keep quiet and continue to pretend that she hadn't heard anything. Each option had its own pros and cons, but option one carried the greatest risk. If Emily hadn't misunderstood—if Zaron's people did indeed drink blood, and he'd been trying to conceal that from her—he might not let her go as promised. In fact, Emily recalled with a sinking sensation, when she'd tried to question Zaron about her memory loss, he'd explicitly said that he couldn't tell her what she wanted to know without violating the mandate. This must've been the reason for his caginess: the Krinar had to know humans wouldn't be comfortable with vampires coming to their planet.

The upcoming invasion was the equivalent of a pack of wolves settling in a henhouse.

"Emily?" The wall dissolved in front of her, and Zaron stepped through, a frown etched into his inhumanly beautiful face. "Are you okay?"

Emily's pulse spiked as she jumped to her feet. "What?" Did he know? Did he realize she'd overheard?

"I'm sorry about earlier." Moving with his customary flowing grace, Zaron crossed the room to join her by the bed, and this time, there was no doubt in Emily's mind.

His stride was that of a predator, sleek and deadly.

"I didn't mean to snap at you like that," he continued, and Emily realized she'd forgotten about his strange behavior, all her thoughts occupied by his inadvertent revelation.

Pasting on a smile, she managed to say, "That's okay. It's no big deal."

Her palms were sweating, her heart drumming frantically in her chest, and she wondered if Zaron could hear it... if he could smell her fear. Emily was fairly certain the Krinar didn't need to kill humans to drink their blood—at least, Zaron hadn't needed to kill her that time—but just the idea of him preying on her like that was enough to fill her stomach with lead.

A vampire. The man in whose bed she'd spent the last two weeks was a vampire.

Emily should've been terrified, repulsed, but as she stared up at him, all she felt was the familiar dark heat, that humming, buzzing awareness that made her skin prickle and her breath catch in her throat. She was afraid he knew she'd overheard, terrified that he might detain her to keep from breaking their mandate, but she wasn't afraid of *him*. She knew Zaron wouldn't truly hurt her—she felt it with every fiber of her being —and as she saw the answering heat in his black gaze, the anxiety bubbling in her veins transformed into something else... something just as disturbing.

She licked her lips, her mouth feeling dry all of a sudden, and his eyes followed the movement, his jaw tensing and his powerful chest expanding with a deep breath.

"Emily..." Her name was a rough exhalation on his lips as he stepped closer, crowding her against the edge of the bed. "Angel, I need you so fucking much."

"Zaron, I—" She didn't know what she wanted to say, but it didn't matter because he was already on her, claiming her mouth in a deep, demanding kiss. His hands caught her wrists, stretching her arms above her head as he bore her down to the bed, and Emily felt the heat inside her ignite to a blistering flame. He was often like this with her—feral, dominant—yet even during those times, he reined in his shocking strength, careful not to hurt her. It turned her on, this controlled savagery of his, and her sex grew wet, her nipples constricting to tight, aching points. Moaning into his mouth, she arched against his powerful body, desperate to quench the pulsing ache between her legs, and felt the hard bulge in his jeans.

Vampire. The word whispered through her mind, bringing with it a disquieting chill, but it wasn't enough to suppress the fire liquefying her insides. She wanted Zaron, needed him in a way that made her forget everything but the dark, dizzying pleasure of his touch. Nothing mattered in this moment but him, this stranger who'd saved her life and stolen her freedom, who'd become so essential to her in the last two weeks. The way he made her feel was both terrifying and exhilarating, as if she was scaling a cliff with just a thin safety line.

Keeping Emily's wrists imprisoned in one of his big hands, Zaron slid his other hand down her body, delving under her skirt to touch the soft, aching place between her thighs. His eyes were pure black as he lifted his head, holding her gaze, and his skilled fingers parted her folds, seeking the throbbing bundle of nerves within. Emily gasped, her core knotting tight when he pressed on her clit, gently at first, then with rougher, crueler pressure. And all the while his hard-muscled body kept her pinned to the bed, making her feel helpless and small, weak with need.

"Zaron." She wasn't sure if she whispered his name or exhaled it, but his nostrils flared, his gaze sharpening with predatory intensity. There was something in his eyes she'd never seen before, something that frightened her despite the arousal blazing through her body.

"Emily, angel…" His voice was a dark, rough whisper as he held her restrained, his fingers still playing with her clit. It was hunger in his gaze, she realized, and something else, something she couldn't quite decipher. "Don't go tomorrow," he whispered, looking down at her. "I want you to stay."

His words slammed into her like a hammer. Emily froze, unable to breathe, unable to do anything but stare up at him in mute shock. What did Zaron mean by that? Did he know? The panic bubbling through her swept away the haze of arousal, leaving only fear in its place.

"But you promised," she managed to whisper through numb lips. "You promised you'd let me go."

The strange emotion in Zaron's gaze faded, replaced by a cold, hard gleam, and his mouth thinned to a dangerous line. It was like watching a man transform into a granite sculpture—a sculpture that radiated rage.

"Fine," he said harshly. "So be it. You leave tomorrow. But until then, you're mine, and I'm going to show you exactly what that means."

CHAPTER THIRTY-ONE

Zaron knew it was wrong to feel such anger over Emily's refusal, but he couldn't help the volcanic fury that burned in his chest as he gazed down at her, seeing the fear in her blue-green eyes. It sharpened the pain of her rejection, intensified it until he felt like he was bleeding from a thousand jagged cuts.

He might as well have offered Emily poison instead of his heart.

On a different day, under different circumstances, he might've been more rational about it, might've made allowances for the fact that they'd only known each other for a couple of weeks. But the ships were arriving tomorrow, and the knowledge that Zaron was about to lose her, that she was going to walk away and leave him to the agonizing emptiness of the last eight years, was like acid dripping on an open wound. All he could think about was that Emily didn't want him, didn't feel the yearning that twisted him up inside and made him crave something he'd thought he'd never want again.

Having her spread out underneath him, with his hand buried between her creamy thighs, only made it worse. He could feel the slickness between her folds, the liquid heat that signaled her desire, and it added to his fury. Emily's body wanted him, welcomed the pleasure he gave her, but her heart and mind were closed to him. It didn't make sense, but Zaron felt used, betrayed somehow—a feeling aggravated by the lust pumping violently through his veins.

If all Emily wanted from him was sex, that's precisely what she would get.

Rearing up, Zaron used his grip on Emily's wrists to pull her up with him, then flipped her onto her stomach and released her wrists. She gasped, her palms splaying on the mattress as if she wanted to push herself up, but he was already tearing off her dress and stuffing a pillow under her hips to prop up her soft, shapely ass. It obsessed him, that ass, just like every part of Emily's body, yet he hadn't claimed it yet, just as he hadn't done the million and one dirty things he'd been aching to do to her. He'd taken it slow, not wanting to overwhelm the human girl, and that had been a mistake.

She was leaving tomorrow, and Zaron hadn't even begun to satisfy his hunger for her.

Leaning over her, he lowered his head until his lips hovered above Emily's ear. Her soft blond hair tickled his face, and her sweet scent was so intoxicating his cock almost punched a hole through his jeans. "I'm going to fuck you," he said in a hard, thick voice he barely recognized as his own. "Today, you're going to give me everything, angel."

She made a soft, strangled noise—an agreement? a protest?

—but when Zaron reached between her legs, she was scalding hot and wet, ready for him. He pushed two fingers into her, penetrating her silky flesh, and his balls tightened at her gasping moan, at the way her body clenched around his fingers, sucking them in deeper. She was trembling underneath him now, her bare skin hot and damp with sweat, and Zaron knew that she was close to coming, that in another moment she'd be his.

Mine. The word blazed through his mind, bringing with it that intense dark longing. The physical hunger was only part of it; the rest was tangled up with loss and grief and something so bright and incandescent that it made up for all the pain it would bring. Zaron didn't want to name that something, not even in his mind, but he felt it like a living thing inside him, humming and pulsing with each hammering beat of his heart.

No. Stop. This was just fucking, Zaron told himself. He'd clearly restrained himself too much; that's why he couldn't imagine letting Emily go, why he felt so empty at the thought of the days to come. He needed to get her out of his system, to do whatever it took to rid himself of this twisted, impossible longing.

Slowly pumping his fingers in and out of her wet heat, Zaron used his other hand to open the zipper of his jeans. His cock sprang free, so hard and swollen it curved up to his abdomen. Withdrawing his fingers, Zaron wiped them on his shaft to coat it in her wetness. The scent of Emily, warm and sweetly female, was in his nostrils, and it was all he could do to line his throbbing cock against her opening and push in slowly instead of plunging in all the way. In this position, with her legs closed, she was extra tight around him, and he knew he could hurt her if he wasn't careful. But then she moaned, arching her back to take him in deeper, and he couldn't control himself. With a low, harsh growl, Zaron slid his hand under her belly to find her clit and, pressing on it, thrust in all the way.

Emily cried out, her hands fisting in the sheets, and he felt her shudder underneath him, her inner muscles clenching around his cock. "Zaron..." His name was a breathless prayer on her lips. "Oh my God, Zaron..."

He knew the precise moment it happened for her, felt the rippling spasms of her release, and he gritted his teeth to avoid coming too. Reaching for Emily's hair, he twisted the silky blond strands around his fist, forcing her head to arch back. Then, holding himself up on one elbow, he pushed the fingers of his other hand—the fingers that had just been inside her— into her mouth. Her lips and tongue felt amazing on his skin, her mouth as slick and warm as the walls of her pussy, and he pushed his fingers deeper, liberally coating them in her saliva before lowering his hand to her ass.

"Have you ever done this before?" he asked thickly, using his hold on her hair to press her face against the mattress. His saliva-slickened fingers slid between her curvy ass cheeks, finding the tight ring of muscle there, and he felt her tense in shock as he touched the tiny opening. "Has anyone fucked you here?"

"No." She gasped as he applied some pressure, forcing the tip of his finger into her. "I... I never—"

"Good. Then this is mine and mine alone." The satisfaction Zaron felt at the thought was beyond primitive. His cock swelled and thickened inside her pussy until he was on the verge of bursting, but with a massive effort of will, he held back the cresting pleasure. A murmured command to his house in

Krinar, and special lubricant coated his hand, easing his finger's entry into her tight ass.

"Relax," he whispered when Emily whimpered and clenched her cheeks, fighting the intrusion. Her pussy tightened around his cock, massaging him involuntarily, and Zaron groaned as his finger touched his cock through the thin inner wall separating her orifices. "You'll get used to it in a moment."

She was panting into the mattress, her skin sheened with sweat, but he felt the wet heat inside her intensify, coating his cock with more moisture. After a few seconds, the worst of her tension eased, her muscles relaxing slightly, and Zaron leaned down and kissed her ear, crooning, "That's it, angel. There you go..." His soothing words were accompanied by his second finger pressing against her opening. She tensed again, but he'd managed to get the tip of the second finger in, and the rest slid in easily, aided by the lube.

"Okay?" he murmured, feeling her shake, and it seemed to take forever before her head moved in a small nod.

"Good girl." Zaron kissed her ear again and pushed himself up to a sitting position. Fighting for control, he began to move, thrusting into her simultaneously with his cock and fingers. Emily moaned, the painfully erotic sound nearly making him combust. It took all he had to remain gentle, to keep his movements slow and controlled so he wouldn't hurt her. As he kept moving, however, some of her stiffness eased, and her moans grew louder, her pussy squeezing him with slick, silky heat.

Groaning, Zaron gripped her hip with his free hand and started thrusting harder, his fingers inside her moving in rhythm with his cock. He felt like a volcano on the verge of bursting, and he knew he wouldn't last more than a few seconds—and then he didn't have to.

With a thin cry, Emily reached her peak, her inner muscles clamping down on him like a soft, wet vise. He felt the spasms wracking her body, heard her panting gasps, and then he was there, the orgasm sending bolts of ecstasy through his nerve endings. His vision went white as a massive wave of pleasure rolled through him, stunning him with its force, and his seed spurted out, his cock jerking inside her uncontrollably.

Breathing heavily, Zaron withdrew from Emily and pulled his fingers out of her back opening. Then he got up, gathered her in his arms, and carried her to the shower. She seemed dazed, barely able to stand upright when he placed her on her feet inside the shower stall, so he picked her up again, holding her against his chest as the intelligent technology cleaned them both.

He'd give Emily a few minutes to recover, and then it was time for round two.

———

Wrapped in Zaron's arms, Emily felt wrung out and overwhelmed. Her body throbbed in places she'd never felt before, and her muscles seemed to be made of cotton. The razor-sharp blend of ecstasy and pain she'd just experienced was too much to process in combination with everything else.

He was letting her go tomorrow.

Emily should've been relieved, but instead, a heavy pressure settled low in her chest, compressing her ribcage and tightening her stomach. Had Zaron been asking her to stay rather than threatening to detain her? Is that why he'd seemed so angry when she'd reminded him of his promise? For a couple of moments, she'd been afraid he might punish her with sex, but he'd been gentle—well, as gentle as a man who double-penetrated her could be. Her back passage still burned from his fingers, but something about that odd, foreign fullness, that feeling of being completely and utterly taken, had made her orgasm infinitely more intense.

When they were both clean and dry, Zaron carried her back to the bedroom. Emily expected him to put her down and step away, but he placed her on the bed and covered her with his body. Holding himself up on his elbows, he framed her face with his big palms, and before she had a chance to say anything, he kissed her.

His breath was sweet and faintly minty from the cleaning, but there was nothing sweet about the kiss itself. It was raw and passionate, as hungry as if he hadn't just emptied himself inside her. Instantly, Emily felt the curl of heat deep in her core and the pulse of arousal in her veins. With Zaron's muscular body over her, she was cocooned in a bubble of dark sensuality, and nothing existed outside of this kiss: no invasion, no fear, no tomorrow. Everything seemed to fall away, leaving only the man devouring her mouth and the desperate need heating her blood.

The next couple of hours were a blur of sex, of his mouth and fingers and cock all over her body. He fucked her like it was the last time he would ever have sex, and she came again and again, screaming his name. And when Emily thought she couldn't take any more, he poured lube all over his cock, bent her in half by draping her legs over his shoulders, and worked himself into her ass, inch by slow inch. It hurt and burned—his cock was much bigger than his fingers—but she was too dazed from all the sex to put up any kind of protest. All she could do was lie there helplessly, trying to breathe through the cramping fullness, but after the worst of the stinging pain subsided, the dark pleasure returned, aided by his skilled fingers petting her swollen folds.

"Come for me," he whispered, pinching her clit as he thrust deeper into her ass, and Emily did exactly that, her exhausted body shuddering with ecstasy again and again.

She wasn't sure if she slept then, or if she simply zoned out, but when she came to, she was clean, and Zaron was sitting on the edge of the bed holding a tray with berries and roasted nuts.

"Eat," he ordered, holding a strawberry to her mouth, and Emily obediently bit into it, still too tired and overwhelmed to do anything else. Her muscles ached in places she hadn't known she had muscles, and her sex was so sensitive the slightest brush against her clit hurt. Yet when Zaron finished feeding her and reached for her again, she responded, her body conditioned by the mind-bending pleasure his touch had always brought.

They made love again, leisurely this time, and when Emily lay in Zaron's arms, shattered and depleted, she felt a dull ache tighten her chest. It was still early in the afternoon, but the next morning loomed like a dark cloud, the mere thought of it filling her with dread. After what she'd learned about Zaron's people, she was terrified of the invasion to come, but she was even more scared of how it would feel to be separated from Zaron... to know that she would never lie in his embrace again.

What if she did stay? The thought was an insidious whisper in her mind, dark and tempting. He'd said he wanted her to stay. Had he meant it, and if so, for how long? Surely he would get tired of her eventually—if not now, then when her human body began showing signs of aging. And then there was the blood-drinking issue and the fact that his people were about to take over Earth with mysterious—and possibly sinister—intentions.

Stockholm syndrome. Emily knew what it was, had even written a paper on it in her college psych class. Zaron wasn't abusive, but he had been holding her in his house against her will. There was every chance that the captor-captive dynamic had twisted her thinking, amplifying physical attraction until it morphed into an unhealthy addiction. Ever since Emily had woken up in Zaron's house, she'd had to rely on him for everything: food, water, walks… even pleasure and comfort. Right now, he was a god in her world, a ruler with absolute power. He controlled her completely. How could she make a sane, rational decision in this state of mind? How could she trust herself to give up everything to be with an extraterrestrial whose species might harm her own?

She couldn't. It was as simple as that.

The pain pierced her, as sharp as any knife, but Emily knew she had to be strong. It was the only way. Still, she couldn't help the stinging in her eyes as she lifted her head from Zaron's shoulder to meet his glittering gaze.

"I want you to do it," she said, her voice shaking from the effort of holding back tears. "That thing you did the second time we had sex. What you promised you wouldn't do. I want you to fuck me and make me forget."

Zaron's body seemed to have turned to stone, his eyes like black pools in his perfectly sculpted face. "Are you sure?" His voice was low and deep. "Are you sure about that, angel?"

Emily nodded, afraid yet resolute. She was beyond sore and exhausted, but she couldn't keep on agonizing like this until morning. And some part of her wanted to experience it again, that dark bliss, that total loss of identity. She wanted Zaron to drink her blood so she could see what it was like and forget her worries at the same time.

"Do it," she said, and watched his jaw tighten. He moved, and in a blur, Emily found herself on her back again, with Zaron's big body caging her against the mattress. His hands slid into her hair as he lowered his head, his lips brushing over her neck, and then she felt it: that sharp, slicing pain.

It was his bite, she realized, and then she couldn't think at all, all her senses swamped by the explosive ecstasy bursting through her veins.

CHAPTER THIRTY-TWO

*Z*aron watched as Emily stirred, rolling over to expose her full breasts and and the upper portion of her sleek belly. Her pale skin was flawlessly smooth, her pink nipples soft in her repose. She was beautiful, this human girl of his, and he ached for her with a fierceness that stole his breath. Last night hadn't helped; if anything, it had made it worse. The taste of her was still on his tongue, sweet and vital, and the knowledge that he'd never have her again was as agonizing as a *Chironex fleckeri* sting.

She didn't want to stay. He had to accept it, no matter how much the dark voice inside him whispered that he could keep her, that no one would ever interfere. He could make her his charl, and eventually, she'd come to terms with it, maybe even appreciate it over time.

No. Zaron suppressed that voice. He'd promised Emily freedom, and he had to keep that promise. He couldn't live with himself if she grew to hate him; no matter how much he needed her, he didn't want her unwilling and resentful.

Lifting his hand, he gently stroked the satiny line of her jaw. "Wake up, angel. It's time to go if you're to make your flight."

Emily's eyes fluttered open, and she blinked, staring up at him. "What?"

"You have to get dressed and eat, so we can go," Zaron said. Though he'd intended to keep things light, the words came out terse and harsh. "You don't want your plane to leave without you."

"My plane?" Sitting up, Emily pulled the blanket to her chest and gave him a bewildered look. "What do you mean?"

"I bought you a plane ticket to replace the one that expired unused," Zaron said. "Now I need to get you to the airport."

"Oh. Thank you. That's really thoughtful of you." She jumped out of bed, her slender curves making his mouth water as she padded naked across the floor. "I'll be right back."

She disappeared into the bathroom, and a moment later, Zaron heard the shower turn on. The temptation to join her there was strong, but he resisted the urge. If he touched Emily again, there was a high likelihood she wouldn't fly out today.

When she emerged from the shower, still naked, he handed her a stack of clothes and watched her eyebrows crawl up. "These are mine," she said, looking up at him incredulously. "Where did you get my clothes?"

"I took them along with your other belongings from the hotel where you were staying," Zaron said, doing his best to keep his gaze above her neck. "I knew you'd need your passport and such." He'd gone there the day after she'd woken up, when he'd decided to keep her until the ships' arrival.

"So you've had this all along?" Her eyes narrowed. "Why have you kept it from me?"

"You didn't need any of these things here," he said, ignoring the way her mouth tightened at his answer. "I gave you better, more comfortable clothes and shoes."

In reality, Zaron didn't know why he'd kept Emily's belongings from her. She hadn't brought much on this trip— just a backpack filled with essentials—and he hadn't given the matter much thought. He'd simply retrieved the bag from Emily's hotel and stashed it away. The clothes he'd fabricated for her were indeed superior to the primitive human ones, and it had given him pleasure to see her walk around in the dresses he'd created.

Emily's movements were stiff and jerky as she got dressed, but she didn't say anything—which was smart of her, Zaron thought. Given the simmering anger in his chest, it wouldn't take much to push him into an argument.

When Emily was clothed, he handed her a fruit smoothie that his house had prepared, and said, "Let's go."

Grabbing her backpack on the way, he led her out of the house.

———

Her thoughts in turmoil, Emily followed Zaron outside, sipping her smoothie without tasting it. Her regular clothes—a pair of shorts, a T-shirt, and Nike sneakers—felt oddly rough and uncomfortable, as if they belonged to someone else. Her body, though, felt fine, with no traces of soreness from yesterday's sexual marathon. Zaron must've healed her while she slept.

Last night and the rest of yesterday's day were a blur in

Emily's mind, a tangle of barely remembered images and sensations. All she could recall was pleasure that seemed too intense to be purely sexual. It reminded her of the time she'd accidentally tried a designer drug in college. It was as if everything had been enhanced, the ecstasy surreally acute. Was that from his bite, or had he used some kind of alien drug as an aphrodisiac? She wanted to ask, but she didn't dare betray her knowledge of this Krinar trait—not when she was so close to freedom.

"How am I getting to the airport?" she asked instead when Zaron began walking in the direction of the lake. The sun was already high in the sky—Emily must've slept late—and the air was thick and humid. "We can't walk the whole way, can we?"

"No, of course not." His response was biting. "I have a vehicle stashed nearby."

"Oh." He had a car in the jungle? "Where?"

"You'll see."

They continued walking in silence. When Emily finished her smoothie, the cup dissolved in her hand, startling her. She wanted to ask about that, but when she glanced at Zaron and saw his shuttered expression, she decided against it. Her captor —soon to be *former* captor—was not in a good mood.

Before long, Emily's T-shirt was clinging damply to her back. The humidity was such that it was actually hard to breathe. It was going to rain this afternoon, she could feel it, and she wondered if that would delay her flight. Or maybe the alien invasion would, she thought, and couldn't help laughing at the ridiculousness of it all.

"What's so funny?" Zaron gave her a sharp look.

"Did your ships already arrive and make contact?" she asked instead of explaining.

Zaron shook his head. "It's happening in a couple of hours."

"And you're already letting me go?" Emily couldn't keep the sarcasm out of her voice. "What if I talk before then?"

Zaron's jaw flexed, but he didn't say anything, and Emily exhaled in relief when he just kept walking. Why had she just tried to provoke him? She knew he was already on edge. Was some twisted part of her actually hoping he'd get angry enough to force her to stay?

Pushing the thought away, Emily followed Zaron through the thick forest. Before long, he turned west and headed up a narrow dirt path that wound through a tangle of trees and bushes. They walked like that for what seemed like a mile until they entered a clearing.

There, half-hidden under a canopy of trees, was a monster pickup truck.

"We'll take this the rest of the way," Zaron said, fishing a set of keys out of his pocket, and Emily watched open-mouthed as he opened the car, threw her backpack in, and climbed into the driver's seat.

"You drive this thing?" she asked in amazement, and he gave her a puzzled look.

"Of course I drive. How else would I get around on your planet? We're not allowed to use our flying pods yet."

"Right." Emily climbed into the truck—literally climbed, as the step was thigh-high for her—and buckled herself in. "I just never pictured you in something like this." She hadn't pictured her alien captor driving at all, but if she had, it would've been in something sleek and futuristic, like a Tesla.

"Sorry to disappoint." Zaron's expression was unreadable as he started the car. "I needed something sturdy for this terrain."

"Gotcha," Emily said as the vehicle began to make its way

through a seemingly impenetrable wall of tall grass and low bushes. She was grateful for the seatbelt as they hit a ditch and climbed over it. "I see what you mean."

She expected them to continue like that for a while, but within minutes, they hit a dirt path and, other than an occasional pothole, the rest of the drive was smooth. Zaron didn't speak, and neither did Emily. His shoulders were tense as he drove, his knuckles white on the steering wheel. Emily sensed that a single word or gesture from her was all it would take for him to turn back. She could feel it in the electric tension that crackled between them and in the silence that felt as thick and heavy as the air outside.

Biting her tongue to keep from saying anything, Emily looked away, staring blindly out the window. She couldn't let herself weaken now. She had a life back home that didn't revolve around a gorgeous extraterrestrial, a life that she'd worked hard to build. She was obviously not thinking clearly; else she wouldn't be tempted to give in to this madness.

It felt like the drive lasted forever, but when Emily glanced at the dashboard clock, she saw that only two hours had passed since they'd gotten into the truck.

"We're going to the Liberia airport?" she asked as they entered the city bounds, and Zaron nodded.

"It's the closest one with international flights. I got you a direct flight to the John F. Kennedy airport."

"Thank you." Emily didn't know what else to say. For someone who didn't want her to go, Zaron was being incredibly considerate. "I really appreciate it."

He didn't respond, and a few minutes later, they were pulling up to the Departure area. Zaron parked the truck at the curb and jumped out, walking around to open the door for

Emily. She was about to jump down, but he caught her and brought her down, his grip on her waist incredibly strong yet gentle.

"Um, thanks," Emily mumbled when he released her and took a step back. His touch had shaken her, the heat from his palms penetrating the thin fabric of her shirt, and her heart thumped against her ribcage as Zaron reached into the truck and pulled out the backpack, handing it to her.

"Your passport is in the outside compartment, as is your wallet," he said, his expression still closed off. "The boarding pass is inside the passport."

Emily nodded. She wanted to thank him again, but there was a thick knot in her throat, and she knew that if she tried to speak, she'd start to cry. Out of the corner of her eye, she noticed the people around them staring at them—or more specifically, at Zaron. Women of all ages seemed mesmerized by the tall, dark man who could've stepped straight out of their fantasies. Did any of them sense his otherness, Emily wondered dully, or were they all too blinded by his stunning male beauty?

Zaron's eyes were trained on her face, and for a moment, she thought he might again ask her to stay. This time, Emily didn't know if she'd be able to refuse. Now that her departure was no longer hypothetical, she could barely breathe through the crushing pain. The thick, humid air seemed to be pressing in on her from all sides, making her feel like she was locked in a small closet. She hadn't even gotten onto the plane yet, and she was already missing her captor, aching for him in the worst possible way.

But he didn't ask her to stay. "Goodbye, Emily," he said, and before she could gather her thoughts, he climbed into the truck and drove off.

Emily didn't know how she'd made it through security and onto the plane. The tears streaming down her face were blinding, and her throat felt like it was in a chokehold, the sense of loss crushing and all-consuming. She kept reminding herself about all the reasons why this was the right decision, but it didn't matter.

She couldn't logic away the pain.

"Is everything okay, señorita?" a concerned guard had asked in the security line, and she'd mumbled something about separating from a boyfriend. The man had given her a sympathetic smile and waved her through, and Emily had stumbled on, somehow getting on the plane where she now sat, listening to the pilot's pre-departure announcements.

Her ticket was for a business-class window seat—another bit of thoughtfulness on Zaron's part. Under normal circumstances, Emily would've greatly enjoyed the upgrade, but she was too upset to appreciate the gourmet meal and the free alcohol. No matter how much she tried, she couldn't stop the tears from flowing, and the five-hour flight seemed to stretch into an eternity. The only thing she managed to do was plug in her dead phone, so it would hopefully work when she got home.

Finally, they landed in JFK.

Her first clue that something was wrong were the frantic crowds inside the terminal. The always-busy New York airport was packed to the brim, with frustrated-looking passengers occupying every available seat at the gates and lining up along the walls. Each customer service desk had a line of several hundred people, and the airline employees behind those desks seemed frazzled and overwhelmed.

"What's happening?" Emily asked a relatively calm-looking man who was standing next to a snack kiosk.

"Haven't you heard?" he said. "The FAA just grounded all flights. They didn't say why, but the President is going to be holding a press conference this evening."

CHAPTER THIRTY-THREE

The wait time for a taxi was almost two hours, so Emily took the airtrain to the subway, and then the E train to the city. The crowd on the subway buzzed with panicked speculation; nobody knew what the upcoming announcement would be about, but almost everyone thought it had to do with a major terrorist threat. Why else would the FAA ground all planes?

Emily knew the real answer, but she kept her mouth shut and tried to ignore the conversations taking place all around her. New Yorkers were solitary creatures, conditioned not to interact with strangers, but the fear generated by the unusual events seemed to break down those barriers. Everyone was talking to everyone else, putting forth their ideas for whether it was the Islamic State or Al-Queda or something else entirely.

By the time Emily got off at her Times Square stop, her head ached, and she felt sick from a combination of jet lag and hunger. She'd been too upset to eat on the plane, and her breakfast smoothie had been many hours ago. Not that eating would've helped the anxiety that was gnawing a hole through her stomach.

The invasion was happening. It was real. Up until she'd stepped off that plane, some part of Emily had foolishly hoped that something would prevent the Krinar from going through with their plan, that they would change their minds for whatever reason. But of course they didn't. They'd made contact, and the US government had reacted by grounding all flights.

And it wasn't just the US government, she realized, seeing the scrolling headlines on the giant screens in Times Square. Flights were grounded all across Europe and Asia. Emily guessed it was so that civilian travel wouldn't interfere with military air maneuvers, should those become necessary.

Shuddering at the thought, Emily pushed through the crowds in Times Square and hurried to Amber's apartment, which was some five blocks away from her own studio in Midtown West. Thanks to her remembering to charge her phone on the plane, she had a couple of bars of reception, but whenever she tried to call Amber, she couldn't get through. She suspected it was because the cell networks were overwhelmed; everyone was trying to call everyone else to speculate about the mystery threat that had halted all air travel. Hopefully, Amber would be home; it was well after eight p.m. on Sunday, and Amber usually had to wake up early on Mondays for her part-time breakfast cafe job.

Amber's one-bedroom apartment was on 10th Avenue, on the fourth floor of a walk-up building that hadn't been renovated since the eighties. The building looked and smelled terrible, but the rent was low—by Manhattan standards, at least

—and Amber could afford it on her cashier/freelance writer's income.

Feeling utterly drained, Emily trudged up the four flights of stairs and rang the doorbell.

"Emily! Thank God!" Amber all but jumped at Emily, enveloping her in a bone-crushing hug the moment the door swung open. "I was so worried about you!"

"I'm okay," Emily said, smiling at her friend—who, as usual, was wearing a paint-splattered bohemian dress and had flecks of paint in her thick red hair. Amber was an aspiring artist as well as a writer, and she spent all of her free time working on her paintings. "I'm so sorry I got delayed like that. I didn't mean to dump George on you for so long. How is he?"

"Your cat is fine—a total sweetheart, in fact," Amber said, leading Emily into the apartment. "It was no problem keeping him. But tell me, what happened? You were supposed to return two weeks ago; then I get that mysterious little email from you and then nothing."

"Yeah, about that…" Emily put her backpack on the floor. "Can we actually turn on the news first? I think it might be easier to explain after the President gives his speech."

"What?" Amber gave her a confused frown. "What speech?"

"You haven't heard, huh?" It wasn't uncommon for Amber to avoid her phone and computer when she was in the throes of artistic inspiration.

"I've been painting all weekend," Amber said, confirming Emily's guess. "Why? Did something happen?"

"You could say that. Come, let's turn on the TV."

As soon as they entered the living room, a gray ball of fur streaked across the floor, meowing loudly. Laughing, Emily bent down and picked up her cat, who began purring as soon as he was in Emily's arms.

"George really missed you," Amber said, picking up the remote to turn on her TV. "He barely ate the first couple of days, just stared out the window and—oh, shit!"

The news channel was showing stranded travelers in airports all over the world, with people lying, sitting, and standing all over the terminals. Taxi lines outside seemed to stretch for miles, and traffic jams in and around major airports were horrendous.

"Yeah, it's like that in JFK too. I made it in right before they grounded the planes," Emily said. Sitting down on the couch, she cuddled George tighter against her chest, deriving comfort from his warm, furry body.

The news anchor was reporting on the situation and speculating on the content of the President's upcoming press conference. What really puzzled everyone was that it wasn't just the President who was scheduled to speak at nine. All world leaders were expected to address their citizens at the same time.

"What's going on?" The freckles on Amber's pale face stood out in stark relief as she turned to face Emily. "Do you know something about this?"

"Just watch," Emily said as the cameras switched over to the image of the White House, where the President of the United States was walking into the press conference room. Stopping in front of a tall podium, he looked directly into the camera, and Emily noticed lines of tension etched into his normally stoic face.

"Good evening," he said, and Emily had to admire his composure. Despite everything, his voice was calm and reassuring. "I'm sure many of you are wondering what's behind today's extraordinary events, so I'm going to get straight to the point. Earlier today, NASA detected an unusual object in Earth's orbit. Shortly thereafter, we—along with most other developed nations—were contacted by a humanoid extraterrestrial species who call themselves the Krinar. Supposedly, they seeded life on Earth billions of years ago by sending us DNA from Krina, their home planet. Afterwards, they guided our evolution with the goal of developing a species that was similar to them in many ways. *We* are that species, and they have deemed this to be the right time to make contact with us. Their ambassador has assured me that, while they do intend to build a few settlements on our planet, they are interested in peaceful coexistence, not war."

He stopped to take a breath, and the room exploded with questions, the reporters trying to outshout one another.

"How do you know this is for real and not some hoax?" screamed a blond woman.

"What do they look like? Where is their planet?" yelled a tall, balding man.

"Is the object in our orbit their ship? How did they approach unseen?"

"How did they get here? Do they have faster-than-light travel?"

"What kind of technology do they have? What kind of weapons?"

"What are they really after? How do we know their intentions are peaceful?"

"Why do they want to build settlements here? Are they trying to colonize us?"

This went on for a solid minute until the President raised his hand, palm facing out.

"Silence, please," he said in that calming voice of his—the voice that had served him so well during the election and subsequent presidency. Instantly, the reporters quieted down, the frantic roar in the room dying down to an uneasy hum.

"Now," the President said, "I'll do my best to address some of your questions. NASA has confirmed that the object in our orbit is indeed one of their ships. There are several more ships nearby in our solar system. At this point, we are certain that this is *not* a hoax. Their ambassador has told us that Krina is in a different galaxy. Given that, the Krinar must have the means to travel faster than the speed of light. Their technology appears to be far more advanced than our own, and we assume their weapons must be too. However, since we have no reason to believe that their intentions are hostile, that should not be cause for concern. As far as their external appearance, it is human. The image of the Krinar ambassador will be distributed to the news outlets immediately after this press conference. This is all we know at this point; as we learn more, we will disseminate that information. In the meanwhile, I urge you all to stay calm and go about your lives as normally as possible. This is a great turning point in our history. Let's make sure it's one we can look back on with pride. Thank you all, and good night."

The room exploded again, but the President was already walking out, surrounded by his aides. As soon as he left the room, the image on the TV screen split into eighths to show similar press conferences taking place all over the globe, and the anchor—who looked as shell-shocked as the viewers undoubtedly felt—began to summarize the President's speech.

Emily let out a breath she'd been holding and lowered still-purring George to her lap. She felt strangely relieved. Up until this moment, some part of her had feared that Zaron had just been trying to pacify her with promises of peaceful settlement. But he'd told her the truth—or at least the same truth that the Krinar had communicated to the developed nations' leaders. The visitors' real intentions had yet to be determined, especially in light of their secret blood-drinking tendencies, but Emily felt better nonetheless.

Next to her, Amber was watching the news with an expression of stunned disbelief.

"Aliens?" She turned to face Emily. "They're kidding about this, right? It's some kind of super-early Halloween trick?"

"I don't think so," Emily said. Amber was her best friend—they'd been inseparable since freshman year of college—but for some reason, Emily was reluctant to discuss Zaron with her. She wanted to think it was because she was bone-tired from the trip, but deep inside, she knew the truth.

She didn't want to talk to her best friend about her captivity because she felt raw and shredded, torn up by the knowledge that she'd never see Zaron again. Going over the whole story would be like ripping stitches out of a still-bleeding wound, and Emily didn't know if she could bear it—not yet, at least.

"Oh, come on. Aliens?" Amber jumped up and began to pace. "Fucking aliens? There's no way, just no way. It has to be a prank—or maybe they're confused, and it's really the North Koreans or the Chinese trying some kind of new weapon. Or maybe it's one of those hacktivist groups. Maybe they got into NASA's computers and are making them think they're seeing aliens. Or maybe..." She went on and on, coming up with ever more creative alternatives while Emily petted George and listened, too tired and dispirited to do anything else.

Finally, after what seemed like a half hour, Amber realized Emily didn't share her shock and disbelief.

"You don't seem surprised by this," she said, her auburn eyebrows drawing together as she stopped in front of Emily. "Why is that? Did you hear something on the way?"

"I..." As much as Emily didn't want to talk about her trip, she didn't want to lie either. "Sort of," she hedged, stroking George's soft fur.

"Sort of? What does that mean?"

Emily let out a sigh. She should've known Amber wouldn't just let it drop. With her often-dreamy gaze and bohemian sense of style, Emily's friend might've looked like an absentminded artist, but she was as sharp as any detective. It never paid to underestimate Amber—especially since she knew Emily so well.

"Can we talk about it tomorrow?" Emily asked, though she knew the futility of her request. "I'm really tired after the trip and—"

"What? No, of course not! You disappear in Costa Rica for two weeks; then you come back, and there's a freaking alien invasion that you don't seem surprised by?" Amber sat down and folded her arms across her chest. "Spill. Now. You don't have a job, so you can sleep in tomorrow."

"Okay, fine." It had been worth a try. Taking a deep breath, Emily launched into her story, beginning with her fall in the jungle. Amber listened in open-mouthed shock, her hazel gaze trained on Emily's face in horrified fascination. As Emily got to the part where she met Zaron for the first time, the TV began broadcasting just-released images of the Krinar ambassador—a tall, dark-haired man who was as strikingly beautiful as her captor. According to the government officials, he went by the name of Arus.

Amber's attention shifted to the TV. "Holy fuck," she breathed, staring at the photographs on the screen. "Did your Zaron look like this Arus?"

Emily nodded. "Pretty much." Zaron's face was a little leaner, his lips fuller and more sensuous than the ambassador's, but the flawless symmetry of his bone structure and the bronze smoothness of his skin were the same. "I met a Krinar woman too, and she had a similar darker coloring."

"You met *two* aliens?" Amber forgot about the broadcast, all her focus on Emily again. "Oh my God, tell me more!"

Rubbing George behind the ears, Emily continued with her story. She told Amber how Zaron had detained her for seventeen days and how intelligent all of their technology seemed to be. She described his physical appearance and incredible strength, detailed some of their conversations about Krina, and even touched on Zaron's tragic loss of his mate. The only thing she couldn't bring herself to say was how close she'd gotten to her captor during those seventeen days, but as it turned out, she didn't need to.

"You fucked him, didn't you?" Amber said when Emily stopped to catch her breath. Her voice was flat. "You had sex with that alien."

Emily felt heat creep up her neck. To cover up her discomfort, she lifted George to her chest and cuddled him closer. "Why do you say that?" she asked, hoping she didn't look as flushed as she felt.

Amber cocked her head to the side. "Because I'm not an idiot, that's why. The way you talk about him, the way you practically *glow* as you describe him… I've never seen you like that, not even when you were first dating Jason. You're a beautiful girl, and if these Krinar are indeed as human-like as you describe, it's not a stretch to imagine that two attractive people—well, one human and one not-quite-human—might hook up when forced to live in close proximity."

Emily didn't say anything, so Amber reached over and took George from her, placing the cat on her own lap. "You know I'm not going to drop this, so tell me. Did you sleep with this Zaron?"

George let out an unhappy meow and jumped off Amber's lap. Distracted, Emily bent down to retrieve her cat, but he stalked off toward the kitchen, tail raised, apparently displeased with all humans.

"Emily…" Amber's tone held a warning note.

"All right, all right." A determined Amber was hard to resist under normal circumstances, but when Emily was exhausted and heartsick, it was all but impossible. "Yes, we slept together, and before you ask, yes, he has all the same equipment as a human male. Happy now?" Despite her attempt to maintain her composure, Emily's voice sounded brittle, like she was on the verge of crying.

"Emily, hon, that's not why I brought it up." Amber was frowning now. "I mean, yes, I'm obviously curious, but I asked because I'm worried about you. Nobody knows anything about these visitors, and this man—this *alien* who held you captive—healed you with their technology, and then you entered into a sexual relationship with him. You understand how crazy and dangerous that is, right? At the very least, you should get yourself checked out by a doctor, or—"

"No." Emily jumped up, horrified. "That's the last thing I need. They'd want to study me, and—no. Just no."

"But—"

"No. No way. Amber…" Emily gave her friend an imploring look. "You can't tell anyone what I just told you, okay? I don't want people knowing what happened to me."

"Well, obviously, I'm not going to go running to the media." Amber rose to her feet. She was two inches shorter than Emily and had a thinner build, but her outsized personality always made her seem bigger. "What do you think I am, a complete idiot?"

"No, of course not." Emily ran a weary hand through her hair. "But I don't want *anyone* to know, not even your parents or your sister. Can you do that for me?" When Amber hesitated, she added, "Please. It's really important."

"Okay." Amber blew out an audible breath. "I won't tell anyone. But can you please promise me something?" Her hazel eyes were somber. "Go see a doctor, just for a regular checkup. You don't need to say anything if you don't want to, but at least this way, you'll know if you're okay—physically, I mean."

"Amber…" Emily sighed. "If he'd wanted to harm me, he wouldn't have healed me. I'm perfectly fine—healthier than ever, actually."

"He might not have harmed you on purpose, but what if you picked up something that could make you sick later, or cause you to infect others?" Amber said, and Emily realized that her friend was purposefully maintaining some extra distance between them. "Europeans all but wiped out Native Americans with their diseases. Even if the Krinar don't plan to kill us, their germs could. Our immune systems aren't equipped to deal with extraterrestrial flu, you know."

Emily stared at her, struck by the thought. Then her brain started working, and she shook her head. "No," she said. "That's a valid concern, but I don't think Zaron's people would've come here if there was any danger of infecting us. They've been visiting Earth and walking among us for thousands of years. If we were going to catch something from them, it would've happened already. I think their medical technology is such that they can prevent this from happening."

"Okay, that may be true," Amber conceded, looking marginally relieved. "But I'm still worried about you, Emily. Are you really okay? I mean, after that fall and everything…"

"Yes, of course." Emily forced herself to smile. "I'm just tired from the trip. I think it's best if I grab George and go home. It's getting late, and I have to stop by a grocery store so I have breakfast tomorrow."

"Are you sure? Because you're welcome to crash here. I have that futon—"

"What?" Emily laughed. "No, thank you. I can walk five blocks to my own place. I'm not *that* tired."

"Okay," Amber said. "But call me when you get home, all right?"

"I will—if I can get through." Emily went into the kitchen, with Amber following her. She found George on the windowsill, his tail swishing as he stared at the street below. Emily picked up the cat and carried him back into the living room to put him in his crate. Then she grabbed her backpack and headed toward the door.

"Emily, wait," Amber said when Emily was about to step out of the apartment.

Emily turned to face her. "What is it?"

"Do you think…" Amber's voice wavered. "Do you think it's

true what they said on the news about their intentions? Are they peaceful people?"

Emily froze. When she'd described Zaron to her friend, she'd purposefully omitted any mention of his predatory traits and the Krinar's possible vampirism. There was no need to scare Amber when all she had were her suspicions. Besides, even if the Krinar drank human blood, that didn't mean they were out to destroy humanity—or so Emily hoped.

"I think what they said on the news is true," she said after a moment. "At least it dovetails with what Zaron told me. If they're lying, they're consistent about it, but I don't know why they would want to deceive us. I don't know much about their weapons, but judging by everything I've seen in Zaron's house, I don't think we'd stand much of a chance if they decided to destroy us. And if they did decide that, I don't know why they'd bother with this ambassador charade." Unless it was to keep humans calm while they set up their blood farms—but Emily kept that possibility to herself.

"Right, that makes sense," Amber said, though she looked pale again. "But do you think, just in case, we should get out of the city? Maybe go to my parents in Connecticut? In the movies, they always hit the major cities first, and here we are, smack dab in the center of Manhattan."

Emily chewed on her lip. How could she reassure Amber when she felt so uneasy herself? "Look, if you're worried," she said, "you should probably leave. I'm sure your parents would love to see you."

Amber frowned. "What about you?"

"I'll be fine," Emily said. "I just got back, and I really don't want to go anywhere again. The traffic must be insane. Besides, if the Krinar plan to level Manhattan, we've got bigger problems."

"All right, it's your call," Amber said. "I'm going to try to reach my parents and see how they're doing. Let me know if you change your mind and want to come home with me."

"I will," Emily said. "It'll be okay, though. Like the President said, we just need to stay calm, and everything will be fine."

Gripping George's carrier tighter, she opened the door and headed out.

———

Everything wasn't fine, though—something Emily realized as soon as she left Amber's apartment. The panic on the streets was tangible, the pedestrians and bicyclists frantically rushing about while the cars stood bumper to bumper. The drivers were honking and cursing, and a few frazzled-looking policemen were blowing their whistles in a futile attempt to clear the congestion. The usual noise of the city had been amplified tenfold, and Emily's head pounded with agony as she made her way through the crowded sidewalks.

"Just one more block," she told George, whose displeased meows were adding to the cacophony. "We're almost home."

Finally, she got to her building. Like Amber's, it was old and rundown, with no elevator in sight. Though Emily had been able to afford a studio in one of the newer high-rises, she'd been focused on saving money and investing it for retirement—a goal that seemed laughable at the moment.

At least her studio was on the second floor, not fourth.

"Here you go, Georgie," she crooned when she got into her

apartment. Putting down her backpack, she opened the crate and let the cat jump out. "Home, sweet home."

Tail swishing, George stalked off to inspect his territory, and Emily plopped down on the plush armchair that was her studio's equivalent of a couch. She felt so drained she could barely think, but she knew she had to get food for tomorrow. Forcing herself to get up, she grabbed her keys and wallet from the backpack, slipped them into the back pocket of her shorts, and went down to the small grocery store on the next block over.

The owner was already locking up when she got there.

"Wait, please," Emily begged, grabbing the door handle just as he started to pull down the metal shutters. "Please, I just need to buy a few things. I'll be quick, I promise."

The white-haired man hesitated for a moment, then slid up the shutters and unlocked the glass door. "Fine, but hurry," he said gruffly, pushing the door open. "I have to get home to Queens, and it's madness out there."

"No problem, thank you!" Emily was already running down the aisles with a basket, throwing in all the necessities, plus extra food for George. It took her less than five minutes to get everything, but by the time she unloaded her haul at the counter, the store owner was looking impatient.

"I said to hurry," he grumbled as he rang up her purchases.

Pushing her tiredness aside, Emily gave him her brightest smile. "Thank you so much. I really appreciate this. Have a safe trip home!"

Grabbing her purchases, she hurried out of the store, but before she made it half a block, something heavy plowed into her, knocking her down and sending her bags flying. She landed on her hands and knees, the hard asphalt scraping the skin off her palms as she slid forward, and in the next moment, she felt something tugging at her back pocket.

"Hey!" she yelled, jumping up and turning, but the teenage boy was already sprinting away, her wallet clutched in his hand.

"Stop him!" Emily started to run after the thief, but he'd already disappeared into the crowd and no one was paying attention to her, not even the cops blowing their whistles at the traffic.

Shaking, Emily stopped and headed back to pick up her purchases. The rushing pedestrians had already stepped on some of her food, so she scrambled to recover as much as she could, stuffing the groceries back into the bags with shaking hands. Luckily, she hadn't bought anything in a glass jar, so most of the products had survived. Emily herself, however, felt like she might shatter at any moment. Her scraped palms were stinging and bleeding, and her heart was pounding in her throat, the excess of adrenaline combining with her headache to make her feel physically ill.

She didn't know how she made it back to her apartment, but somehow she found herself by her door, keys in hand. She wondered vaguely how they'd managed to stay in her pocket, but she had them, and that was all that mattered.

Entering the apartment, Emily locked the door, washed her bloodied hands, put the groceries away, and poured dry cat foot into George's bowl. She held it together until she stepped into the shower, but the moment she felt the hot water spray on her skin, all remnants of strength deserted her.

Sinking down to the floor, Emily wrapped her arms around her knees and cried.

CHAPTER THIRTY-FOUR

"Good evening, folks. Our show tonight marks the seven-week anniversary of K-Day, and amazingly enough, we haven't been vaporized yet," the late-night TV talk show host said as Emily stared listlessly at the screen. "For those of you who have been living under a rock, seven weeks ago today, the Krinar—or the Ks, as they're colloquially known—arrived and turned our world upside down. To celebrate that momentous occasion, today we have a special guest, Dr. Edmonds, who's here to tell us the latest theories on the visitors' biology."

"Thank you, James," the guest said, sitting up straighter as the camera swung toward him. "Glad to be here, and glad to see so many of you stayed in the city and came out to the studio today. You're all very brave—or very stupid."

The audience laughed and clapped in response.

"Now," Edmonds continued, "as all of you know, it is

suspected that the Krinar may have a significantly longer lifespan, as well as greater speed and strength. James, if you don't mind putting on that video…"

The image changed to show a grainy smartphone recording of a blurringly fast fight punctuated by flashes of gunfire and explosions. Without slowing the recording, it was impossible to figure out what was going on, but Emily, like everyone in the audience, already knew what the video was about.

The recording was of a dark alley in Riyadh where a band of thirty-three Saudis, armed with grenades and automatic assault rifles, had attacked a small Krinar delegation some two weeks earlier. They'd managed to injure the six unarmed Ks, and that's when things had gotten hairy. The wounds hadn't prevented the visitors from ripping the Saudis to pieces—literally in some cases. The blurring speed with which they'd moved and their incredible strength—one K had thrown two men sixty feet into the air, one with each hand—had stunned the human population, as did the sheer savagery of the fight.

As Emily had sensed during her time with Zaron, the Ks had a terrifying penchant for violence.

The video had made her sick when she'd first seen it, and she wasn't the only one. The exodus out of the major cities—the reverse migration that had begun on K-Day—had picked up speed in the last two weeks, with traffic jams again threatening to choke all travel. For some reason, people thought they'd be safer in small towns and rural areas, and they fled the cities despite the UN announcing the Coexistence Treaty last month.

"Oh, please," Amber had snorted when Emily had spoken to her on Skype after the announcement. She'd left the city the day after Emily's return and was staying with her parents in Connecticut. "Everyone knows that treaty is a sham. The UN just tucked their tails between their legs and rolled over, throat bared. You heard what they're saying about the nukes, right?"

"Yes, of course," Emily had said. The Internet was rife with rumors that China had tried to launch a rocket carrying a nuclear weapon at one of the Krinar ships, and the aliens had retaliated by vaporizing all of Earth's nuclear arsenal. Nobody knew if that was actually true—the government officials were denying everything—but every couple of days, some anonymous source would pop up with new details, and the story would get new legs.

Conspiracy theorists were having a field day.

"So yeah, they don't have any weapons left now, so they just gave in," Amber had continued in disgust. "Cowards."

"Well, what else are they supposed to do? Go to war with the Ks?" Emily had asked, but Amber hadn't wanted to listen to reason. It was easier to think of the government leaders as cowards than to accept the scary truth that the Krinar were so technologically superior that any military resistance was futile.

Not that people didn't try to resist on an individual level. The vicious fight with the Saudis was one of many such skirmishes that were occurring all over the world as people came into contact with the invaders. Nobody was happy that the aliens were planning to build their colonies on Earth for some unknown purpose, and many groups were downright hostile. Fights with the invaders kept breaking out in various parts of the globe, and with each one, the humans learned just how dangerous and violent the Krinar truly were. Though the visitors' intentions were supposedly peaceful, the death toll attributed to the Krinar was in the hundreds, and there was no sign that the violence would abate any time soon.

The situation was further exacerbated by the doomsday-like

panic that kept sweeping through the population as different stories, some true, some false, circulated on the net. The most recent rumor—which Emily suspected might actually be true—was that the Krinar were planning to shut down major industrial farms and force meat and dairy producers to switch to growing fruits and vegetables. As a result of that rumor, many had begun hoarding animal products, and the prices for chicken, beef, and milk were skyrocketing, leading to more hoarding and an even greater incidence of looting.

And that was the biggest problem of all: the governments' inability to control and police their panicked citizens. Emily's mugging on K-Day had been just the start of an unprecedented crime wave that had swept cities and towns all over the globe. New York, which had lost over half of its population, was now dangerous enough that Emily no longer ventured out of her apartment after dark. However, it was nothing compared to places like Moscow, Beijing, and Johannesburg. It was still possible to buy a few groceries in Manhattan, and most local businesses, including banks and media companies, continued to function, but those other cities had descended into chaos. Some pundit had dubbed the weeks following the Ks' arrival "the Great Panic," and the name had stuck.

It wasn't the end of the world like some had predicted, but in some places, it was close.

While the vast majority of the population obsessed about the invaders, Emily watched the news with a disinterest that bordered on depression. She knew she should care, and sometimes she considered going to the authorities with the little extra knowledge she had, but most days, she felt too listless to do more than get out of bed, take care of George, and fill out a couple of job applications. Not that anyone was actually hiring in this climate. Stocks, bonds, and other securities had crashed immediately after K-Day, and every new story about the invaders caused the markets to oscillate wildly, resulting in a volatility that far exceeded the worst months of the Great Recession. Trillions of dollars in invested funds had been lost in fear-driven selling, and Emily personally knew at least ten hedge funds that had collapsed in recent weeks, unable to sustain the heavy losses. There was no refuge anywhere, not even in AAA-rated government bonds—typically the safest of all investments. When one didn't know whether the United States would exist next month, it didn't matter that something was backed by the full faith and credit of the US government.

Emily's own investment portfolio, already decimated by the recession, was now pitifully tiny, and her savings were shrinking at an alarming rate. Or at least it was a rate that would've alarmed the old Emily, the one who didn't feel so empty inside. The Emily who had returned from Costa Rica couldn't work up the energy to care about any of it—simply *existing* took everything she had.

Her longing for Zaron was like a wound that refused to heal. No matter what she did, she was cognizant of missing him—his smile, his laugh, his touch... even the predatory intensity that had scared her at times. The horrifying stories on the news should've made her hate him—hate all Krinar—but all she could think of was the way he'd held her at night and how she'd felt closer to him than to any man she'd known.

She'd tried to go out once. Two of her girlfriends from work had stayed in the city, and the three of them had gone bar-hopping the weekend before the crime wave had gotten really bad. Emily had laughed and flirted with the men who'd hit on her, but all of them had left her cold, and she'd returned home alone, feeling even emptier than before.

If she could've gotten into a time machine and gone back to the moment when Zaron had asked her to stay, Emily would've made a different decision. Maybe her feelings for Zaron were a result of her captivity, but that didn't make them any less real. Her leaving hadn't been a rational move; Emily realized that now. All her rationalizations had been an attempt to justify something irrational, to suppress and ignore the fear she'd carried with her since her parents' deaths.

She'd been so afraid that Zaron would leave her that she'd pushed him away—just as she'd done with Jason.

Groaning, Emily turned off the TV and got up to pace around her tiny studio. Though she'd gone out to buy groceries just a few hours ago, she was beginning to feel cooped up and claustrophobic. She wanted to go for a run, to do something to force away the depression that sucked all life out of her, but it was too dangerous to go out at this time of night. To make matters worse, thinking of going outside reminded her of how much she'd enjoyed the lush nature of Costa Rica during her walks with Zaron through the jungle.

How much they'd enjoyed it *together*.

A sharper ache pierced her chest at the memories, and scorching tears stung her eyes. To combat the urge to cry, Emily pulled out her yoga mat and began doing sit-ups. It wasn't the same as a run outside, but it was better than nothing —and it was certainly better than another crying fit in the shower. She could get through this; she *would* get through this.

She was a survivor, and she was determined.

It was on her twenty-seventh sit-up that an idea came to Emily. She didn't have any way of reaching Zaron—he hadn't left her an email or a phone number or whatever the Krinar used—but she did know the approximate location of his house. Could she do it? Could she swallow her pride and beg him to take her back? Yes, there was a risk that he wouldn't want her, that he'd found someone else during this time, and yes, they'd have only a few years together before Emily started to age, but weren't a few years better than nothing?

Wasn't it better to know happiness, even if just for a short while, than to go through life experiencing only this draining loneliness?

Suddenly energized, Emily jumped up from the mat and ran to her computer. Civilian air travel was allowed again, and though plane tickets had skyrocketed in price due to overwhelming demand, there was nothing preventing Emily from using her remaining savings to buy a one-way ticket to Costa Rica.

To hell with her fear and pride. She was going to hop in that time machine and try to undo her mistake.

She was entering her payment information on the United Airlines' website when her doorbell rang. Puzzled, Emily walked over to the door to look through the peephole, and her heart flew into her throat.

Two men dressed in suits were standing on the other side of her door. One was of average height and lean, while the other one was nearly as wide as he was tall.

"Yes?" Emily called out without reaching for the lock. Her palms were sweating, her stomach tight with a sickening premonition. "How may I help you?"

"Miss Ross, I'm Agent Wolfe, and this is Agent Janson," the lean man said, holding up an official-looking badge. "We're from the Department of Homeland Security. If you don't mind, we'd like to talk to you about a call you made to the United States Embassy in Costa Rica several days prior to K-Day."

CHAPTER THIRTY-FIVE

*T*he *shari* plants were adapting well to the Costa Rican soil. The roots were thick and healthy, and the scan showed that within a few months, they would flower and bear fruit. In general, it appeared that Zaron had chosen this Center's location well. The climate was pleasant, and the soil welcoming. As Zaron had hoped, upon arrival, the Council had decided to use this Center as their primary base of operations. They named it Lenkarda, meaning "a triumphant start." They also praised Zaron and his team for the other Centers' locations. This should've pleased Zaron, but all he felt was a kind of bleak indifference—the same dull numbness that had gripped him since Emily's departure.

Leaving the farming area of the developing Center, he went back to his house. Even moving at his natural speed, it took him over an hour to get home on foot, but Zaron didn't mind. He could've relocated closer to Lenkarda, but he liked the isolation. Being around other Krinar was uncomfortable, almost painful these days. On the rare occasions when the numbness gripping him receded, he felt raw inside, like a tree stripped of its protective bark, and interacting with people seemed to make it worse.

Losing Emily was as devastating as he'd feared it would be.

Entering the house, Zaron took a shower and went into Emily's room. Her scent still lingered there, in the sheets that he'd forbidden his house to change. He lay down and breathed it in, closing his eyes to pretend that she was still with him, that if he reached out, he could touch her... hold her.

But of course he couldn't. Not because she was far away—a couple of thousand miles meant nothing to the Krinar—but because he'd made her a promise.

"You can get her back, you know," Ellet had said last week, dangling the temptation in front of him again. "Just go to New York and bring her back. Who knows? Maybe she'd be glad to see you. You know what the situation in those human cities is like. Do you really want her living there?"

Zaron had snapped at his colleague, telling her to mind her own business, but a similar thought had occurred to him more than once—on a nightly basis, in fact. He missed Emily so acutely that he sometimes thought he'd go mad from the intense longing. In some ways, it was even worse than when Larita had died. Then, he'd had no choice but to accept that his mate was gone, that he'd lost her forever, but with Emily, the knowledge that he could have her back taunted him, made him want to forget all about his principles and the promises he'd made.

He could have her—all he had to do was go against her wishes and deprive her of her freedom.

Pushing the thought away, Zaron closed his eyes and tried

to fall asleep. To his annoyance, the sleep wouldn't come. He tossed and turned for a solid hour before giving up. Getting up, he touched his wrist computer and said, "Show her to me."

A three-dimensional image of Emily's apartment appeared in front of him. The day after she left, Zaron had accessed the camera on her laptop, telling himself that, given the humans' panicked reaction to the Krinar arrival, he needed to make sure Emily got home safely. It was his responsibility to her; after all, he'd been the reason she couldn't return to New York earlier.

To his relief, she'd been in her apartment that evening, watching TV with a gray feline curled up on her lap. It was her cat George, Zaron had realized, hungrily taking in the image. After a few minutes, he'd forced himself to turn off the recording, telling himself that he had to leave her alone, but the next day, he'd accessed the camera again and watched Emily eat a sandwich while reading a book. The day after that, she'd been out, and he'd been frantic, worrying that something had happened to her, but she'd come home after an hour, and he'd relaxed again. Enough, he'd told himself then, but the computer kept luring him back, and every few days, he'd slip up and watch her as she slept, ate, played with her cat, or searched for jobs on the human Internet. It was a terrible invasion of her privacy, he knew, but he couldn't stop himself.

Seeing her on those recordings was the only thing that brought Zaron joy these days.

So now he greedily studied the image in front of him, searching for signs that Emily was home. Sometimes she was in the bathroom, and he wouldn't see her right away, but she always came back into the main room after a few minutes. Emily's entire apartment was that room, so if she was home, Zaron would see her soon enough.

But he didn't see her. Only her cat was there, sitting on the floor and licking its paw, then swiping it over its furry face. Zaron had to admit the animal's antics were fascinating, and on a different day, he would've enjoyed the show, but Emily's absence was making him uneasy. It was already late, and she'd stopped going out in the evening in recent weeks—likely because of the growing crime rate in her city. So where could she be? What could she be doing?

He waited for an hour and a half, his unease growing with every second, but she still didn't come home.

Zaron checked the time. It was well after midnight in New York. There was no reason for Emily to leave her apartment so late. She had to know it was dangerous for a young woman to wander around the city on her own these days.

Unless… unless she wasn't on her own.

Everything inside Zaron jolted at the thought, the fury like a blast of fire through his veins. He'd known Emily would find a mate eventually—she was far too smart and beautiful not to— but there was a world of difference between knowing something and confronting it. Emily, *his* Emily, might be with another man at this very moment, and Zaron couldn't bear it. He pictured her sleeping in some human male's embrace, and his fists clenched with the urge to kill the man, to rip him into pieces with his bare hands. It didn't matter that Zaron had let Emily go; the ancient territorial instinct within him insisted that she was his—that she would *always* be his.

His rage was so strong he was barely cognizant of issuing the order to his computer. It was only when Emily's texts and emails appeared on the three-dimensional image in front of him that Zaron realized how insane he was acting. Still, he couldn't make himself stop. He read through all of her recent communications, searching for any clue as to where she might be and with whom, but to his disappointment, there was nothing there—no agreed-upon assignations, not even a hint of flirtation.

Zaron's jealousy gave way to worry.

"Track her cell phone," he said sharply, and his computer obeyed, pinging off the human satellites to triangulate the GPS signal.

But there was no signal—at least none that his computer could detect.

Frowning, Zaron tried again. And again.

Nothing.

It was as if Emily's phone had vanished.

"Access her laptop," Zaron ordered his computer. "Search her browser history."

And it was there, in Emily's browser, that Zaron saw it: a partially finished order for a one-way plane ticket to Costa Rica.

His pulse stopped for a second, then roared back to life, his heart slamming into his ribcage.

Emily was returning.

She was coming back to him.

For a second, the elation was almost blinding, but then Zaron realized that Emily hadn't completed the order.

She'd left before buying the ticket, and he was no closer to figuring out where she was and what had happened to her.

CHAPTER THIRTY-SIX

"I've already told you everything I know," Emily said, unable to contain her frustration. They'd been interrogating her in this small, stuffy room for hours, and she could feel the walls starting to close in on her. She tried to manage her claustrophobia by taking deep breaths, but nothing was helping. To make matters worse, she was so tired it took all her energy just to remain upright in her hard metal chair. What time was it now? Two in the morning? Three? There was no clock on the wall, and they'd taken away her cell phone. She'd always thought government employees worked nine to five, but that clearly wasn't the case with Homeland Security—or at least with this particular branch.

Emily strongly suspected the agents who came to her house weren't run-of-the-mill border patrol.

"You've hardly told us anything, Miss Ross," Agent Wolfe said, his narrow face expressionless. "You fell, you were saved by a Krinar who then detained you for two and a half weeks, and you returned home on K-Day. Do you honestly expect us to believe that this is the whole story?"

"It *is* the whole story," Emily said wearily. "Yes, I knew the invasion was coming—that's why I called the embassy—but that's it. I don't know anything else about their plans. I haven't kept in touch with Zaron. The moment he released me, I went back home. I don't know anything about their weapons, and I already described to you what I saw of their technology—which wasn't much, as all of it was inside a residential house."

"Yet this Zaron brought you back from the brink of death with medical technology he had inside that house," Agent Janson said, his double chin quivering with each word. "Healed your broken spine, you said?"

"Yes." Emily regretted telling them about that, but when they'd first begun questioning her, she'd been too intimidated to come up with a plausible lie. As soon as she'd opened her door, they'd marched her downstairs, stuffed her into a black car, and brought her to this rundown warehouse in Queens—or rather, the facility that was in the basement of said warehouse. Emily had barely had time to grab her wallet, keys, and phone—items they'd confiscated before putting her in this room and questioning her as though she were a terrorist.

At least she'd had the presence of mind not to say anything about the sexual nature of her relationship with Zaron and her suspicions about the Krinar being a vampiric species. The latter omission was because she still wasn't sure she was right, and because she feared what would happen if those types of rumors began circulating. Would the panic on the streets and the guerrilla attacks on the Krinar get worse? Could an actual war break out?

She couldn't bear it if she were somehow responsible for

more violence. This "peaceful" invasion was already far too bloody.

"Miss Ross…" Agent Wolfe leaned in. "You're not helping your case by being evasive. It's obvious that you know more than you're letting on. You've spent two and a half weeks with one of *them*. You need to tell us everything you've seen and heard—every detail, no matter how small. You might not think it's significant, but it will help us form a more complete picture of the enemy."

"The enemy? I thought we were at peace," Emily said, too tired to conceal her sarcasm. "Isn't that what the Coexistence Treaty is all about?"

Janson folded his arms, resting them on the mountainous mound of his stomach. "Don't be naïve, Miss Ross. The Krinar are not our friends, nor will they ever be while we know next to nothing about them. Why are they here? What do they want from us? We don't know, and we won't until they deign to tell us. But you may know something, and if you do, it's your duty as an American citizen—as a *human* citizen—to tell us."

"I don't know anything more than what I've already told you," Emily said for the fifteenth time. The walls seemed to be creeping closer with each second, and she was finding it hard to breathe. If they didn't let her out of this room soon, she'd go insane. "You have the whole story."

"No," Wolfe said. "We don't. But if you'd rather not talk to us tonight, that's fine. We'll continue this tomorrow. In the meantime, we'll see if we can't get answers some other way." He got up and turned to the other agent. "Janson, please take Miss Ross to Medical. Let's see if this alien healing left any traces."

"Wait, no. You can't do that," Emily said, drawing back when Janson stood up and stepped toward her. Her heart was pounding so fast she thought she might be sick. "I'm not consenting to this. I want a lawyer."

But Janson just wrapped his thick fingers around her arm and pulled her to her feet. "Let's go," he said, his palm damp and clammy on her skin. "It's time we learned more about your ordeal."

CHAPTER THIRTY-SEVEN

"You want me to find a human girl?" Korum frowned, his unusual golden-colored eyes narrowed. The Councilor seemed equal parts puzzled and displeased by Zaron's request. "Why?"

"Because she's mine, and I want her back," Zaron said. There was no time to play games and pretend his request was anything other than a personal favor. He couldn't shake off the feeling that something was terribly wrong. Every second that he couldn't locate Emily felt like an hour, the fear inside him growing uncontrollably. "I saved her when she got hurt, and she stayed with me for a while," he explained. "However, I made the mistake of letting her go back to New York, and something's happened to her. I can't find her anywhere."

Korum's frown deepened. "So how do you expect me to find her?"

"Through the nanocytes in her body," Zaron said. The idea had come to him early in the morning, and he'd instantly requested an in-person meeting with the Councilor. "I learned that your company designed the jansha device I used to heal her. I don't have the code to activate the tracking feature on the nanocytes, but I know there is such a feature. Isn't there?"

"There is," Korum confirmed. "All nanocytes have a unique signature that can be detected. But I'd need to see the jansha to figure out which specific batch of nanocytes was used on her."

"Here it is." Zaron extended his hand and opened his palm to show the small, tubular healing device. "I figured you might need it."

"All right," Korum said, taking the device from Zaron. "I'll look into this for you. It might take a few days, so—"

"No," Zaron said sharply, his muscles tensing with a surge of fury. "I don't have a few days."

"Excuse me?" Korum's gaze hardened.

"It's important," Zaron said, forcing himself to moderate his tone. He couldn't afford to antagonize the one person who could help him. "*She's* important."

"More important than my duties on the Council and the designs I'm working on?" Korum's nostrils flared. "I understand that you want your human pet back, but—"

"She's my charl." Zaron held Korum's icy gaze, refusing to back down. The notoriously ruthless Councilor wasn't someone to be crossed, but there was nothing Zaron wouldn't do to get Emily back.

He'd challenge Korum to the Arena if he had to.

"Your charl?" Some of the cold anger left Korum's voice. "Like Arus's Delia?"

"Yes." Zaron didn't see the need to explain that Emily wasn't his charl yet. She would become one as soon as he found her; he'd decided that last night. She'd chosen to come back to him

—that was what that half-finished ticket purchase was about—but even if she still had some reservations about belonging to him, Zaron would overcome them.

Once he had Emily, he would never let her go again.

"I see." A tinge of amusement appeared in Korum's gaze. "I didn't realize you and Arus had so much in common. I'll never understand a charl's appeal, but if you want a human, I guess it's your choice."

Zaron did his best to conceal his relief. "So you'll help me? Today?"

"Yes, I will," Korum said. "Come back in two hours. I should have her location by then."

———

The two hours crawled by at a glacial pace. To distract himself, Zaron went to the lake and swam fifty laps, then ran twenty miles through the jungle. Despite not sleeping at all last night, he felt wired, his body buzzing with violent energy.

If he came across any human guerrilla fighters, they'd be in trouble.

But Zaron didn't come across anyone, and exactly two hours after the conversation, he was back at the Council meeting hall in Lenkarda.

Korum was waiting for him in front of a three-dimensional floating image.

"She's in there," he said without preliminaries, pointing at a crumbling warehouse on a trash-littered street. "It's a building in a semi-abandoned industrial area of Queens, one of the New York City boroughs. I did some digging on it for you. It turns out the building is owned by the US government. They used several shell corporations to conceal that fact, which makes me think it's not one of their official locations."

"A government building?" Zaron frowned at the image. "Why would she be there?"

"I don't know," Korum said. "Maybe she decided to talk to them about you, tell them what she's learned during her time with you. How long did you keep her?"

"About two and a half weeks. But she's only seen our most basic home technology, so I doubt she can tell them anything useful."

"You shouldn't have shown her even that," Korum said, and the image winked out of existence. "The non-disclosure mandate is no longer in place, but we're still bound by the non-interference mandate. We can't give or show them anything that would alter the course of their natural technological development. In general, it's a problem that the government has her. The nanocytes are inactive, but she still has them in her body, and that's not a technology we're going to be sharing with the humans any time soon."

"Don't worry. It won't be a problem for long," Zaron said. "I'm going to get her back." He doubted the humans had sufficiently advanced technology to do anything with the nanocytes, but he didn't argue.

He had Emily's location, and that was all that mattered.

Korum gave him a hard look. "You know you can't just show up and drag her out of there. They might have security measures in place that aren't apparent from the outside. If this really is some kind of government facility, you could cause a major interplanetary incident if you storm in and get hurt."

"So what do you suggest?" Zaron asked, suppressing a flare

of impatience. Now that he knew where Emily was, he couldn't wait to get to her.

"Arus can put in a request for you through the proper diplomatic channels," Korum said. "It'll probably take some time, but—"

"No." Zaron's rejection was instinctive, a gut feeling born of his need to have Emily back that very instant, but when he saw Korum's expression, he knew he'd have to provide a reasonable explanation. "If we ask for her, they'll think she's important," he said. "They might deny that they have her or delay returning her to me so they could question her. It would be much easier if I went there by myself and retrieved her. If I break in like a human burglar, they'll never know that a Krinar was involved, so—"

"No." It was Korum's turn to interrupt. "That's not the way to handle it. If this Emily of yours told them everything, they might expect us to come for her. You can't go in unarmed and unprepared. If you really can't wait, I'll help you. I have a couple of designs I've been itching to test out."

The Councilor explained the plan, his golden eyes gleaming, and as he spoke, Zaron felt the knot of tension in his chest start to loosen.

One way or another, he was going to get Emily back.

It was time for his angel to come home.

CHAPTER THIRTY-EIGHT

*H*er heart thudding in an erratic rhythm, Emily stared at the white-haired nurse who was getting ready to stick yet another needle into Emily's arm. The older woman had a kind face that reminded Emily of the actress Betty White, but so far, she'd ignored all of Emily's entreaties to stop and let her call a lawyer.

The initial round of tests had consisted of them taking several vials of Emily's blood, X-rays of every part of her body, a CT scan, and an MRI. Afterwards, they'd let Emily pass out for a few hours on a hard cot in a tiny gray room, and she'd woken up feeling like she was suffocating. She'd needed fresh air, needed it so badly she'd felt like she was dying, but instead of letting her out, they'd given her a sedative to keep her calm. She'd floated in a drugged haze for a while, dreaming of Zaron coming to save her, but the drug was starting to wear off and the claustrophobia was back, along with nausea from the sedative and a churning sensation in her empty stomach. Emily had thrown up the coffee and donuts they'd given her a half hour ago, and the hunger intensified the headache throbbing in her temples.

"Don't do this, please," Emily begged again as the Betty White lookalike approached her with the syringe. Her tongue felt thick and unwieldy inside her dry mouth. "Please. I'm a US citizen. I haven't done anything wrong."

The nurse ignored her, her kindly face set in stoic lines. Emily tried to jerk her arm away from the syringe, but the padded handcuff around her wrist kept it in place. Two male nurses had cuffed her to a metal chair after she'd tried to resist the second round of tests, and the restraints had worsened her claustrophobia, making her pulse beat sickeningly fast. She was strapped down as securely as in a mental asylum, unable to get up or get away. Emily had never been a fan of needles, going so far as to avoid getting flu shots, but there was no avoiding this.

She was a prisoner, and there was no escape.

The nurse gripped Emily's arm to hold it still, and the needle went into her skin, piercing the vein on the inside of her elbow.

"Stop," Emily moaned, bile rising in her throat as her blood flowed into the vial attached to the syringe. "I'm going to be sick."

Holding the syringe in place with one hand, the nurse reached for a nearby plastic tray. "Here," she said, thrusting the empty tray under Emily's chin. "You can vomit into this if you need to."

Emily was shaking, her skin covered with cold sweat, but she managed not to throw up. Seeing that the tray was not needed, the nurse put it back. Removing the needle from

Emily's arm, she put a cotton ball on the wound and taped a Band-Aid over it.

"All done for now," she said. "Sit back and relax. Agent Wolfe and Agent Janson will be in to see you shortly."

She exited the room without unlocking Emily's cuffs, and two minutes later, Wolfe and Janson walked into the room. Neither agent batted an eye at seeing Emily restrained in a chair, and she realized that to them, she wasn't a person.

She was the enemy, and they'd go to any lengths to break her.

"Please take these cuffs off," she said. It took all her strength to keep her voice steady. She was dizzy, and it felt like all oxygen was leaving the room. "I'm not going to attack you."

Wolfe gave her a thin-lipped smile. "I'm sure you won't, but the nurses might need to run a few more tests, so it's more efficient if we keep them on for now. I'm sure you understand."

"No, I don't understand," Emily said, unable to contain her anger and desperation. "I haven't committed a crime, but even if I had, there is due process in this country. If you're going to hold me like this, I demand to see a lawyer, and—"

"Miss Ross, please." Janson sat down on a chair across from her, his fleshy jowls quivering with the movement. "You're a smart young woman. I'm sure you know that the Patriot Act gives us a lot of leeway when it comes to threats to national security. You must also know that the Krinar are the biggest threat we've ever faced. Since you're refusing to cooperate with us—"

"I'm cooperating with you!"

"—we have no choice but to keep you here," Janson continued as if Emily hadn't spoken. "The preliminary tests show that you were indeed healed by a technology that far

exceeds anything we know. Your dental records, for instance..."
He droned on, listing everything they'd discovered so far, but
Emily was no longer listening.

A humming sound—something resembling the distant
buzzing of a beehive—had caught her attention.

Suddenly, the lights flickered and went out, and the buzzing
sound intensified.

"Fuck," Wolfe said, pulling out his phone and using it as a
flashlight. "Janson, you all right?"

But Janson wasn't paying attention to him. He'd fallen silent
and was holding his phone above his head, shining its light
straight up at the ceiling.

"What is that?" Wolfe asked, tipping his head back, and
Emily followed his gaze.

The ceiling looked like it was shimmering—no, like it was
melting.

Wolfe jumped to his feet, pulling his gun out, but it was too
late.

A large portion of the ceiling disintegrated, the thick layer
of concrete evaporating as if it were made of smoke. Sunlight
poured through the opening, blinding Emily for a moment, but
then she saw it.

A tall, broad-shouldered figure of a man standing on the
edge of the opening.

The bright sunlight from above cast his face into shadows,
but there was no mistaking the catlike grace with which he
moved.

Stunned, Emily stared at Zaron, fierce elation sweeping
through her.

Her alien captor had come for her.

He wanted her back.

"Stop right there!" Janson shouted, raising his gun, but Zaron was already jumping down into the room.

The deafening *pop-pop-pop* of gunshots filled the air, and Emily stopped breathing, her heart plunging in icy terror. She knew the Krinar were fast and strong, but that didn't mean they couldn't be hurt or killed. If something happened to Zaron... Before the fear could choke her, she saw that he'd landed on his feet, unharmed.

The seconds that followed were a blur. Zaron moved like a deadly tornado. In what seemed like a blink of an eye, both agents were on the floor, screaming in pain, and Emily watched in paralyzed shock as Zaron lifted Janson by his throat, holding him up with one hand as if the three-hundred-pound man weighed nothing. Janson's right arm was hanging at an odd angle at his side, but his left hand clawed at Zaron's fingers in frantic terror, his feet flailing in the air with desperation.

Zaron was literally choking the agent to death.

"Stop!" Emily yelled, horrified. "Zaron, please, stop!"

Her lover froze, and she saw a shudder ripple through his powerful body. His face was turned away, so all she could see was the taut line of his jaw, but she could feel his barely restrained rage. Violence thrummed in the air, dark and toxic, and Emily knew that if she didn't do something, Zaron would murder these two men.

Like the K in those videos, he'd rip them into pieces.

"Zaron, please." Swallowing her panic, Emily softened her voice, making it gently cajoling. "Put him down."

Janson's struggles were already weakening, his legs kicking with less force, and for a moment, Emily thought Zaron wouldn't listen to her. But then his fingers loosened, and the agent fell to the floor, audibly gasping for air. Wolfe lay next to him, whimpering, both of his arms bent at unnatural angles.

Nausea rolled through Emily again, but she forced herself to look up at Zaron as he stepped over Janson's cringing bulk and came toward her, his black gaze burning with something dark and frightening.

"They hurt you." His voice was thick with rage as he stopped in front of her, and she realized he was looking at the needle marks and bruises on her arms. "Those bastards hurt you." He was all but shaking with fury, his big hands unsteady as he undid her restraints and pulled her to her feet.

"They just took some blood," Emily said numbly, but Zaron was already bending down to lift her into his arms. Despite his anger, his grip on her was gentle, his inhuman strength tightly leashed as he held her clasped to his chest.

Engulfed by his warmth and familiar scent, Emily began to shake. Winding her arms around his neck, she buried her face against his shoulder, trying to hold back the tears that burned her eyes. She felt both euphoric and overwhelmed, the searing joy of seeing Zaron again battling with the horror of what he'd done.

After nearly two months of agonized longing, she was with the man she loved—an extraterrestrial predator who'd come within a hairbreadth of killing two human beings.

"Hold on," Zaron said, and Emily felt his muscles bunching. Instinctively, she tightened her grip on his neck, and then they were flying—or so it seemed for a second. Before she could process what was happening, they were on the first floor of the facility, standing on the undissolved portion of the ceiling.

Zaron had jumped up from the basement while holding her, Emily realized dazedly. On any other day, she would've marveled at this inhuman feat of athleticism, but that wasn't what held her attention now.

All around her were bodies—human bodies. Tall and short, fat and skinny, armed and unarmed, they lay on the floor in strange poses, their slack faces illuminated by the sunlight streaming through the now-nonexistent roof.

"Are they..." Emily couldn't even pronounce the word. Shuddering, she pushed at Zaron's chest to look up at him. "Zaron, are they—"

"They're asleep," Zaron said, tightening his grip on her. "I knocked them out to avoid casualties."

Emily lay her head on his shoulder and drew in a shaky breath, relief sweeping through her like a tidal wave. She didn't know if she could've lived with herself if the Krinar she loved had turned out to be a mass murderer.

"Where are you taking me?" she asked as he stepped over a couple of bodies, carrying her in his arms.

"You'll see," Zaron said, and she felt his muscles bunch for another superhuman jump.

They landed on the remaining portion of the roof, and Emily felt the warm summer breeze on her skin. Her lungs expanded, drawing in air, and the claustrophobic tension constricting her ribcage melted away, taking her remaining doubts with it.

She was finally back with Zaron.

He had come for her.

"How did you find me?" she asked, pulling back to meet his gaze, and her pulse jumped at the look in his eyes.

Zaron was staring at her with uncompromising possessiveness, with a hunger so intense it made her insides turn to mush.

"The nanocytes used to heal you," he said, and it took Emily a second to realize he was answering her question. "I was able to track them."

"Oh." Unease fluttered through her, but before she could question Zaron further, he turned to the left, holding her, and she saw something odd.

On the remaining roof of the warehouse was a spherical pod made of some strange ivory-colored material. It was only a few feet in diameter and had no visible windows or doors.

"Is that—"

"Our way of getting home, yes," Zaron said, walking toward it. As he approached, the wall of the pod disintegrated, creating an entrance for them.

Stepping in, Zaron carefully lowered Emily onto a floating plank—one of the two that were inside the pod. Instantly, the plank conformed to her body, molding itself to her back and the curve of her butt. The comfort was incredible, and for the first time, Emily realized how much she'd missed the intuitive Krinar technology.

"Are we flying somewhere?" she asked, looking around. The walls of the pod were see-through from the inside, giving her the illusion that she was sitting in a giant glass bubble. It should've scared her, but instead, it made her feel light and free. She didn't feel confined in these transparent walls, though she was as much of a prisoner now as she'd been in the basement below. Zaron wasn't going to let her go again—she knew that with a certainty that transcended all reason—but the knowledge didn't scare her.

She never wanted to be without him again.

"We're going back to Costa Rica," Zaron said, sitting down on the other plank. "There's a new Krinar settlement there called Lenkarda. It's not far from my home—which is your home now too."

"What about my cat?" There were a million other questions Emily probably should've asked first, but concern for George was uppermost in her mind.

"We'll swing by to get him," Zaron said with no hint of surprise or hesitation, and she knew he must've been prepared for this.

Her intuition had been right: he wasn't going to let her go.

"What about my apartment?" Emily asked, the logical questions finally coming to her. The adrenaline rush from her violent rescue was fading, and she was beginning to feel overwhelmed again. "What about my things? What will I live on if—"

"Emily." Zaron swiveled on the plank to face her. Clasping her hand between his large warm palms, he said softly, "You have nothing to worry about, angel. I'll take care of everything."

Emily stared at him, her mind whirling. Nobody had taken care of anything for her since her parents' deaths. "But—"

"Hush," he murmured, raising his hand to stroke her cheek, and she saw that the possessiveness in his gaze was edged with tenderness, the hunger tempered by something soft and warm. "You don't have to be afraid, angel. You're not alone anymore."

She inhaled, her eyes prickling with sudden tears. "Zaron…"

"We'll talk more when we get home," he said, and she nodded, too overcome with emotion to argue.

With a light, soundless push, the pod took off, rising into the air. Emily's breath caught as they whooshed over New York, covering the distance from Queens to Manhattan in less than a minute. Accelerating so fast should've given her whiplash, but she didn't feel any discomfort from the speed.

The ride was as smooth and easy as if they were flying at five miles an hour.

They landed on the rooftop of her building, and Zaron jumped out of the pod as soon as the wall opening appeared. "Stay here. I'll be right back," he said, and before Emily could object, he disappeared behind a chimney.

Emily got out of the pod and started to follow him, but before she could take more than a dozen steps, Zaron returned, carrying a wild-eyed George in his arms. Seeing her, the cat let out a loud meow, and Emily grabbed him from Zaron, laughing as the cat swatted her with a paw to express his indignation at being taken by a strange man.

"What about his litter box?" she asked, looking up at Zaron when George settled in her arms and started purring. "And his food and toys and—"

"I'll provide everything your pet needs," Zaron said, placing his hand on the small of her back to lead her back toward the pod. "We should go now. I think your air authorities spotted us."

Sure enough, Emily could hear the distant roar of helicopters and the whine of sirens. Did the agents at that Queens facility report Zaron's attack? Would this be considered a violation of the treaty? Emily wanted to ask, but Zaron was already shepherding her into the pod and sealing the entrance. She barely had time to sit down on the plank with George secured on her lap when the pod lifted off, swiftly rising high above the city.

The clouds below them turned into a blur, and George meowed, clawing at Emily's leg in distress. She stroked him soothingly, knowing how scary all of this must seem to a cat who'd never been outside of Manhattan. Even to her, flying in a glass bubble at this insane speed was utterly surreal.

"How long until we get there?" she asked, and Zaron's full lips curved with amusement.

"We're there," he said, and she realized the pod was already descending into the green canopy of the rainforest, having covered the distance from New York to Costa Rica in a few short minutes.

They landed in a clearing next to the small mountain into which Zaron's house was embedded. To Emily, it felt strangely like coming home. She'd spent less than three weeks here, but the fresh, humid air and the lush vegetation called to her, making her feel alive and whole in a way that the crowded streets of New York City never could.

Stepping out of the pod, she held George against her chest and followed Zaron into the hidden cave he'd made into his home.

Inside, everything was as she'd left it, from the floating furniture to the clean ivory walls. The wall opening closed behind Zaron, sealing them inside the house, and Emily bent down to put George on the floor. The cat looked uncertain for a moment, but then his normal fearlessness kicked in, and he stalked off to explore his new home.

Straightening, Emily faced Zaron, her pulse speeding up with nervous excitement. Zaron's gaze was hooded as he watched her, his beautiful face set in taut, hard lines.

This was it. They had nowhere to hurry, no other place they needed to be.

It was just the two of them and the tension that simmered in the air, a mutual attraction so potent Emily could feel it like an electric current across her skin.

"Zaron…" She didn't know if she stepped toward him, or if he moved first, but it didn't matter because somehow she was in his arms, his mouth devouring her with raw, demanding hunger as his hands roamed across her body. His taste, his scent, his touch—it was everything she'd dreamed of these past seven weeks and more, the reality sharper and more intense than her recollections. His tongue plunged between her lips, taking her mouth with unrestrained passion, and she felt the hardness of his erection as he lifted her against him, spreading her thighs wide to grind his pelvis against her aching sex. His jeans and her yoga pants were between them, but they might as well have been unclothed. Emily felt like she'd been set aflame, each grinding roll of his hips sending shards of sizzling pleasure through her body. Her erect nipples ached inside her bra, and her clit felt swollen and sensitized, her underwear damp with pulsing need.

Moaning into Zaron's mouth, Emily gripped fistfuls of his thick, silky hair and tried to get even closer, needing more of this, more of him. Distantly, she registered some ripping sounds; then both of their shirts were on the floor, and her naked breasts were pressed against his chest, the relief of skin-to-skin contact almost orgasmic. Their pants were still on, however, and Emily couldn't bear that. Any barrier between them was too much. As if sensing that, Zaron lowered her to her feet, letting her slide down his muscular body, and in the next instant, she found herself with her yoga pants and underwear around her ankles.

She kicked off her shoes and stepped out of the pants, and Zaron spun her around and bent her over, positioning her on all fours on the floor. She heard the slide of his zipper, and then he was behind her and over her, one muscled forearm snaking under her hips to keep her still while his other hand gripped her hair. His hold was rough and possessive, his breathing harsh and heavy against her neck, and her muscles tightened with instinctive unease as she felt the smooth, broad head of his cock prodding at her folds. He was so much bigger than her, so much stronger. Even if he were human, she'd be helpless in his embrace.

"You're mine," he rasped into her ear, making her shiver. "This pretty pink pussy is mine. All of you is mine. I'm going to fuck you until you forget what it's like not to have me inside you, angel... until you never, ever want to leave again."

His graphic promise both scared and thrilled Emily, but before she could reply, he drove into her, his thick cock spearing her in one hard thrust. The air whooshed out of her lungs, her delicate inner tissues quivering at the shock of his entry. She was wet, but she still felt stretched and overtaken, her body no longer used to his size. And yet the heat inside her remained, the pleasure battling with the discomfort of his rough invasion.

"Zaron, please..." She didn't know what she was begging for, but he seemed to, because his arm under her hips shifted and his fingers landed on her sex, parting her slick folds to find her aching clit. Unerringly, he located the most sensitive spot, and Emily's discomfort vanished, her breathing picking up and her spine tightening as he began thrusting at a steady pace, each powerful stroke of his cock pushing her clit against those clever fingers.

"Mine," he breathed, his teeth grazing over the sensitive skin of her neck, and the tension inside Emily gathered into an impossibly tight coil, the heat transforming into a scorching conflagration. For a moment, she couldn't breathe, couldn't see, and then the orgasm exploded through her, the pleasure dark and incandescent, shattering in its intensity. It seemed to go on forever, the steady thrusting of Zaron's cock intensifying and prolonging the sensations. Sweat trickled down Emily's back, and her toes curled as Zaron continued fucking her through her climax, and just when the agonizing ecstasy began to ease, his fingers pinched her throbbing clit and hurled her straight into her second release.

The waves of pleasure were so overwhelming Emily was caught off-guard when Zaron thrust deep into her with a savage groan, and she felt his cock thicken and jerk inside her. His grinding motions sent aftershocks rippling through her body, and she moaned, her inner muscles clenching as his seed filled her in several warm spurts.

Exhausted, she tried to sink to the floor, but Zaron didn't let her. Picking her up, he carried her to the shower and washed every part of her body, his touch achingly tender on her sensitized flesh.

———

Clean and wearing a pink dress Zaron had given her, Emily had just enough energy to sit upright at the floating kitchen table while Zaron ordered his house to prepare a meal for her. It took only a couple of minutes to get the food, and she fell on it the moment it appeared, as ravenous as if she hadn't eaten in weeks.

"How did you know I was hungry?" she asked after she'd devoured most of her salad and a big bowl of some delicious stew. It was a trivial question, but she couldn't bring herself to ask the important things, like why Zaron had come for her and what he wanted. The food had given her a burst of energy, but her body still throbbed from his possession, and her cheeks warmed as George jumped onto her lap and sniffed at her crotch before letting out a loud meow. Emily guessed the cat could smell Zaron on her, and he wasn't sure he liked it.

"Your stomach was rumbling earlier," Zaron answered, watching George's antics from across the table. Like her, he was dressed in a fresh set of clothes—a pair of jeans and a white T-shirt—and he looked stunningly sexy as he sat there, his dark eyes trained on her with possessive intensity. "They didn't give you any food, did they?"

"They gave me some this morning, but I threw up," Emily admitted. "The drugs they gave me made me sick."

Zaron's jaw tightened. "You shouldn't have stopped me from killing them."

Emily's pulse lurched, and she bent down to lower George to the floor. "Zaron..." She straightened to face him. "What exactly are your people?"

"What do you mean?" He frowned.

"Are you..." She could barely bring herself to say it. "Are you some kind of vampires?"

His gaze sharpened. "What makes you ask that?"

"I overhead you and Ellet talking," Emily said, pushing her plate aside. "And then..." She bit her lip. "Well, I'm pretty sure whatever you did to me the night before I left wasn't normal sex."

"You knew, and you still wanted me to do it?"

"What exactly is 'it?'" Emily asked in frustration. "Am I right about the blood-drinking thing?"

Zaron folded his arms in front of his chest and leaned back. "Yes... and no." His eyes gleamed like dark gems. "Human blood contains a hemoglobin that we once needed to survive, but we altered our genetic makeup so we don't need it anymore—biologically, at least. Some psychological hunger for it remains, however, and in the absence of a biological need, we get a kind of high from it—a pleasure that's almost sexual in nature."

Emily's mouth went dry. "You... You get high off my blood?"

"Yes—but only if I take it during sex. So don't worry, angel. I won't just randomly bite you—though if I did, I'm sure you'd find it pleasurable. Our saliva has a drugging effect on our prey, which is why you enjoyed it when I took your blood those two times."

Our prey. A shudder rippled down Emily's spine, and she had to fight not to recoil. It was one thing to have her suspicions, but to have Zaron confirm them so casually...

"I don't understand," she said, her mind racing. "How could human blood contain a hemoglobin your species needed? We would've had to evolve side by side with you, but you said the Krinar are much older than my kind. Unless..." She inhaled sharply. "Unless you had a species comparable to humans on your planet, and you manipulated our DNA so we'd be like them?"

"Very good," Zaron said approvingly. "You'd make an excellent biologist. Yes, that's exactly right. On Krina, there was a primate-like species called the lonar that my ancestors used to hunt. Their blood had the hemoglobin we needed. Unfortunately, they were weak and fragile creatures, with low birth rates and short lifespans, and when a plague nearly wiped them out, we realized we needed an alternative. Humans—or rather, your ancient primate ancestors—were supposed to be that alternative. As it turned out, we didn't need them; by the time Earth primates had evolved enough to have the hemoglobin, we had come up with synthetic blood substitutes and also altered our genes to get rid of our reliance on it."

"So then why did you continue manipulating our evolution?" Emily asked, confused. "You did do that, right? Because how else could humans be so much like you?"

Zaron nodded. "Yes, you're right. Once we no longer needed your blood, the intent of our experiment shifted. Our scientists decided to see if they could create a Krinar-like species by nudging along the evolution of one species of Earth primates."

"The species that became the modern-day *Homo sapiens?*"

"Yes, precisely." He looked pleased that Emily understood, and she wondered if that meant he was surprised at her intelligence. Then a horrible thought occurred to her.

What if Zaron saw her as an unusually smart monkey or some type of genetic experiment?

Her lungs seized, her stomach cramping for an awful moment, but then she remembered how Zaron had confided in her about his mate, how he hadn't wanted Emily to leave but had respected her wishes regardless.

No. She began breathing again. That particular worry was unfounded. However the Krinar felt about her species, Zaron didn't view Emily as a lab animal—that much she was certain of.

As if sensing the direction of her thoughts, Zaron leaned forward and took her hand. "Emily... Listen to me, angel." His voice was soft, but there was no escaping the intensity in his gaze. "I know that what I am—what my people are—is still new to you, and that it must seem frightening at times. But you have nothing to fear, believe me. I will take care of you. I will give you whatever you need, and I will do everything in my power to make sure you're happy and safe." His eyes glittered dangerously as he added, "Nobody will ever hurt you again."

Emily dragged in an unsteady breath. "Zaron..." There was a growing lump in her throat. "Why did you come for me?"

"Because you're mine," he said, his hand tightening around her fingers. "Because you've been mine from the moment I saw you lying on those rocks, broken yet clinging to life with all your strength. I didn't know it then, but when I saved you—when I gave you your life back—you gave me back mine, Emily."

The lump in her throat expanded, and her eyes began to burn as Zaron got up and stepped around the floating table, using his grip on Emily's hand to pull her up and draw her against him. Gazing down at her, he took both of her hands in his palms, bringing them up to his chest, and the raw vulnerability of his expression pierced her to the core.

"After I lost Larita, I lived in darkness," he said quietly. "I existed in a world so bleak and gray it took everything I had to get up each morning. There were days I thought I wouldn't make it and nights when..." His powerful throat moved as he swallowed. "When I didn't *want* to make it."

"Oh, Zaron." Emily felt like her chest had been ripped open. "I'm so, so sorry—"

"No, don't." He gave her hands a gentle squeeze, his fingers strong and warm around her palms. "You don't understand, angel. I'm not telling you this to solicit your pity. I just want you to understand."

"Understand what?" Emily whispered, blinking to clear the veil of tears from her eyes. Her heart pounded in a fast, shallow rhythm, the warm glow in his gaze making her breath tremble in her throat.

"Understand why I love you," he said. "Why I want you with me every day for the rest of my life. You gave me back what I thought I'd never have again, and I can't bear to lose it, Emily. I can't bear to lose *you*. I let you go before because I'd made you a promise, but I can't do it again. I need you, angel. I need you with me forever."

"You—" Emily's voice broke, the tears streaming down her cheeks. "You have me, Zaron. I'm here. I love you, and I'm yours for as long as you want me. I'm sorry. I'm so sorry I left before. I thought I had to—I told myself it was the rational thing to do— but that was just fear talking all along. I didn't want you to leave me, so I left first and—"

"And I didn't stop you because *I* was afraid," Zaron said, squeezing her hands tighter. "I was scared I would lose you like I'd lost Larita, so I didn't try to explain, to make you understand what I could give you." His mouth twisted bitterly as he released her hands and dropped his arms to his sides. "I should've said to hell with the mandate and told you the truth, but instead, like a coward, I kept silent and let you walk out of my life."

"What are you talking about?" Emily whispered, blinking up at him in confusion. She felt bereft without his touch, as lost as an abandoned child. "You did ask me to stay. What does the mandate have to do with anything?"

"It doesn't—not really." Self-recrimination tightened his voice. "It was an excuse all along. I thought I couldn't tell you everything because if you'd then refused to stay with me, I'd have broken the mandate. But that was my own fear talking, nothing more." He drew in a breath. "I'm sorry, angel. The truth is, I let you walk away because I fell in love with you, and I couldn't face the thought that I could lose you someday... that some freak accident could claim your life when I was least prepared."

"Oh, Zaron..." Emily couldn't bear to listen any longer. Stepping closer to him, she clasped his large palms in her hands and brought them to her chest, mimicking his earlier hold on her. The tears were choking her again, the bittersweet joy of his confession making her throat ache. "You *are* going to lose me; it's inevitable," she said hoarsely. "But that doesn't mean we can't be together until then... doesn't mean we can't love each other until then. Even a few years is better than—"

"No, angel." To Emily's surprise, the corners of Zaron's mouth lifted in a faint smile. "You still don't understand." Gently extricating his hands from her grasp, he gripped her shoulders, his touch warm and tenderly possessive. "It's not a few years, you see—not when you're fully mine."

"What?" Emily stared at him. Surely he couldn't mean...

"There's another type of nanocytes—one much more advanced and complex than what I used to heal you," Zaron said, his eyes gleaming. "These nanocytes are designed to repair cellular and DNA damage for as long as they're inside a living human body."

Emily opened her mouth, then closed it. Shaking her head, she took a step back, moving her elbows in a circle to break Zaron's hold on her shoulders. "Repair DNA damage? You..." She could barely speak. "You're talking about biological immortality."

"Yes." He came after her and caught her wrist, stopping her from backing away. "So you see, angel, it doesn't have to be a few years—not if you're my charl."

"Your what?" Emily's head was spinning.

"Charl," he said. "That's what we call humans we bring fully into our society. The label is irrelevant, though. What matters is what it can give you: access to those nanocytes and a life free from the ravages of disease and aging—a life that can go on for millennia or longer at my side."

"Oh my God, Zaron..." What he was telling her was utterly unbelievable, but if it was true... "Your people can grant us immortality?"

He shook his head. "Not all of you, no. Only those we claim as charl—like I'm claiming you."

"But if you have this technology—"

"Emily." He let go of her wrist to frame her face between his palms. Gazing down at her, he wiped the tears off her cheeks with his thumbs and said softly, "Listen to me, angel. I understand how it must seem to you, but there's nothing I can do for the human race as a whole. That's up to the Council and the Elders. Maybe one day they'll share this technology with your kind, but until then, we can only give these nanocytes to our charl. *I* can only give them to you."

Staring up at him, Emily wrapped her fingers around his wrists. His bones were thick and sturdy, as strong as the man himself. She didn't know what to think, how to process what he was telling her. Should she be selfishly glad that Zaron was going to give her this incredible gift, or horrified that the Krinar were withholding it from the rest of Earth's population? How many lives could be saved with the Krinar technology? How much suffering prevented? Her heart ached as she pictured all the sick and dying around the world, and realized she wouldn't be one of them.

She would never be one of them because she would belong to Zaron.

Instead of the few short years she'd pictured them having together, they would have an eternity.

"Don't cry, angel," he whispered, and Emily realized that the tears were running down her face again, her hands trembling as she held his wrists. Bending his head, he kissed the tears from her cheeks, but they just kept coming, the flood of emotions impossible to control. Her joy was mixed with guilt, her happiness tainted by the knowledge that she would be one of the privileged few, that her friends would age and pass away as she remained unchanged with the man she loved.

She tried to stop crying, to turn her face away from Zaron's soothing kisses, but his lips captured hers, and the dark heat that burned between them ignited anew, weakening her knees and muddling her thoughts. A moan vibrated in her throat, and his kiss turned savagely demanding, his tongue invading her mouth as he backed her up against a wall, one of his hands pinning her wrists above her head while the other fumbled with the zipper of his jeans, freeing his erect cock. Still kissing her, he released her wrists and lowered his hands to grip her thighs and lift her off the ground. Overwhelmed, Emily clutched at his shoulders. She wasn't wearing underwear, and the thick crown of his shaft pressed against her naked sex, stoking the pulsing heat inside her.

"Zaron," she groaned, arching her head back as his lips trailed over her jaw, leaving a hot, damp trail on her skin, and then she felt it: the sharp, startling slice of his teeth across the delicate skin of her throat.

"Mine," he rasped, his mouth latching onto the wound, and her world spun away, consumed by the white-hot ecstasy that overtook them both.

CHAPTER THIRTY-NINE

*I*t wasn't until the next morning, when Emily woke up next to Zaron, that she had the chance to process everything.

He was lying on his side watching her when she opened her eyes, and the possessive warmth in his gaze filled her with a confusing mix of joy and unease.

She belonged to Zaron now. Forever. He hadn't said so explicitly, but she knew that even if she begged, he wouldn't let her leave again, and it wasn't just because he'd broken the mandate by telling her about the full capabilities of Krinar medical technology.

He was going to keep her because he needed her—and because he knew she needed him.

"Good morning, angel," he murmured, brushing a strand of hair off her face, and Emily's skin heated as she remembered what had taken place yesterday. He'd taken her blood again, and the sex that followed had been out of this world. She remembered more of it than after the first two times—maybe because her body was growing used to whatever it was his saliva did to her—and the recollections sent a surge of liquid warmth to her sex. Zaron had been insatiable, taking her in every way possible, and she'd enjoyed all of it, her body craving every dirty, depraved thing he'd done to her.

"Are you hungry?" he asked, and Emily nodded, pushing the graphic images out of her mind.

"I'll be right back," she said and jumped off the bed, ignoring the hungry way his eyes tracked her as she walked naked to the bathroom.

When she emerged a few minutes later, she found Zaron dressed in an unusual outfit: a sleeveless ivory-colored shirt and a pair of loose white shorts that ended at his knees. The simplicity of the clothes highlighted his powerful build, the soft-looking material draping over his muscles in a way that made her mouth water. He looked strikingly gorgeous, the light color of the outfit highlighting the deep bronze hue of his skin, and Emily sucked in a breath as he came toward her, his mouth curved in a sensuous smile.

"I'm wearing Krinar clothing," he explained as she continued to stare at him. "Here, I made you some, too."

He handed her a pale peach dress with thin straps and a deep plunge in the back. Emily put it on, marveling at the way it fit her so well. The lightweight, fleece-like material was similar to the dresses he'd given her before, but the style was different. The bodice of the dress both concealed and revealed, emphasizing the shape of her breasts without showing her nipples, and the skirt floated prettily around her legs, stopping a couple of inches above her knees.

"It's beautiful," she said as Zaron gave a command in Krinar and one of the walls turned into a mirror, showing Emily her reflection. "Thank you."

"You're welcome." He came up behind her, resting his hands on her shoulders, and a tremor rippled down her spine as she felt the warmth of his palms on her bare skin. The reflection in the mirror highlighted their differences. Standing behind her, Zaron was a full head taller and uncompromisingly male, his thickly muscled shoulders twice as wide as her slender frame. Though Emily had never considered herself particularly small, she looked tiny next to him, her pale skin and blond hair making his dark coloring appear even more exotic.

For the first time, it struck her that she would be a foreigner among Zaron's people. No, not a foreigner—an alien, a member of a totally different species.

Her stomach tightening with anxiety, Emily turned around to face her lover. "Zaron…" Her voice was unsteady. "Where do you intend for us to live?"

"For the next year, here, near Lenkarda," he said, smiling down at her. "Afterwards, when I'm no longer needed to oversee the settlement process, we can decide on our next home together. We can choose to stay here or go to Krina. Or we can live in one of your cities if you wish, though I'd much prefer the first two options."

"You'd come to New York with me?" Emily asked, surprised. Given the general public's fearful and hostile attitude toward the Ks, the idea of Zaron joining her in Manhattan had never crossed her mind.

"If things settle down, yes. Otherwise, it wouldn't be safe for you."

"For me?" Emily frowned. "I don't think those agents would

dare come after me again. I was worried about you, with all the unrest in the streets and—"

"Oh, I can take care of myself," he said, waving his hand dismissively. "And no, I don't think your government will mess with you again, but that doesn't mean some foolish human resistance group won't."

"Oh." She hadn't considered this aspect of the situation, but Zaron was right. If anyone found out about Emily's relationship with Zaron, she'd become a target for K haters. They'd label her a traitor—and they wouldn't necessarily be wrong, she thought with a pang of guilt.

She *was* sleeping with the enemy—an enemy who was planning to give her an unimaginable gift as a result.

"Don't worry," Zaron said, misreading the dismay on her face. Raising his hand, he gently stroked her cheek. "Nobody will harm you, angel. I promise you that."

"I know." Emily covered his hand with her own, pressing his palm against her cheek. Warmth filled her chest at the unconcealed love that shone in his gaze. "I know that, Zaron."

His smile reappeared, brighter than she'd ever seen it. "Good. Now, come, let's eat—and locate your cat."

———

They found George relaxing on one of the floating couches in the living room. He seemed quite content as he lay there, and when Emily asked Zaron about the cat's food, he told her he'd given his house orders to ensure that the feline would be fed regularly and provided with the appropriate bathroom situation.

"What kind of bathroom situation?" Emily asked, amused,

and Zaron explained that the house had created a special nook where the cat could do his business. Emily insisted on seeing it, so Zaron took her to a room she'd never been in before—one with a floor made entirely of dirt.

"Zaron, this is huge," she said, looking around in amazement. "Did your house build this room just for George?"

Zaron nodded. "I want George to be happy here too," he said with utmost seriousness and bent down to pick up the cat, who'd followed them to the room. "Later today, I'll take him hunting for mice and birds. His species needs that."

Emily's mouth fell open. "You're going to take my cat hunting? In the jungle?"

"Yes, but don't worry." Zaron held George against his chest, ignoring the cat's attempts to jump out of his arms. "I'm fast enough to make sure he won't run off or get hurt in any way. I know your pet is a domesticated creature."

And that was that. As they ate breakfast, Zaron kept George on his lap, letting the cat get used to him, and after a few loud meows and one thwarted attempt at scratching, the cat settled down, letting Zaron stroke his fur and scratch behind his ears. By the time they were finishing their meal, George was full-on purring.

It seemed even cats were not immune to her lover's forceful tenderness.

After the meal, they went for a walk—without the cat, as Emily was definitely *not* fast enough to catch him if he ran off—and she brought up the other problem that had been weighing on her this morning.

"Zaron... Can I tell my friends where I am and with whom?" she asked as they passed under a guanacaste tree on their way to the lake. "Amber might worry when she can't reach me, and the others will probably start wondering about my absence after a while."

Zaron glanced at her. "You can tell them you're with me in Costa Rica. But you'll have to keep quiet about the nanocytes and pretty much everything else you see and learn going forward."

Emily swallowed. "I understand." Her life would diverge drastically from those of her friends; it was already happening, in fact. Thanks to Zaron, she'd survived the fall off the bridge, but her old life had ended on those rocks. Even before he'd come back for her, she'd been different, irreversibly altered by the experience of meeting and falling in love with a man so extraordinary she could've never imagined he existed.

No wonder she'd felt like a zombie during those seven weeks in New York. She'd been trying to resurrect the old Emily instead of coming to terms with the person she'd become.

They walked in companionable silence until they reached the lake. It was hot and humid, and when they got to the clear water, they both gladly dove in, swimming for well over an hour until Emily got tired.

"Will I be stronger when I have the nanocytes?" she asked, holding on to Zaron's shoulders as he swam toward the shore, towing her on his back from the middle of the lake without any sign of exertion. "Will I be able to keep up with you in this and other activities?"

"No, I'm afraid not," he said, stopping and bringing her around to face him. His strong legs scissored in the water below to keep them both afloat. "You won't age or get sick, but you'll still be human, with all that it implies. But because the nanocytes will rapidly heal all damage inflicted on your cells, no matter how minute, you'll recover faster from intense exercise and will have greater endurance. So if you exercise a lot, you could become as strong and fit as any of your top athletes in a much shorter period of time."

"Oh, wow." Just thinking about that made Emily's heart beat faster with excitement. "I can't wait."

"You won't have to wait long," Zaron said, a warm smile appearing on his lips. "You're getting the nanocytes tonight."

And drawing her to him, he kissed her with such passion she was surprised the water didn't boil around them.

CHAPTER FORTY

"*A*re you ready?" Zaron asked, holding Emily's hand. He could see the fear in her eyes, but she lifted her chin and smiled brightly.

"Yes, of course."

"Good." Zaron gave her hand a reassuring squeeze, then turned to face Ellet. "Is everything set?"

The human biology expert nodded. "I've run the simulations, and everything is ready to go. Emily, I'll be putting you under now, okay?"

"Okay." Emily's smile dimmed slightly, her hand tensing in Zaron's grasp. "It'll be just for a short while, right?"

"Yes, don't worry." Ellet approached her with a small jansha-like device. "It'll feel just like a dream."

"Okay, then, go for it," Emily said, and Ellet pressed the device against her neck. Instantly, Emily's hand went slack in Zaron's hold, her eyes closing as she fell into a drugged sleep.

"Everything is normal," Ellet said, switching the jansha-like device for a more sophisticated nanocyte-dispersion tool, and Zaron realized some of his worry must've shown on his face. He knew the procedure was safe—it had been done to humans for thousands of years—but it still made him uneasy to see Emily like this: unconscious and acutely vulnerable.

It reminded him of how she'd been in those first couple of days in his house, when she'd been healing from her fall.

Of course, this wasn't his house. It was Ellet's new lab in Lenkarda, a place equipped with the latest Krinar medical technology. Even the most basic device here was infinitely more advanced than anything Zaron had at home.

That knowledge should've calmed him, but the anxiety remained, gnawing at him like a parasite. The risk of something going wrong during the procedure was about the same as that of the world ending tomorrow, but that didn't lessen his irrational worry. If anything happened to Emily... No. He couldn't think that way.

He couldn't let fear dictate the course of their relationship again.

"You love her, don't you?" Ellet asked as the procedure continued, and Zaron tore his eyes from Emily long enough to glance at the Krinar woman and nod tersely.

"Of course I do," he said, his voice tight. "Why else do you think I'm here?"

Ellet smiled, her hazel eyes filled with gentle encouragement. "It'll be all right. You'll see," she said, and he knew she wasn't just talking about the procedure.

"I know." Turning his attention back to Emily, Zaron stroked the inside of her palm with his thumb. "I know that."

And he did. Losing Emily would always be his greatest nightmare, but he'd never let that drive them apart again.

Their time together was too precious for that.

Emily's hand twitched in his grasp, yanking Zaron out of his thoughts, and he realized she was already waking up.

"It's all good," Ellet said when he glanced at her in concern. "The nanocytes are in place and functioning as intended. Here, I can show you." She reached for a small knife, likely intending to scratch Emily to prove her point, but Zaron caught her arm before she could get anywhere near Emily's skin.

"Don't," he said harshly. He knew he was being insanely overprotective, but he couldn't bear the thought of Emily getting injured in any way.

Nobody would ever hurt her on his watch.

Ellet looked startled but recovered quickly. "Of course, whatever you wish." Pulling her arm out of his grasp, she put the knife back on the floating table. "She wouldn't have felt it— she's still a little numb—but if you don't want me to do it, I won't."

"That's right." Zaron's muscles were coiled tight. "I don't want you to do it."

"Zaron?" Emily's voice was soft and sleepy-sounding, but it acted on him like a lightning bolt. His attention instantly snapped back to her, his hand tightening around her slender palm.

"I'm here, angel," he said, watching her eyes flutter open. "How are you feeling?"

"Um…" Looking disoriented, she tried to sit up, and Zaron helped her, wrapping his arm around her back. Her long hair tickled his face, the soft blond strands silky and fragrant, and he inhaled deeply, drawing in her delicate scent before pulling back to meet her gaze.

"I don't feel any different," Emily said, blinking at him in confusion, and Zaron smiled, joyous relief filling his chest.

The procedure had gone well. His angel would be healthy for centuries and millennia to come.

"You're not supposed to feel any different," Ellet said as Zaron lifted Emily into his arms. "At least not right away. Over time, you'll notice some improvements. You won't get colds, for instance, and if you ever injure yourself, you'll heal faster."

"Thank you, Ellet," Zaron said, regretting his harshness with her earlier. "I really appreciate it."

"My pleasure," she said with a warm smile, and Zaron headed out, holding Emily cradled against his chest.

———

George greeted them with a loud meow as they entered the house, and Zaron carefully placed Emily on her feet, letting her walk on her own. She no longer looked woozy, but she was a little quiet, and he knew she was still recovering from the procedure.

He let her pet George for a couple of minutes, and then he couldn't wait anymore.

"Come," he said, taking her arm and leading her to the bedroom.

"Again?" she asked, her eyes wide. "But we just had sex before dinner."

"I know," Zaron said, pulling off her dress. His body hardened at the sight of her slim, naked curves, but sex wasn't what he was after—not at this moment, at least. Removing his own clothes, he picked Emily up and placed her on the bed, then lay down next to her, pulling her into his embrace.

Understanding what he wanted, she nestled against him, laying her head on his shoulder and draping her leg over his thighs. Her breasts were soft and full against his side, her body fitting against his like she'd been made for him. Ignoring the lust lashing at his body, Zaron held her tight and let himself feel the dizzying perfection of simply being with her... of loving her. Happiness, fragile but real, was within their grasp, and he was no longer afraid to reach for it. The pain of losing Larita would never go away completely—his former mate would always have a piece of his heart—but loving Emily made the grief bearable.

Loving Emily made his life worth living again.

"I love you, Zaron," she whispered, lifting her head to gaze at him, and he smiled, knowing she'd somehow sensed the direction of his thoughts.

"I love you too, angel," he said softly, looking into her bright, clear eyes. "You're mine—now and for all eternity."

EPILOGUE

Ten Months Later

"Are you okay?" Zaron asked, his dark eyes trained on her face, and Emily nodded, though her heart was jackrabbiting in her throat. George meowed in her arms, so she bent down to put him on the floor. The cat instantly jumped up onto a floating plank—his new favorite piece of furniture—and started licking his paw, displaying none of the nervousness Emily was feeling.

The last year had been utterly surreal, but the adventure she was embarking on now superseded her wildest imaginings. In less than two minutes, the Krinar spaceship they were on would leave the Earth orbit, carrying Emily, Zaron, George, and hundreds of Krinar scientists to Krina.

In less than two minutes, Emily and her cat would be on their way to their new home in a different galaxy.

Zaron had gotten the three of them a private room near the hull of the ship—so Emily would have the best views, he'd explained. From the outside, the bullet-shaped ship didn't look particularly futuristic, but inside, it was like Zaron's house on steroids. Everything was light and airy, filled with floating furniture, exotic-looking plants, and intelligent Krinar technology. The best thing of all was that the outer walls were transparent from within, enabling Emily to see Earth from an astronaut's vantage point.

Turning, she stared at the pretty blue ball that was the birthplace of humanity. "You said we'll fly at subluminal speeds at first, right?" she said, tearing her eyes away from the mind-blowing view to glance up at Zaron. "We won't go straight into the warp jump, correct?"

"That's right," he confirmed, his beautiful lips curving in a smile. "We'll first spend several days flying away from Earth. That's to avoid causing disturbances when we warp space-time."

"Okay, got it. Just a little run-of-the-mill warping of space-time. No biggie," Emily said, trying not to sound as anxious as she felt. "It will be just like going for a walk."

"It will be," Zaron promised, tucking a strand of hair behind her ear. "You'll adapt to space travel just as well as you've adapted to everything else."

His words—and the warm look in his eyes—calmed her a bit. Zaron was right: Emily had acclimated to her new life with him with surprising ease. Far from missing New York and her career in finance, she'd thrived in Costa Rica. Within a month, she'd grown as comfortable with basic Krinar applications as she'd been with human technology, and with the aid of a neural language implant—which she'd gotten a week after her nanocytes—Emily had spent the last ten months learning everything she could about Krinar science and society.

Her knowledge base had grown so rapidly she was seriously considering exploring her childhood dream of being a scientist.

She'd expected Zaron to laugh when she'd mentioned the idea, but he'd been overjoyed and had immediately set out to teach her all about the different species of plants and animals on Krina. His passion had been so infectious that Emily was now thinking about being a biologist like him.

"You don't have to decide now," Zaron had said when she'd told him about that idea. "In fact, you don't have to decide at all. Many of us dabble in different fields, and you can too. It's all up to you. I know that whatever you choose to do, you'll be successful at it."

It was that kind of encouragement and unwavering support from Zaron that had given Emily the courage to agree to move with him to Krina. Zaron had been offered a new research opportunity there, and he was looking forward to reconnecting with his family and mending the rift between them—something Emily very much approved of. It had bothered her that Zaron had parents who loved him, yet he was estranged from them. She'd encouraged him to make up with them, even though she'd worried they might disapprove of his relationship with her. However, Zaron had spoken to them in virtual reality last month, telling them all about her, and he'd told her afterwards that nobody had a problem with her being human. They were all eager to meet her, he'd said, and Emily was now excited to meet them. Still, she was more than a little nervous about leaving Earth.

It didn't help that her friend Amber had told her she was being insane.

"You're already living next door to an alien colony—*with* an alien," she'd hissed at Emily when they'd met in person in New

York last month. "And now you're thinking of going to Krina? What the fuck are you going to do there? You don't even speak their language!"

Emily couldn't tell Amber that, thanks to the language implant, she *did* speak Krinar, so she'd kept quiet and Amber had railed on, making all kinds of dire predictions about Emily's fate on Krina. Emily had taken her warnings with a grain of salt; like most people in the wake of the Great Panic, Amber feared the Krinar so much she'd refused to meet Zaron. Unfortunately, Emily couldn't dismiss her friend's concerns out of hand, either.

Not all Krinar were as enlightened in their attitude toward humans as Zaron; that was why she'd been worried about Zaron's family. Even in Lenkarda, where most residents had spent time among humans, Emily had encountered quite a few Ks who seemed to regard her as a cross between Zaron's pet and sexual possession.

If she hadn't been certain that Zaron both loved and respected her, she wouldn't have agreed to go to Krina.

"Angel..." Zaron framed her face with his palms, and the heated intensity in his gaze chased away the anxiety that had swept through her again. "You have nothing to worry about. I'm with you, and I won't let anything happen to you, okay?"

"Okay," Emily whispered, further reassured by his words, and Zaron wrapped his arm around her shoulders, pressing her against his side as a soft chime sounded, marking the start of the ship's journey.

Mesmerized, Emily stared through the transparent wall as the ship began moving, carrying them away from Earth. The pretty blue ball that was her home planet was getting smaller with each second, but the journey ahead no longer frightened Emily. Whatever the future held, she'd face it together with the man who embraced her with such tender possessiveness, the Krinar who'd saved her life and captured her heart.

She was with Zaron, and that was all that mattered.

THE KRINAR EXPOSÉ

With Hettie Ivers

Part One

THE X-CLUB

CHAPTER ONE

$\mathcal{T}$wo years since the invasion.

I couldn't believe it had been two years since the invasion, and we still knew next to nothing about the aliens who had taken over Earth.

Frustrated, I removed my glasses and rubbed my eyes, feeling the strain from staring at the computer screen all day. Over the past two weeks, ever since I'd decided to prove myself by writing an insightful piece about the invaders, I'd pored over every bit of information available on the internet, and all I had were rumors, a number of unreliable eyewitness accounts, some grainy YouTube videos, and as many unanswered questions as before.

Two years after K-Day, and the Ks—or the Krinar, as they liked to be called—were nearly as much of a mystery as when they'd first arrived.

My computer pinged, distracting me from my thoughts. Glancing at the screen, I saw that it was an email from my editor. Richard Gable wanted to know when I'd have the article on conjoined puppy twins ready for him.

At least it wasn't another one of those "sky is falling" emails from my mom.

Sighing, I rubbed my eyes again, pushing away distracting thoughts about my insane parents. It was bad enough my career still hadn't taken off. I had no idea why all the fluff pieces landed on my desk. It had been that way ever since I'd joined the newspaper three years ago, and I was sick and tired of it. At twenty-four years of age, I had about as much experience writing about real news as a college intern.

Fuck it, I'd decided last month. If Gable didn't want to assign me real work, I'd find a story myself. And what could be more interesting or controversial than the mysterious beings who'd invaded Earth and now resided alongside humans? If I could uncover something—anything—factual about the Ks, that would go a long way toward proving that I was capable of handling bigger stories.

Putting my glasses back on, I quickly wrote an email to Gable, requesting a couple of extra days to finish the puppy article. My excuse was that I wanted to interview the veterinarian and was having trouble getting in touch with him. It was a lie, of course—I'd interviewed both the veterinarian and the owner as soon as I got the assignment—but I wanted to avoid getting another fluff piece for a few days. It would give me time to explore an interesting topic I came across in my research today: the so-called x-clubs.

"Hey there, baby girl, any plans for tonight?"

I looked up at the familiar voice and grinned at Jay, my coworker and best friend, who'd just stepped into my tiny office. "Nope," I said cheerfully. "Going to catch up on some work and then veg out on my couch."

He sighed dramatically and gave me a look of mock reproof. "Amy, Amy, Amy... What are we going to do with you? It's Friday night, and you're going to stay in?"

"I'm still recovering from last weekend," I said, my grin widening. "So don't think you can drag me out again so soon. One night of Jay-style partying a month is plenty for me."

Jay-style partying was a unique experience consisting of multiple vodka shots early in the evening, followed by several hours of club-hopping and a dinner/breakfast at a twenty-four-hour Korean diner. I wasn't lying when I said I was still recovering—the combination of vodka and Korean food had given me a hangover that was more like a bad case of food poisoning. I'd barely crawled out of bed on Monday to go to work.

"Oh, come on," he cajoled, his brown eyes resembling those of a puppy. With his thick lashes, curly brown hair, and fine features, Jay was almost too pretty for a guy. If it hadn't been for his muscular build, he would've seemed effeminate. As it was, however, he attracted women and men alike—and enjoyed both with equal gusto.

"Sorry, Jay. Another week perhaps." What I needed to concentrate on now was my article about the Ks... and the secretive clubs they supposedly patronized.

Jay let out another sigh. "All right, have it your way. What are you working on right now? The puppy piece?"

I hesitated. I hadn't told Jay about my project yet, mostly because I didn't want to appear foolish if I couldn't come up with a good story. Jay didn't get a lot of meaty assignments either, but he didn't mind it as much as I did. His goal in life was to enjoy himself, and everything else—his journalism career included—came second. He thought ambition was something that was only useful in moderation and didn't apply himself more than necessary.

"I just don't want to be a total bum—for my parents, you know," he'd explained to me once, and that statement perfectly summed up his approach to work.

I, on the other hand, wanted more than to not be a bum. It bothered me that the editor had taken one look at my strawberry-blond hair and doll-like features and had permanently slotted me into fluff-piece land. I would've thought Gable was sexist, except he'd done the same thing to Jay. Our editor didn't discriminate against women; he just made assumptions about people's capabilities based on their looks.

Deciding to finally confide in my friend, I said, "No, not the puppy piece. I've actually been researching a project of my own."

Jay's perfectly shaped eyebrows rose. "Oh?"

"Have you ever heard of x-clubs?" I cast a quick look around to make sure we wouldn't be overheard. Thankfully, the offices around mine were largely empty, with only an intern working on the other side of the floor. It was nearly four p.m. on a Friday, and most people had found an excuse to leave early this summer afternoon.

Jay's eyes widened. "X-clubs? As in, xeno-clubs?"

"Yes." My heartbeat sped up. "Have you heard of them?"

"Aren't they the places those alien-crazy people go to hook up with Ks?"

"Apparently." I grinned at him. "I just learned about them today. Do you know anyone who's been to one?"

Jay frowned, an expression that looked out of place on his

normally cheerful face. "No, not really. I mean, there's always that 'friend of a friend of a friend,' but no one I know personally."

I nodded. "Right. And you know half of Manhattan, so these clubs, if they exist, are a closely guarded secret. Can you imagine the story?" In my best broadcaster's voice, I announced dramatically, "Alien clubs in the heart of New York City? *The New York Herald* brings you the latest in K news!"

"Are you sure about this?" My friend looked doubtful. "I've heard those clubs are near K Centers. Are you saying there are some in New York City?"

"I think so. There's some chatter online about a club in Manhattan. I want to find it and see what it's all about."

"Amy... I don't know if that's such a great idea." To my surprise, Jay appeared more disturbed than excited, his uncharacteristic frown deepening. "You don't want to mess with the Ks."

"Nobody wants to mess with them—which is why we still know nothing about them." My earlier frustration returned. It bothered me that everybody was still so intimidated by the invaders. "All I want to do is write a factual article about them. Specifically, about some places they allegedly frequent. Surely that's allowed. We still have freedom of press in this country, don't we?"

"Maybe," Jay said. "Or maybe not. Personally, I think they erase whatever information they don't want to be public. Used to be, once it's on the internet, it's there forever, but not anymore."

"You think they might suppress my article somehow?" I asked worriedly, and Jay shrugged.

"I have no idea, but if I were you, I'd focus on the puppy piece and forget about the Ks."

———

It was almost eight in the evening by the time I came across it: a mention of the x-club's location on an obscure online sex forum. It was buried within someone's lengthy—and rather improbable-sounding—account of his hook-up with a group of Ks. The feeling of ecstasy the man described sounded suspiciously like a drug-induced high to me, though similar tales littered the web, giving rise to all sorts of rumors about the invaders... including that of vampirism.

I didn't buy it, but then again, thanks to my mom's obsession with wacky conspiracy theories, I had a natural distrust of rumors. I liked facts; that's why I'd gone into journalism rather than choosing to write fiction.

According to this man's account, he had gone to the club right after his dinner in the Meatpacking District. He named the restaurant where he'd had dinner, and then he wrote that the club was directly across the street from it.

And just like that, I had a lead.

Jumping to my feet, I grabbed my bag and hurried out of the office, nodding to the janitor on the way.

It looked like my Friday night was about to get a lot more exciting.

CHAPTER TWO

"*Y*ou don't have to come with me," I repeated for the fifth time, giving Jay an exasperated look. I'd made the mistake of texting him about my plans, and he'd showed up on my doorstep twenty minutes later, dressed for clubbing but doing his best to dissuade me from going.

"If you're going, I'm going," he said stubbornly. "I don't think either one of us should be doing this, but baby girl, you're crazy if you think I'll let you go there by yourself."

"You just want your name to be on the story," I joked, flipping my shoulder-length hair upside down to work in some mousse. My reddish-blond strands were naturally fine and straight, but if I put enough product in them, I could achieve some sexy waves. Sexy wasn't a look I normally tried for, but in this case, it was important. The Ks were not only humanoid in appearance, but downright gorgeous... and according to what I'd read online, they liked their human sex partners to be nearly as good-looking as they were.

I was fairly certain I didn't fit that criteria, but I was hoping that with enough makeup—and with contacts instead of glasses—I'd look pretty enough to be allowed into the club.

"Our names will *be* the story," Jay said darkly. "I can see it now: *Two Missing Journalists, Last Seen Hunting Aliens in Meatpacking District.*"

"Oh, please." I straightened and began applying mascara to my long brown lashes. "Since when are you afraid to go to a club? You do crazy stuff all the time—"

"Yes, but I do it for fun, not to prove myself to our idiot boss. And no amount of drinking or partying compares to trying to infiltrate an alien sex club. You do see the difference between a little recreational weed and this, don't you?"

"Yeah, yeah," I muttered, swiping blush onto my pale cheeks. "Like I told you, I only texted you about this so someone would know where I am. You don't have to come with me."

"Yes, I do." Jay gave me a "get real" look. "You're my only female friend. You think I'd let you get spirited away on some spaceship?"

"They live in K Centers on Earth, silly." I grinned at him in the mirror. "Why would they take me on a spaceship?"

"Who knows?" he said, plopping down on my couch. "Maybe they like cute, green-eyed blondes who wear glasses to work to seem smarter."

"Mmm, yes. I'm just their type." Laughing, I smoothed my hands down my blue, form-fitting dress. With my curvy hips, I wasn't exactly model material, though I was generally happy with my figure. It helped that my ex-boyfriends seemed to enjoy a rounder ass; one of them even claimed it was his favorite part of my body.

"You never know," Jay insisted. "Seriously, Amy, I wish you'd reconsider. Do you realize that they can do absolutely anything to you in that club, and nobody would stop them? Our laws don't apply to them. They can kill you, and nobody would blink an eye, treaty or no treaty. You understand that, right?"

"Of course I do." I was beginning to get tired of this conversation. Sometimes Jay could be like a dog with a bone. "I wasn't born yesterday. I know how dangerous the Ks can be. I've seen those videos of them ripping people to shreds, and I've read the eyewitness accounts. But we're journalists. We're supposed to investigate stories, to uncover important truths and bring them to light, even if there's risk involved. We didn't choose this profession so we could be writing about puppy twins or socialite weddings or whatever bullshit Gable assigns us. We need to be doing real reporting, Jay—and this is our chance."

Pausing, I gave him a level look. "I'm doing this—and you can either join me or go home."

CHAPTER THREE

"Okay, this is the restaurant," I said when our cab pulled up in front of a fancy-looking hotel. According to Google, the restaurant was on the rooftop of the building. "Now what?"

"Now we go to some real nightclubs and forget this insanity," Jay said, climbing out of the cab and opening the door for me. "You're already dressed up; it'll be perfect. We'll have a blast, just like last weekend."

I blew out an exasperated breath. "I'm not repeating last weekend for a good long time. I already told you that. And we're not here to party; we're here to observe."

"Right, of course." Jay sounded morose. "We're just going to quietly observe some aliens—who won't mind at all that we want to publicize their secrets."

I ignored him, trying to figure out where the club "across the street" could be. All around me, the area swarmed with beautiful people. Meatpacking was *the* clubbing district of

Manhattan. Models, celebrities, Wall Streeters, and everyone else mingled on the cobblestone streets and in edgy-looking club-lounges, trying to outdo each other with designer bags and clothing. Music blared out of several open doorways, and drunk girls stumbled around in sky-high heels, giggling and flirting with every guy in sight.

I had to admit that the Ks were smart to locate their club here; with all the glittering crowds, even a Krinar could go unnoticed.

Studying the building across the street, I saw a group of tall, leggy women approaching an unassuming brown door. There was no sign above it, nothing to indicate what kind of establishment it was. One of the women knocked, and the door swung open, letting the group in. Then the door closed immediately.

My story-sniffing instincts went on full alert. "There," I said, grabbing Jay's arm and practically towing him across the busy street.

"How do you know?" His voice held an undertone of anxiety. "Did you see one of them?"

"No." I ignored the honking of cabs as I cut in front of several cars. "But I think I saw some women who might be their types."

"Their types?"

"Krinar-like," I explained, weaving through the crowds on the sidewalk. "Tall, gorgeous… like supermodels."

"That doesn't mean anything—"

"Look, let's just try this and see," I interrupted, stopping in front of the brown door. Turning toward Jay, I said, "Ready?"

"No," he said glumly, but I was already knocking on the door.

For a few seconds, nothing happened. Then the door quietly opened, revealing a narrow hallway.

"Okay, here we go," I whispered to Jay, and stepped inside.

He followed me in without another word.

As we walked silently through the hallway, I could feel my heartbeat picking up. Was it possible I would actually get to meet them in person? The invaders I'd only seen on TV?

The hallway ended in front of another door—this one metallic gray in color. It was locked, so I knocked again, not knowing what else to do.

Then I waited.

And waited.

And waited.

"I don't think they're going to let us in," Jay whispered after a minute. "Maybe we should leave."

"Not yet," I whispered back. I didn't want to admit it, but now that we were here, I was starting to get nervous as well. The full enormity of what we were doing was beginning to dawn on me. If this was indeed the x-club I'd heard about, then on the other side of that door were beings from another planet —from an ancient civilization that had supposedly seeded life on Earth.

My heart was now throbbing in my throat.

Gathering my courage, I knocked again and called out, "Hello?"

Jay gulped audibly next to me, his face turning pale.

"Hello?" I called out again, louder this time. Nervous or not, I wasn't leaving until I gave this my best shot.

"Amy, let's go—"

The door quietly slid open.

A man stood there, his tall, broad-shouldered frame taking

up most of the doorway. In the low light, all I could see of his face were high cheekbones and a jaw that looked like it had been carved from granite. His eyes glittered darkly underneath thick eyebrows, and his clothes were pale, almost white.

Stunned, I stared at him. Could it be…? Could he be…?

The man smiled, his teeth flashing white in his bronzed face. "Welcome," he said softly, and stepped aside, motioning for us to come in.

CHAPTER FOUR

$\mathcal{M}$y heart was beating furiously in my chest as I stepped through the doorway, with Jay on my heels.

Inside, the room was large, dimly lit, and completely empty. No furniture and no people—except the man who'd opened the door for us. He stood there calmly, watching us with his dark gaze.

The door behind us slid shut.

I surreptitiously wiped my sweaty palms on the front of my dress, hoping the man didn't notice my nervous gesture.

"Hi there," Jay said, stepping up to stand next to me. To my surprise, my friend's voice was steady, and there was a flirtatious smile on his face. "We heard there's a party here. Is that true?"

The man didn't reply for a moment, causing my anxiety to spike. Then he spoke, his deep voice filled with amusement. "You could say that."

"Great." Jay beamed at him. "That's what we're here for."

I felt a wave of admiration for my friend. I'd always known Jay was great in social situations, but this was far from a typical party setting. For all his reluctance to be here, Jay had clearly brought his A-game.

"Both of you?" the man asked, still sounding amused.

"Yes." I forced a bright smile to my lips. If Jay could do this, so could I. "We're very... curious."

"Ah." The man laughed, a low, sensuous sound that sent a shiver down my spine. "Curious, indeed. Well, follow me."

He turned and began walking toward the far side of the room. My heart skipped a beat. Like the Ks I'd seen on TV, the man didn't just walk; he flowed, his every movement filled with inhuman power and grace.

There was no longer any doubt.

I'd just met my first Krinar.

Jay touched my arm, and my gaze flew up to his. On his face, I could see the same awe and excitement I was feeling. "Oh, my God," I mouthed at him, and he nodded, his eyes wide with shock.

"Come on," I mouthed again, jerking my chin in the direction of the K, and we both hurried after him, nearly running to keep up.

The K stopped in front of a wall at the far end of the room and waved his hand in a brief motion. To my shock, the wall dissolved, creating an oval, man-sized opening. I barely suppressed a gasp. I'd known that the Ks had more advanced technology, of course, but I'd never seen it in action.

This was definitely going into my article.

As I mentally composed the first paragraph of my story, the K stepped through the opening and disappeared inside. Not wanting to lose him, I stepped through the opening too, with Jay following.

We ended up in a darkened hallway. After walking a dozen feet, we found ourselves in front of another wall. The K waited for us to catch up, and then he created a second opening, through which I could see multi-colored lights and hear pulsing music.

"Here we are," the K said, his English as perfect as any American's. I had always wondered about that—how the aliens knew Earth languages so well. It was speculated that they had some kind of neural language implants, but no one knew for sure.

It might be another thing for me to investigate tonight.

"Wow, how cool," Jay exclaimed, playing his role of a ditzy party-goer to perfection. "I love the way you do that, man."

The K lifted his eyebrows but didn't dignify that statement with a response. Instead, he went in, walking with that startling, animal-like grace. Jay, who seemed to have gotten over his cautious spell, followed him without hesitation. After a momentary pause, I went after them, my heart pounding with a mixture of trepidation and excitement.

We were officially inside an x-club.

———

The first thing I noticed was the music. Outside the opening, I'd caught just the pulsing beat, but as soon as I stepped inside, I could hear the weeping undertones of some unknown instrument mixed in with the sharper vibrations. The music wasn't particularly loud, yet it enveloped me, made me feel cocooned within the melody.

Over the music, I could hear laughter and a hum of conversations. The spacious room was filled with people— although I wasn't sure "people" was the right term, given that many of the individuals present were Krinar. The aliens were easy to spot: all of them were tall, dark-haired, and had the kind of stunning beauty one usually observed in supermodels. For a while, there had been rumors that the Ks weren't biological beings at all, and I could see how those rumors had originated. Not only were the Ks incredibly strong and fast, but they were also almost too perfect to be real.

Or at least too perfect to be human.

The room itself was sparsely furnished, with circular tables standing in each corner. They appeared to be the K version of bars. I could see both humans and Ks milling around those tables, holding glasses with various drinks.

The lighting in the room was soft, several hues of warm colors blended together. It flattered the light-colored clothing worn by the Ks. The clothes themselves weren't particularly exotic—pale, floaty dresses for women and shorts with sleeveless shirts for men—but they suited the aliens, emphasizing their golden skin tone and fit, graceful bodies.

Before I could absorb any more details, the K who'd brought us in turned to look at me. There was a mocking half-smile on his full, perfectly shaped lips.

"Curiosity satisfied?" he purred, staring at me, and my breath caught in my throat as I got a good look at him for the first time.

The Krinar standing in front of me had a dark, satyr-like beauty that was both alluring and disturbing. His black hair was glossy and straight, long enough to cover his ears and fall carelessly across his forehead. With his masculine nose and

319

strong jaw, he could've posed for an army-recruitment ad—except no soldier had a mouth so wickedly sensuous or eyes that spoke of such carnal pleasures.

Beautiful, thickly lashed black-brown eyes that were even now traveling over my curves with unabashed male interest.

For the first time in my adult life, I blushed. I couldn't help it. It felt like the K was stripping me with his gaze, leaving me standing there naked and vulnerable. My body felt uncomfortably warm, and my breathing quickened, my pulse speeding up.

The K wasn't just looking at me; he was devouring me with his eyes—and my body was reacting to his stare as if to a physical touch. My nipples hardened, and liquid heat began to gather between my thighs. The air was so thick with sexual tension I could practically taste it. As the K's eyes came up to rest on my face, all I could do was stare at him, hopelessly caught by that dark, all-consuming gaze.

"And who is this, Vair?" A woman's voice broke the spell, intruding into the sensual bubble that seemed to have formed between me and the K.

Grateful for the interruption, I drew in a shuddering breath and tore my eyes away from the Krinar, turning toward the newcomer.

It was another K. The woman was smiling seductively, her attention focused on Jay—who was gaping at her with the same helpless fascination I had just experienced.

Crap. This was not good. This was not good at all. Jay wasn't exactly known for his self-control around temptation—and the female Krinar standing next to him was nothing if not tempting.

Dressed in a short white dress, she was nearly six feet tall, with bronzed, toned legs that seemed to stretch into infinity. Her body was perfectly proportioned, slim and feminine at the same time, with a waist that was almost too small for her frame. "Alien Barbie" was the thought that popped into my head.

A *very sexy* alien Barbie.

"These are a couple of strays I found in the hallway," the K—Vair—responded to the woman's question. His lush lips curved in a sardonic smile as he said, "Shira, meet curious girl and curious boy. Delicious, aren't they?"

Before I could figure out how to react to that insulting—and rather alarming—statement, Jay stepped forward and extended his hand. "I'm Jay," he said in a husky tone. "It's a pleasure to meet you... Shira, is it?"

The woman laughed, her voice low and throaty. "Yes, indeed, sweet thing. It's Shira. Why don't I show you around?" And clasping Jay's proffered hand with her long fingers, she led my friend toward one of the bars, her body moving as sinuously as a cat's.

Jay went with her without a word of protest, apparently too mesmerized to remember his earlier concerns—or the fact that he was here to help me with the story, not to be some K Barbie's sex toy for the night.

"Don't worry," Vair said, as though reading my mind. His voice was filled with dark amusement. "Shira will take care of him."

Reluctantly, I turned toward him, my heartbeat accelerating as our eyes met once again. "I'm not worried," I managed to respond. "We're here to have fun, after all."

"Of course you are, darling." Vair's teeth flashed white. "And fun you shall have. Would you like something to drink, or would you prefer to dance?"

I blinked at him. "Dance?" The music had a good tempo, but it wasn't exactly dance-floor loud. And no one around us was dancing.

Not to mention, I wasn't going within touching distance of Vair if I could help it. The club may have been a place to hook up with Ks, but that wasn't what I was here for.

"Yes, dance." His smile widened at my incredulous look. "Like this." He made a small gesture with his hand, and all of a sudden, the room darkened, the soft light taking on a reddish-purple hue. The music picked up the pace and grew in volume, the throbbing beat permeating my body. All around us, I could feel the energy of the room changing as conversations trailed off and groups coalesced into pairs, beginning to sway in unmistakably dance-like movements.

Startled, I stepped back. "What? How—"

"I own this place," Vair murmured, moving closer to me. "Did I neglect to mention that?"

I swallowed. "Um, yeah. I think you did." *Holy fuck.* This was the club owner—and he seemed to want me for some reason. This was either a big problem or a big opportunity.

"How long have you owned it?" I asked, my inner reporter deciding that it was the latter. This was an excellent chance to get some information—even if it meant I'd have to put up with an alien's sexual advances.

Which weren't nearly as unwelcome as I would've liked.

"A while." Vair stepped even closer, stopping less than a foot away from me.

I sucked in my breath, tilting my head back to gaze up at him. It was like looking up at a mountain. I'd known he was tall, of course, but I hadn't realized how freaking *large* he was. The K was well over six feet in height, with muscles that would've

322

done a bodybuilder proud. He towered over my five-foot-five frame, making me feel as tiny as a child. Even as a human man, he would've been incredibly strong, and the Krinar were known to be much, much stronger than humans.

My belly clenched with fear and arousal as I reflected on the fact that he could do anything he wanted to me. *Anything at all.* Like Jay had said, the Ks were, for all intents and purposes, above the law.

"How long is a while?" I persisted, doing my best to ignore my skyrocketing pulse. "Ever since you guys arrived?"

He laughed. "No. Only since things settled down."

Ah. We were finally getting somewhere. I guessed that "things settling down" was a euphemism for the end of the Great Panic—the dark months that had followed the Ks' arrival on Earth. By that timeline, the club had been around less than eighteen months.

Mentally jotting down that tidbit, I gave Vair an encouraging smile. "How amazing. And what prompted you to open one in New York? I thought that you don't like our cities—"

"Why wouldn't I like your cities?" He quirked his eyebrows.

"Not you personally. I'm talking about your people. The Krinar."

He looked amused. "I can't speak for the Krinar as a whole, darling, just like you can't speak for the entire population of Earth. I'm just one individual, and I happen to like this city of yours. I find it very… stimulating." His eyes slid down my body again, leaving no doubt about the kind of stimulation he had in mind.

A treacherous warmth kindled in my cheeks as my body reacted to that look again. "Right, of course," I murmured, racking my brain for a way to turn the conversation to a less sexually charged topic. "So why—"

"Why don't we dance?" Vair interrupted, and I realized that nearly everyone around us was swaying and gyrating to the music—including Jay and his Barbie on the other side of the room.

And before I could figure out how to refuse, Vair closed the remaining distance between us, pulling me into his embrace.

CHAPTER FIVE

*a*s Vair's powerful arms closed around me, drawing me against his muscular body, my breathing turned fast and irregular. I could feel his warmth, smell his clean masculine scent, and a wave of heat spread through me, making my inner muscles tighten with need.

Shocked and embarrassed by the potency of my reaction, I attempted to pull away, splaying my palms on Vair's chest to keep him at a distance. "Wait, I'm not good at dancing—"

"You don't need to be." He smiled down at me, ignoring my weak attempts to push him away. "I'll lead."

"But—"

"Just relax, darling," he murmured, beginning to move to the pulsing beat. The steely muscles in his chest flexed under my fingertips, and his thigh brushed against my legs, causing my heartbeat to spike. "Isn't this what you came for?"

I drew in a shaky breath, my mind racing as I stared up at his dark, sensual gaze. *No,* I wanted to scream. *No, it wasn't.*

"I just wanted to see how things were," I whispered instead, hoping the half-truth wouldn't get me kicked out. My voice sounded breathless, as if I'd sprinted a mile. "I'd never seen one of you in person, and I was curious, like I told you…"

"Ah, yes, that infamous curiosity of yours." His smile took on a mocking edge. "You do know what this place is for, don't you, little human?"

I moistened my lower lip, willing my frantic heartbeat to slow. "Of course. But I'd like to just observe this first time. I hope it's not a problem." If it was, I'd have to leave, as I had no intention of sleeping with anyone to get a story.

I wasn't *that* dedicated to my career.

At my response, Vair's eyes darkened, and the smile faded from his lips. "I see."

I waited for him to say something else, but he didn't. Instead, he kept his hold on me, leaving me no choice but to move with him to the music. His hands were gentle on my waist, yet every time I tried to pull away, his grip tightened, making it clear he wasn't quite ready to let me go. After a couple of attempts to discreetly extricate myself from his embrace, I gave up, not wanting to cause a scene.

Just a dance, I told myself. *It's only a dance.* I was fine with a dance if he didn't insist on anything more—and he didn't seem inclined to, for now at least. He held me at a careful distance, close enough for me to be acutely aware of his warm, muscular body, but not so close that I'd be plastered against him. A couple of times, I thought I felt something hard brush against my belly, but I couldn't be sure as the contact was brief.

Still, the idea that it could've been his erection—*that he wanted me like that*—was nearly as exciting as it was scary.

Article. Focus on the article, Amy. "So, Vair, tell me a little bit about yourself." I kept my gaze locked on his face, hoping that talking would distract me from the growing ache in my core. "What made you decide to come to Earth?"

He smiled, his eyes gleaming. "I was bored."

"Bored?" I hadn't expected that. "Why?"

"Because I ran out of ways to amuse myself on Krina. I require a lot of amusement, you see."

I wet my lips again. I had a feeling we were once more venturing into dangerous territory. "What did you do on Krina? Professionally, I mean?" Did the Ks even have jobs? I wasn't sure, but it seemed like a safer topic than whatever it was Vair did to "amuse" himself.

"Professionally?" His smile turned sardonic. "Not much. Or too much. Depends on your perspective, I guess."

"Oh." I stared at him, puzzled. "You mean you changed your career?"

"You could call it that." He laughed softly, looking down at me. "What about you, little human? What is it that you do... professionally?"

"I'm a grad student," I lied. "I'm getting my Master's in English Literature."

"Your Master's?" He lifted his eyebrows.

I felt myself flushing for some reason. "It's an advanced degree one gets after college," I explained, unsure if Vair was messing with me or if he was genuinely unfamiliar with the term. "One step above a Bachelor's degree."

"Ah, okay." His eyes glittered as he shifted his grip on me, his hands moving lower to rest on my hips. "One step above a bachelor. I get it."

He *was* messing with me. "Yes, that's right," I said smoothly, trying to ignore the fact that his large palms were essentially on my ass. "What kind of degrees do you guys have? Do you have college and such?"

He shook his head. "No, we don't. We learn throughout our lives."

"But how do you train for work?" I persisted. "Surely you're not born knowing how to do everything. And what about math, science, history? How do you learn all that?"

"You *are* a curious little creature." He regarded me with a strange half-smile. "You want to know everything about us, don't you?"

"Of course." I gave him a bright smile. "Who wouldn't?"

"Most humans who come here," he murmured, looking at me. "Nearly all of them, in fact. They're interested in only one thing—and that thing has nothing to do with our educational system."

"I guess I'm an exception then," I said, my heart jumping at the odd intensity in his gaze. Was it possible he suspected me for some reason? "I've always loved learning about other cultures—the more exotic, the better."

He laughed softly and stopped, letting me go. Before I could breathe a sigh of relief, I saw that we were standing in front of one of the bars. Somehow Vair had maneuvered us there without my noticing.

"A drink?" he asked, reaching for a glass filled with a purple liquid.

I hesitated. "What is it? Wine?"

"No, just a special type of fruit juice mixed with mild alcohol. It's safe for human consumption."

I considered that for a moment, then accepted the drink from him, trying not to react when I felt his fingers brush against my own. But I couldn't control a slight hitch in my breathing, and I saw the corners of his lips lift in a knowing smile.

Vair could sense the impact he had on me, and he was obviously enjoying it.

Seeking to hide my discomfort, I lifted the glass to my lips and took a sip. My taste buds exploded at the sweet yet zesty flavor. I could feel the bite of the alcohol, but it was too subtle to detract from the unusual taste of the juice. "What fruit is this made from?" I asked, and Vair grinned at me, sipping his own drink.

"You wouldn't recognize the name if I told you. It's a plant we brought from Krina."

"Oh, wow." I tried the drink again, attempting to memorize the complex flavor so I could describe it in my article later. It made my mouth tingle and my throat feel warm, though that could've been from the alcohol. A part of me wondered if I should've been more careful about trying an exotic drink—or drinking with Vair in general—but I could see other humans in the club holding similar glasses, and it would've been suspicious if I'd refused to so much as take a sip.

Especially given my act as a party girl interested in all things Krinar.

Casting a quick glance around the room, I spotted Jay dancing on the other side. This time, in addition to the K Barbie —Shira—there was a male Krinar there. The three of them were grinding against each other, and the expression on Jay's face left no doubt that my friend was in seventh heaven, his earlier worries gone.

"Are you involved with him?" Vair stepped in front of me, blocking my line of vision. His tone was casual, but there was an odd expression on his face. "With that pretty boy human?"

I blinked. "With Jay? No."

"Why not?"

"I don't know," I said honestly. "We've just never connected on that level, I guess."

I'd met Jay during our internship at the newspaper, and gotten to know him better when we'd both ended up working there full-time after college. For some reason, Jay—who did his best to have sex with anything that moved—had never tried to hook up with me, and as time passed, I'd found myself soliciting his advice on everything from vacation destinations to boyfriend troubles. In return, I'd lent a sympathetic ear whenever he'd needed to gripe about his overachieving family, and offered him a woman's perspective on clinging one-night stands. Over time, we'd become surprisingly close friends—and all without the attraction that typically accompanied such male-female relationships.

"That's good," Vair murmured, placing his empty glass on a nearby table. "I'm glad to hear that."

I, finishing my own drink, nearly choked on the sweet liquid. There was something almost *possessive* in the way Vair was looking at me. His stare spoke of heated male intent and something more.

Something that disturbed me greatly.

Placing my drink on the bar table, I gave him a cautious smile and took a couple of steps back. "Thank you for the drink and the dance, but I think I have to get going now." My voice sounded steady, even as my heart hammered in my throat. "It's getting late, and I have a lot of work to do tomorrow."

"I thought you were a student." Vair stepped closer, ignoring my obvious desire to maintain a distance between us. "Getting your Master's, isn't that right?"

I swallowed. "Yes, of course. I just meant that I have a lot of work to do on my thesis." *Shit.* He did suspect something—or else he simply enjoyed toying with me, making me nervous. Either way, I needed to get Jay and get out of here.

I was starting to have a bad feeling about all this.

"I don't think your friend is quite ready to leave," Vair said, glancing at Jay—who was happily sandwiched between the Barbie and the male Krinar. "In fact, I'm pretty sure he'd prefer to stay." Vair's voice was filled with amusement, but his eyes gleamed darkly as he turned his attention back to me and said softly, "You should stay as well, darling—learn some more about us."

I opened my mouth to decline his offer, but at that moment, the lights dimmed further and the music changed, becoming twice as loud. I could no longer see my friend on the other side of the room; the dark red glow barely allowed me to discern Vair's features, and he was standing right in front of me.

"Wait—" I began, unnerved by the sudden change of atmosphere, but Vair was already pulling me into his arms again and maneuvering us back into the dancing crowd.

CHAPTER SIX

*S*tartled and alarmed, I pushed at Vair, but it was like trying to move a wall. All I could do was follow his lead as he swayed in a sensuous rhythm, keeping me pressed tightly against him. The music blared all around us, the beat fast and exotic, and his heat, his scent, surrounded me, entangling me in a darkly seductive web. He was so strong my feet barely touched the floor as he held me; it was as though I were a rag doll, an inanimate object he could move about at will.

This time, he didn't bother keeping any distance between us. I could feel every inch of his powerfully muscled body, and I realized with a jolt of panic that he was already hard, his erection pressing into my belly. Gasping, I tried to push at him again, but he ignored my ineffectual struggles, holding me contained without any apparent effort. His eyes glittered in the darkness, watching me with obvious hunger, and my heart thumped harder in my chest as I realized he had no intention of letting me go this time.

Not until he got what he wanted from me.

The thought should've been terrifying, but my body's response had nothing to do with fear. My nipples pebbled within the confines of my bra, and I could feel warm moisture dampening my underwear. My body wanted him with a primitive animal instinct, and it didn't care about the fact that this was happening against my will—that my mind wanted nothing to do with Vair.

As our forced dance continued, the night took on a surreal feel for me. Everything about this place felt like a dream, from the flickering red glow emanating from some invisible light source to the stunningly beautiful man who held me trapped in his embrace. The music pulsed in tune to the throbbing in my body, and my head spun, my senses utterly overwhelmed. The drink, I thought vaguely, staring up at him, but I knew alcohol was only partially responsible for the haze clouding my brain.

It was *him*. Vair was the reason I was feeling like this. My attraction to him was more potent than anything I had ever experienced—and judging by the hard bulge pushing against my stomach, he wanted me just as much. His gaze spoke of dark pleasures and twisted sheets, of ecstasy and lust. My hands moved up to rest on his shoulders as I stopped trying to push him away, and his eyes gleamed brighter at my tacit surrender.

I wasn't sure how much time passed as we danced like that. All of my senses were focused on him—on the hard press of his body against my own and the warm scent of his skin... on the way he held me, with one hand splayed on my upper back and another arm wrapped around my waist. We moved as one, our bodies seemingly in tune, though I didn't have the freedom to move any differently. After a while, his hand slid from my upper back to my neck, his fingers delving under my hair and stroking the bare skin of my nape, and the heat inside me intensified, my breathing coming faster.

When he bent his head and claimed my lips, it was almost a relief, though it added to the tension building inside me, sharpened my need even more. There was no uncertainty in the way he took my mouth, no hesitation of any kind. Vair kissed like he danced—with dominant expertise and calm force, his lips and tongue teasing and invading at the same time. He didn't ask for my response; he demanded it, and I couldn't help but give it to him, my hands clinging to his shoulders and my lips parting to let him in.

My back met a hard surface, and I realized we'd somehow ended up near a wall. Before I could gather my wits, one of his hands slid into my hair, cupping my skull, and his other hand traveled lower, to the curve of my ass. Still kissing me, he lifted me off the ground with one hand, holding me pinned up against the wall so he could grind his erection into the soft notch between my legs. The hard pressure added to the tension in my core, and I moaned into his mouth, unable to control myself.

"Yes, that's it, darling," he whispered, his breath hot on my ear as his mouth trailed over the side of my face. His lips nibbled at my earlobe, and then he bit it lightly, sending goosebumps over that side of my body. "Such a beautiful, delicious little darling…"

I moaned again, my eyes closing and my head arching back as he began kissing the underside of my jaw, his mouth leaving a warm, moist trail on my skin. Rationally, I knew this was wrong, but rationality was not what ruled my mind at the moment. My body was on fire, and my sex pulsed with an empty ache. "Please," I whispered desperately. "Please, Vair…" I didn't know if I was asking him to stop or to continue, and ultimately it didn't matter. I was completely in his power, my body his to play with and manipulate at will.

He chuckled, the sound low and dark, and then his mouth moved lower, to the sensitive curve of my neck. I felt his teeth graze my skin, and the slight pain somehow only added to my arousal, making me writhe against him. "Yes, that's it," he muttered thickly, his hand tightening on my ass. "That's it, darling..."

Lost in my heated need, I barely registered the fact that the wall behind my back seemed to disappear. It was only when I found myself stretched out on some sort of comfortable surface that the warning bells rang in my mind.

Where was I?

Panic swept through me, temporarily clearing away the haze. Gasping, I opened my eyes and saw Vair's bronzed face looming over me. The music still played, the lights still flickered, but we were no longer among the dancing crowd. Instead, we were in some private space, with me laid out flat on a bed-like surface.

"What... where—" I began in shock, and he lowered his head, taking my mouth again. At the same time, he captured my wrists, stretching my arms up over my head before transferring both of my wrists to one of his large hands.

I was now completely helpless, restrained and utterly at his mercy.

The realization should've cooled my desire, but as soon as he started kissing me again, a melting languor spread through my body, sapping my inclination to fight. Waves of heat rolled over my skin, and my nipples throbbed, becoming acutely sensitive. Warm slickness gathered between my legs, and as

Vair ran his free hand down the front of my dress, I unconsciously arched into his touch, desperately craving more.

As my eyes drifted shut, the sense of unreality that had engulfed me earlier returned. It felt like it was all a dream, a dark fantasy playing out only in my mind. When Vair hooked his fingers into the top of my dress and ripped it down the middle, I jerked at the sudden violence of the movement, but even that was not enough to pull me out of my sensual daze. All that existed in my world was heat and pleasure, his touch and the weight of his body over me.

My bra and panties suffered the same fate as my dress, and then he slithered down my body, releasing my wrists to cup my breasts in both of his big hands. His mouth latched onto my nipples, first one, then the other, making me cry out at the sharp, pulling pressure. My hands, finally freed from his restraining hold, somehow found their way to his head, and I clutched fistfuls of his silky hair, not knowing if I was trying to push him away or bring him closer.

He moved up over me then, covering me with his huge, naked body, and I realized that his clothes were gone too, though I didn't remember seeing him remove them. I didn't have a chance to ponder the mystery, though, because everywhere our skin touched, my flesh tingled, as if electrified. Opening my eyes, I met his gaze and saw the same desperate hunger reflected on his face.

He wanted me.

He wanted me, and he was going to take me.

His knees wedged themselves between my legs, spreading them open, and my breath caught as I felt the smooth, broad head of his cock brushing against my inner thigh. Though I couldn't see it, his erection felt massive, and my muscles tensed with a purely feminine fear. Would he hurt me? What if our species weren't as sexually compatible as I'd heard?

It was too late to worry about that, however. Before I could say anything, he kissed me again, claiming my mouth with devastating expertise, and guided himself to my entrance.

His penetration was slow and careful, giving me time to adjust to his girth. Nevertheless, I felt almost painfully stretched as he worked himself in, inch by thick inch. My hands tightened in his hair, and I would've cried out, but he kept his mouth on me, distracting me with delicious, drugging kisses. It wasn't until he was all the way inside me that he let me come up for air, and all I could do at that point was stare at him, panting, my body full and overtaken, completely overwhelmed by his possession.

He stayed still for a moment, holding my gaze, and then he began to move, his strokes leisurely at first and then gradually picking up pace. After a few moments, my discomfort lessened, replaced by steadily growing heat. My eyes closed again, and my hands slid down to his sides, clutching at them as the tension inside me intensified, every thrust sending me spiraling higher and higher. I could hear my own cries and gasping moans, and my knees came up, my legs folding around his hips, bringing him deeper into me. The sensations that rocked my body were so intense I felt as if I would fly apart… and finally, I did, the orgasm rushing through me with unbelievable, shattering force. My body convulsed, my inner muscles contracting around him, and I heard him groan, his cock jerking within me as he reached his own peak.

It's over, I thought dazedly, too stunned to move. Tiny aftershocks of pleasure still rippled through my body, and I felt as if my muscles had turned to jelly. My hands were still grasping at his sides, my nails digging into his skin, and I forced myself to lower my hands to the mattress—or to whatever comfortable surface I was lying on.

Then I slowly opened my eyes and looked at Vair.

He was propped up on his elbows, staring down at me. His breathing was heavier than normal, and his somewhat softer cock was still buried deep inside my body. As our eyes locked, I saw that the heat in his gaze had cooled only slightly—and much to my shock, felt him stiffening within me once again.

"Are you all right?" he asked softly, and I nodded automatically. My body still pulsed from my release, my flesh slick and swollen around his hardening cock, and my mind was in complete turmoil.

I, who had always been so careful and cautious about bed partners, had just had sex with a man I barely knew.

No, not with a man. With a male K—an alien who had invaded my body as unceremoniously as his species had taken over my planet.

"Good," Vair whispered, a dark smile playing on his lips as he began to move inside me again. "Because I'm not done with you yet, little human…"

Mute with shock, I stared up at him, unable to believe this was happening—and that my body was responding again. Even the soreness I was beginning to feel didn't seem to matter; every stroke of his cock was reigniting the fire within me, making me burn with need once again. My hands instinctively rose, gripping his sides once more, and my bent knees tightened around his hips.

"Yes, just like that, darling," he murmured, lowering his head to nuzzle at my neck. His warm lips pressed against the sensitive skin just below my earlobe, and I shivered with pleasure, arching toward him in a silent plea for more. "So sweet, just like I knew you would be…"

As he continued thrusting with a steady rhythm, his mouth teased and nibbled at my neck, and one of his hands worked its way between our bodies, delving into my wet folds. My clit throbbed at his touch, and I tensed as I felt another orgasm approaching. Before I could go over the edge, however, I felt something slice across my neck—a stinging burn that was as painful as it was shocking.

Startled, I cried out, bucking against him as I felt his mouth latch on to the wounded spot. *Those vampirism rumors*, I thought in panic, *they had to be true…* and then I couldn't think at all as my senses exploded in white-hot ecstasy. The climax that had hovered so near swept over me but didn't stop; the sensations intensified instead of ebbing as I screamed out my release. My skin burned, my heart raced, and I was cognizant of nothing but the intense, mind-shattering pleasure. The sucking pull of his mouth at my neck, the driving force of his cock—those were the only things real in my world, and I screamed as my body convulsed over and over again in unrelenting, agonizing bliss.

I wasn't sure how long that went on. It could've been hours or days. All I knew was that the ecstasy seemed to go on forever, until my body and mind couldn't cope with it anymore, and I passed out in Vair's dark embrace.

CHAPTER SEVEN

*T*he alarm buzzed insistently, dragging me out of a sound sleep. Groaning, I rolled over and smacked the annoying clock, desperate to shut it up. The buzzing stopped, and I groaned again, pulling my covers over my head.

Ugh. I really didn't want to go to work. How could it be Monday already? It was just Friday—

Friday! Jackknifing to a sitting position, I gaped at my bedroom walls, my heart beating wildly in my chest as memories of Friday night flooded my brain. I'd gone to an x-club with Jay... I'd danced with a K... I'd had *sex* with that K, and then—

Holy fucking shit. Had Vair bitten me? My hand flew up to my neck, but all I could feel was smooth skin. In general, my body seemed to be free of any pain, though I distinctly remembered feeling sore after the first fucking last night—and if my blurry memory of the second, third, and fourth encounters was in any way accurate, I should've been in serious discomfort. Had I dreamed up the whole thing, and if not, what the hell had happened and how had I ended up in my own apartment?

Jumping out of bed, I ran to the dresser, where my small handbag was sitting. Grabbing it, I fished out my phone and stared at the screen, my breath whooshing out in relief as I saw the date.

It was Saturday. I hadn't lost the entire weekend; I must've simply forgotten to turn off my alarm before I went to bed last night.

Except I didn't remember going to bed last night, I thought with a deep inner chill. The last thing I recalled clearly was that strange, mindless ecstasy after Vair had bitten me—or whatever it was that he'd done to my neck. A cold shudder ran through me at the memory, and it was only then that I realized I was standing there naked.

Completely naked—when I usually slept in a tank top and cotton briefs.

Someone had put me to bed last night... and that someone hadn't been myself.

For the first time, it dawned on me that someone—most likely the K—had been to my apartment.

Maybe was still *in* my apartment.

I nearly hyperventilated at the thought.

"Hello?" I called out, my voice shaking. Frantically opening the dresser, I grabbed the nearest T-shirt and a pair of yoga pants and pulled them on. "Hello? Anyone there?"

Silence was my only response.

Picking up the phone, I opened the bedroom door and crept out into my tiny living room, trying to convince myself not to panic. Maybe it all *had* been a dream, and I'd just had too much to drink with Jay again. Maybe I'd fallen into bed naked and simply didn't remember it. Weird things happened when Jay-style partying was involved.

Jay! My pulse spiked again as I remembered that he had been there with me—and that when I'd seen him last, he'd been gearing up for a close encounter with not one but two Krinar. What happened to him? Where was he now?

To my tremendous relief, the living room was empty—as were the kitchen and the bathroom. My apartment was tiny, just a converted studio, so there weren't many places a K could hide. I was alone and safe for now.

Still shaking from the surge of adrenaline, I sat down at the kitchen table and dialed Jay's number. He didn't pick up right away, and just when I thought I would go out of my mind with panic, I heard his sleep-roughened voice answer, "Hello?"

"Jay!" I almost broke into tears. "Jay, are you okay?"

"What? Oh… Amy?" He sounded disoriented. "What—what's going on?"

"Jay, what happened last night?"

"Last night?" I could practically hear the wheels starting to turn in his sleep-fogged brain. "Last night… Oh shit, baby girl, we went to the club! The fucking x-club! Are you okay? You disappeared with that K and then—"

"What happened to *you*?" I interrupted, not wanting to talk about my experience quite yet. "Did you sleep with those two Ks?"

Jay laughed with delight. "Sleep with them? Baby girl, we did everything *but* sleep, and it was the most intense shit I'd ever experienced—like Ecstasy combined with heroin and amplified tenfold. I don't even know how I ended up home. We must've been partying all night 'cause I don't remember a thing right now."

"Right, uh-huh." I rubbed the bridge of my nose, the adrenaline draining out of me. It sounded like Jay had gone through the same experience that I had. Whatever had happened to us last night was far outside the realm of normal sex, corroborating all those stories I'd read online.

I was certain now that the night had been real—which left the mystery of how I'd ended up back home after passing out at the club.

Or at least I assumed I'd passed out at the club, as my last memories were of non-stop sex and impossibly intense pleasure.

As Jay continued to talk, telling me all about how the K Barbie had gone down on him while she was being fucked by the male Krinar, I tried to work through the possibilities. The only thing that made any sense was that Vair had brought me home... which meant he knew who I was and where I lived.

He must've found my driver's license in my purse, I decided after a moment of uneasy contemplation. If he knew more than that about me—if he knew I was a journalist—I doubted he would've let me go so easily.

I got lucky, and so did Jay.

When he finished describing his sexcapade, I told him about what had happened to me, leaving out the forceful nature of Vair's seduction and my own helpless reaction to it. The fact that I'd ended up having sex against my better judgment—and that it had been the hottest sex of my life—was not something I wanted to analyze too closely.

"Wow, you go, baby girl," Jay said admiringly when I was done telling him the night's events in broad strokes. "You really let loose this time. I'm proud of you. So what's next? Are you going to go back to the club?"

"No," I said. One night of out-of-this-world sex was plenty for me. "Next, I write the story."

It was time for my real career to begin.

Part Two

VAIR

CHAPTER EIGHT

The memory of his hands gripping and positioning my hips encroached upon my mind as my fingertips clacked noisily against the keyboard. The words on the screen in front of me blurred, and I yet again lost focus on the article I was writing as I recalled the way he'd slowly rocked his impossible girth into me from behind, how his tongue had licked between my shoulder blades and his teeth had teased my earlobe, his fingers circling maddeningly, teasing my drenched clit until I'd—

Fuck.

It had been happening all day. One minute, I would be on my virtual soapbox espousing the benefits of eating bone broth and bacon, citing Paleo diet research and case studies, and the next, I'd be in a near frenzy—skin flushed, thighs rhythmically clenching beneath my desk as I remembered the inconceivably rapturous sensation of having him inside me.

God, it had been like nothing I'd ever felt before.

Or would again.

Because I'd fucked an alien.

It was a hard fact that played on a loop inside my head throughout the day.

Every day.

All day.

In the morning as I ate my breakfast, while I sat in meetings at work, when I rode the subway, as I was washing my hair in the shower—*particularly while in the shower.* Even in sleep I would dream about him.

It had been a month. Four weeks, two days, and thirteen hours since I'd ventured into an alien sex club in the Meatpacking District of New York City.

The gravity of what I'd done that night confounded me daily still, but it was the magnitude of the situation I had since trapped myself in that was becoming more suffocating by the hour.

I couldn't forget about it for a moment, and the knowledge that my present predicament was entirely my fault didn't help.

Because the truth was, I could've walked away. Twice. Before I'd slept with the gorgeous x-club owner, and then afterward.

I could've locked that absolutely mind-blowing experience away, never letting a soul other than my coworker and partner in alien-sex-clubbing, Jay, know about anything that had happened.

But instead, I did what any ambitious twenty-four-year-old with a mountain of student loan debt would've done.

I'd penned an alien sex tell-all article for *The New York Herald.*

Only... I hadn't exactly told *all*. I'd done what good journalists are supposed to do. I'd removed myself personally from all events revealed in my alien sexposé and reported that it was based off of my interviews with *other* undisclosed humans.

And I'd gotten away with it. *So far.* Which was what confused and concerned me most, feeding my paranoia and driving my fear of imminent alien retaliation to new heights with each passing day.

My computer pinged, and a small email alert popped up in the lower right-hand corner of my left screen. Noting the sender, I clicked the "x" button at the corner of the pop-up to dismiss it. I had a deadline to meet and couldn't afford to be by ridiculous emails from my mom tonight—any more distracted than I already was, that is.

Another ping sounded, followed by another pop-up alert. I sighed and waited it out as eight more pings and pop-ups appeared. She was on a roll for a Friday night. After the eleventh pop-up, I went to my browser and logged out of my personal Outlook account.

My mother had been a "sky is falling" Chicken Little type long before the Krinar had actually fallen from the sky two years ago to take control of Earth. Her initial "told you so" victory dance amid the early invasion panic had been quickly followed by daily email forwards from random online "news" sources predicting all of the horrible ways humans were bound to be mistreated and ultimately killed by the Ks.

My mother's propensity for readily embracing irrational and absurd media sources *might* have played a small role in influencing my desire to seek and report the facts above all else in my career as a journalist.

Unfortunately, facts were often slanted by other factors. And truth came in shades beyond black and white.

As "accurate" as my alien sexposé had been, it hadn't exactly been impartial.

Not only had my acclaimed article omitted all culpability on my part as a willing participant in the best sexual experience of my life, but it had also painted the Ks in a rather negative light, showcasing them as sexual predators whose blood-drawing had an Ecstasy-like, aphrodisiac effect upon humans.

In quieter moments, I could admit that perhaps that specific slant was driven by my own ego's need to rationalize my embarrassing response to Vair that night.

Throughout my college years, I'd always been so careful, so cautious about the few men I'd dated. I'd become friends with all of my boyfriends first, getting to know them well before things had become sexual. I'd never even come close to having a one-night stand.

And then, a month ago, the very first time I'd let loose and allowed passion to dictate my actions, I'd gone and had a one-night stand with a deadly, vampiric extraterrestrial who'd sucked my blood and fucked me until I'd literally collapsed unconscious from sexual exhaustion.

My phone buzzed to life on my desk, startling me. My mother's number lit up the screen.

Oh, what the hell. Not like I was getting work done anyway. Talking to my mom would be the fastest, surest way to get my errant mind off sex.

I hit the speaker button. "Hey, Ma."

"Did you read my email?"

"You mean the *dozen* emails you sent me ten seconds ago?"

"Yeah." She said this with zero hesitation or apology.

I bit the smile forming on my lips and shook my head at the ceiling. "Nope. Still at work. Got an article deadline."

There was a sharp intake of breath from the other end of the line, followed by a clattering noise and then muffled shouting for my dad to come quickly.

"You're not still working there, are you?" She sounded out of breath now. "I thought you decided last week you were going to quit *The Herald* and go into hiding?"

"No. *You* decided I should quit and go into hiding." I lowered the speaker volume. I was pretty sure I was the only one still working on my side of the floor, but just in case.

"You're not writing another E.T. article, I hope?"

"Yep. That's sort of my thing now, Ma. I get all the Krinar stories."

Another sharp inhale, followed by a wheezing sound. "Have more victimized xenophiles come forward with their sex-clubbing stories?"

I winced. Xenophiles—or xenos for short—was the derogatory term for humans who lusted after Ks and sought out sexual relations with them. "K addicts" was another, more neutral name for them. It was that disturbing phenomenon that had spawned the xeno clubs—a.k.a. x-clubs—that I'd reported on in my article.

"No." I cleared my throat. "This one's about their forced vegan lifestyle and how it's not only robbing humans of our free will but potentially damaging our health and the health of future generations, simply for the sake of satisfying *their* preferences."

Two years ago, when the Krinar species had invaded and assumed control of Earth, they'd inserted themselves into all aspects of our world—down to the foods readily available for consumption. They had immediately shut down our industrial farming industry and forced meat and dairy producers to grow fruits and vegetables instead. Nowadays, any meat or dairy products to be found were sold at an outrageous premium.

The Ks claimed to have done this for our own benefit, to prevent us from further destroying our already weakened, sickly bodies and our even sicklier planet with our overproduction and overconsumption of meat and dairy.

And this had pretty well set the tone for how we could expect to be viewed by our new overlords—as a lower life form not intelligent enough to make even the most basic daily choices about the foods we put into our bodies.

"But you've been a vegan for eight years." My dad's voice sounded confused.

"Oh, hey, Dad. Yeah, that's true. But that's not the point. The point is, it's our right to—"

"The point is, why should *we* have to give up pork fat when they're eating humans at dance clubs," my mother cut in with exasperation.

Oh, Jesus. "Listen, I've got to get back to work. I'll call you guys on Sunday, all right?"

"Amy." My dad's voice was calm but weighted with concern. "We think you need to stop antagonizing the Ks with these articles. From what little we know of them, they're a violent, dangerous species... capable of anything. It isn't wise to risk—"

"You have to stop!" My mother's frantic pitch was approaching E-flat range. "Your dad and I are worried sick that those E.T.s are going to come to kill you and eat your brain any minute now."

I knew I shouldn't have picked up her call. "It's blood they like, Ma. Not brains."

"They eat brains too," she insisted. "I sent you a YouTube interview on it."

Here we go. "Okay, remember when we discussed YouTube not being the most reliable—"

"The YouTube video of those Saudi resistors being massacred by Ks was confirmed to be legit," my dad reminded me. "No one thought that footage could possibly be real at first either."

He had a point, although I wouldn't concede to it just now. "That was different, Dad."

The memory of that early video footage of the Ks never failed to induce an internal shudder. During the first few weeks of the Krinar invasion, guerrilla fighters in the Middle East had ambushed a small group of unarmed Ks. The gruesome event that ensued had been captured via iPhone, showing the whole world exactly what kind of genetically advanced—and positively ruthless—species had taken over planet Earth. Thirty-some Saudis armed with grenades and automatic assault weapons had been no match for six unarmed Ks capable of moving at inhuman speed and strong enough to literally tear their human attackers apart with bare hands—and throw them as far as sixty feet with minimal effort.

"Sources say they're constructing human labor camps in Costa Rica," my dad continued.

I sighed and let my eyes roll. *"Sources"* indeed.

"They're developing torture and execution facilities for miscreant humans," my mother interjected.

This was too much. I needed to get back to work.

"Your mother read that they publicly behead criminals on their home planet of Krina."

"And then they have a feast where they drink their blood and eat their brains and other organs," she chimed in.

Ugh. My empty stomach churned in revolt. "Guys, I really have to go now; my boss just emailed me for an update."

"All right, honey, but your mother and I are very worried. We respect what you're trying to do for the good of the public, but we think it'd be better if you went into hiding and wrote for one of the underground news sources we subscribe to."

Of course they did. "Thanks, Dad. But you don't have to worry about me. Everything's fine. Believe me, if the Ks had been upset over my x-club story, they would've pulled it from circulation as soon as it was released. They never would've let it get so much press and media attention." At least I hoped so. *I had been banking on that theory.* "It's not like *The New York Herald* is beyond their reach or influence. It's been pretty well confirmed that Ks monitor and control the world media at this point."

"You say that now, but what happens when they come after you and cart you off to a K torture camp"—my mom's voice cracked on an exaggerated, hysterical sob—"and we're left wondering how many aliens ate our little girl's brains for supper?"

With a poorly muffled wail of distress, she sobbed out a melodramatic goodbye and audibly stomped off.

That was my mother. If there was one thing she could always be counted on for, it was her penchant for high doomsday drama and her knack for saying the most unhelpful, inappropriate, and terrifying things at inopportune moments.

A long, awkward pause on the line followed. Twenty-seven years of marriage and my dad had never quite learned how to react to my mom's special brand of crazy. It was an odd thing between the two of them that had grated on me immensely growing up.

Eventually, he said, "I should probably let you go now."

"'Kay, Dad. Call you on Sunday."

"Talk to you then. Be careful, Amy."

CHAPTER NINE

I disconnected the call and resumed typing, pushing my parents' dysfunctional relationship and my mom's crazy K fears far from my mind as I quoted research from the Weston A. Price Foundation extolling the merits of lard, full-fat butter, and cod liver oil consumption.

The Krinar were a highly intelligent, ancient species that clearly held a genetic advantage over humans, given what we had witnessed as far as their physical capabilities, not to mention what we had been told of their extended life spans. They'd taken over Earth in a matter of weeks, wielding technology more impressive than anything our science fiction novels had ever contemplated. And although we were similar in appearance to them—albeit far less beautiful and perfect-looking—by the Krinar's own admission, our human DNA was actually more similar to that of a gorilla than that of a Krinar.

Therefore, who the hell were they to decide what *we* should eat?

I chose to ignore the fact that gorillas were herbivores—because it was irrelevant to my point. *Sort of.*

And besides, if a vegan diet was so fulfilling to them as a species, why did they crave our blood so much? Maybe it was *they* who were missing something from this perfect vegan diet of theirs that they'd now subjected our entire planet to. And what if the same missing link in their diet led to humans eventually craving blood as well?

Fuck. I removed my glasses and rubbed my eyes. I was going off the rails and reasoning like my mother now.

My mind drifted to thoughts of Vair—specifically, the way he'd bitten me that night at the club—and I wondered what my blood had tasted like to him. Just thinking about the way his bite had *felt* always got me uncomfortably aroused. It was a memory I'd pleasured myself to on more than one occasion—more often than I cared to contemplate.

What if I was becoming a xeno?

The notion terrified me—and turned me on.

I couldn't stop thinking about him.

Too often I'd lie awake at night, wondering what he was doing at that very moment. I'd even go so far as to run through alternate scenarios in my head about how things might play out if I ever got the courage to get out of bed, get dressed, and go back to his club.

Proof-positive I was going insane.

In some scenarios, I imagined him being terribly angry with me for the article I'd written about his club—possibly reacting with violence. That potential alone was enough to keep me from ever venturing back. Other times, I envisioned him mocking me for coming back, laughing in my face and tossing me out of the club.

Yet somehow I felt it was more likely he'd forgotten about me altogether by now—too busy sucking and fucking New York City's finest supermodels, no doubt.

Ironically, rather than ruin business for Vair, the article I'd written had made his x-club the most sought-after secret sex club in Manhattan. Instead of being warned away, humans were more curious than ever to explore the sexual proclivities of the Ks, resulting in more eager xenos than before.

I shook my head. I'd inadvertently done Vair a favor with my article. He had no reason to be mad.

But beyond that, I doubted he'd be too terribly concerned with me one way or another, based on the fact that I *had* heard from Vair—just once—right after my story was printed.

An enormous exotic fruit basket had been delivered to me at *The Herald.* And by exotic, I mean the basket was filled with fruits that couldn't have been grown anywhere on Earth. I'd been terrified to even touch it, but Jay had dug right in, rummaging through and examining each unusual, delicious-looking piece of edible perfection.

There'd been a note with the basket. And the few words written in bold, black scrawl on the rectangular-shaped, cream-colored cardstock had nearly sent me into cardiac arrest.

DELICIOUS THESIS, DARLING. CHEERS TO EARNING YOUR MASTER'S!

I'd reread those words only a few thousand times, making myself—as well as Jay—a nervous wreck by analyzing every possible overt and hidden message contained therein, only to resign myself to the fact that Vair was once again messing with me, teasing me and fucking with my head like the inferior human specimen that he clearly took me for.

No wonder he'd seemed so amused when I'd lied about being a grad student earning my Master's.

I decided his note was Vair-speak equivalent for: *"Congratulations. I was on to you all along from the moment you entered my club, and I played you right back."*

Because he *had* played me.

I'd succumbed all too easily to his undeniable sexual thrall.

And he was letting me know that he didn't give a fuck about my little article, while making it painfully clear that he still held all the power—and that he could use it to crush me if he chose to.

He knew where I lived. Where I worked. He knew the truth of what had happened between us. He was above the law—as were all Ks—and far higher up on the food chain than I was.

But he let the article run and my white lie stand because he simply didn't care one way or another.

That conclusion alone should've been a relief to me.

But it wasn't. For some reason, it infuriated me to my very core.

Against Jay's protests, I'd pitched that giant, fancy exotic fruit basket straight down the incinerator chute along with Vair's mocking card that same evening.

And I'd committed myself to writing any and every anti-K story that *The Herald* would print going forward.

———

My fingers were flying over the keyboard when both of the computer screens in front of me flickered, then went dark.

My palm connected with the wood laminate desktop as I

silently cursed *The Herald's* quest to cut costs and their ever-cheapening technology systems.

I glanced at my watch. It was after seven p.m.

Great. No one in IT would be around.

Leaning forward, I reached behind the monitors to fiddle with the connection, hoping it was just a loose cable, when my screens abruptly came back on, along with my speakers—at max volume.

I froze, my heart seizing in my chest at the sights and sounds that assaulted me.

The right monitor displayed footage of me from my night at the x-club—my writhing body held high in Vair's arms, dress hiked up to my waist, back pressed against the wall. My lust-dazed face was plainly visible, my plaintive cry of "Please, Vair" distinctly audible over the pulsing background beat of club music as the gorgeous alien ground himself rhythmically between my spread thighs.

The incriminating scenes playing out on the left monitor were far worse, the sounds more embarrassing still. I stopped breathing as a high-def montage of our tangled, glistening naked bodies copulating in every manner and position imaginable streamed across my screen.

I was *so* fucked.

CHAPTER TEN

"*C*ab!" I yelled at the security guys in the lobby downstairs over the file boxes balanced precariously in my arms. "Please," I appended when out of the corner of my eye, I saw one of the guards literally jump and scramble for the phone next to him at the front desk.

In my effort to keep my voice from cracking, I'd managed to sound like a royal bitch.

The other guard rushed forward to help me with my boxes, and I lost my composure again, barking, "I got it!"

I was too close to an epic meltdown for any sort of interaction, and the file boxes packed to the gills with my personal belongings were a physical barrier I wasn't willing to part with at the moment. They were heavy and awkward, but I needed some sort of energy outlet for the adrenaline coursing through me.

"I'll wait outside," I announced, cutting the first security guard off as he started to say that a cab was on its way.

Utilizing what my ex-boyfriend had often said was my strongest asset, I hip-checked the swinging glass exit door wide —with more force than was probably necessary—before guard number two had a chance to get it for me.

"Thanks," I muttered in a belated effort at politeness as I plowed through, rear first.

The scents of early fall in New York City filled my lungs as I backed my stack of haphazardly packed belongings out onto the sidewalk on wobbly limbs.

"Hey! Watch where you're going!" a woman snapped at me when I spun around without looking and nearly rammed into her with my awkward burden.

"Sorry."

Jesus, I needed to pull it together. I had to figure out what to do next, where I could go for help.

Could anyone even help me?

How bad was my situation? How many news stations and social media outlets had already received that footage?

Would my mother see it?

My dad?

My eyes burned with unshed tears, and my stomach lurched. *Great.* I was about to vomit all over Broadway.

Where was that cab?

I forced in a calming breath as a cool evening breeze whipped my hair. Peering around the side of my boxes as best I could to avoid colliding with another pedestrian, I inched closer to the curb. Twilight was waning, and while the street was active, I was grateful that there were far more popular spots than Lower Manhattan's Financial District for the masses to seek early entertainment on a Friday night.

Tires rolled to a stop a few feet from the curb in front of me, and I craned my neck enough to make out a black stretch limo —not the cab I'd been hoping for. I started to amble on farther down the sidewalk to where a cabbie would be better able to spot me, when I heard the sound of car doors opening.

Sure, rapid footsteps fell smoothly upon the concrete in my direction.

Too smoothly.

Some innate self-preservation instinct made my pulse quicken. I had a mad compulsion to drop my boxes and flee, but I was wearing my practical two-inch heels paired with a very impractical pencil skirt. It was doubtful I'd be able to outrun a K.

A second later, it was too late entirely as I sensed *his* heat at my back—running along the entire length of my body, blocking out any trace of the evening breeze. I froze as the familiar scent of inhuman male perfection assaulted my olfaction, bringing with it the memory of the most carnally gratifying night of my life.

Oh, fuck.

My stomach clenched. My nipples hardened. The rest of my body seemed to have a vivid memory of that night as well, judging by its immediate—and mortifying—Pavlovian response to Vair's mere presence. My inner muscles fluttered in anticipation, slick heat rushing to lubricate my sex.

I reminded my stupid sex that this was the same alien who had just destroyed my career and my life. He was the enemy who had invaded my planet. *An enemy who was possibly about to kill me as well.*

Or worse—turn me over to Krinar authorities.

But when warm, long fingers encircled my right bicep, another jolt of sexual electricity shot through me. And when his other hand latched onto my left hip, it felt oddly reassuring, momentarily calming and centering me as a second set of unseen hands pulled the file boxes from my grasp.

"This way, darling," Vair's deep voice instructed from above my head as he bodily steered me in the direction of the stretch limo.

To the person who had confiscated my file boxes, Vair spoke rapidly in a foreign, guttural-sounding language that I couldn't place. Over my shoulder, I glimpsed a tall, beautiful male K in a black suit nodding in assent as he effortlessly hauled my boxes back in the direction of the building where I worked.

Had worked. Wait…

"That's my stuff," I protested a little too late. "Where's he going? Why's he taking my stuff?"

"Get in the car, Amy." The command was accompanied by gentle pressure at my crown as Vair physically maneuvered me into the limousine before I had sense enough to put up a fight.

He followed closely behind, folding his huge form gracefully into the luxuriously upholstered passenger cab and taking the seat across from me. The car began moving while I remained stock still—frozen in place amid a mixture of heart-pounding shock, fear, and anticipation.

The moment Vair was settled and his full attention was fixed upon me where we sat face to face, I blushed. And not just a little flush that could pass for nervousness or be attributed to recent exertion from the heavy boxes I'd carried, either. It was the kind that made my skin feel sun-blistered and my head dizzy. The kind that screamed "guilty" in a court of law.

The sort of blush that broadcast exactly how well I remembered the sensation of him plunging deep inside me and the sound of his masculine groans and grunts as he spent himself in me... in my mouth... across my back, my stomach, my...

I broke eye contact—for fear of passing out—and let my eyes roam about as if investigating my surroundings. But I barely took in any of it. Every cell and fiber of my being was too acutely aware of the god-like alien sitting across from me.

Watching me.

God, he was so much better-looking than my masturbatory sessions had given him credit for. So much bigger. More predatory.

Way more dangerous.

There was too much room in his enormous limo for just the two of us. Yet not nearly enough space for me to avoid the sight, the scent, the very vibration of his essence in the air surrounding me.

He could be taking me anywhere. Planning to do any number of terrible things to me.

Pull it together, Amy.

"You look hot." His deep voice was light and playful, but it startled me just the same. "Shall I adjust the temperature?"

My eyes snapped back to him and found that he was staring down at his palm—tracing something there with the forefinger of his other hand and not looking at me at all. He was wearing casual slacks, a simple white T-shirt that accentuated his bronzed skin tone, and loafers, and he managed to look fresh and chic—more sophisticated than I'd looked first thing this morning in my pencil skirt and silk blouse... *before* I was rumpled and disheveled from my day.

"What are you going to do to me?" My voice betrayed me, emerging too high-pitched and with a slight quiver. Pitiable-sounding. *Damn it.*

He seemed taken aback by my question at first—or perhaps by my tone—as he returned his attention to me, but then a slow, sensuous smile spread across his wide mouth and full lips. "What indeed?" His forefinger brushed absently across those gorgeous lips, and I had to remind myself to focus on his mocking tone—and on finding a way to live through this.

"What would you do if you were in my shoes?" He sighed, and his face was suddenly devoid of humor. "I'm afraid several very powerful Krinar Council members were rather displeased with your article."

There it was. My very worst fear realized. I was a dead woman.

And it was bullshit. My mother could *not* be right about this.

"What?" I feigned shock. "What do you mean?" I blustered, a surge of adrenaline fueling me. "I was simply presenting factual information about your club... about the sexual habits of your race. I mean... you can't be serious? You're not serious, are you?" I latched onto the offensive and ran with it. "My God, your club is now the most sought-after best-kept secret in town. I've got New York's hottest supermodels calling me, begging for your address!"

I'd failed to mask the jealousy in my voice at that last part, so I quickly rambled on. "And anyway, I was under the impression that your powerful Council members controlled our media. I thought they'd simply squash the article—erase it from online circulation entirely—if they didn't like what I'd written."

Vair's features remained impassive. Uncompromising.

Fuck.

Fear and panic had my mouth working overtime. "They *let* it run," I emphasized, as if that alone signified their tacit endorsement of it. "Well, I'm sorry; I had no idea anyone would be offended." I threw in a huff of confusion. "If they disapproved, why didn't they just pull it? It can't be my fault they failed to pull it? I mean, they could've just called *The Herald* and asked them to pu—"

I stopped at the sound of Vair's slow clapping and the look of mocking amusement in his dark eyes.

"Thank you for that lovely, very insincere apology, Ms. Myers. A pity you didn't take up acting while you were at NYU earning your degree in journalism."

Shit. I really was in trouble.

He held my gaze in silence, and the air around me seemed to grow colder with each passing second.

"So… what then?" I raised one haughty, exasperated brow and emitted a dry chuckle that came out sounding far too nervous to support my bluff. "You going to cart me off to K jail? Or is capital punishment customary for alien-sexing-n-telling?" *Oh my God, shut up!*

"Mmm… a bit of torture, a decade in a Krinar hard labor camp, and then public beheading. *Customarily.*"

This couldn't be happening. My mother's wacky sources could not be accurate. There was no way. He was messing with me. I was sure of it.

Almost.

I released a nervous laugh. His expression remained stoic.

"Y-you're not serious…"

He frowned and ran a hand through his tousled hair. Now he looked pissed. "I convinced them it would be bad PR to torture and kill you."

"Oh?" My monosyllabic response somehow managed to

affect effortless nonchalance—while my heart began to pump overtime.

Was he fucking with me or was he serious? I'd lost the ability to gauge.

"The Council agreed that I would be allowed to... handle the situation with you. Directly." His eyes had darkened at "handle," sending an involuntary shiver through me.

"W-what does that mean?" That he personally got to torture and kill me? *Somewhere away from prying human eyes?* Was that where we were headed now?

My face must've projected my train of thought because he rolled his eyes in a surprisingly human-like manner, then muttered something in that guttural foreign language he'd used before. Probably Krinar cuss words, judging from the angry set of his jaw and the way his big hands had balled into fists against the seat on either side of him.

But when he addressed me again, his voice was gentle. Patient. "We don't practice capital punishment on Krina. Our methods for reforming those who break our laws are very different from what you're accustomed to in human society. No Krinar will harm you. Least of all me."

His eyes on me were thoughtful as he said it. Forthright. They didn't look like they wanted to hurt me at all. Those bottomless eyes looked like they wanted something else entirely. And in my haze of relief, I suddenly wanted to drown in them—to cast years of sanity and sound judgment aside and believe anything they said.

I blinked and looked away, breaking the connection as I recalled the grainy YouTube footage of those Saudis being torn apart.

"Ks *have* killed humans," I pointed out. *Because facts were facts*

—no matter what voodoo his eyes made me feel. "It's been documented. Graphically," I added with a grimace of disgust.

"Yes, it's true," he acknowledged. "We have killed humans when necessary. Mostly in self-defense as a last resort."

It was my turn to roll my eyes. But I chose not to debate it further, my mind shifting to my initial cause for panic this evening.

The video footage.

If they didn't intend to harm me physically in retaliation for my article, then there was another reason for this meeting. And for that footage.

My pulse raced as it hit me. *They were blackmailing me?*

Horror and excitement gripped me at once. If I was right and they intended to blackmail me with it, then there was a chance the video hadn't been released to the masses yet. And I would do anything to prevent its release. Even if it meant...

Fine. It was inevitable.

"You want me to retract what I wrote in my article," I stated, my voice flat. My career as a journalist would be over, but at least I'd walk away with some shred of dignity if I could keep that sex tape out of circulation.

He frowned. "Of course not. Your exposé was brilliant. And"—his tongue ran casually across his full bottom lip as his gaze swept over me—"enlightening."

The heat that pooled anew in my belly was as untimely as it was unwelcome.

I gave myself a mental shake. "You don't want me to retract what I said?" A sense of dread crept up my spine at the realization that I might not have any bargaining chip at all.

"No." His lips parted in a lazy smile as his dark eyes held mine.

Then his gaze fell to my breasts.

My palms were slick with sweat where they gripped the leather seat beneath me. I swallowed. Breathed. "Why the video footage then?"

He leaned forward, his expression deathly serious as reproving eyes returned to mine. "You didn't call, Amy."

It was as if all the air had suddenly been sucked out of the limo.

"You never came back to my club."

I'd soaked through my panties by "Amy"—in spite of the confusion and mild terror that his abruptly accusatory tone evoked.

"I didn't know you wanted me to." The truth tumbled out defensively, faster than I could process what he'd said as conflicting emotions flared to life within me. "I mean—I didn't mean for anything to happen... with you... that night at the club."

What the hell was I saying?

What was he saying?

A bead of sweat trickled down between my shoulder blades, causing me to shiver in my silk blouse. It was freezing in the limo now.

"I see. You were a victim then?" His tone was earnest, but his eyes appeared amused. Smug.

I felt my anger rising. There was no easy answer to his question. I kept my knees glued together and my sweaty palms planted on the seat in an effort to subvert my shaking.

"I never meant for anything to happen between us that night," I reiterated, my words clear and firm despite the dryness now choking my throat.

He sighed. "Humans complicate the most basic emotions by

experiencing them through extraneous social filters." His eyes projected a strange sort of pity—and a measure of quiet disappointment that was somehow unsettling.

I needed water. *I needed out of Vair's limo.*

I needed answers more.

"Is it on the internet already?" I blurted, my heart pounding in my ears.

"Is what on the internet, love?"

"You know what!"

"Answer my question, and I'll answer yours," he countered.

"I'm not a victim."

"Good." He gave a curt nod and proceeded to retrieve a glass bottle of clear liquid from a refrigerated side compartment. "I don't play well with victims."

He uncapped the bottle and held it out to me.

"I'm not drinking that."

"It's water, Amy."

"And what else?"

He smirked and shook his head, murmuring, "Whatever else you want, darling." He proceeded to give me a lazy, blatant once-over reminiscent of the flirtatious, teasing manner he'd taken with me during our initial meeting at his club.

His all-consuming gaze held the promise of so much more than water. And it had the same spellbinding effect as before, drawing me in and making me want things I rationally shouldn't, leaving me feeling confused, vulnerable, and exposed.

He shifted his big body forward to the edge of his seat, grazing my bare knee with the cold bottle in the process, and I jerked back reflexively.

With a chuckle, he tipped the bottle up to his own mouth,

and I found myself riveted by the sight of his lips pressed against the bottle's opening, of his throat muscles working as he gulped down half the contents of the glass container.

When he'd drunk his fill, he offered it to me again with a raised brow, and I didn't hesitate to wrench it from his grasp. I rationalized it was because I was parched, and not because I was answering his unspoken challenge—or because I had some mad impulse to put my mouth where his had been.

It was a safe bet it wasn't poisoned. A powerful alien didn't need poisoned water to get whatever it was he wanted from me. I just needed to figure out what that something was, if it wasn't the retraction of my x-club story that he was after.

Brazenly wrapping my lips around the bottle's opening, I tipped my head back and chugged the remains of the container in one noisy, unladylike pull. *Because fuck the Ks with their constant superiority bullshit and their ongoing intimidation of my race.*

My thirst quenched and a sliver of my dignity returning, I lowered the bottle along with my chin, releasing an uncouth, open-mouthed sigh of satisfaction in the process. Only to have my stomach fall straight through the floor at the look on Vair's face.

It was the look of a jungle cat ready to pounce. The face of a starving man intent on his favorite meal.

I cleared my throat. Gripping the empty glass bottle with both hands, I held it primly in front of me—suspended above my lap, as if it might shield me from him.

"The internet," I prompted. "I answered your question. Now answer mine."

"No."

My stomach twisted at his brusque reply. "No? You won't answer?"

"No, it's not on the internet," he clarified, his face suddenly a stone mask, his tone formal. Irritated. "Yet."

I swallowed. "I see. So"—I rolled and squeezed the glass bottle between clammy fingers—"is it on its way to being released to the media then?"

"No."

My immediate sense of relief was fleeting as I summoned the courage to push forward and ask, "So what do you want from me? In exchange for keeping it off the internet?"

He laughed. It was a throaty, dark chuckle that sent goosebumps flowering over my skin. He waved his hand, and a three-dimensional video image appeared out of thin air directly between us. A perfectly detailed, lifelike hologram proceeded to play, as if from an unseen projector.

A hologram of me.

"Let's discuss this video first, shall we?"

It was footage of me in my office from not more than thirty minutes ago. Multiple camera angles had captured every embarrassing moment, from my stunned reaction to the sex montage when it had first appeared on my desktop screens, to the freak-out that had ensued as I'd attempted to shut the videos off to no avail—first by disconnecting the monitors, then disconnecting my computer, then yanking every cord from the wall outlet, until finally I'd succumbed to full meltdown panic and resorted to smashing both monitors to pieces with the closest thing to a weapon that I'd been able to get my hands on: my Swingline twenty-sheet, three-prong hole puncher.

Not my finest moment under pressure.

CHAPTER ELEVEN

I wasn't sure what was more disturbing: seeing myself flip out and destroy the newspaper's property in a fit of panic, or knowing that Vair—and perhaps other Ks—had been invading my privacy and spying on me.

Definitely the latter, I decided—although the former was more mortifying in the moment.

I was speechless as I watched the hologram version of myself calm down enough to realize what I'd done and allow a new sense of horror to take hold.

"Imagine how it hurt my feelings," Vair's smooth voice cut in as the hologram "me" proceeded to dash about, packing up my personal belongings as quickly as possible, "to see this—your violent reaction to my favorite compilation of our intimate moments together?"

He was messing with me again.

Or he was a psycho.

Leave it to me to have my first one-night stand with a *Fatal Attraction* vampire alien.

It should've been a tip-off when he'd told me on the dance floor that he'd come to Earth out of boredom. He'd said he required a lot of amusement, and that he had run out of ways to amuse himself on Krina. *So he'd left his home planet to open a sex club in NYC centered around Ks sucking and fucking willing humans?*

And I'd viewed my ex-boyfriend's lack of direction in life as a red flag of things to come.

"You threw out the exotic fruit basket I sent you." His voice held a note of censure.

Vair just *had* to be messing with me. I tried to tune him out and focus on the hologram version of myself shoving papers and mementos into emptied file boxes. My hologram was out of breath.

I was out of breath. I shut my eyes as my head began to spin.

"Amy?"

I shook my head, unwilling to open my eyes. I didn't want to see him.

But then I heard him. *Grunting.*

Followed by the sound of a woman moaning.

And I knew without looking that it was another hologram version of me that was playing now. Of us. From our night at the club.

"Oh, please, Vair. Right there... yesss..."

The sound of slick flesh slapping together filled the limo at high volume, along with the sound of my own whimpered pleas and cries for more.

Oh, God.

The bottle slipped from my fingers.

"Amy?" Present-moment Vair's calm entreaty was overlaid by the sounds of my unseen hologram self reaching orgasm.

I couldn't breathe. I pressed my fingers to my temples.

"You're so wet," his hypnotic voice spoke from across the limo.

My inner muscles contracted, clenching around emptiness.

"So ready for me."

Fuck. *I was very wet.*

I could feel his eyes on me, sense his essence calling to me— his sexual hunger a visceral thing that pulsed and tugged at my core as his need became my need, magnifying it tenfold.

"I've thought about you." His voice was low and hoarse. "Did you think about me?"

I'd thought about him nearly every moment of every day for the past month.

"Take your clothes off."

I shook my head at his directive, even as I reached for the buttons of my blouse and began to undo them with trembling fingers.

"That's it... Such a beautiful, delicious little human," he purred at me over the background sounds of my hologram's moaning and soft sucking noises.

Recorded Vair was grunting louder now, and my sex throbbed in reply, aching with an intensifying need at his growled commands for me to suck him harder. *Deeper.*

My mouth watered. My fingers fumbled desperately, tugging at the stubborn buttons.

This was madness.

"Amy," Vair called quietly to me again.

I opened my eyes at last.

The lighting had changed. The limo's tinted windows had

darkened to black, and a soft, flickering red glow similar to the lighting in his x-club illuminated the alien predator seated across from me.

Naked.

Stroking the biggest erection I'd ever seen.

And between us, the projected 3D recordings of our naked bodies were 69-ing like starved animals.

"Come here." One hand fisted the base of his massive cock while he crooked the finger of his other hand at me. "Show me you're not a victim."

The strange sense of unreality I'd experienced in his club came over me again, and I found myself on my knees between his muscled thighs a moment later, stretching my lips around the thick, wet tip and sucking him into my mouth—*because attacking his cock with my tongue was apparently the way my brain and body instinctively chose to demonstrate non-victimhood.*

"Ahh—good girl," he hissed, raising his hips toward my mouth while pressing down on the back of my head, quickly filling me to the back of my throat, yet still barely fitting half of his thick length inside.

He pushed deeper. I gagged. He eased back, then shoved forward to the same point again. "That's it, darling…"

My eyes watered as he took up a steady, insistent rhythm, rocking his hips up while restricting the position and motion of my head with his hand, fucking my mouth without ceremony or pretense. Driving into me as far as my gag reflex would allow while his other hand squeezed and stroked the length of him that I was unable to take.

"Yes… just like that," his gruff voice coaxed as crude slurping noises began to escape me—the sounds becoming beyond my ability to control as he pumped faster, taking my mouth with a primal urgency that *was* oddly empowering.

His sharp, short intakes of breath and guttural grunts of satisfaction had me aroused to the point of near orgasm as I was swept up in the paradox of feeling so powerfully in control of delivering his most critical, basic need, while at the same time being dominated by the situation.

"Amy... *Amy*..." He groaned my name like a dirty prayer as his thrusts became erratic.

I was sure he was about to come.

I was on the brink of flying apart myself; even without any physical stimulation, it was all so fucking hot.

His blunt fingertips spread and dragged back and forth across the back of my scalp, sending delightful shivers through me before he fisted the roots of my hair in a near-painful caveman grip.

Knowing he was about to blow in my mouth at any moment, I succumbed to temptation, slipping my hand between my thighs and up my pencil skirt—desperately seeking my own fulfillment.

The moment I pressed my fingertips to my soaked cotton underwear, I came undone.

I'd been hoping to get myself off discreetly while he was caught up in his release—ideally, without him even knowing it. But as soon as I began to detonate, he tugged me sharply up by my hair, pulling himself from my mouth and wrenching my head upright.

My eyes opened wide as my body twisted and convulsed, the carnal sounds erupting from me rivaling those from the recorded hologram playing in the background.

Caught red-handed, with my fingers up my skirt and

rubbing in a frantic motion, my flushed face sloppy wet with drool and residual tears from gagging on his cock, I was helpless to halt the sheer force of my own orgasm as he absorbed every brutally raw detail.

I couldn't have pulled my fingers away from my slit if I'd wanted to.

I didn't want to.

The sly, slight smile on his lips was the only thing darker than his eyes as he watched me bare my wanton soul, his jaw tight and his fist locked in a death grip around the base of his massively engorged erection, preventing his own explosion.

CHAPTER TWELVE

"May I?" He swiped his thumb across my bottom lip, wiping the dampness from my chin as his fingers massaged the part of my scalp where he'd pulled my hair.

I wasn't sure how long we'd faced one another in silence in his darkened limo. He'd squeezed the base of his cock until the pained look in his eyes had finally subsided and he was able to release it—still fully erect and loaded—while I had yet to rein in my breathing and get my emotions under control.

The video hologram no longer played. And the limo had stopped moving several minutes ago. But I couldn't bring myself to ask where we were.

I remained mute with shock, still kneeling on the carpeted limo floor between his legs, as he proceeded to pull my hand from between my thighs. He brought my fingers up to his mouth and licked them clean with a satisfied hum. He then tugged my skirt back down into place and buttoned up my blouse, studying my features closely as he did this—as if I were a puzzle he was working out.

"Are you all right?"

I didn't answer him, too baffled by his seemingly solicitous gestures. Using the pads of his thumbs, he dabbed the dampness from my cheeks just below the rim of my glasses where my eyes had leaked.

What the hell had just happened?

He hadn't even come. He was still sporting monster wood that had to be causing him discomfort. Like *major* discomfort.

Nevertheless, he was calm and in control as his fingertips brushed aside the strands of loose, fine hair that had fallen across my forehead. The last time we'd been together, he'd been insatiable, unable to stop himself from taking me over and over... and over again.

Was he not into me anymore?

His forefinger traced a line between my brows, drawing my attention to the fact I was frowning.

"It's all right, you know," he said gently. "Your responses are perfectly healthy and normal." His smile was kind—genuine and surprisingly open—as he brushed the backs of his knuckles down my jawline. "I like it when you're honest with yourself. I like that light that comes on in your eyes when you see something you want." He bent closer and pressed a small kiss to my cheek. His breath warmed my ear as he murmured, "But what I love most of all is watching you take it."

What?

"Next time"—his voice dropped an octave—"I hope you go for the intimacy you truly crave... that you climb onto my lap and take what you want from me."

Want from him?

Intimacy?

He had me all wrong. I didn't want *anything* from him, least of all intimacy.

I drew my face away, shaking my head minutely as I pulled my shit together about five minutes too late. "That's not... This wasn't—"

"Wait, don't tell me..." His lips quirked as he raised a silencing forefinger. "You never meant for any of this to happen just now, did you?" Mocking Vair was back. "You were simply curious? You only wanted to *observe* this first time, right?" He threw my own words back at me—the excuses I'd given him at the club.

I rolled my eyes away, muttering *"Sonofabitch"* under my breath.

His hand snaked out and fisted the back of my hair with jarring speed, forcing my eyes back to his.

He leaned closer. No longer smiling, he looked like the dark predator he was. He canted his head at me.

I swallowed. *Gulped.*

His long, dark lashes lowered as those deep-set brown eyes dropped to my throat. His gaze settled upon the wild pulse point that had to be visible in my neck, given how frantically I could feel it beating.

He licked his lips. And stared.

And stared.

My breath came in rapid, shallow pants despite my effort to remain calm. Because the more I tried to calm myself, the harder I could feel my heart racing.

His nostrils flared. His face inched ever closer, then dipped to my neck until the tip of his nose grazed my jugular.

He was going to bite me.

Butterflies thrilled in my belly. I braced myself for impact. But he simply inhaled deeply and exhaled. "Delicious."

He released my hair and abruptly pulled away, while I fought yet again to get my breathing under control.

"I'd like for you to come to my club tomorrow night. My driver will pick you up at eleven."

He'd phrased the first part as a request, the second as a directive. Was he giving me a choice or not?

"What if I don't want to come to your club?"

He leaned back against the plush leather seat cushions, linked his fingers behind his head, and shrugged—utterly unconcerned with the fact that his giant erection stood straight and proud in my direct line of sight. "What if I get lonely and my nostalgia drives me to play home videos of us in Times Square?"

Ass. "What do you want from me?"

"I've just told you, love. I want you to come back to my club."

"For what purpose?"

Another shrug. "I need you there."

My throat felt suddenly tight. I was exhausted and emotionally wrecked from all of Vair's mind games.

"Why?"

He smirked. "Plenty of reasons."

He was planning to humiliate me publicly. It was the obvious conclusion. I bit the inside of my cheek to keep myself from getting emotional. Stoically, I asked, "Is there an option B?"

His perfect, straight white teeth practically glowed in the darkness as he shook his head and chuckled. "No. But I'll hear your suggestion if you have one."

"I'll retract everything I said in my article," I immediately offered.

"No."

"What if I amended it to paint Ks in a more favorable light?"

"No."

"Fine, I'll issue a public apology to all Ks and xenophiles!" I all but screamed at him.

I couldn't go back to his club. I couldn't spend any more time with this man—*alien.*

"No."

"Why not?"

"None of those things are of any interest to me."

"Then what is of interest?"

The electronic limo door swung up, revealing the front entrance of my apartment building. The sight of it was a blessed relief. And at the same time, it was somehow unnerving that this was where he'd taken me.

We were done?

"You're a smart, curious girl, Amy. I'm sure you'll figure it out."

Just like that? He wipes my drool, then kicks me to the curb while calmly sitting back and driving off with a ginormous erection?

Whatever. I scrambled to the door and climbed out with as much dignity as possible, praying that none of my neighbors would be around to see me—*or the monster alien wood dismissing me.*

Thankfully, no one seemed to be around. I swung my head back around to deliver a scathing parting remark, but the limo door was already closing in my face.

Apparently the Krinar weren't big on goodbyes.

I turned and took a step in the direction of my building, only to find the gorgeous male K who had taken my file boxes blocking my path. He held my small purse and my keys out to me.

Oh. Right. Those had been tossed into one of the file boxes he'd confiscated.

"Um. Thank you." I took them from him.

He smiled. His unnaturally perfect face was a vision of symmetry. "You're welcome. Your computer screens have been restored and your office items returned to their usual places," he informed me.

Then he walked off, leaving me standing on the sidewalk more confused than ever.

CHAPTER THIRTEEN

"*I*ntimacy! Can you believe it? He said I craved intimacy. Intimacy from *him*, of all absurd things. As if, right?"

Jay's eyes were the size of saucers. "Could we back up to the part where Vair said several powerful Krinar Council members were upset about your article? Did he assign a number to several? Or did he just say several?"

"Just several." I frowned at the empty wine glass in my hand from my seat on the couch as Jay nervously refilled his own at the kitchen island. "Did you hear what I said about the intimacy part?"

Jay nodded absently and took a liberal sip of red wine.

After Vair had dropped me off, I'd stayed in my own apartment only long enough to pack an overnight bag and to obsess over the many places where Ks could've hidden cameras. Then I'd hightailed it over to Jay's Soho micro-loft. The unit his parents had bought for him was in a swanky building with twenty-four-hour doormen. And while logically, I knew no one was safe from a K, rich people places always *felt* safer somehow.

"I have a friend from college who wound up at the CIA... I think," Jay mused aloud, pacing the small space of his living room with a full wine glass in his unsteady hand. "Maybe he can help us?"

"Um"—I waved my empty glass in the air—"you mind?"

"You can't go back to his club tomorrow night."

"Duh!"

"He could be planning anything."

"Agreed."

"You'd be walking into a trap."

"No shit."

"He could do anything to you in that club and no one would stop him."

"Jay, my insufficient buzz is already wearing off. This conversation isn't helping." I tilted my glass in indication once more.

"We've got to get you out of town tonight, baby girl." He grabbed the wine bottle from the kitchen island and came toward me. "Tomorrow morning at the latest."

"It's not that simple," I said as he refilled my crystal stemware. "I can't risk that video footage being released."

"But it doesn't add up." Jay shook his head. "Why wouldn't he just let you retract what you said or issue a public apology? How does you going to his club appease angry Council members more than a retraction would?"

I managed a shrug as I tipped my wine back.

"It doesn't," Jay concluded, his brow furrowed in concentration as he sank down onto the coffee table in front of me. "You know what I think? I think he knew we were reporters the moment we arrived at his club."

"I've thought that, too. He did personally let us in and escort us inside. How many club owners do that?"

"Exactly. And then he was all over you the whole time. I mean the guy never left your side for even a minute. If I hadn't been so distracted by Shira—fuck, do you suppose he meant for Shira to distract me?"

It had never occurred to me, but Jay was right. He and I had been more or less separated immediately upon entering Vair's club. The alien Barbie had captured Jay's attention and swept him away from my side within moments of Vair introducing her to us.

A strange, disconcerting realization seemed to cross Jay's features as he slowly eyed me up and down. It looked out of place on his characteristically jovial, pretty-boy face.

"What?" I glanced down to check that I hadn't spilled red wine on myself or on his cream-colored couch. "Why are you looking at me like that?"

He chewed his lip, his frown deepening.

"You're freaking me out, Jay."

"I'm remembering an exchange between Shira and Kyrel," he answered slowly, as if he was still processing the memory. "You know, the male K she and I hooked up with?"

I smiled as a welcome giggle bubbled up in my chest, alleviating some of the tension in the air. "Oh, I remember. You've over-shared quite a few memorable stories about him as well as Shira."

Jay didn't laugh. Or even crack a smile as he scanned me up and down again, as if he were seeing a problem. "Fuck. You really *are* hot, Amy. You know that, right?" He said this like it was bad news.

"Um... yeah? I'm okay-looking, sure. Thanks. So? What did Shira and Kyrel say?"

"When I was dancing between Kyrel and Shira, and I first realized you'd left the dance floor with Vair and were nowhere to be seen, I panicked. I tried to break away, saying I had to find you. Shira stopped me, telling me not to worry, that Vair would take great care of you. Then Kyrel laughed and said, 'Yes, for all eternity, in fact.' I didn't think much of it at the time, assuming it was just—I don't know, the alien expression equivalent of Kubrick's 'me love you long time' joke or something."

I released a breath as my stomach settled in relief. *"That's* what you're freaking me out over?"

"No, it was the part that came after that. Shira laughed along with him, and then she said something about how Ks could be exceptionally possessive. She joked that I was lucky I hadn't been holding your hand in the hallway outside the club, or else I might be dead or minus a hand at the very least."

"What?" My sense of relief was short-lived. "She actually said that? And you took it as a joke—coming from a female alien who literally *could* tear your hand off?" My eyes flew to the ceiling in disbelief. "And you still hooked up with her."

"Look, give me a break. I'm pretty sure her hand was already on my junk at that point. Anyway, who am I to judge an extraterrestrial's quirky sense of humor? Besides, she was a fucking goddess. Hottest woman I've ever seen up close."

"Krinar," I corrected him. "Hottest Krinar."

"Whatever. She was all woman, believe me. And she was warning me about Vair's possessive tendencies, not her own. Because Kyrel cautioned me a moment later that I should be careful never to lay a hand on you if I wanted to go on living. He said"—Jay's brow rose meaningfully, as if this were the key part—"that he'd had to calm Vair down by pointing out that our body language quite obviously said we weren't together when Vair first spotted us waiting in the hallway."

Vair had questioned me directly about my relationship with Jay that night. In truth, it *had* felt strangely possessive at the time—given the fact we'd only just met. But clearly, he'd merely wanted to hook up with me and hadn't wanted any obstacles in his path.

"So... Krinar males are competitive and susceptible to male ego and pride, same as human men? Got it. I'll make that the topic of my next K article."

Jay let out a huff. "Don't you see? Vair saw us before he let us in. As did Kyrel, apparently. So they must've been viewing us on surveillance cameras as we were waiting that long-ass time in the entry hallway."

I recalled how Jay and I had stood there, staring nervously at the big metallic gray door for what had felt like an eternity. I'd had to work up the courage to knock several times before Vair had finally answered and opened the door for us.

I didn't get what Jay thought was so revealing in all of this, though. It was hardly unusual to screen visitors via hidden surveillance at an exclusive Manhattan club, let alone a K sex club.

He groaned at my nonplussed expression, setting the wine bottle down next to him with a heavy thud. "Amy, what if Vair staked his claim on you before we even entered his x-club? What if this blackmail thing has more to do with him wanting you than it does the Krinar Council being upset over your article or wanting to exact some sort of punishment for it?"

My stomach flipped with a level of schoolgirl excitement that was disturbing and altogether embarrassing, given the absurdity of Jay's theory, not to mention the sheer sordidness its entire premise was built upon.

It wasn't as if I actually wanted Vair to want me.

No, what I was feeling was simply the natural relief that anyone would draw from the notion of someone wanting them versus the scarier and yet more likely notion of someone planning to ship them off to a Costa Rican alien labor camp. Because from a purely logical standpoint, this made the terrifying prospect of having to go to Vair's club tomorrow night seem a bit safer—albeit more nerve-racking at the same time.

I shook my head. "I really don't think that's the case, Jay."

"Why not? Hell, he's already caught on to your intimacy issues."

My jaw dropped and I whacked him squarely in the shoulder, coming dangerously close to sloshing my wine all over us both in the process. "Take that back!"

"Annnd"—Jay laughed at my attack, wielding a triumphant forefinger—"he didn't come in your mouth tonight. Baby girl, that alien has got it bad for you."

"Oh, my God, shut up!" I'd known I'd regret telling Jay too many details from my limo encounter with Vair. But I'd been in a vulnerable state and had needed to vent to someone. "That is the most absurd logic ever."

To redirect the conversation away from aborted blowjobs and my perceived intimacy issues, I asked, "Why didn't you tell me about what Shira and Kyrel said?"

"Don't know. Guess I just didn't think of it after everything else that happened that night. It was already a lot to talk about.

Like being bitten by a K." He wagged his brows. "That shit was like the best drug ever. Besides, nothing ever came of it. We both made it home safely from the club, and aside from the fruit basket after your article came out, you hadn't heard from Vair until today."

I nodded. It was all too much to contemplate. I felt my body crashing, the adrenaline that had fueled me all evening rapidly waning. Yet my mind remained keyed up. No doubt I'd enjoy a special state of exhaustion combined with insomnia tonight.

"Look, it's just a theory. Don't panic, okay? We'll figure something out."

I closed my eyes, pulled my glasses off, and pinched the bridge of my nose. "Got any Advil? Tylenol?"

"I'll do you one better. Hang on." I heard Jay rise and cross in the direction of the bathroom.

I chuckled dryly to myself, betting he'd be back with some proprietary blend of pharmaceutical-grade marijuana oil.

Blindly, I set my glasses down on the coffee table in front of me. Those things had been bothering me for weeks. I likely needed a new prescription. My vision somehow seemed to be worse whenever I wore them lately, and it was causing me headaches.

What if Vair actually did want me?

Though why would he? For what? He had NYC supermodels and actresses clamoring for his attention.

Besides, it wasn't as if our species were compatible. At least, I didn't think we were. Not really. I pushed aside the memory of how "compatible" we'd felt sexually. It was irrelevant. A farce.

He'd bitten me. That was what had caused the aphrodisiac high I'd experienced with him.

"You look flushed." Jay's voice pulled me from my thoughts as he reentered the room. "I'll get you some water."

He returned with a glass of water and offered me a Xanax pill.

"Jay, I can't take that."

"It's the best thing for my headaches."

"Yeah, 'cause you're passed out."

"It'll help with your anxiety. Amy, we've got less than twenty-four hours to come up with a plan. You can't go back to Vair's club tomorrow night."

"But I've had wine."

"So have I, and I'm taking one. It's the lowest dose. My doctor says it's fine with a little alcohol."

I was about to ask whether that advice was from the same doctor who prescribed his medicinal marijuana, but instead, I gave in and downed the little white pill before I lost my nerve. It was doubtful I'd get any sleep tonight otherwise, and I needed all the mental sharpness I could muster tomorrow to devise a way out of going to Vair's club.

"Take my bed," Jay offered. "I'll take the couch."

"No way. I'll sleep on the couch." Lord only knew who and what had happened in Jay's bed this week and whether his cleaning lady had washed the sheets since.

I was already feeling woozy and swaying on my feet as I brushed my teeth and washed up in Jay's bathroom.

I'd just managed to pull my pajamas on and climb atop the couch Jay had made up for me when I succumbed to the state of blissful, dreamless darkness that only pharma-induced sleep provides.

CHAPTER FOURTEEN

$\mathcal{I}$ awoke to a light shining directly in my eyes as someone pried the lids open. I grumble-moaned my displeasure.

"Relax," Vair's voice soothed in my ear. "Let us have a look, darling." I felt his arms around me. They felt so good, so comforting as they held my dead weight upright in his lap.

I was dreaming. And I didn't want to interrupt what I already sensed was going to be a pleasant dream about Vair.

Even in my dream state, I felt drugged—unnaturally exhausted—making it easier to do as he'd asked and relax into his embrace despite the blinding light presently in my eyes. I reveled in the masculine scent of him, in the sensation of his full lips pressing against my temple and his warm fingers gently stroking the side of my head.

My eyelids were released and the light extinguished. It occurred to me that someone other than Vair had been holding them open. He was talking in that foreign language of his again.

And not to me, I deduced when a female voice responded in kind.

Cool, feminine fingers palpated the glands on either side of my neck next, and an irrational sense of jealousy washed over me when Vair laughed softly at whatever the woman who spoke his language had said.

"No," I murmured. "Not funny." I wasn't sure why. And my words came out slurred. Garbled.

They both laughed this time.

"Agreed," Vair said. "It's not at all funny how you make me worry. Never mind the way you disregard your liver."

He was chastising me. But any sense of indignation I might've felt was forgotten as he hugged me tighter against the warm, solid mass of his chest.

Because in that moment, he felt safe. Normal. Better than normal. *Nearly human.*

And in my dream, I believed him. I believed Vair truly was concerned with my well-being. And it felt... nice. So nice that I didn't object when a glass was pressed to my lips and Vair told me to drink.

I swallowed all of the strange-tasting, sweet liquid as he stroked my hair and made promises that I was safe with him, that he would never do anything to harm me.

After a while, I got the sense that we were alone. I didn't open my eyes, though. I was too afraid that the dream would vanish and I'd wake up.

My brain felt more lucid after the drink he'd given me, my tongue certainly more adroit as I mumbled in response that I would never harm him either, and assured him that he was also safe with me... *if* he turned over all copies of that video footage he was blackmailing me with.

My declaration was met with a barely suppressed shout of laughter. I felt his body quake beneath me.

"Clever, delicious little minx," he half-chuckled, half-growled against my neck.

My equilibrium shifted and I found myself flat on my back, trapped beneath him. His weight settled between my legs.

My nipples instantly tightened.

I moaned as his lips brushed mine, his tongue flicking out to tease me as the hard length of his erection did the same, grinding into the soft, pulsating notch between my thighs.

In my dream, I lacked the arm muscle strength and coordination to reach up and pull his head down to me. But I wanted him to kiss me. *Really* kiss me.

So badly.

Who was I kidding? I wanted him to fuck me. *Consume me.*

I told him so.

He groaned and told me to "shut the fuck up." It sounded so out of calm, collected alien character for him that I giggled. And then he shut me up with his hard, insistent mouth.

The sensation of his tongue thrusting between my lips to stroke my own was torture, especially coupled with the masculine grunts of arousal that reverberated to the back of my throat as he ground his massive cock where I wanted him most.

Torture of the best kind.

"I *should* fuck you," he managed between kisses. He sounded angry.

I liked it.

My inner muscles squeezed in anticipation. My pajama bottoms were already soaked.

"Until you can't"—he thrust his pelvis against me just right —"fucking walk."

"Who's stopping you?" I gasped out.

He growled and rotated his pelvis hard into me once more. Then twice. And by the third time—

Oh, God...

I was on the brink of orgasm when he stopped, released my mouth, and abruptly pulled his delicious weight from me.

My hands that had been too weak to lift a moment ago were somehow gripping his T-shirt in an effort to halt his retreat. I made a wounded sound that didn't even sound human as his panted breaths fanned my forehead.

"Don't want you to go." My voice emerged shaky. I sounded so forlorn. Lost. So... *needy.*

So god-awful!

I opened my eyes to end this dream-turned-sudden-nightmare and found Vair's hungry gaze studying me through the darkness surrounding us—a pained, vulnerable expression on his face that somehow mirrored my own tortured emotions.

I couldn't decide if I should take comfort in that or feel worse about it.

His irises were so black they were nearly the same shade as his pupils, making him look scary. *And yet hot.*

Creepy otherworldly.

Still hot.

But most of all, he looked real. Very real. Felt real. Smelled real.

"I'm dreaming." *Please say yes. Please say yes.* "This is a dream."

He simply stared. Didn't answer. Eventually, he told me to close my eyes.

I did.

His lips brushed my forehead. He told me he had to leave so

I could finish dreaming—neither confirming nor negating whether I was, in fact, dreaming at present.

I was still clutching his T-shirt. He told me to let go, joking that even aliens needed rest on occasion.

"I promise you, I don't want to leave you. But you need your rest now."

He told me he hoped I was brave enough to come to his club that evening. *Way to throw down the gauntlet.* His implication that I had a choice in the matter was as odd as my feelings and behavior toward him in that moment, further corroborating that I *had* to be dreaming.

I felt him gently removing my fingers from his shoulders.

He told me he would stay until I fell asleep. I told him I *was* asleep.

The last thing I remembered was letting him know that he was wrong.

I didn't have an intimacy problem.

CHAPTER FIFTEEN

Someone was singing "Bad Romance." That someone was also cooking eggs and bacon. And hash browns. More importantly, I smelled coffee.

I smiled and rubbed my eyes open. Jay was preparing breakfast less than fifteen feet away in his open kitchen, using animal products that only wealthy people like his parents had easy access to.

"You're an angel," I called out to him, stretching as I rose from my makeshift bed. I felt surprisingly well-rested and energized, my mind clearer than it should've been, my head and body suffering none of the aches and pains I would've expected after consuming wine and Xanax and sleeping on a couch. Even my looming anxiety over the prospect of going to Vair's club tonight had somehow abated during the night, because I felt markedly less panicked over the whole situation.

"So I've been told. Breakfast is in five." He waved a spatula at me. "Chop-chop."

I hit the bathroom, washed up, and was back in ten to take a seat next to Jay at his island countertop. He had already shaved, showered, and dressed for the day—which was atypical Jay behavior for nine a.m. on a Saturday.

"The hash browns, fruit, and coffee are all vegan," he announced proudly, making me laugh as he bit into his bacon.

"Look who's a funny man this morning," I teased, picking up my fork and digging into the hash browns Jay had plated for me.

He seemed to be in remarkable spirits, full of energy and beaming from ear to ear like he couldn't wait to get going with his day. Or to tell me something?

"Did you go out partying after I went to bed last night?"

"Without you?" he exclaimed with a look of mock horror. "I slept great is all. You?"

"Surprisingly excellent as well. Thanks again for letting me stay with you. And for making breakfast."

"My pleasure. Can't let my only female friend face Ks on an empty stomach." He glanced at his watch. "But hurry it up; we've got less than fourteen hours to figure out what you're going to wear tonight to the club, not to mention come up with brilliant interview questions."

I frowned. "I'm sorry, did I miss something? Last night we were plotting my escape from the city. Now you want me to go to Vair's club?"

"I know, I know, but I feel better about the whole situation after sleeping on it. Because guess who's going to the x-club with you?" He raised his brow and gestured to himself.

My eyes popped. "Jay, I can't ask you to do that."

"You're not. I'm crashing your party." He grinned. "I took it upon myself to contact Vair this morning to let him know I'd be coming. Also, to negotiate our terms."

My fork slipped to the quartz countertop with a clatter. "You what?"

"Told him you were only going if I came with you and if he guaranteed our safety." His puppy-brown eyes lit with excitement. *"And* if you got to interview some Ks."

"You spoke with him?"

"No, we texted."

"Texted?" My jaw dropped. "You have Vair's phone number?"

He shrugged, looking sheepish. "I swiped it from your exotic fruit basket."

"What?" There had been no number written on the card included with the basket Vair had sent me. I'd read that note over a thousand times. "Jay, there was no number anywhere on his card."

"Not on the personal card, no. But there was a business card tucked inside the basket that included a phone number."

"And you kept it all this time and never told me?"

He held his palm up. "You wanted nothing to do with that basket, Amy. You were spazzing out and didn't even want to touch it, remember? I barely had time to look through the cool fruit and snag the card for safekeeping before you tossed the whole thing into the incinerator."

"So you just woke up this morning and texted a K?" I couldn't process it. "You texted Vair?"

He nodded, his mouth now full from the bite of eggs and bacon he'd taken.

"And he responded?"

Another nod. He raised his finger as he finished chewing.

"Yeah. He said I could come tonight." He paused to take a sip of coffee. "I asked about the Council members, too. He said everything was cool and he was handling it."

"He said everything was *cool?*"

"I'm paraphrasing. He said you aren't in any danger from them or any other Ks offended by your article as long as you stick close to him. You know, so that he can look out for you. That's why he wants you to come to his club."

Jay said this like it made perfect, rational sense. As if Vair was blackmailing me into coming to his alien sex club for altruistic reasons.

I couldn't decide if I should be relieved and embrace my best friend's abrupt change of perspective on my situation, or be alarmed that I might be living the Krinar version of *Invasion of the Body Snatchers.*

"Come on, eat up. Everything's going to be fine." Jay gave me a reassuring smile. "Think about it: this will be way better material for your next K article than the veganism stuff."

I shook my head, my appetite gone. "What deal did you make with Vair about me interviewing Ks?"

"Like I said, I told Vair you'd come to his club tonight if I came with you, and if you got to interview some Ks who frequent the club for your next article."

"This is a bad idea, Jay." Writing articles about Ks is how I'd gotten myself into this whole mess.

"Will you stop shaking your head at me and listen for a minute? Vair gave me his word that we'd be safe under his protection at the club." He spoke slowly and clearly, as if he thought I wasn't getting it. *As if Vair's word on this was somehow gospel.*

"He also agreed to let you interview Ks, but only Ks of his

choosing." Jay scrunched his nose at the last part—like it was the most regrettable news. "And only on his terms, which include him being present for any and all interviews with these other Ks. For your protection, of course."

Once again, Jay was quick to present Vair's actions as considerate—practically noble. What the heck was going on?

"To be honest, I got the impression Vair just wants you to interview him, actually."

Great. "Jay, you know I want to help get factual information about the Ks out to the public more than anyone, but don't you think I should avoid pissing off the Krinar Council any more than I already have at this point? What if Vair's lying and this is all a trap?"

Jay cocked his head, studying me with a distracted expression.

"If you come with me, we're both endangering our lives," I pointed out. "We could disappear off the face of the Earth, and no one would ever know what happened to us."

Jay's eyes widened, like he'd just had an epiphany. "Hey, you're not wearing your glasses. And you're not squinting at everything like you normally do without them."

"Did you hear anything I just said?"

"I heard it. Are you wearing contacts? I thought you'd lost your last pair weeks ago and hadn't reordered them yet?"

I was about to flip out on him over his bizarre behavior when I realized he was right; I wasn't wearing my glasses. I *had* lost my contacts weeks ago. Over four weeks ago, to be exact— the night I'd hooked up with Vair.

And I could see fine without glasses or contacts right now. *Perfectly,* in fact.

I could see flecks of gold and black in Jay's brown irises that

I'd never noticed before. I could read the tiny print on the dial settings on the small Viking convection oven nestled within the wall of cabinets that was well over six feet behind Jay's back.

"Oh, my God…"

I hopped off my stool and dashed over to the couch. I found my glasses right where I'd left them on the coffee table the night before and put them on.

Then I took them off. And put them back on again.

I couldn't see for shit with them on.

It wasn't a new prescription that I needed. Apparently, I didn't need glasses at all? Something wasn't right.

Then it hit me. *His scent* hit me.

My heart thudded in my chest. I dropped to my ass on the couch, balled the mess of tangled sheets between my hands, and raised them to my face, inhaling deeply as I recalled my dream.

"Um… what are you doing?"

I looked up at Jay. "I think Vair was here."

"Don't be silly. We have doormen downstairs."

"Like that matters. Jay, we watched him disintegrate a wall right in front of us at his club, remember?"

"Point taken." He joined me on the couch. "But maybe it's just my cologne you're smelling." He attempted to pull the sheets from my grasp, and I jerked back reflexively, clutching them to my chest.

Like a possessive, K-sniffing xenophile. A crazed K addict.

I tossed the sheets at Jay like they were on fire.

Subtle.

"No—I mean, it's not, um… your scent." I took my glasses off and busied my fingers by fiddling with the hinges. "You can sniff for yourself." I sounded like a lunatic.

The look on my best friend's face confirmed my worst fear. I put my glasses back on.

Perfect vision was overrated.

He stood. "Okay. Ah, suppose it's from your limo ride yesterday then? You didn't shower last night, right?"

It was a perfectly plausible explanation. But somehow I knew my gut was right this time. Vair had been here. And I had very confusing mixed feelings about that.

My body did too.

"You're probably right."

"Of course I'm right. I'm always right," Jay said with a forced laugh, doing his best to lighten the mood. "But why don't I try to connect with that friend of mine from college anyway?" He tucked the crumpled-up sheets under his arm. "The one I think ended up at the CIA. You know, as a precaution."

I nodded. Maybe the government was quietly working on a Krinar vaccine that could make me immune to Vair? I'd gladly volunteer to test it.

"I think that'd be a good precaution," I said, though I doubted any human could protect us from Ks. "Especially if we risk going back to Vair's club tonight."

"Baby girl, I know we were both pretty spooked last night, but I feel better about the situation this morning after texting with Vair. I really don't get the sense that he intends to harm you. Think about it: he would've done it already. And besides"—Jay puffed his chest out, assuming a comical stance—"you'll be with me! What could possibly go wrong?"

I had to laugh. "What indeed."

"I mean, look," he said with a shrug, "maybe Vair wanting you at his club isn't about angry Krinar Council members *or* about Vair wanting to love you long time. Maybe it's as simple as Vair wanting to reignite the buzz about his club that your last article created."

"Maybe," I said doubtfully.

"It's just possible that not all vegan, bloodsucking alien overlords are villains, right? Vair could simply be opportunistic and capitalist-minded—like everyone else in this city."

I snorted. "One can hope."

"Atta girl!" He reached down and chucked me under the chin. "Do you want"—he held the balled-up sheets out to me —"your K blankie back?"

"Ugh, my God." I rose from the couch, shoving a laughing Jay from my path. "I'm going to shower now."

"Good idea," he called after me. "Wash that alien stink out of your hair."

CHAPTER SIXTEEN

"You can't wear that."

"Why not?"

"You'll look like a young MILF who got lost on her way to PTA night."

I rolled my eyes and held up the next dress option in front of me. "This one?"

Jay made a retching sound. "Are you going to a wedding or a sex club? I've said it before, I don't believe in puce."

I groaned and fished the last of my dress options from my TJ Maxx shopping bag. "How about this?"

Jay made a "meh" noise and gave it a "so-so" hand gesture. "I need to see what it looks like on. My hunch is that if Diane von Fürstenberg and Tory Burch had a bastard lovechild who designed cheap, slutty wrap dresses for Bebe, that's about what we've got here."

I flung it onto the chair next to his bed and tossed my hands in defeat. "Well, I'm out of options."

"Because you insisted on shopping where there were no options."

Jay had wanted me to shop in some trendy place in his Soho neighborhood, saying he envisioned me "braving Vair's club wearing an edgy, slinky, minimalist, bodycon Helmut Lang-esque number"—a.k.a. something way too expensive for my budget.

And given the fact that the last time I'd gone to his club, Vair had torn the nicest clubbing dress I'd owned to shreds, along with my bra and panties, I was not about to spend half of my paycheck on a designer dress that might suffer the same fate.

So I'd purchased six dresses from TJ Maxx instead, and I planned to take them all back—ideally, even whichever one I wore tonight to the club if I could manage to hide the tags.

"Did you get in touch with your friend at the CIA?" I asked.

"No, but I confirmed with a mutual friend that he does work there, and I got his number and left him a message."

It was progress, I supposed, but not all that comforting, given that we'd be back at Vair's club in less than five hours. Anything could happen to us tonight, and no one would be the wiser.

"And while you were out making substandard dress selections, I brainstormed some K interview questions." Jay pulled his phone from his pocket. "Want to hear them?"

I really didn't. "Sure. Lay them on me," I said brightly anyway.

My stomach was in knots, and I'd barely eaten all day. I'd stopped by my apartment after shopping to pick up my makeup bag, a selection of shoes, and other necessities for getting ready at Jay's place, and the entire time I'd been there, I hadn't been able to shake the paranoia that I was being watched. It was nerve-racking to think I might never have a sense of privacy in my own home again.

Jay sat on the edge of his bed and read from his iPhone. "What are the Krinar's ultimate plans for us as a society?"

I made a face. "Pass. Reasonable question, but too vague and easy to dance around answering. Besides, they obviously don't want us to know all of their intentions. Highly doubtful we'll get any worthwhile answer out of a K to that one." I could already envision Vair deflecting such a question with humor and sexual innuendo. "Next?"

"Why intervene and insert yourselves into our society now if you've had the ability to do so for thousands of years? If you were concerned about the health of our planet, why didn't you come to its rescue sooner?"

"Exactly!" I nodded. "Why indeed? I like it, but Ks aren't likely to answer that one either. Maybe we should start with x-club-related questions and try to pepper others into the convo as we can?"

"We?" He shook his head. "Baby girl, I'm afraid you're on your own with this. I'm dying to interview a K, but Vair was clear about only you doing the interviewing at his club."

Naturally. "Fine. *I'll* start with x-club-related questions. Got any of those?"

"Do I evah," Jay sing-songed. "Here's one that I wrote for Vair: It's rumored that more and more humans are frequenting your x-club. Many humans have shared stories on online forums about how addictive the experience of being bitten and having their blood sucked by a Krinar alien is. Is drinking human blood equally addictive for a Krinar?"

"Nice. Definitely an important, key question." *Professionally and personally.* And it was possible Vair or other Ks would entertain that one and perhaps provide some response from which I'd be able to extract a half-truth or two.

"You'll like this next one for Vair even better. While the Krinar continue to preach the merits of veganism and have strong-armed the entire planet into a predominantly vegan lifestyle, you've established an exclusive club where Krinar may access the fresh blood of willing humans—because apparently, the Krinar version of 'veganism' includes the blood of mammals? Care to explain that hypocrisy for the human public?"

I giggled and bounced in place on the balls of my feet. "I'll have to tone it down a bit, but I love it. What else?"

"How many other women have you been with in the past month?"

"Jay!"

"What?" He looked up from his phone with a devious grin. "Okay, so I admit that as I was writing these, they somehow became a bit more Vair and Amy hook-up specific than general K and x-clubber questions." His finger tapped and scrolled down the screen. "Let's see... I'll just skip over the next few," he said with a chuckle. "We can come back to the ones about how your blood tastes later."

"Ew! *Not* funny."

Jay got his laughter under control, cleared his throat, and continued. "I've heard that Krinar can be highly possessive. Does that mean that Krinar pair off and mate for life, like penguins, coyotes, and termites?"

I covered my face with my hands.

"What does it mean when a Krinar says that they're going to 'take great care of someone' for *all eternity*? Is that like a Krinar euphemism for engaging in an extended sexual encounter?"

"Oh, my God." I flopped down onto the chair laden with my "substandard" dress choices. "I am not asking those questions. Let's move on. How about asking about their language? Or about how they're capable of understanding all of *our* languages so readily? Or about their technology and whether they ever plan to share any of those advances with us?"

Or if they intend to just keep using them against us—for control, intimidation, general spying, and the occasional sex tape compilation.

"Lame and lamer. Consider the venue, Amy. We're not meeting up at an Apple store. You're interviewing Vair and other horny Ks in a sex club. Besides, Vair said no boring, safe questions would be answered."

"What?" I jerked upright in my seat. "You talked with Vair while I was out?"

"Texted again."

"I want to see!" I demanded, reaching for the phone in his hands. "Show me the texts from this morning, too."

"I'd show you, but they've been erased."

"Bullshit." I jumped up and snatched the phone right out of his hands. "Why would you erase them?"

"I didn't. Vair did. Or *something* did. Because they disappeared seconds after I read them."

I scrolled through his recent text messages and confirmed that it was true.

"It's something with their technology, I'm sure."

"No doubt," I muttered, nodding absently. A new wave of anxiety curled in my gut as I heard my mother's voice in my head. *They wouldn't want to leave evidence behind of how they lured two unsuspecting human reporters to their beheading.*

I shook it off internally. I couldn't afford to go there. Jay seemed certain that we'd be safe tonight at Vair's club, and I had to trust his instincts on this. I knew that my own instincts were flawed—warped by years of my mother's constant fearmongering and "sky is falling" proselytization.

I'd seen a therapist about it in college. Being at school and away from my mom's influence for the first time had made me recognize just how poor my ability to judge the inherent danger of situations was. I'd learned in therapy that kids who were raised to fear everything in life were more likely to be victimized as adults—because being taught to see danger everywhere in the world, *including in places and situations where there was none,* left them with no reasonable gauge for identifying true danger when they were faced with it.

According to my therapist, when danger becomes normalized, people stop hearing their intuition, until eventually they can't differentiate between the nebulous daily "sky is falling" threats and the "obvious to everyone but you creeper at the bar blatantly plotting to roofie your drink" threat.

My therapist had also cautioned me that sometimes those who were raised to see fear everywhere became subconscious thrill-seekers or adrenaline junkies in adulthood.

Knowing my instincts might be faulty, I relied on observation and fact as much as possible. And on the instincts of people I trusted.

Jay had been adamantly against the idea of me going to investigate and report on x-clubs at first. However, once we'd gotten in and were standing face to face with Vair, it was I who had become half-immobilized by fear and shock, while Jay had warmed to the situation, his instincts telling him that the threat was not as great as he'd initially feared. And he'd been right.

That time, my mother's voice warned in my head.

I handed Jay his phone and stood silently by the bed, lost in my thoughts.

"You want to text him for yourself and see?" he offered after a beat, awkwardly extending it back out to me.

"Oh, no. Definitely not."

"I could give you his number and you could use your own phone to text—"

"I'm good!" I snapped, then caught myself. "Sorry. Can we just veg out for a while? Watch a movie or something? I need to get my mind off things."

"Sure. I got *Men in Black, Alien vs. Predator, Independence Day*—"

"You're about to be strangled with a puce dress."

And as he erupted with laughter, I threw said dress at him.

CHAPTER SEVENTEEN

I opted to wear the von-Fürstenberg-Burch bastard lovechild to Vair's club.

The perfectly symmetrical-faced K who'd confiscated and subsequently restored my boxes of office belongings the day before was waiting outside of Jay's building to collect us at exactly eleven p.m. He was driving a sleek but understated hybrid Lincoln Town Car. We learned that his name was Zyrnase.

Zyrnase seemed easygoing and friendly enough, chatting with us about how he liked living in the city, until Jay made the horrendous faux pas of asking if allergens were a common problem on Krina like they were on Earth—and followed it up with a joke about how "Zyrnase" sounded like the K might've been named after an antihistamine drug.

I cringed and slunk low in my seat as Zyrnase stoically informed us that no such ailment existed on Krina because allergens weren't the problem, our feeble human immune systems were. We fell silent for an uncomfortable length of time before Zyrnase activated the tinted glass divider and blocked us out entirely.

"Really? An antihistamine?"

"What? It was funny. Good clean K humor. Guy needs to lighten up," Jay grumbled under his breath. "Perfect facial structure gets dull fast when a person can't laugh at himself."

"I knew it!" I whisper-exclaimed. "You're into him."

"Duh. He's hot. *Was* hot. Before his personality disorder crashed our limo party. Which, by the way, sucks. There's no alcohol or even any snacks back here." Jay proceeded to rummage through all of the compartments he'd already ransacked. "You know, I get why drinking alcohol before getting your vein sucked might be a bad call, but how about offering your human suckees some frigging apple slices or mixed nuts? Even the shittiest blood bank offers crackers and cheap cookies to donors."

"Oh, God, you're nervous, aren't you? You're totally regretting coming tonight. Do you really think they're planning on biting us? I'll understand if you want to back out and not go in with me when we get there, okay? Zero judgment."

"What are you talking about? Of course I'm going in with you."

"You don't have to. I'm serious, Jay. This is my problem. *I* insisted on going there the first time. I'm the one who wrote the article that pissed off the Krinar Council."

"Well, *I'm* the best friend who insisted on coming with you that first time. And I had the hottest sex of my life that night, thank you very much. I'm also the same friend who negotiated this evening's reprise, and I'm not missing it."

"But, Jay—"

"But nothing." He pressed his fingers and thumb together in front of my face in the "zip it" gesture. "If you think I'm letting you hog all the hot aliens for yourself, you're blinder than those blinder glasses you're still wearing for no rational reason. Vair said I could come, and I'm going. End of discussion."

"Aw, Jay…" Blinking rapidly to stave off the tears stinging the backs of my eyes, I scooted closer and linked my arm through the crook of his. Leaning my head against his shoulder, I told him, "You're the best—you know that? Thank you."

The words sounded lame to my ears. They were grossly inadequate, given all that Jay was risking on my behalf. But I was never good at expressing such things. And I couldn't afford to get emotional tonight.

I knew Jay had always gotten that about me, because he never pushed emotional topics like some of my other friends did. Sure, he might tease me about having intimacy issues, but he always kept it light and playful. And he backed off whenever he sensed my discomfort. It was one of the qualities that made him such a remarkable friend.

"Yeah, yeah," he muttered. "So I've been told." He leaned his head on top of mine and gave my arm a squeeze.

We traveled for several blocks in contemplative silence.

"But for real," he broached as we passed through Greenwich Village, "why are you still wearing those glasses if your vision is worse with them on?"

I sighed and straightened in my seat, unlinking my arm from his. "Because it doesn't make sense. I've worn glasses since second grade. Vision doesn't just get better on its own."

"What if it did?"

"It's not possible."

"So you're still wearing them out of denial?"

"No, of course not. Look, maybe I just like the way they feel?" My statement had meandered into a question by the end.

Jay's blossoming lopsided grin said he wasn't buying it.

I couldn't blame him; I didn't either.

"What? They go with my dress!" I insisted with a giggle. "I like wearing glasses, okay? Can we drop it?"

He shrugged. "Whatever you say, baby girl." He gave me a wink. "Totally your business if you want to hide those gorgeous green eyes behind spectacles you can't see out of." His amused expression turned to puzzlement and his attention shifted to the window beside me when the car made a right turn. "Why is he turning here? This isn't the way we came last time."

I swiveled my head and saw that we'd turned down an alleyway. I didn't have the world's best sense of direction, but this definitely didn't look familiar to me. Granted, I couldn't see much between the darkness of the dimly lit alley and the blurriness my glasses created. "No," I said worriedly. "Doesn't seem like it."

My heart began to pound in my throat as all sorts of awful scenarios sprang to mind. I wished I'd been paying better attention to the route Zyrnase was taking.

"Well, I suppose it makes sense," Jay said as my panic was setting in. "He must be taking us through the super-secret high-profile celebrity entrance in the rear."

I forced out a nervous, half-assed chuckle. Jay took my hand in his and gave it a reassuring squeeze as our car came to a stop alongside the back of a nondescript, old brick building.

"What now?"

I'd barely whispered the question when, to my

astonishment, the brick wall next to our car began to dissolve, creating an opening large enough for a car to drive through. And that's exactly where Zyrnase steered our car.

Darkness engulfed us as we drove straight down a ramp and into what appeared to be an underground tunnel. We proceeded to journey at slow speed with only the car's headlights to illuminate our way. I tried to remain calm, but after we'd driven for what felt like three whole blocks, I began to feel like I might hyperventilate.

"Okay, maybe I shouldn't have compared him to an antihistamine," Jay mused quietly next to me. I knew he was attempting to inject some humor into the tension-filled moment for my sake, but I heard the apprehension and alarm beneath his joking words as he asked, "Shall we jump out and make a run for it?"

"Somehow I doubt we'd get very far," I told him truthfully. "Let's not panic."

"Who's panicking?" he muttered. "No one in this car. You and I are not the panicking types."

I laughed so I wouldn't piss myself from fear.

My pulse jumped when our tires rolled to a stop once more in the middle of the darkened tunnel.

"On second thought—"

Jay's words were cut short as a reddish-purple light suddenly flooded the passenger cab. A large hole had opened up in the side of the tunnel where we'd stopped. Zyrnase drove us through it, and we found ourselves inside a subterranean parking garage.

About twenty feet later, we rolled to a final stop in a parking space marked with the letter "Z," and Zyrnase cut the engine.

"Jesus." Jay exhaled an exasperated sigh of relief as Zyrnase hopped out of the driver seat and made his way around the car to my door. "That was just a little over-the-fucking-top dramatic cloak-and-dagger, don't you think?"

It was an understatement. But I shushed Jay and quietly reminded him to play nice with the K as Zyrnase opened my door for me.

"Thanks... um... for the ride," I said as graciously as possible as I stepped out of the car, my legs as unsteady as my pulse after our unnerving journey. I extended my shaky hand to him, and his eyes widened strangely. Then he backed up a step, eyeing my hand like it was a poisonous snake.

"You're quite welcome," he said politely. *Without taking my outstretched hand.*

I dropped my arm and stepped aside.

When Jay climbed out of the car after me and held his hand out, Zyrnase shook it without hesitation.

Wow. Sexist much?

"Hey, thanks for the ride, man. Sorry about the bad joke before," Jay said.

Not for the first time, I marveled at how calm and collected my friend always managed to be—or at least seem.

"What joke?" Zyrnase responded, stone-faced. "I don't recall anything humorous." He shut the car door and turned his back on us. "Follow me."

"Um. Right. Hence the *bad* part—"

"Drop it," I told Jay with a sharp elbow jab to his ribs, and we followed after Zyrnase.

He led us through a hole he created in the parking garage wall. That took us down a long, gray hallway, and then through yet another hole he made in another wall, which led to another long hallway.

"Seriously, are we there yet? This is just overkill now," Jay complained loudly enough for Zyrnase to hear, prompting me to shush him again even though my stiletto-clad feet were beginning to agree.

I was also freezing, practically shivering in my short, sleeveless wrap dress as we walked through the cold, barren hallways.

We were silent as we took a small elevator up two levels, before trailing after Zyrnase down another long, sterile, industrial-looking hallway.

"Hey," Jay piped up softly, leaning closer to me and slowing his pace. "Can't believe I forgot to tell you. I heard back from Stephen while you were getting ready. Slipped my mind as we were rushing out the door."

"Who?" I mouthed back.

"CIA friend," he mumbled covertly out of the side of his lips. "He wants to talk to you. Said your name is on a list."

"What?" I mouthed, aghast.

He nodded and then jerked his head in Zyrnase's direction, murmuring, "Let's talk about it tomorrow."

"My name is on a list? What kind of list?"

Jay's eyes flashed in warning, but he shook his head and whispered back, "No idea. Said it was classified."

"Are you serious?"

"Later," he insisted, pressing his forefinger to his lips.

I shut up, but my mind was whirling.

How could I have gotten onto a classified government list?

We turned a corner at the end of the hallway, and my heart

tripped when I spied Vair standing there, not more than twenty feet away—his tall, commanding, bronzed presence a thing of surreal beauty that sent a purely feminine thrill through me.

"It's nice to see you again, little human," he said. "Welcome back to my club."

CHAPTER EIGHTEEN

I should've been insulted by his "little human" remark. But his tone was so warm, and the enchanted look he was giving me made it seem like the greatest of compliments.

"Hi."

I couldn't think of anything more eloquent to say as I stood there staring at him—feeling the strain in my cheeks from the goofy grin that had spread, unbidden, across my face. I knew exactly which grin it was, too. It was the same one found in every one of my elementary school photos—before I'd learned with age and good sense how to rein it in and smile like a normal person.

It was my overly excited, unrestrained smile, and it had absolutely no business staging an appearance now—in front of the mocking, domineering, sexy bastard of an alien who had used incriminating sex tape footage to blackmail me into coming to his x-club tonight.

As Vair walked toward me, it became easier to control my exuberant grin, while harder to will the rest of my features into a semblance of something subdued and appropriate. With each graceful step he took in my direction, his sheer size and otherworldly magnetism had me feeling torn between turning around and fleeing, and leaping into his arms to climb him like a tree.

Even at a distance, and with me wearing my blurred-vision glasses, those dark brown eyes of his were drawing me into their infinite depths, making me forget all the reasons I hadn't wanted to come to his club tonight—all the reasons that he was a danger to me and to the human race.

In that moment, there was only the chemistry between us: a force that defied logic and reason, scoffed at the inherent differences between our species, and disregarded the complications of our interplanetary politics.

"Hey, man. Great to see you again." Jay stepped directly in front of me, obstructing Vair's path in what was at once the most badass and foolishly suicidal best-friend cock-blocking move ever. "Thanks for having us back to your club."

I had completely forgotten that Jay and Zyrnase were even standing in the hallway with us.

Jay's height and musculature may have been impressive for a human male, but Vair's Krinar physique dwarfed his easily. And Vair did not appear happy with Jay for interrupting our moment. His mercurial dark eyes had gone from warm and effusive as they'd stared at me to possessive and forbidding as they'd narrowed on Jay.

My concern for my friend prompted me to find my voice at last. "Vair, you remember my best *friend*, Jay," I said, putting added emphasis on the "friend" part.

His jaw tight, an imitation of a smile on his lips, Vair clapped Jay none too gently on the shoulder and bit out a curt welcome, before bodily steering my best friend aside, out of his way.

My grade-school grin came back, accompanied by the most embarrassing schoolgirl blush, as Vair stood directly in front of me—his imposing presence once again blocking out all else, the heat emanating from his powerful body burning straight through every part of me.

"Hi," I said stupidly again.

He laughed softly and parroted, "Hi."

He took both of my trembling hands in his, warming them and chasing away the last of my fear. Replacing it with a different brand of excitement as he brought each of my hands to his lips, one after the other, depositing scalding kisses that made me regret I hadn't stashed an extra pair of panties into the tiny evening bag hanging from my shoulder.

"You look very nice, Amy." His deep, lulling voice was hypnotic as his lips brushed across the sensitive skin of my knuckles. "It's good to have you here."

My whole body came alive at his slightest touch, my muscles tightening with anticipation and my insides turning to liquid fire. My eyes fluttered shut and I swayed closer, breathing in his scent like the xenophile that I was for him.

"I'm glad you were brave enough to come tonight, darling."

The familiar words he'd used in my dream the night before proved to be the figurative bucket of ice water I needed.

My eyes flew open as it hit me: I had been right. Vair *had* visited me inside Jay's condo last night. That hadn't been a dream.

I gave myself a mental slap.

What the fuck was wrong with me?

I yanked my hands from his grasp. He relinquished them with a frown, and I took a step back, putting much-needed space between us.

I'd been standing there *blushing*. Gazing into Vair's eyes, stealing whiffs of his heavenly K scent, acting as if we were a couple out on our second date, when this was the same mocking, stalking, wall-dissolving-and-entering, videotaping, blackmailing K who was a threat to both my career and my life.

"Brave?" Jay interjected with a laugh, stepping up to my rescue when I remained at a loss for words. "Vair, man, no offense, but Amy and I have been to waaay crazier sex clubs than yours."

I nearly choked on my own spit as my head whipped in my friend's direction. Either Jay was the bravest person I knew or he seriously had a death wish.

"Is that right?" Vair said softly.

"Yeah." Jay shrugged, looking unperturbed by the cold promise of murder that had bled into the K's tone. "We're reporters, as you know. Goes with the territory."

I cringed internally.

Oblivious, my coworker proceeded to double-down on his sex-clubbing boast, beaming as he confided with a chuckle, "Since Amy and I are the youngest and best-looking journalists at *The Herald*, we're the logical choice to go undercover to research the most exclusive sex clubs in the city." He gave another shrug. "When duty calls," he sing-songed. "So here we are. No longer undercover and ready to roll whenever you are with those interview questions you promised you'd allow Amy."

I gulped. Vair was looking at Jay like he might end my friend on the spot.

But then Vair smiled thinly and responded with a nonchalant, "Of course. And I'm happy to oblige. But first, I think you should have a look around and maybe spend some time behind the bar to gain a better sense of some of the inner workings of our club—see how it compares to all the others you've been to."

He wanted us to bartend?

"Awesome," Jay agreed with enthusiasm. "Lead the way."

"I'm afraid I have other business and guests to attend to for most of the night. Zyrnase will show you around."

I tried to ignore the abrupt sense of disappointment—not to mention, anxiety—that spiked in me at the prospect of not actually spending time with Vair while in his club tonight.

If my dejection showed on my face, Vair didn't see it. Because he wasn't looking at me—adding another unwelcome layer of rejection to round out this unsettling turn of events. Only yesterday, Vair had professed in the limo that he *needed* me back at his club. He'd expressed to Jay that we would be here under his protection. Now he was simply casting us out on our own?

Vair's focus was on Zyrnase as he directed, "Take them to the upstairs bar, and see that Tauce looks after them. Let him know who she is, and tell him I said she was free to interview him." He spared only the briefest glance in my direction as he said this. "I'll send Shalee to speak with her as well, when she's available."

Zyrnase nodded, but I got the sense he wasn't exactly thrilled with what seemed to me like a newly hatched arrangement. And I couldn't shake the suspicion that we were about to be thrown to the wolves.

"Wait. You don't need to be present for her interview with this Tauce guy?" Jay asked. "Or Shalee?"

Vair smiled. "I'm sure Tauce and Shalee will manage fine without me."

"But I thought you were concerned about Amy's protect—"

"It's fine," I cut Jay off. "I'll be fine."

I hoped.

I wasn't about to let Vair think that I needed or wanted him to babysit me at his club. And I was perfectly capable of interviewing Ks on my own, without his supervision—or interference.

Vair smiled at me—a predator's grin—his teeth gleaming white within his smoothly sculpted, bronzed face. "Of course you will be."

He stepped closer and grasped me by both shoulders, the heat of his palms branding my bare skin as he invaded my personal space. His lips ghosted over my cheek before dipping to my ear to whisper, "I'm counting on you to play nice with the other aliens, darling. Don't disappoint me."

The hell?

What did that mean?

Vair traded quick words in his own language with Zyrnase as he backed away from me, a sexy, disarming grin gracing his perfect face.

When Vair was gone and we were continuing down yet *another* hallway several safe paces behind Zyrnase, I socked Jay in the bicep and hissed in his ear, "Quit antagonizing Ks!"

"Me? You started it."

"What did I do?"

"Girl, you've got to get your lust under control around Vair. You can't just look at a guy like that."

Crap. "Like what? How was I looking at him?"

"Like you wanted to make alien babies with him."

"I did not."

"Did so. And like make them right there in the hallway in front of me and Zyrnase."

"You were imagining things."

He laughed. "Well, I wasn't the only one imagining things. Pretty sure Vair was about to take you up on your unspoken offer before I stepped in between you two."

"Yeah, well... thanks for that. I appreciate it. But it was foolish and dangerous. Which reminds me..." I punched his arm again. "Are you trying to get yourself killed boasting about our fabricated sex-clubbing experience?"

"Oh, come on, it was great. And now we know that Krinar can get butthurt just like humans can. I'm thinking of making that the topic of *my* K exposé."

———

We entered the upstairs bar at Vair's x-club through one final hole in the last hallway. The multi-colored lights that greeted us brought back memories of our first visit, as did the ethereal, weeping musical undertones of some mysterious instrument playing amid the sharper vibrations and pulsing background beat.

The bar area looked similar to the one we'd been in before, but it was definitely not the same space, making me wonder just how large the entire club was. This room was a little smaller than the one we'd been in during our first visit, but with more intimate lounge seating areas featuring privacy drapes along the walls rather than the circular tables that had served as bars. The dance floor here was slightly elevated, and there was a large, futuristic-looking circular half-bar composed of what appeared to be metal and white molded glass lit from within.

The Krinar were easy to spot in the room, their superior height, bronzed skin, and stunning supermodel attributes setting them apart from even the most beautiful of the humans present on the dance floor. As before, the Ks were dressed in simplistic, light-colored clothing that accentuated their healthy-looking, tanned skin, and in fabrics that seemed to conform to their bodies in a way that emphasized their graceful, impressive physiques—causing me to feel a moment of inadequacy and regret over my outfit selection as I covertly wiped my damp palms on the skirt of my dress.

After a month of obsessing over my last visit, I was officially back inside Vair's x-club. I was just beginning to get my nerves under control and my game face on when a ruckus started on the dance floor.

"I told you not to come back here!"

CHAPTER NINETEEN

*T*he music cut off and the lights brightened, illuminating the kerfuffle that had erupted.

An enormous Krinar male with a completely shaved head and striking greenish-yellow eyes was holding a tall, clean-cut-looking young human man up by his throat with one hand. As huge as Vair was, this bald K looked even bigger—maybe a few inches taller and packing another thirty pounds of muscle.

If I'd noticed him on the street in broad daylight carrying a bag of groceries, I might've been alarmed enough to walk briskly in the opposite direction. Seeing him holding a struggling human in the air with ease was positively terrifying.

"Who *the cusack* let this guy in here again?" the scary K demanded. His eyes—more yellow than green now—casually scanned the room in accusation before returning to regard the man in his grasp with renewed disdain. "Last call. Any Krinar want to claim him?"

Those stark yellow eyes, set amid perfectly symmetrical,

sharp features, and so pronounced against his deeply tanned skin, reflected zero compassion for the victim in his grasp, who was turning purple for lack of air and clutching desperately at the massive hand around his throat.

And I mean zero.

I tugged Jay's elbow. "We have to do something."

"I know, but what?" he whispered, his face pale. "Get ourselves killed?"

"Tauce won't kill him," Zyrnase reassured us, his voice devoid of concern.

That was Tauce? The K Vair had elected to "look after us" was this crazy-eyed killer alien choking a man to death in the middle of a dance floor?

Thrown to the wolves, indeed.

"Are you shitting me?" Jay exclaimed. "That's the guy she's supposed to interview? *Alone?* Where's Vair? I want to talk to him."

"There's no need for that. Tauce!"

At Zyrnase's sharply spoken call, the giant K let the poor human man drop to the floor in a semiconscious heap.

"Don't come back," Tauce coldly told the man, who was now twitching and coughing on the ground, holding his throat as he struggled to take in air again.

The K's words held the promise of certain death should the man be foolish enough to disobey.

But why?

What on earth had the man done? He didn't look much older than early to mid-twenties. And he was obviously no match for a K. What could possibly have gone down to warrant such treatment?

Pushing my fear of the yellow-eyed K aside, I took a step

forward as Jay and Zyrnase started arguing over Vair's choice of babysitter and interviewee for me.

Other Ks came and removed the human man from the dance floor, the lights dimmed, and the music resumed as Tauce stomped off, heading over to the bar, a disgusted, angry look still etched on his face. Which, for all I knew, might've been his normal expression.

My heart fluttered in my throat as I took a second step, and then another.

I told myself it was because I was curious. That it was simply the reporter in me driven to know the facts of the situation—to understand what a human could've possibly done at an alien sex club to deserve to be attacked and threatened in the way I'd just witnessed.

It wasn't because I felt challenged by Vair's "play nice with the other aliens" remark, or because I wanted to show Vair that I was brave enough to confront whatever scary alien dares he was willing to dish out.

And it certainly wasn't because his influence called to the subconscious thrill-seeking adrenaline junkie in me who lacked the good judgment to gauge true danger when faced with it. This was about getting the facts straight and having my interview questions answered by a K for my next article.

Summoning all of my nerve, I cautiously ambled closer until I was standing in front of the great beast of a K who was angrily stewing behind the bar. He glanced up at my approach and smiled. *And somehow managed to look even more frightening when he did.*

"Well, hell-o there, sweetness." Lascivious green eyes had my wrap dress off in seconds flat. "I'm Tauce." He reached across the lit bar between us, offering me his ginormous throat-choking hand. "First time at the club?"

"Yieeeccch!" Zyrnase released a bizarre-sounding distress cry from behind me, where he'd been arguing with Jay. "She's Vair's human!"

Tauce withdrew his hand at unnatural speed, exclaiming something that sounded like "fuck," but with more syllables. His eyes were wide and disbelieving as they looked over my shoulder in Jay and Zyrnase's direction. "Charl?" he asked.

"Uh, no, name's Jay." Jay rushed forward to stand protectively next to me. He extended his hand to Tauce. "I'm assuming you already know Zyrnase?"

Tauce didn't take Jay's hand. The scornful look he leveled at my friend made me like the K even less than I had ten seconds ago. "I was referring to the lady," he said, his wide, square jaw jutting in my direction.

"Her name's not Charl, either," Jay told him. "It's Amy."

Tauce's eyes turned a shade that was almost neon yellow as his annoyed glare transferred from Jay to Zyrnase. "Don't even say it, Z. Not tonight."

"Vair wants you to look after them."

"Aw, *cusack!*"

I decided "cusack" must be the Krinar equivalent of "fuck"—or something along those lines. In any case, it wasn't a happy word.

Zyrnase and Tauce argued in Krinar. It didn't last long, and I knew Tauce had lost his case when he scrubbed an enormous hand over his face and groused "cusack" three times in rapid succession.

———

Zyrnase left us in Tauce's capable killer hands. Tauce spent the better part of the first twenty minutes with us serving drinks and ignoring our presence as we stood idly behind the bar, keeping out of his way as much as possible.

When he wasn't procuring a beverage for someone, he was tracing things into his palm with his pointer finger—usually with his nostrils flared and his upper lip curled in contempt. Sometimes he appeared to be reading things from his forearm. I couldn't decide if he was still pouting over his missed homicide opportunity on the dance floor, or if all his emo alien ire was for us.

Jay attempted to engage him in conversation, but to no avail. It wasn't until we decided to leave him sulking by himself in favor of exploring the room on our own that he chose to interact—*to stop us.*

He corralled us back behind the bar, and let it be known that we were not to leave his presence. It became clear that Vair had designated Tauce as our bodyguard-slash-babysitter—a revelation that was somewhat reassuring in the sense that it meant Vair seemingly did want to keep us safe while we were in his club. And yet it was also disappointing.

Hanging out with Grumpy K while he was working and moping was very anticlimactic after the amount of speculating and stressing that Jay and I had done in the past twenty-four hours.

"We walked through twenty wall dissolves for this?" Jay complained.

He pointed out that if we had to watch angry paint dry for the rest of the night, we had better start drinking. Unfortunately, the x-club bar wasn't stocked with Jay's usual vodka shots. In fact, it wasn't stocked at all—it was literally an empty bar.

Tauce would simply wave his hand or ask for a certain drink, and it would appear—rising up from hidden compartments below the white glass surface of the bar. Making his "bartender" role seem a tad superfluous, in my opinion.

The exotic purple fruit juice mixed with mild alcohol that Vair had given me the last time I'd been here seemed to be the most popular choice for the human clubgoers. Jay began referring to it as an "alien Shirley Temple" after he consumed two glasses and failed to catch a buzz.

"I think they do it on purpose," Jay said, noisily slurping down the remains of his second glass in vain while Tauce brooded and kept watch over us from the other end of the bar.

"Do what?"

"Serve such mild, benign drinks that after a while, you're so desperate to catch a high you'll willingly sign up for a vein tapping by any K available. Makes sense, right?"

I laughed and shook my head. "I don't know. I'm still on my first glass, and I can feel the alcohol a little. I definitely feel something... like some kind of warmth or energy flowing through me. Maybe it's just the music." Or my waning adrenaline rush.

"I think it's Tauce's laser eyes burning into your rear. Seriously, I'm about to throw down in your honor if he doesn't quit staring."

"Shhh, keep it down; he'll hear you."

"That's the point. I'll tell you, the very last thing I expected was to be bored tonight." Jay set his empty glass onto the bar. "It's literally the only scenario I never contemplated in coming here."

I had to agree. But it felt wrong to be disappointed about that. We should've been relieved to be bored.

"Hey, at least we're safe," I reminded Jay. "That's the most important thing. This is a way better outcome than any other scenario."

"Speak for yourself. Not all of us value safety above all else in life, baby girl." Jay waved his hand over the top of his glass the way we'd seen Tauce do.

Nothing happened. When Tauce had done it, the bar would open up and pull the glass down below the surface.

"I command you to take the glass away," Jay intoned in a ridiculous voice, loudly enough to garner a scowl from Tauce.

"Cut it out. He'll think we're making fun."

"Good. Vair implied we'd get to work the bar. He said we'd get to look around and gain a better sense of the inner workings of his club. Nothing we've done with Tauce so far remotely qualifies." Jay shouted the last part in Tauce's direction. "He also said we'd get to interview Tauce, but the guy won't even speak with us. He just stands there pretending to doodle on his palm and read things from his forearm."

I swore I could hear Tauce's teeth gnashing from ten feet away as Jay continued his tirade. The K looked like he was angry-tracing on his palm now.

"And anytime another K or human tries to interact with us, anti-soc baldie over there scares them away. Vair's treating us like children, Amy. Either we get some real drinks and a real interview with a K, or I say we get out of here."

Right. Like it was that easy. Vair was up to something with this arrangement; I just couldn't figure out what. In the interim, I needed to calm Jay down and get him to shut the hell up before he pushed our alien babysitter too far.

But then Jay stopped talking on his own, riveted by the sight of a statuesque brunette K approaching the bar.

Her glossy, shoulder-length hair fell in loose, natural waves, and she was wearing a body-hugging white, short, asymmetrical tank dress that was the perfect, effortless marriage of casual sexy and haute couture chic. Her gaze paused briefly as it swept over Jay before meeting mine. She smiled and extended her hand to me, and I noticed how her brown eyes had striking shades of amber in them.

"I'm Shalee."

I took Shalee's proffered hand and gave it a firm shake. Tauce made no attempt to stop me.

"Nice to meet you. I'm Amy."

"I know. I work very closely with Vair. It's a pleasure to meet you, Amy."

My heart sped up and something in my gut twisted at her words, even as I kept a pleasant smile on my face. "Oh? How nice. For how long?"

I hadn't meant to voice that question, but seeing as I couldn't take it back, I decided to expand on it. "What kind of work? What do you do with him?"

Are you sleeping with him?

"Research." She canted her head, studying me with squinted eyes as the right side of her mouth curved up. "Mostly."

Bitch.

"I'm Jay." My best friend thrust his hand forward, practically shouldering me out of his way to get directly in front of Shalee.

I took the hint and stepped aside.

Shalee's smile widened. "Hi, Jay." She took his hand, and I watched as normally suave, socially sophisticated Jay just stood there, speechless, staring at Vair's gorgeous coworker like he might drool on himself at any moment.

"We're not together," he finally spoke up with a nod in my direction. "In case… in case you were wondering." He was still holding her hand.

"I know."

"This is going to sound like the world's cheesiest pick-up line," Jay began, then paused to catch his breath.

I thought about shoving him back out of the way to save him from himself, but I didn't know if I'd be able to break the hold he had on Shalee's hand. And some small, evil part of me did want to hear Jay's cheesiest pick-up line for humor's sake.

"I swear I had a dream about you last night," Jay confessed in total sincerity.

Lordy.

Shalee's brow lifted—in apparent genuine interest, too, not in a "you've got to be kidding me" way. "Really? What were we doing?"

She wasn't serious, was she? She seemed way too smart to fall for that. Had they never heard that tired line on Krina?

"In my dream, you were a nurse." Jay cleared his throat. "And you made… a house call."

I coughed. Loudly. But Jay didn't look away from Shalee to catch my signal.

"You don't say?" She sounded legit intrigued. *There was no way she was going for this.* "What was the treatment?"

"You gave me some kind of hangover prevention medicine."

She bit her lip, assessing him with a sexy smile. "Did it work?"

This was like watching bad porn. She *had* to be messing with him.

He nodded. *And blushed.* I had never seen my friend blush before.

"Very well, actually." He gestured to the dance floor. "Would you like to—?"

"Yes," she answered. "I would."

No way.

She looked to me. "You don't mind if I borrow him for a bit, do you?"

Yeah, I did, actually. I pinched Jay's elbow to gain his attention. He didn't even flinch. It was as if he was hypnotized by Shalee's face.

"Oh, well, I think Tauce wants us to stay—"

"Take him," Tauce intervened, shutting me down. "It's fine."

CHAPTER TWENTY

I lost sight of Jay and Shalee after their second dance, when they moved to the lounge seating area along the wall and drew the privacy curtains. From the way they'd been all over one another on the dance floor, I didn't expect that I'd see either of them again very soon.

It felt uncannily like the last time I'd been here, when Jay had abandoned me for Alien Barbie Shira, only worse, because Vair wasn't by my side. And Jay's departure and subsequent love fest on the dance floor with Shalee had made Vair's absence feel all the more pronounced.

It had also made hanging out alone with Tauce nearly unbearable.

But at least I was safe, I reminded myself.

Safety was key.

I'd given in and taken to wearing my glasses on top of my head instead of over my eyes in order to scan the crowd and people-watch rather than observe Tauce staring at his own hand. I was beginning to come to terms with the fact that I really couldn't see well with my eyewear on anymore.

Another thirty minutes and an "alien Shirley Temple" later, my stilettos were killing me. My night was going nowhere fast and I had nothing to lose, so I decided to try and throw out a few of the interview questions Jay had come up with.

"Hey, so um, Vair said... he said that I could interview you. Is that... is that okay?"

Tauce didn't react. He didn't even twitch an eyelash. He just stood there, staring me down.

I fidgeted on my feet, tucking my hair behind my ear. "So what are the Krinar's ultimate plans for us as a society?"

I'd known it was a bad question. Tauce confirmed it.

His eyes widened. Then he slow-blinked. "You do this for a living? And they *pay* you?"

Ass.

Fine. "What's with pushing veganism on the planet when you're all here getting high on human blood? That hardly qualifies as a vegan diet."

He made a soft grunting noise and pinched the bridge of his nose, shaking his head.

Fuck.

"How long have you worked here?"

He gave me his back.

Not even that one he'd answer?

"How do you like living in New York City?" I called after him as he walked to the other end of the bar.

"Hi, Tauce." A striking blond woman strolled up to where he had gone to ignore me and leaned across the bar, spilling ample boobage from her ultra-sexy, barely-there dress. "Will I see you in the basement later?"

I thought she might be a Krinar at first, but then I saw that she was too short. As I studied her closer, I realized she looked vaguely familiar, but I knew I didn't know her.

As I watched Tauce's apathetic response to her flirting, it hit me where I'd seen her before: gracing the covers of tabloids in the supermarket checkout line. She was a well-known soap opera star who'd been on the same show for ages. I was pretty sure she'd won numerous Daytime Emmy Awards. I couldn't think of her name, though, as I'd never seen the popular show she was on.

She gave up trying to entice him and strutted off when Tauce ignored her boobs in favor of drawing on his palm with his finger in that weird way he'd been doing.

I rushed over to him once she was gone. "Oh, my God. Was that—"

"Yes," Tauce cut me off with an eye roll. "It was. Yes, she's some kind of… television personality." He said it like it was the dumbest job a person could have, or be impressed by. "All the humans ask that when she comes in."

It was reassuring to know I was just like every dumb human Tauce encountered in Vair's club. "She comes here a lot?"

He shrugged, and I thought that he was done with the conversation. But after a beat, he offered up: "She's a nymphomaniac; likes a K in every hole when she comes here. I enjoy taking her in the ass."

Alrighty. It was my turn to slow-blink.

I resisted. Because this was a Tauce breakthrough. Maybe he would talk if the topic was sex?

"Are you a polyamorous society on Krina?"

His yellow-green eyes raked me up and down. "We like to have sex. Sometimes in groups. More often in pairs."

Interesting. *Which did Vair prefer?*

"We don't suffer the prudish social constraints that plague your society."

"Plague?" I had to giggle. I was nearly giddy with excitement that he was finally engaging with me and answering my questions. "That's a tad dramatic."

He gave me his best stone-faced Tauce look in reply.

Okay, then. "Do Krinar ever pair off for life? You know, get married? Or something similar to that? Like humans do?"

He made a face like he'd just smelled something awful. "If they're unlucky."

Right. And I'd bet my left kidney the K who ended up saddled with Tauce for life would consider herself the unlucky one in that arrangement.

"So is it more of a societal arrangement then? Not because the Krinar pair wants to?"

"No. They do it because they want to." He looked down at his palm, becoming distracted with whatever he was seeing there.

I was losing him. I needed to steer the conversation back to sex.

"I overheard the blond actress ask whether she'd be seeing you in the basement later. Is that where you've, um... hooked up with her before?"

Tauce looked up from his palm, his brow arched in amusement. "Hooked up? You mean fucked?" He shook his head. "I can't believe you're Vair's human."

"And what does that mean?" I failed to keep the affront I felt at his tone from my voice. Zyrnase had referred to me in those same terms when I'd been introduced to Tauce. I hadn't wanted to read into it or analyze its meaning too closely at the time.

"Do you mean I'm Vair's human guest when you say that?" I asked hopefully.

He smirked. Some guys managed to pull off "cocky-sexy" when they smirked; Tauce just looked like a dick.

"No, little reporter, it means you're Vair's property. It means that he owns you."

I forced a breath as I felt the blood draining from my face.

Don't panic, don't panic. It's not what it sounds like he's saying.

"You mean while I'm here at his club? Like in an erotic power-exchange kind of deal? Dom and sub stuff? Because I haven't—I didn't agree to do anything... like that..." I trailed off, swallowing hard at the nasty look of amusement that spread across Tauce's features.

He bent his head closer to mine, his penetrating yellow-green eyes staring me down. "Ks don't need permission from humans," he informed me in a cold whisper. "We take what we want. We keep what we claim as ours."

My face burned with indignation. "No one owns me, Tauce."

He laughed. His laughter came off even worse on the bastard scale than his smirk.

Recognizing the futility of continuing to argue this point with him given my present predicament, I decided to change the subject.

"So what was with that guy earlier on the dance floor?" I shifted my glasses back down over my eyes, not wanting to see any more than I had to of Tauce's face. "What happened?"

"He was warned not to come back here."

"Yeah, I kind of caught that from your exchange. But why? What did he do to get banned from the club?"

Not surprisingly, I was met with blurry stone-faced Tauce in response, followed by him ignoring me to fiddle with his palm.

"What is up with the damn palm business, already?" I was beyond over it.

His head jerked up at my tone. "I'm working," he said, as if stating the obvious.

"You're working? On your palm?"

"Yes."

"I'm sorry." I shook my head. "I'm not following. How is that working?"

"The same way you humans work on your cellular devices."

"You have a tiny phone in your hand? Where?" I moved closer, grabbing for his hand as curiosity got the better of me.

He pulled back before I could touch him. "Not a phone. And it's not for your human eyes to see."

Ah. Right. The 'ole *Emperor's New Clothes* deal—a K device that was invisible to unfit humans. Made total sense within their technologically advanced world of dissolving walls.

It was the perfect segue to broach the topic of K technology and to ask Tauce whether the Krinar ever planned to share any of their advances with us. But instead, I found myself asking, "You got anything stronger to drink in this place?"

I set my glasses back atop my head and rubbed my sore eyes.

What I really wanted to ask was what time my shift ended tonight. Because that's exactly what this felt like: working a shift at a shitty clock-watching job where you lost hours of your life talking to people you'd never willingly engage with had you not been coworkers.

"Not for you," Tauce replied.

I nodded, putting my glasses back in place. "Figures."

"How about a change of scenery instead?" Tauce suggested.

"Yes!" I agreed, a little too enthusiastically. "I mean, yeah, that'd be great. I'd love to tour other parts of the club."

I pushed my glasses up again so that I could see his face and gauge his sincerity, but he was busy messing with his stupid palm once more. When he was done, he glanced up and gave me a stoic, "Come with me. I need to work the downstairs bar now."

We walked through a hole Tauce made in the wall behind the bar area, down a surprisingly short, dark hallway, and into a small elevator.

I felt a little anxious about leaving Jay behind in the upstairs bar, but I had a feeling he'd be safe with Shalee. And I wouldn't be gone long, I rationalized—even though I had no idea how long Tauce was supposed to work this downstairs bar we were headed to.

When the elevator opened at the basement level, I was expecting to find a hallway or at the very least another wall that Tauce would need to dissolve before we reached our final destination. But instead, the doors opened and we were thrust smack-dab into the middle of a busy club scene.

A scene that I was woefully unprepared for.

People—and aliens—were having sex. *Everywhere.* In cages suspended from the ceiling, in cages on the ground, on the dance floor, against the wall—*suspended by chains in some cases.*

A woman was being eaten out on a table mere feet from where we were standing!

My mouth went dry as I met Tauce's smug eyes. He was clearly enjoying my discomfort.

"I'd rather work the bar upstairs," I managed to say.

He gave me a look that said I wasn't getting anything I wanted—at least not from him.

"I want to speak with Vair about this."

He smirked. "You're in luck. Vair's the reason you're down here. Follow me."

He took off at an easy stride, and I was torn between not wanting to be left alone in this triple-X basement bar scene and not wanting to follow and see how much worse it might get. When I didn't immediately follow, he turned around and made a hissing sound at me.

An actual. Hissing. Sound.

Oh, my God. This guy. I rolled my eyes and bit my lip to keep from telling him to *cusack* the hell off.

He was in front of me in a blink, with that perpetually irate, constipated-looking expression that I'd privately dubbed "resting Tauce face" during the hour and forty-three minutes I'd endured with him.

"Do you not understand the word *follow*, human?"

"Oh, was that what you said? I couldn't hear you over the music and screaming down here."

His hiss morphed into a growl. Then he seemed to make an attempt to compose himself.

"Listen, *Amy...*" He addressed me by my name for the very first time, and managed to make it sound like a foul disease he didn't want to contract. "Someone's liable to suck and fuck you and ask questions later if you don't stick close to me down here."

He had me at "suck."

I held my palm up in surrender. "Got it. Lead the way. I'll *follow.*"

I stuck close to Tauce as he wove a path through the

basement of Sodom and Gomorrah. As horrified as I was by the sights and sounds that surrounded me, I found myself unwittingly turned on by some of them as well.

Any fledgling hope I'd quietly harbored about Vair not being into the really kinky stuff was squashed as we passed by naked people gagged and bound to sex furniture and tied to x-shaped Saint Andrew's crosses.

Why, oh why hadn't I kept my mouth shut and stayed upstairs in the safe bar?

My system was on overload, my shaky fingers continuously sliding my glasses up and down between the bridge of my nose and the tip, torn between wanting to see and not wanting to know.

I was so disoriented I barely noticed my steps, much less paid attention to where we were going, and before I knew it, I'd walked through an opening in a wall that Tauce had made. In front of me was the famous blond actress from the bar upstairs —engaged in a scene I could've gladly gone my whole life not knowing about.

CHAPTER TWENTY-ONE

*M*ultiple men—Krinar—were touching her. *And were inside her.*

At once.

Others were waiting their turn. And judging by the euphoric, inhuman sounds coming out of her, the beautiful Emmy award-winning actress was one hundred percent down with this. Then again, they'd likely bitten her, and as Jay had said, a bite from a K was like the most potent drug.

Tauce nudged me from behind and I stumble-entered the room—having tripped over my own slack jaw as I tried to block out the sounds I was hearing. To un-see what I was witnessing.

Vair was seated in an elevated white lounge chair at the edge of the bed. His chair appeared to be floating above the floor—in the same manner the circular platform bed was doing. Upon my clumsy entrance, his floating chair swiveled in my direction. He looked like the Greek god Dionysus himself, sitting on his throne, all dark and gorgeous, casually observing the orgy before him. *Buck-naked.*

I spun on my heel, intending to flee back upstairs to the bar, only to find Tauce already gone and the opening in the wall I'd come through sealed off.

"Come, now, don't be shy." Vair's arms were encircling me from behind in an instant, his throaty laughter just loud enough to be heard above the panicked blood roaring in my ears and the woman having an orgasm behind me, as he half-dragged, half-carried me over to the chair he'd vacated. "I want you to observe and take notes for me."

Take notes?

He pulled me straight into his lap as he reseated himself, his arm wrapping firmly around my waist so that I couldn't have moved an inch even if I hadn't been rendered stiff from shock. "This is your opportunity to get answers. You like observing and reporting facts, remember?"

He was mocking me again. But I was too scared shitless to care. I was in his naked lap in a sealed room where an alien orgy was taking place.

My fight reflex belatedly kicked in, and I struggled wildly against him. "No, I can't! I'm not wired like that. I don't do group sex. Please, I'm a terrible multitasker!"

"Shh-shh—calm down." His palm clamped over my mouth. "I asked you to observe and take notes." The genuine annoyance in his voice did more to soothe me than his actual words. He tipped my head back at an awkward angle until I found myself staring up into his glaring countenance. "No one touches you but me, little human. Understand?"

His proclamation was delivered in a tone that was

downright grumpy—nasty even. "Little human" falling from the twisted line of his angry lips sounded more like a slight than the endearment it had seemed to me earlier. So it made no sense when my heart warmed at his words and the paralyzing fear I'd felt abruptly abated.

No one touched me but him. I could get on board with that—for the moment, at least.

His fingers flexed, biting into the hollow planes below my cheekbones, silently demanding my response. I nodded against his palm and his eyes softened, if not his mouth.

Removing his hand, he yanked me upright in his lap and dropped an odd-looking electronic notepad into my sweaty hands. It was slightly larger than my phone, but lighter. I dazedly listened to his brusque instructions as he relayed the features, showing me how I could take notes manually or via the recorder feature.

Oh, my God, he was serious about me taking notes?

Fine, I could do this. I was a *reporter.* Taking orgy notes was better than being expected to participate in one.

I swallowed and forced my eyes up from the electronic device in my hands to the group of perfectly formed naked male bodies undulating and thrusting directly in front of me.

Just disconnect emotionally and report the facts, Amy.

Far be it for me to judge another person's "fantasy," but Jesus —it was a lot to take in once I stopped trying to block it out.

The genetic male perfection of a Krinar whose dick Ms. Emmy was riding was gently fingering her clit and worshipping her nipples, sucking on one perfect, pink areola at a time. But the things he was saying to her in between his nipple play belied the apparent sweetness of his touch. Because he was calling her a dirty slut. Telling her what a greedy whore she was being.

In contrast, the alien gripping her hips, controlling her positioning for his maximum penetration as he fucked her rear entrance, was groaning about how beautiful and precious she was, telling her what a good girl she was being for them and how sweet her tight asshole felt gripping his dick.

And still a third K was playfully taunting her as he fisted the roots of her hair and stroked his giant erection right in her face. "Show me how a good alien cumslut begs," he'd coax, before letting her lick the precum. He would allow her to wrap her bee-stung, begging lips around the fat head of his dick before yanking her by the hair off of him again and proceeding to stroke his cock just out of reach of her extended tongue until he was satisfied with her begging again.

My cheeks were so hot they hurt. My eyes burned from not blinking. This was so utterly twisted.

Positively horrific.

And horrifically hot.

I was so turned on I was sure Vair could feel it on his thigh through the thin fabric of my tags-still-on TJ Maxx dress. Definitely wouldn't be returning it for a refund now.

Focus on the facts. Just dictate the facts.

"Are you asking me for help with the facts?" Vair's chin settled on my shoulder.

Shit. I'd said that out loud?

"Feel free to interview me," he offered. His hard chest pressed along my spine, and the arm banded around my waist drew me deeper into his lap until my ass was nestled against his groin.

On the one hand, his proximity felt safe and comforting within the small room presently dominated by naked, huge, aroused male Ks wielding inhuman erections on the floating bed/stage in front of me. At the same time, the alien erection I felt hardening against the cleft of my ass was equally disruptive to what scant peace of mind I was clinging to. Then the palm of his other hand settled on my lower thigh just below the hem of my dress, and his finger began tracing lazy circles on my inner knee.

I couldn't get my brain and mouth to formulate a reply. Nor could I get my hands to stop shaking enough to make use of the electronic notepad he'd given me.

"Fact." Vair's low voice filled my ear as his lips brushed against it. "Human female has been enjoying extended orgasms at the hands, mouths, and cocks of multiple male Krinar for over thirty minutes now."

Was I supposed to jot that down?

I didn't. I was having difficulty just forcing enough air into my lungs.

"Fact: Female human has been injected with Krinar saliva at her own behest," Vair continued, "making her more receptive to orgasm, her body primed to engage in prolonged sexual intercourse with numerous partners."

K saliva—injected?

His slow circles were drifting higher up the inside of my leg.

"They didn't bite her?" I tried to sound analytical. Detached.

I totally failed.

"No. They did not."

Interview him like a reporter. You're a reporter. "Isn't the whole point of this club so Ks can drink human blood?"

"Yes. And no."

Helpful. "What—why a saliva injection?" I was panting now.

"Our saliva in your bloodstream is what induces the Ecstasy-like sensation and aphrodisiac effect that you so fondly wrote about in your article."

Was that a hint of bitterness I detected? Score one for Amy.

And this was valuable intel. *Focus on the intel.* "How? Why would your saliva—"

"Your blood contains the same hemoglobin characteristics as the Krinian primates who used to be our primary source of sustenance on our home planet before we hunted them into extinction millions of years ago."

Not the explanation I was prepared for.

His muscled thighs flexed and shifted beneath me, parting my legs as they did so. His hand drifted higher beneath my dress as if it had every right to, sending a thrill of anticipation straight to my lower belly—a thrill that contrasted sharply with the rush of fear that tripped my heartbeat.

"There's a chemical found in our saliva that was originally designed to make our prey feel drugged and docile, allowing us to feed from them without resistance."

This was fucked up with a capital F.

"That same chemical now has the effect of enhancing your human sexual experience when we bite you."

I was officially *prey.*

And I'd just spread my legs wider for the predator holding me.

"With the advent of synthetic hemoglobin substitutes and the manipulation of our own DNA over the past million years or so, we no longer require the blood of a sister species for survival."

Now they just did it for fun?

It was all so disturbing. Yet somehow hot... in a really wrong and dirty science-of-evolution kind of way.

"But w-why inject it?"

His hand was so close now. The heat coming off of it between my thighs was sending my clit into a mad, fluttering frenzy.

"Because this way, the Krinar males remain in control of their own desires." His voice was patient as the tip of his knuckle made contact with my soaked underwear at long last— finding the evidence of my instinctive "prey" response. "They don't have to worry about getting carried away and fucking a human female too hard. Too fast. Humans are a fragile species. We've learned to be gentle with our food."

Cute. My E.T. had a sense of humor. *A sick one.*

"Makes it easier for them to focus solely on the human client's needs."

"Client?"

"Patron, subject, patient—whichever you prefer. We're also less territorial when we don't drink our prey's blood. Makes it easier to share."

Patient? Share?

I could feel my heartbeat in my sex as his knuckle began to lightly stroke me.

"How... that's not—this isn't sexy"—I gasped for air as he added more pressure—"at all."

Oh, God, who was I trying to convince? Myself? Vair? The three aliens waiting for their turn with the soap star who were now all watching me with hungry eyes as they stroked themselves, relishing the scent of my fear and arousal?

"Mmmm." Vair inhaled deeply against my neck. "I disagree, love."

"You aren't the food," I pointed out, directing a back-the-fuck-off glare at one of the Ks when he had the audacity to lick his lips while eyeballing me.

"Humans are obsessed with vampires." Vair's voice was amused. "They've romanticized them for centuries." His lips caressed my ear. "Fantasized about being their prey."

Damn, this was true. "Not all of us."

"Of course. Not *you*, Amy." He chuckled. "Never you. My turn to ask questions."

I didn't argue. I again was in Vair's world, playing by his rules, swiftly falling under his spell.

"Have you ever fantasized about being shared?"

I shook my head, relieved that it was an easy question.

He was still stroking me. Barely. *Lazily.* Just enough to keep me uncomfortably aroused and on edge.

"That's good. Because I'll never share you."

I was so hot I was melting.

"Tell me, are you enjoying the other male eyes on you right now?"

"No," I admitted breathlessly. "Not at all." Another easy one.

"Very good. I'm not enjoying it either."

He said something in his K language, and the air shimmered and rippled in front of us as if it were water, before taking on a silvery, translucent quality that expanded the length of the room to form a wall between us and the other occupants—a wall that looked similar to a two-way mirror.

I hadn't a moment to ponder this crazy-impressive phenomenon, though, because Vair's finger hooked inside my underwear and tore the crotch clean out in one swift tug.

The cool air hit me where I was exposed and desperate to feel his hot fingers.

And so much more.

"Better?" he asked as he spread my legs wider with his knees and slipped his hand up over my breasts and around my neck.

I didn't answer. My heart hammered in my chest as his lips pressed to my ear and his fingers tightened around my throat.

"Fact: You're ready for me to fuck you now. So ready you're praying that I'll do it without you having to ask. You're hoping I'll bite you, aren't you? Give you the excuse you need to lose control and beg me to fuck you until you forget why you ever thought that playing it safe in life was a good idea.

"That's why you've been rocking back and forth, rubbing against my knuckle, grinding your perfect, luscious ass into my erection, isn't it? You've been hoping I'd lose control. Hoping I'd turn into a wild, savage predator who takes what he wants so you don't have to admit that you want it.

"Well," he continued with a dark chuckle, "you're in luck. I've been a very patient savage, Amy. For *a whole month*. I gave you time. Time to write your article. Time to sort things out in your mind. Time to come to me on your own terms. You didn't. Now it's happening on mine.

"I'm going to fuck you." He spoke the words slowly, his breath hot against my ear as my pulse beat frantically against his fingers. "Then I'm going to bite you." His voice was calm and even, belying the violent urgency radiating from him. "And then I'm *really* going to fuck you."

Immobilized by fear and excitement, I remained mute as his other hand pried the electronic notepad from my sweaty fingers. I didn't bother to notice what he did with it.

He removed my glasses next.

I didn't object.

"Take the dress off if you want to keep it."

I didn't move.

My body jerked reflexively as my dress and undergarments were shredded off of me seconds later.

CHAPTER TWENTY-TWO

*V*air stood, unseating me from his lap. My naked body pitched forward, and I stumble-stepped, thrown off-balance in my high heels, until my palms found purchase against the strange glass wall separating us from the soap star's orgy.

I knew a moment of panic at being so completely exposed, standing there naked in my heels, my nose inches from the glass surface that felt solid and yet somehow alive—as fluid as water, moving and vibrating with energy beneath my palms—as I was afforded a front-row, up-close, and graphic view of the alien group sex session that was getting wilder by the minute.

No one on the other side of the glass was looking at me, though. I told myself they couldn't see me—that it had to be a two-way mirror given what Vair had said about not enjoying other male eyes on me. Still, I'd never felt more naked and vulnerable.

I took a step back, pushing off against the glass. But I didn't get far as my ass collided with Vair's hard thighs. His hands were suddenly everywhere, his body rubbing against and covering the length of mine from behind.

And my hands were... stuck.

Literally stuck.

That alien glass *was* alive. It had wrapped around and shackled my wrists to its surface. My hands were positioned at chest level, and I could see where the glass had morphed into thick, clear restraints around my slender wrists.

"Vair?" I sounded terrified.

I *was* terrified.

His right palm closed over mine atop the glass as his mouth brushed my cheek, whispering reassurances that failed to register as I continued to struggle in vain.

I immediately understood why people used safe words.

Because I needed one. And I didn't have one.

"Easy, darling." He linked his fingers with mine against the animated glass as his left hand fisted in my hair. "It's all right. The wall won't harm you." He tilted my head back. "I'd never let anything harm you."

"I don't like being restrained!" My eyes beseeched his—two dark pools of lust that studied me, and not without compassion, I noted, as he seemed to genuinely consider my plea. *Briefly.*

Then his lips brushed over mine in the first true, conscious kiss we'd shared since being reunited. "You'll like it this time," he promised softly. He nipped my bottom lip, tugged it gently between his teeth, and sucked. "Because you're with me." He leaned into me, his erection pressing unmistakably against my ass—so hard and huge it sent another wave of apprehension through me. "And you know I'll always keep you safe."

I didn't know that.

Why the hell would I know that?

His species was my planet's enemy. He was blackmailing me. He was restraining me against a moving, translucent wall straight out of a science fiction horror story, planning to fuck me while I was forced to watch the crazy erotic alien orgy taking place mere feet away on the other side of said creepy wall.

I'd never been so terrified and turned on in my life.

"I adore you, little human."

"Little human" was back to being an endearment, and he kissed me with none of the aggressiveness I'd anticipated when he'd first announced that he was going to fuck me, bite me, and then "really" fuck me—in that order. His gentleness took me by surprise as his lips caressed and nibbled until my own relaxed and allowed him to deepen the kiss.

"I worship you," he murmured before slipping his tongue inside my mouth in a languid, drugging kiss that made my whole body feel so heavy with need I was almost glad the wall restraints were there to hold me up. "Never harm you."

His words were nonsensical. Ks didn't worship humans. And he was sure to harm me.

My body didn't know the difference. Didn't care that he was the obvious threat that even my faulty instincts should've recognized.

I sagged into him, my nipples painfully erect and yearning for friction where the cool air was hitting them. Arousal flooded my sex and dripped down my inner thigh, my core clenching with the need to have him fill me. To push his alien cock in deep where it could never belong.

My body didn't care about the obvious facts of the matter—

that this was completely dangerous and untenable territory. It wanted to lose control.

Because screw danger and consequence; sometimes a girl just needs to get fucked.

So I kissed him back the way a woman kisses a man when she wants exactly that, silently daring him to give it to me. Knowing Vair would deliver.

I swallowed his groan of approval as his hands skimmed over my goose-pimpled skin at last, his touch too light and brief against my trembling stomach and aching nipples to satisfy.

I spread my legs and tilted my ass into his groin in supplication.

He broke our kiss, his breathing labored as he said, "So sweet. Just like I knew you'd be."

His hand skated down my lower belly to touch between my drenched thighs before moving around to grip my butt cheek.

"This ass has haunted me for a month," he confessed, kissing his way down my spine until he was on his knees behind me, kissing, licking, and sucking the underside of my rear into his mouth in a way that was sure to leave marks.

As much as my ex-boyfriends had raved about my booty, none of them had ever given me a hickey there before. There was something so erotic, slightly taboo, and oddly humbling about the way Vair was worshipping my backside.

Hearing the noises that he was making and knowing how turned on he was just to be kissing my ass pushed me past the brink of my own long-held preconceived notions of decorum, well past caring that I was restrained by an animated glass wall and about to get eaten out from behind by a scary, dominant alien. I went up onto my toes in my heels, angling my ass higher for him as his fingers spread my fleshy cheeks apart to make way for his exploring tongue.

When that hot tongue made contact, licking the length of my slit from clit to anus, I lost it. And by "lost it," I mean I got loud.

As Vair proceeded to nibble, suck, and lick every millimeter of my exposed, over-stimulated privates, I threw years of well-ingrained, safe, proper behavior aside and started making noises that rivaled those coming out of the soap star on the opposite side of the glass—who was high on K saliva and getting fucked by a whole roomful of hot, hung Krinar aliens.

When all orgy eyes shifted in my direction, I realized that although they might not be able to see me, they were most definitely hearing me. And they liked what they were hearing. A lot.

I could tell by the way their irises glowed with excitement, the way their pupils dilated, and the way their movements accelerated—whether stroking their own cocks or moving inside the human client-slash-patron-slash-patient they were attending to—that the noises I was making turned them on immensely.

Their hungry eyes stared unseeingly in my direction, and I knew they were imagining the things that Vair might be doing to me behind the two-way glass partition.

I wanted to quiet down, but I couldn't.

It was all too fucking hot. So dirty and exhilarating I could scarcely believe it was happening.

And it was happening all right.

It was all too much to resist: the pressure of Vair's tongue moving against my clit, his fingers squeezing and holding my ass cheeks apart, his thumb stroking shallowly into my center.

And then his long, slickened finger began pressing inside me where no man had dared venture before, setting off a string of begging interspersed with profanity as I came apart against his face.

CHAPTER TWENTY-THREE

I had no time to get my bearings. My orgasm had barely receded and Vair was already standing behind me, his thick girth pressing steadily into my slick channel despite the residual contractions working against him.

My legs were shaking so badly they could no longer support my weight. The wall restraints and Vair were holding me upright—his big hands wrapped around my waist, his strong thighs pressed against the backs of mine as he drove his full length to the limit inside me.

A noise that was a cross between a grunt and a gratified scream escaped me when he bumped up against my cervix.

He felt bigger than I remembered. *Huge,* despite how wet I was from my orgasm and the fluid still rushing to lubricate my sex for his entry.

But this was no mere entry.

It felt like primal possession—a deep and all-consuming

invasion—as his fingers tightened around my waist to the point of discomfort.

A growl of contentment reverberated from his chest. I felt it resonate through me from the bottom of my toes to the tips of my imprisoned fingers. And I knew…

This was a claiming.

Any slim doubt I held of that fact was eradicated the moment he began to move. He plunged to the hilt with every thrust, his strokes controlled yet brutal—at once tender and ruthless in the way that he rammed deep, filling me to the point of distress even as gentle fingers continued to coax my slick bundle of nerves, his words of praise encouraging me to take more, to accept all of him.

He began spouting nonsense behind me, saying that I belonged to him, that I was made for him. Assuring me that I would mold to him—that my body was meant to accept his inside it for all eternity.

I knew that he was serious. Instinctively, I sensed that this was not standard K pillow talk or hyperbole he was engaging in when he promised that he was keeping me this time—that he intended to fuck me like this *forever*.

The realization of that fact wasn't something I could logically define. It was a deeper awareness—a visceral knowing. Something I felt in the thrust and drag of his cock as he filled places inside me no man had ever reached before. In the warmth that expanded within my chest as I sensed how much he wanted me—*needed me*—with him.

It was terrifying and wonderful.

Intoxicating and sobering.

But mostly, I was ill-prepared to process such complicated, dichotomous emotions while being restrained and getting plowed from behind as I watched an alien orgy in the basement of an x-club.

So I pushed it aside, chalked it up to my faulty intuition, disconnected and isolated it within the gray matter of my mind for further evaluation at a later time.

It was just sex.

Kinky, hot-as-fuck, earth-shattering blackmail sex.

There was no need to delve into unwelcome, confusing emotions, to try and discern the meaning of Vair's words or fathom any deeper intentions he held beyond fucking me into oblivion. Not when my whole body was taut with tension, my sex keyed up and primed for an explosion I was helpless to contain.

I was emitting primitive keening noises and panted grunts in time to the slapping sound of Vair's balls against my ass. Shouting things that were nonsensical. My pussy had never felt so used and so treasured.

And every single K in the divided room was getting off on the collective anticipation of my next orgasm. I'd somehow managed to upstage a gorgeous soap star for their attention.

They knew from the noises we were making just how well and good I was getting fucked on the opposite side of the mirror as Vair made up for lost time, and that knowledge was hotter than it should've been.

In general, the realization of how much I was enjoying this whole scene disturbed me greatly. *But not enough to stave off the swiftly approaching freight train of my orgasm.*

"That's it, darling. Let it out. Show me who you really are."

I shattered.

Violently.

Squeezing around the biggest cock I knew I'd ever have

inside me, I felt the contractions deep within—stronger than I'd ever experienced. My inner muscles fluttered and squeezed and locked, wave after wave, milking and claiming Vair right back—demanding his capitulation.

Shackled to a scary, animated wall in the bowels of an alien sex club, bent over and getting fucked harder than I'd ever been in my life, I felt like anything but a victim as Vair's strokes became short and punishing, his breaths ragged, his Krinar curse words disjointed and loud.

I suddenly felt like *I* was the savage predator—the dominant, conquering species holding Vair and every other K in the room captive and at my mercy as my orgasm tore Vair's from him, sucking every drop of his essence from his powerful Krinar body and taking it deep within me... where I wanted it to belong.

CHAPTER TWENTY-FOUR

$\mathcal{H}$e collapsed into me.

Or maybe it was I who'd collapsed?

For a moment, I thought I'd blacked out, but then I realized the glass wall had simply gone dark—completely opaque. The sounds of the other Ks grunting and of flesh slapping on flesh had also been snuffed out, because my own labored breathing suddenly sounded overly loud in the too-quiet room that I shared only with Vair.

I could hear his breaths as well. Feel them fanning the top of my head.

The wall had released my wrists. I was sandwiched in between it and Vair, his arm around my waist holding me upright against him, his semi-hard cock still buried deep inside me.

His lips skated down the side of my sweat-dampened face, pressing kisses as he murmured, "Are you all right?"

I didn't have an answer.

I wasn't sure if I was all right.

I wasn't sure of what had just happened to me—if I would ever be all right again.

"I need you to be," he told me when I didn't respond. "Because we're not done, darling."

My muscles pulsed and tightened around him in reaction.

"That's my good girl," he purred in my ear. I felt him harden and lengthen within me in turn. "Always ready for me."

I winced as he withdrew; I was sore from our rough coupling. But more than that, it was the loss of him inside me that chafed. Even though it was only for a moment as he turned me in his arms so that I was facing him.

His hands gripped beneath my ass, and my heeled feet left the ground as he lifted my legs to wrap them around his waist. The wall felt cold against my damp back as he pressed me flush against it.

"I missed you," he said as his lips connected with mine. Tasting. Then *devouring*.

The tip of his hard cock prodded the tender folds between my thighs, and I clutched his shoulders, urging him closer, feeling my body melt into him as the gentle, erotic thrust of his tongue mimicked that of the thick organ working its way into me.

Arching my back against the wall for leverage, I angled my pelvis forward, rocking and grinding into him, encouraging his possession despite how sore and swollen I felt inside.

My need for him was stronger than the discomfort.

I felt crazy for wanting him so much. Crazier still at the prospect of this night coming to an end.

And it would have an end. It was virtually the only certainty that existed within this unsustainable dance we were engaging in.

Yet I wanted the moment to go on. Wanted these feelings and this connection between us to be real. To hold a place of permanency within me where I knew they had no right.

He thrust deeper, penetrating me to the hilt and making me gasp at the fullness. He stilled, letting me adjust.

Our foreheads met. His nose nuzzled mine as our breaths intermingled.

"Did you miss me?"

I wasn't sure what he was asking. Was he asking if I'd missed him since we'd seen each other earlier tonight? Or if I had missed him for the past month?

Either way, I didn't have an answer. Vair wasn't someone I could afford to miss.

"Do you remember this room from your last visit?"

I shook my head. I'd been in the basement of his x-club during my last visit? This was news to me. But not entirely unbelievable, considering that many details about the events that followed after he'd bitten me remained hazy in my otherwise-potent memories.

What stood out were the sensations I'd felt at his touch. The scent of his skin, the taste of his mouth and his sex, the sounds he'd made. I recalled, too, the many positions in which he'd taken me, but they were only snapshots of colorful imagery in my mind's eye, interspersed within the powerful waves of lust I'd ridden, over and over again.

I felt his smile against my lips. "Would you like to see *my* favorite memories?"

It was one of those Vair-speak questions that didn't require answering. He was going to show me, whatever it was.

I heard Vair's "memories" before I saw them as three-dimensional video images came to life all around us in the previously quiet space.

A nervous giggle bubbled up in my chest—more giddy than anxious—though there was nothing funny about the erotic images of us on display when I turned my head to take in this new footage from my first x-club visit.

To my surprise, I saw that I'd had sex with Vair while restrained before tonight.

And I had definitely liked it.

There was footage of Vair taking me from behind while I was bent over and tied to what looked like a padded sawhorse. Images of him fucking my upside-down mouth while I was bent backward, strapped to a bench.

My sex fluttered around him as I watched the shocking videos play out.

He began to move inside me. Slow and easy, but at an angle that was *so* deep.

My thighs flexed; my ankles tightened around his waist.

"You see how good we are together?" His teeth nibbled my earlobe. "How perfect?" His questions were delivered as statements of fact.

What I saw was that my E.T. was a kinky motherfucker—beyond anything my limited vanilla sexual experience had ever contemplated.

We were wholly incompatible.

In another hologram, I was restrained to one of those x-shaped Saint Andrew's crosses, moaning and screaming my head off as Vair knelt in front of me—his mouth and hands working my sex without mercy.

My insides clenched around Vair at the sight of it. I rotated my pelvis into him.

It might've been the hottest visual I'd ever seen. It was an image that I knew would stay with me. One that I couldn't— *didn't want to*—unsee.

We were clearly wrong for one another.

"You see why I had to have you back at my club?" His mouth was laving my throat now, his fingers tugging on my nipples.

I did see.

And yet I didn't.

"Are you all right, love?"

I nodded. Feeling overwhelmed. Needing more. Wanting less. Craving everything my scary alien lover had to give.

"Is this okay?" He dragged in and out.

Stretching me.

Soothing me.

Burning me up inside and making me ache for more.

I couldn't speak. I nodded again.

"I'm going to bite you, Amy."

It was a statement. But the way he announced it let me know that he would give me a choice in the matter—an opportunity to tell him no if I didn't want that.

It made me want it even more.

I nodded, tilting my throat up into his marauding mouth. My fingers slid through the silky hair at the back of his head, coaxing him closer as my hips ground and rotated against him, meeting his too-slow, too-gentle thrusts.

"Yes… that's it, darling. Show me. I'll give you everything you want."

His movements sped up, his hips thrusting and rolling

between my thighs with renewed urgency as his mouth latched onto the column of my neck and his hand stole between our bodies to finger my throbbing clit.

I felt the sting of his bite and cried out, a sliver of fear racing through me as the slicing pain of his sharp teeth rent my fragile flesh. It hurt, burned in a perversely carnal way, and before long, the erotic, sucking pull of his lips and tongue wrenched an orgasm from me with a white-hot force that caused my vision to fade, my skin to burn, and my heart to race.

After that, I knew nothing but mindless pleasure, my body convulsing over and over through all-consuming climaxes, lost in a world where there was only Vair, only us, reaching for ecstasy that was nothing short of divine.

———

I was vaguely aware of Vair bathing me at some point ages later —it might've been hours or days. Of Vair's coworker Shalee examining me afterward and taking my vitals in odd places and with foreign medical devices as she and Vair spoke in hushed tones.

I remembered being beyond wrecked, exhausted yet fighting the call of sleep, not wanting my night with Vair to be at an end. I remembered embarrassing myself by telling Vair so, saying that I didn't want to fall asleep and wake up alone inside my apartment again—like the first time I'd gone to his club. Then I tried to cover it up by complaining that it was his K saliva that had made me say it.

He kissed me and promised to be there when I woke up as

he tucked me into the most comfortable bed I'd ever lain upon. I fell asleep shortly thereafter to the lulling sound of his deep voice speaking in Krinar, and to the sensation of his fingers combing lazily through my hair.

CHAPTER TWENTY-FIVE

*M*y new sheets were rubbing against me in the most sensuous way. Lightly caressing and molding to my bare legs in a manner that was heavenly. My God, but they were soft. I would have to order another set of these—if I could remember when and where I'd gotten them.

Wait... had I gotten new sheets?

I noticed the room was too bright behind my closed eyes. My bedroom never got this much sunlight in the morning. Then I remembered that I'd been staying with Jay. Sleeping on his couch so that we could figure out what to do about me going to Vair's x-club the next—

Shit!

I jackknifed to a sitting position.

My heart racing, I gaped at my unfamiliar surroundings. I wasn't at Jay's. I was in a massive bedroom, with floor-to-ceiling windows along one wall revealing gorgeous views of clouds and sky. In a mad moment of sleep-deprived idiocy, I feared Vair had abducted me on his alien spaceship.

Then I jumped out of bed and saw the blessedly familiar skyscrapers of NYC below.

Below?

Jesus, I was high up. In a penthouse somewhere.

"Good morning."

At the sound of Vair's voice, I spun around so fast I nearly toppled over.

"Hi," I said automatically, my face flushed and my eyes wary as they met his. He was leaning casually against the wall by the door, and I realized that I must be in his bedroom.

Crap. I'd spent the night at Vair's place?

I glanced down and was relieved to note I wasn't naked. I was wearing a very soft, very *large* man's shirt. Vair's shirt, no doubt.

Vair was dressed for the day already, looking polished and elegant—and devastatingly attractive—as he stood staring at me with his dark, assessing gaze.

"Good morning," I said, sounding like an imbecile. I was out of sorts; I didn't know what to say or do.

He smiled. "The bathroom is that way if you need it." He pointed to my right. "You'll find towels and whatever toiletries you require."

"Great!" I practically shouted the word as I beelined in the direction he'd pointed, doing my best not to run, and also to mask my freak-out when I noticed that the bed and nightstands were floating above the floor in the same manner as the furniture in Vair's x-club basement room.

"Oh, and Amy," he called out just as I reached the open door to his lavish bathroom.

"Yeah?" I jumped and spun around, releasing a startled gasp when I found him standing directly behind me.

He caught me by the shoulders and steadied me on my feet, a frown marring his brow. He looked like he was about to ask me if I was all right in that way that he always did, so I headed him off.

"I *really* have to pee."

"Of course." He released my shoulders. "I only wanted to tell you that the bathroom, like the rest of the apartment, is intelligent. Equipped with Krinar technology that's programmed to respond to my voice, gestures, and mental commands. I haven't programmed it to respond to you yet, so you may need some help getting the shower settings the way you want them if you decide you'd like to shower this morning."

I'd stopped taking his words seriously after he'd referred to his penthouse as an "apartment." I'd shut down and disregarded them completely at the point when he'd implied he was going to program his shower to respond to my commands—like I'd be here using it so often that it'd be necessary.

I shook my head and waved him off with a shaky smile. "I'm just going to hit the head and be on my way, okay? I'll just… shower at home."

I shut myself inside the bathroom and locked it before he could get another word in. Then I forced in several calming breaths as I counted to ten.

Vair's bathroom was, in a word, ridiculous. My eyes feasted on black-and-white marble, an enormous sunken tub, and a walk-in shower sized for twenty people, with a wall of glass overlooking the city.

I couldn't deal. And I actually did have to pee.

There was no normal toilet, but there was an upright

porcelain hollow cylinder with rounded edges where a toilet should've been. It was missing several critical toilet components, though—namely, water and a flushing mechanism.

Oh, what the hell. I sat on it and relieved my bladder anyway. I realized when I was done that there wasn't any toilet paper in the bathroom either. I cast my eyes to the ceiling. *Typical bachelor pad oversights apparently extended to aliens, too.*

I was contemplating my options when a warm breeze blasted my ass without warning. I leapt off the cylinder with a yelp.

Looking down into the white porcelain, I saw no trace of urine, even though there was still no water in the cylinder and there had been no flushing sound. I also felt clean and dry.

Well, it was different, but pretty darn handy, I had to admit.

The sink looked slightly more normal, but there were no controls or buttons on the faucets. Assuming it had motion sensors, I waved my hands under it. A soap-like substance came out, followed by water a few seconds later.

Huh. Neat.

After washing my face, I inspected it in the mirror, noting that I looked far better than I felt on the inside. My skin was clear and healthy-looking, and I didn't have terrible dark circles under my eyes, as I would've anticipated.

There was a brand-new toothbrush and a travel-sized toothpaste on the counter that I made use of. It'd looked as if they were there just for me, making me wonder what the Krinar did to clean their own teeth.

Despite all of the sweating I'd done the night before, I noted that I didn't stink. In fact, my hair and body felt freshly washed.

Disjointed memories surfaced of Vair bathing me at some point during the night.

And of Shalee coming to check on me.

Even amid my waning bite-induced haze in the early morning hours, I remembered thinking that her methods for "checking my vitals," as she'd called it, were fairly unorthodox.

My pulse spiked as I recalled her inserting a slim medical device about the size of a tampon inside me. I plopped down onto a marble bench by the shower's entrance, hiked my feet up, and spread my knees wide.

After the amount of intense, rough sex I'd had with Vair—who was by any human standard, *huge*—it should've been painful merely to pee this morning. But I felt perfectly fine. And I looked perfectly fine down there—just like the first morning after I'd hooked up with Vair at his club. It had puzzled me that time as well, initially causing me to wonder if I'd only imagined the events of our first club encounter.

It was widely presumed that the Krinar had advanced healing technology, given what humans had been told of their extended lifespans. Was it possible that Vair and Shalee had utilized their Krinar medical technology on me? Just to heal my vajayjay faster?

As crazy as it was, it seemed like the best explanation for how I'd managed to avoid soreness. But why would they do that? And without my consent?

Had they done other things to me?

Stripping off Vair's shirt, I stood and inspected the rest of my body in the wall mirror, noting that I had none of the marks or bruises that should've come with the way Vair had been holding and touching me the night before—squeezing and gripping my flesh like he couldn't get enough of it. There were no bite marks on my neck, either.

Nor on my ass.

As I scanned every inch of my person, it dawned on me how well I could view every detail, each tiny pore on my blemish-free skin.

My eyesight!

I wasn't wearing my blinder glasses. I had no idea where they'd even ended up after Vair had removed them along with my clothes.

Holy shit, had they done something to correct my lifelong vision impairment as well? Was that why I had been seeing better without glasses these past weeks?

But why would they do it? *Why me?*

I sat back down on the marble bench, rested my elbows on my knees, and dropped my forehead in my hands as Tauce's awful words about me being Vair's property swam in my mind. *About how Ks take what they want and keep what they claim as theirs.*

Oh, God. It was no more than what Vair himself had said while ramming into me from behind in the x-club basement. He'd said that I belonged to him, that he was keeping me this time, and that he intended to fuck me for all eternity.

"Amy?"

I jumped at the sound of Vair's voice and his soft knock on the bathroom door.

"Are you finding everything you need in there?"

"Yes!" I called out. "Everything's fine. I—I'll be right out."

I slipped his shirt back on and exited the bathroom. He was standing outside waiting for me, his eyes soft, a subdued smile on his lips. It was almost as if he was *trying* to appear nonthreatening.

As if the predator that he was had scented my fear and panic.

He held his hand out to me. "Come. I'll show you around."

I slipped my hand in his and did my best to keep my cool as he led me through the grand opulence that was his "apartment."

The place was enormous. It had to have been the entire top three floors of the building.

Sleek and modern, elegant and minimalist, with floor-to-ceiling windows that stretched three stories high, the penthouse was a study in clean lines and architectural symmetry. And Vair's futuristic furnishings and technologically advanced appliances and equipment somehow complemented the more conventional marble surfaces and oak herringbone floors that were reminiscent of traditional Park Avenue residences.

As stunning as the space's interior was, the views from the windows were awe-rendering. We were no longer in the Meatpacking District—that much was certain. The view from the main room faced north, and we were high enough up that I could see clear across Central Park to the George Washington Bridge.

There were no words. But I found one.

"Wow," I breathed, my quiet morning voice lost in the grand space.

Much like me.

"Do you like it?" Vair's thumb stroked back and forth against the sensitive skin of my wrist.

I nodded. "It's... breathtaking."

It was a work of architectural genius. *On Park Avenue.* A coveted NYC residence that likely traded somewhere near the hundred-million-dollar range. And I was standing in it, looking out across Central Park—holding hands with the alien invader sex-club owner who lived in it.

I needed to leave.

He gave my hand a gentle squeeze. "Thank you."

At his words, I turned away from the view to find him smiling at me as if he was genuinely pleased by my reaction. "I'm glad you approve."

He didn't sound the least bit sarcastic.

I swallowed, fighting down the panicked voice inside me that was screaming, *"Run."*

"You hardly need my approval," I said with an anxious laugh, feeling small as I stood there in Vair's oversized shirt—and gargantuan penthouse.

His hand shifted against mine, his fingers repositioning to link between my own.

"You don't need to be nervous, Amy." His thumb resumed its idle stroking.

My heart rate spiked. Blood pounded in my ears and my face prickled with heat. My stomach roiled and dark spots began to invade my vision. I suddenly felt more terrified standing there holding Vair's hand than I had been in the basement of his x-club, surrounded by aroused male Ks and restrained by an animated glass wall.

The fear was ludicrous—but also very real.

I knew Vair sensed it, too. Heard the concern in his voice that sounded so far away through the blood rushing in my ears as he asked me if I was all right.

Sheer will and the greater fear of embarrassing myself kept me from fainting on my feet as I closed my eyes and nodded.

"I'm afraid of heights," I mumbled, knowing that I had to tell him something. "I shouldn't have come so close to the window."

I was off my feet, cradled in his arms, and being carried across the room before I'd taken my next breath. He set me down on a white, floating couch-like surface and said that he'd be back. A moment later, he returned with a glass of light pink liquid, and I drank it all without even asking what it was.

That was the moment I knew the truth.

I was no longer afraid of Vair.

It wasn't the scary Krinar alien in him that I was panicking over.

It was the alien feelings and reactions he was inducing in me.

I needed to get it together and get the hell out of his penthouse.

I felt the weight of his warm palms on my knees as he knelt in front of me. I met his dark gaze—and immediately regretted it.

It wasn't the concern that I saw there that unsettled me, nor was it the sincerity. It was the understanding. The quiet knowing in his bottomless eyes that wordlessly projected that he totally got that I was full of shit. *And he was okay with it.*

"I know you're afraid of many things, Amy." His voice was low and gentle. "But I don't believe fear of heights is among them."

Neither of us dared to speak. You could've heard a pin drop. But it wasn't a pin that I heard; it was the theme song to *The X-Files* playing quietly in the distance.

My phone.

CHAPTER TWENTY-SIX

*J*ay had been messing with my ringtone settings while I'd been at his place yesterday. He'd reset my ringer to *The X-Files* theme song in an attempt to lighten the mood over my predicament with Vair.

My phone was ringing in my purse now. *Somewhere.*

"Ah… that's my purse," I said, setting my empty glass onto the floating coffee table next to me. "I mean, my phone in my purse. May I have it? I think I hear my phone ringing."

I'd had my phone inside my tiny evening bag when I'd gone to Vair's club. Tauce had stashed it in a hidden compartment within the upstairs bar last night, and I hadn't thought to bring it downstairs with me when we'd left for the basement.

"Of course." Vair stood with that catlike grace of his, and left the room. My phone had stopped ringing by the time he returned and handed the purse to me.

My first shock in retrieving my phone from my bag was in seeing the time.

"Can it really be after eleven?" I protested, more to myself than to Vair. "I can't believe how late I overslept."

"You didn't fall asleep until almost four in the morning. You could use a few more hours of rest still."

"I'm fine. How much sleep did *you* get?" I countered defensively, sounding like an ornery child—and feeling like a scolded one. "You couldn't have gotten much more than I did."

"I slept three hours. Krinar don't require the same amount of sleep as humans."

They didn't? Oh. Well, that was convenient for them. Humans probably would've made more advances as a species too if we didn't need to sleep so much.

I stood and walked to the windows, tired of feeling Vair's eyes staring down at me. I needed space to think.

I began to pace back and forth as I flipped through my recent phone activity. There were two missed calls from Jay, twenty-nine from my parents, and eight new voicemail messages.

Fuck. It was Sunday. I'd told my parents I would call them, and I always called them before ten a.m. on Sundays. They'd probably called the NYPD, FBI, and National Guard by now. I'd long considered it a personal blessing that, barring evidence of violence or unusual circumstances, an individual had to be gone for twenty-four hours before they could legally be considered a missing person. Regardless of how many times my mother had been told this by law enforcement personnel, she persisted in trying to report me as a missing person whenever I failed to check in with her as scheduled.

There was a text from Jay saying to disregard his voicemail because he'd already spoken with Vair, which meant that the other seven voicemails were from my mom.

My eyes rolled. I couldn't decide whether it was over my mother's seven voicemails or the fact that Jay had been in touch with Vair while I'd been sleeping.

As I was concocting a plausible explanation—*lie*—for my parents, *The X-Files* theme song sounded again.

Shit. It was my mother. I didn't want to take it with Vair listening in, but I knew she would just keep calling and freaking out if I didn't. *And start calling everyone she knew in NYC to organize a search-and-rescue party.*

"Hey, Ma."

"Amy, is that you?" Her hysterical voice came through the connection at such high volume I jerked the phone from my ear.

"Yeah, Mom, who else would it be?"

"It's almost eleven-thirty," she shrieked. "Where have you been?"

"Oh, hey, sorry I missed your call. I, um… went to an early morning hot yoga class. It was great, but super-intense. And then I was so tired afterward that I crashed. I didn't even hear my phone ringing until I woke up just now."

I rationalized there was a partial truth in there. But I knew I sounded like a compulsive liar. I snuck a peek at Vair. His expression was stubbornly blank as he watched my pacing, his forefinger rubbing absently back and forth across his full bottom lip.

"Hot yoga?" My mom sounded confused on the other end of the line. Or horrified. I couldn't quite tell which as she repeated, "Hot yoga? You've been doing hot yoga?"

"Yeah, hot yoga. It's my new thing. Hey, so it's not a good time right now. I've got all these errands I'm behind on and that article I told you about that's due Tuesday. I'll call you guys later tonight, okay?"

"Amy, do you know how many people have died doing hot yoga? Didn't you read the articles I sent you about that Bikram guru who was sentenced to prison?"

Oh, geez. Why hadn't I fabricated a story about a community gardening project or something? I heard her yelling for my dad in the background and knew I couldn't do this right now.

"I've got to hang up now, Ma. I'll call you later." I disconnected the call and powered my phone off, then turned to face Vair.

"What?"

His expression was still annoyingly blank. "I didn't say anything."

"But you're judging."

"If you say so, love."

"You don't understand. You don't know my parents, okay? Sometimes it's better to tell a white lie with them." Why was I explaining myself? I didn't owe him an explanation.

He laughed. "On the contrary. I have a very good understanding of them. I must confess, your mother terrifies me."

"Ha! Right." The idea of Vair being terrified of my mom was comical.

"I mean it. Those emails she constantly sends you..." He shook his head, one brow arched high. "It's disturbing. Even for human behavior."

My breath caught. I felt like I'd been punched in the gut. He'd accessed my personal email account? Jesus, why was I even surprised? The man—*alien*—had videotaped me without my knowledge or consent. I should've realized he'd have tapped into everything of mine that was personal and off-limits. Still… "You read my personal emails?"

"Of course, darling." Not a trace of contrition.

"I am not your darling. And my family's behavior is none of your business." How dare he judge my mom?

His smile slipped, his military-poster jaw tightening sternly. "I beg to differ. Everything about you is my business. Everyone who affects you is my business."

My stomach took another dive. He was one hundred percent serious.

"Rather high-handed, don't you think? Oh, right, you're a Krinar. Invading a lowly human's privacy is no big deal—totally within the realm of Krinar everyday behavior."

Protective and defensive instincts for my parents aside, his "even for human behavior" remark was gutting on another personal level, because it demonstrated just how low his view of my race was—and by extension, of *me*. Though, of course, how could someone who lacked the basic respect for my right to privacy view me as anything but inferior?

His eyes were thoughtful, yet his tone direct. "I only hope you understand that every time your parents say, 'Be careful,' they're saying, 'I love you.' You do know that, right?"

This conversation was not happening.

"Once again, Vair, what I do understand is that anything my parents say to me is my business and none of yours." I heard the echo of my words in the enormous room, and realized how much I'd raised my voice.

I needed to calm down.

"It's the only way they know how to express their affection

for you—by constantly warning you of dangers and over-sharing their fears for your well-being."

I swallowed the unwelcome lump forming in my throat and forced a laugh. "Of course I know that. That's Psych 101 stuff. You should really stick to being superior at wall-dissolving and other K technology and leave emotional understanding to therapists."

He grinned, showing his perfect white teeth as he chuckled dryly. "Believe me, I wish I could at times. But there are many other Krinar with superior wall-dissolving skills and too few inclined to study human behaviorism."

I felt like I was missing an inside joke.

"Your parents programmed you to respond to fear. To constant threats of danger and intimidation. And you've grown up to be as terrified as you are fascinated by those threats." He shook his head and took a step in my direction. "You seek the truth above all else, and yet you lie most easily—especially to yourself. It makes you quite an interesting, delicious paradox, Amy."

He was fucking with me again.

Or maybe not?

He took another step closer. The space between us suddenly felt charged with sexual energy. I knew I had to dispel it.

"Fine." I tossed my hands in defeat. "You're right. I'm not afraid of heights. So I'm a bad liar? What the hell do you want from me?"

He didn't respond, so I filled the silence. "Look, I'm just an only child from Skaneateles with overprotective, paranoid parents. I probably should've taken the scholarship I was given and gone to college at Syracuse, close to home, like my parents wanted me to," I rambled as he stalked nearer. "But I wanted to get away on my own. So I spent too much on my college degree at NYU as a result. And now, at twenty-four years old, I'm just trying to make a go of it here in the city and work my way out of debt."

He kept moving fluidly closer. I retreated another step, then stopped myself.

"I'm not really even a very good reporter. Yet," I appended. "And when my boss kept giving me nothing but stupid fluff pieces, I got desperate."

He was close enough to touch me now. I knew I should stop all of my justifying and apologizing, but his soft black eyes encouraged me to continue.

"So I came to your x-club. I never meant to offend you or to upset the Krinar Council. I was just looking for an 'in'—a lucky break. A chance to write a real news story that would give the human public more helpful information about Ks than we've gotten in the two years since the invasion. Can't you try and understand that and stop punishing me for my article?"

His sigh fanned my forehead. "Amy, I already told you, I thought your exposé was brilliant. I have no desire to punish you for it, nor will I allow anyone else to."

"Then why are you doing this to me?" I blinked against the traitorous sting of tears. "Why are you blackmailing me?"

"I've already explained that as well, darling. You didn't come back to my club, and I needed you to."

"But *why?*"

"Because…" He smiled and brushed a stray wisp of hair from my forehead. "I'm an eight-hundred-and-forty-seven-year-old only child from Krina who came to Earth to try and help out with the transition and assimilation of our species. But after I saw you, I lost focus on all else. I found myself only interested in assimilating with you."

I heard the blood rushing in my ears again. I'd known that the Krinar were long-lived, but I'd never really contemplated it in quantifiable terms.

He was eight hundred and forty-seven years old?

And he wanted to assimilate with *me?*

Neither of us spoke as his fingers traced my jawline and stroked down the column of my throat, his feather-light touch sending a delightful thrill through me. So many questions swirled in my head. I posed the least significant one.

"You're an only child, too?"

He nodded, his mouth twitching at the corners. "Yes." He leaned into me, his lips ghosting over my brow. "As a result, I'm afraid I'm used to having my way, and I don't like to share." His tone, which had been light and playful, became stern and fervent as he said, "Which reminds me, I don't want you spending the night at Jay's anymore."

My back stiffened. I pulled away from him as my spine straightened. "I'm sorry... how is that your business? How do you even know—? Have you been spying on me?"

It was a dumb question. We both knew the answer was yes. We both knew he'd visited me the night before at Jay's. But it required asking nonetheless.

"Jay told me when he texted yesterday that you'd stayed with him Friday night."

Oh.

"But yes, actually, I have been spying on you," he continued matter-of-factly. "Quite intensely. It's my second-favorite pastime."

My stomach flipped at his admission. And the craziest part was that I wasn't sure if it was nausea or butterflies I felt.

I had been right. Vair had been keeping tabs on me everywhere.

And he didn't seem the least bit repentant about it.

CHAPTER TWENTY-SEVEN

"So... there *are* hidden cameras set up at my apartment, too? Just like at my office?" Another dumb question, but I needed to have it spelled out.

He stared me dead in the eyes as he answered without apology, "Yes. Several."

"Why?"

"I like watching you, Amy." His knuckles grazed my cheekbone. "A lot."

I swallowed. "In every room?"

"All the important ones."

What did that mean? "I don't understand."

But I did. I just didn't want to.

"It's simple, Amy." His lips dusted my forehead as I felt the weight of his words brand me in other places. "I like recording you. I enjoy watching you." He kissed my lids, my nose. "Especially when you touch yourself. In your bed. The shower. That one time in the living room..."

Oh, God.

"I like to imagine what you might be thinking. About me."

This wasn't hot.

"The naughty things you fantasize about us doing."

It wasn't hot.

My nipples disagreed. My pussy did too.

Everything about Vair that should not have been a turn-on to me somehow was. And there was nothing about it that I could rationally reconcile.

His arm locked around my waist, and his other hand slipped under my oversized shirt, between my ass cheeks, to cup my bare center from behind. I pressed both hands to his chest, pushing against him. He didn't move. "We have to stop," I protested. "We have nothing in common."

"You just said it yourself: We're both only children. As solid a foundation as any for a relationship."

I groaned. *This was all madness.*

"This can't work."

"My darling, it's already working." His mouth dropped to my neck, kissing and sucking the sensitive skin there. "You're dripping wet."

"But we're not... compatible." I moaned as his fingers found my drenched center.

My hands had found their way to his shoulders, but they were no longer pushing him away.

They were clawing him closer.

"I'm not a sex-club person," I tried to argue through the haze of lust swiftly enveloping me. "I'm not into all that... kinky... stuff."

I heard the quiet laughter deep in his chest, felt it in the quaking of his shoulders beneath my grip. "Of course you aren't, darling. Yet you endure it so well for me."

Before I knew it, I was being held high in his arms. We'd both been stripped naked by some force of K technology, and my legs were locked around Vair's waist. His hot tongue rhythmically stroked the depths of my mouth as the blunt tip of his erection pressed into my entrance.

And then he kept me there, his cock barely inside me, while he whispered filthy promises, his fingers teasing back and forth along the cleft of my ass to the point where we were joined— until I was desperately wiggling against his hold in my effort to shimmy down and impale myself.

Still, he didn't relent.

I took to begging when his fingers slipped between us and he proceeded to tease my clit until my insides clenched, my arousal dripping down to coat the stubborn, hard cock lodged too shallowly within.

But begging didn't satisfy.

No, only when I began to admit, at his prompting, to all the things that I liked about his club, to confess to my dirtiest masturbation fantasies, did he slowly lower me onto his thick shaft.

By that time, I was so thankful that I cried out with every inch given. I whimpered and arched my pelvis into him as he lifted and lowered me, going a little deeper each time, my body welcoming and worshipping his length as it stretched my walls and split me open until finally he was fully inside.

Then he seated us both in one of the floating chairs and told me to take what I wanted from him.

And I did.

With my legs astride his hips, my knees dug into the soft but firm surface beneath us, and I began to ride him, my hips circling, moving up and down, raising and lowering. He groaned as I sucked his tongue into my mouth, kissing him with a wanton abandon that matched my body's movements.

His fingers dug into my ass cheeks. His hips tilted up to deepen the penetration as I impaled myself over and over again. "So tight." He grunted. "So perfect."

His hands grew rough and urgent on my breasts as I bounced and rolled my body up and down, lost in the sensation of his cock spearing me so deeply, relishing the freedom and control I had over our union.

His fingers pressed urgently against my clit, and I muffled my cries against his neck, my mouth latching on, sucking and savoring the scent and taste of his skin.

"That's it..." His voice was hoarse. "Just like that, darling. Mark me."

My inner muscles clenched harder at his words, gripping him possessively as I came undone.

"Fuck. You're all mine. *Forever*," he growled.

My internal walls seized around him and my teeth sank reflexively into his neck as my body flew apart, convulsing in orgasm.

He took control of our movements then, ramming his length into me, his big hands on my ass jerking me up and down in a rapid frenzy as he roared and cursed, emptying everything he had to give deep within me.

––––––––

After my mind-blowing orgasm had receded and my brain was able to process things beyond blind lust, I settled into a bout of post-coitus remorse once more. Vair's "all mine forever" proclamation may have had something to do with it—reminding me of Zyrnase and Tauce's remarks about me being "Vair's human."

Krinar property.

I remained quiet as Vair and I showered together. After our shower, he insisted on shining a strange red light from a thin silvery medical device over any areas where he feared he'd left bruises or scratches on my skin. He explained that it utilized nanocyte healing technology.

I allowed it. But when he wanted to insert the tampon-sized healing device Shalee had used on me in order to heal any potential internal abrasions, I snapped and more or less told him to chill his shit, saying that my pussy and I weren't that fragile and that I didn't mind having an ache to remember him by for the next few days.

I probably should've left it at that when he backed off and didn't press the issue, but instead, I brought up the mystery of my improved eyesight, and asked him point-blank whether he had done something to heal my vision.

His answer was an unapologetic yes, confirming what I had already pretty much known.

Once again, I fell silent, conflicted over whether to be grateful or angry about his interference.

I watched with detached fascination as he fabricated clothing for me to wear out of thin air—a long-sleeved, lightweight casual tunic dress in a pale shade of blue, along with a pair of nude low-heeled shoes. This explained his ability to make those rapid wardrobe changes I'd witnessed. Or more accurately, his ability to get naked in seconds flat.

It was all very surreal. So foreign and overwhelming that I

felt myself detaching more and more to avoid freaking out. Because in the back of my mind, I was growing increasingly afraid that he wouldn't allow me to leave.

"So… what happens next?" I finally worked up the courage to ask as I slipped on the shoes he'd made me.

"Well, I was thinking we might eat a very late breakfast together," he proposed with an adoring smile. "Maybe go for a stroll. Talk. We could also stay here," he offered, a hint of something carnal in his dark eyes. *The alien was insatiable.* "What would you like to happen next, Amy?"

His indulgent smile and the gentle way he'd asked that almost made me want to go for that stroll with him.

But I had to know where I stood.

I swallowed. "Um… I'd like to go home. To my apartment. Alone?"

He stared at me for a beat, pursed his lips, and nodded slowly. "Okay. Zyrnase can take you. Or Robert. But I'd like for you to eat something before you go if you're up for it."

He was going to let me go? Just like that?

And there was a Krinar named Bob?

"And then I can go? If—if I eat first?"

His dark eyes turned stony. "Amy, you can go now, without eating, if you like. But I think you'll feel better if you get some food into your stomach. We had a long night together. And morning."

He was really letting me go?

"But what you said before about, um… me belonging to—I mean, being *all yours*—"

"You're not my prisoner, Amy." His voice was flat, his tone weary. "I'll get Robert for you." He left the bedroom.

And he didn't come back. Not even to say goodbye.

Eventually, Zyrnase came to tell me that my ride was downstairs.

The Krinar named Bob wasn't actually a Krinar at all. He was a middle-aged human guy from Queens. He drove me back to my apartment.

Alone.

CHAPTER TWENTY-EIGHT

*A*fter Bob dropped me off, I went to Jay's place to grab the stuff I'd left there the night before. I ended up listening to him rave about Shalee, Vair's gorgeous and brilliant Krinar medical associate, for hours.

Jay was utterly smitten with her, even though he continued to profess that it wasn't serious, that they were only planning on having some fun together.

"You know, it's just that she's bi and I'm bi, and we're both into science and medicine and all—"

"You're into science? Since when? And *medicine?* Jay, having a lot of prescriptions in your bathroom cabinet doesn't count."

"Whoa!" He laughed and made an angry cat noise, throwing the claw gesture my way. "Someone didn't get bitten hard enough at the club last night."

He rambled on about Shalee some more, then offered to let me crash at his place again, but I declined. Not because I feared Vair's disapproval, but because I needed to be alone for a while.

Exhausted, I made my way home, and after calling my parents back and listening to my mom lecture me on the dangers of hot yoga for over forty minutes, I climbed into bed early.

And then I stared at the ceiling, wide-awake for most of the night.

I got through Monday in a constant state of exhausted panic, expecting Vair to show up any minute and demand that I get into his limo and go back to his club. I imagined Tauce's angry yellow eyes following me around every corner, heard his nasty voice in my head, sneering that I was Vair's "property."

I couldn't eat. I didn't sleep well the next night. And I couldn't write.

When Tuesday came and I'd failed to finish my article about the Ks' forced vegan diet, I turned in the article I'd written weeks ago on the conjoined puppy twins—a month after my editor, Gable, had wanted it, and after every other news source in the city had already covered it.

I was probably going to get fired.

Meanwhile, Jay surprised everyone at *The Herald* by turning in a well-written opinion piece on the similarities between Krinar and humans, highlighting universal traits of emotional intelligence that both species shared. He even worked in anecdotal evidence of Krinar "butthurt" behavior, changing names and descriptions of key Krinar, of course, in order to "protect the innocent"—*and his ass.* Jay's K article was probably the only thing that saved *my* ass for the week with our boss.

By Wednesday, I'd started panicking that Vair *wouldn't* show up demanding that I get into his limo. By Thursday, the fear that I'd never see him again had crept in.

But then he texted me that evening. He sent a video. *Of us.* With a message to watch it and to think of him... because he was thinking of me.

I didn't text back.

But I watched the video. And I ended up fingering myself on my living room couch. Knowing that Vair was watching. And likely recording it.

I'd reached the pinnacle of dysfunction.

By Friday, my stomach was in knots as I anxiously awaited Vair's next move—quietly hoping that he would call or text, and, ideally, blackmail me into going back to his club that weekend.

I made a mental note to call my therapist and see if she would still see me on a sliding scale.

A little after three in the afternoon on Friday, Jay poked his head into my office and told me to grab my purse and meet him by the rear stairwell in ten. Thirteen minutes later, we were meeting with Jay's college friend and CIA agent in a little rundown coffee shop located on the fringe of the Financial District.

"Great to see you, man," Jay told him with a grin before turning to me. "Amy, this is Stephen, my friend from college that I told you about. Stephen, this is Amy."

We shook hands, grabbed coffees, and found seats at a quiet corner table. Jay's CIA friend, Stephen, was a tall, blond-haired, blue-eyed all-American type who looked like he should be in NYC hitting casting calls rather than working for the CIA National Clandestine Service. But then he started talking, and I totally got it.

"As I'm sure you know, Ms. Myers, two years ago, after the Great Panic, our world governments entered into the Coexistence Treaty with the Krinar, allowing them to establish settlements across the globe. We've since done our best to cooperate with the Krinar Council in order to coexist with these Ks. For the most part, they chose warm climates and isolated, sparsely populated areas to construct their main K Centers." Stephen paused his slow, monotone delivery to take a sip of his black coffee, and I slipped Jay my most discreet side-eye.

"They built settlements in Costa Rica, Thailand, and the Philippines. But there are also some K Centers here in the U.S. There's one in New Mexico, Arizona—"

"Stephen, man," Jay interrupted. "This is intel that we can get on Wikipedia or a general Google search. Can you tell us why Amy is on a government list?"

Thank God.

"Right. I was just getting to that. As you well know, while many humans despise the Ks and remain fearful and resentful of their sovereignty, there are those who view them as gods, and worship them as such." His speech and posture mimicked that of an unhip fifty-year-old. It was hard to believe he was our age. "Xeno-clubs, or x-clubs, sprang up almost immediately outside of the K Centers as places for Ks and K-worshipping humans to… interact." He made air quotes at "interact," prompting unwelcome flashbacks to the four-hour conversation in which my mother used nothing but euphemisms to explain the act of sex to me.

Then he paused, turning his attention fully to me. "Ms. Myers, I understand that you are familiar with these x-clubs. Is that correct?"

"Stephen, you know she is. She's the Amy Myers who wrote *The Herald* article on the x-club located here in New York City. Can you please speed it up? We have to get back to the office sometime tonight."

"Of course. Of course. In the past two years, there have been more and more troubling cases of Krinar and humans *overindulging* in these x-club... interactions."

He made air quotes again at "interactions," and I nearly got up and left. I settled for furtively checking my phone for new text messages from Vair.

Damn it. Still nothing.

I blew on my coffee and took a sip.

"At first there was concern over the addiction aspect and the potential long-range effects of these K interactions. But then there were fatalities."

The coffee I'd just swallowed turned sour in my stomach. "I'm sorry—*what?*"

"Fatalities?" Jay shot me a nervous look. "You mean... from K bites? Humans have died? At x-clubs?"

"K *addicts* have died," Stephen stressed. "Xenophiles."

I couldn't help but notice he'd said it in a way that made it seem as if he felt they deserved it.

"How?" Jay asked, his face paling as he absently palmed the side of his throat. "From blood loss?"

"We aren't certain."

"From withdrawal?" I had to ask it. My cheeks reddened as Stephen shot me a scandalized look.

"We don't know." To his credit, his monotone didn't falter. "The Krinar Council gave our government very little information. But they assured us that the Krinar researcher they were sending here would investigate the matter thoroughly and implement strict controls for all x-clubs going forward. Our government agreed to provide whatever support was needed for the K researcher and his team to establish an underground x-club here in the city, and to prevent human interference with the organic selection process necessary for their study. The idea being that New York City's dense, diverse population provided access to a broader human gene pool for Vair to analyze than the rural, remote areas around the K Centers where these fatalities had occurred."

"Vair?" In my shock, I think I whispered it. At the same time, Jay had nearly shouted it.

"Yes, that's the name of the head Krinar researcher the Council sent." Stephen turned to me. "I believe you know him, Ms. Myers." His tone and expression didn't alter, but I knew I saw judgment in those blue eyes. "From what we understand, he's a behavioral scientist. Isn't that correct?"

My lungs felt compressed. I shook my head and struggled to breathe as I stuttered, "I—I don't know... anything... about him. Behavioral—?"

"We aren't certain of his exact title or position within Krinar society," Stephen explained, "but we've been led to believe that he is more or less the Krinar version of an esteemed psychologist or behaviorist."

"Wait a minute," Jay interjected. "You're telling us that Vair is a sex therapist on Krina?"

"No. I'm telling you he's the head researcher that the Krinar Council sent to collect empirical data on the short- and long-term effects of blood and saliva sharing between Ks and humans."

"Empirical data?" Jay intoned with disbelief. "From a sex club?"

Stephen paused to take an annoyingly long sip of coffee before answering. "Yes. Testing the side effects of Krinar saliva on humans. Recording withdrawal symptoms, measuring how quickly humans become addicted. Also measuring how quickly Ks become addicted, researching potential cures—that sort of thing."

Oh, my God. I was a guinea pig?

An alien sex-lab rat?

Pieces began to fall together in my mind, forming a most disturbing puzzle. I recalled Vair's offhand remark on Sunday about too few Ks being inclined to study human behaviorism, and the way that he'd referred to his human clubgoers as *subjects* and *patients.*

"So what's the government list that Amy is on?" Jay asked, bringing me back to the point of this meeting.

"It's called the *charl* list," Stephen answered.

"Charl?" Jay's eyes lit up. "Amy, remember when Zyrnase and Tauce—"

"What does it mean?" I cut in.

"Charl are a class of humans under Krinar protection. Our government no longer has any jurisdiction over them. Actually, neither does the Krinar Council, it would seem, without the express permission of the Krinar whom the charl belongs to."

"Belongs to?" Jay gaped at his college friend. "Excuse me?"

"Our division intended to squash Amy's article, fearing that it would interfere with Vair's testing—give the whole x-club research program away. It's unusual enough having an x-club here in the city, so far from a K Center. According to my sources, the Council was in agreement and didn't appreciate her article drawing attention to Vair's testing facility either. But Vair stepped in and claimed Amy as his charl, forbidding both the Council and our government from doing anything to obstruct the circulation of her x-club exposé."

Vair had let my article run? He had opposed the U.S. government *and* the Krinar Council in this? More importantly, he'd *claimed* me as belonging to him and gotten my name on some government "off-limits" list?

"How many humans are on this charl list?" Jay asked.

"I'm not at liberty to divulge those statistics."

"How can a K just claim a human being?" Jay objected. "And how the hell can our government go along with that?"

I loved Jay for asking it, but I feared the answer was obvious: Ks were above our human laws. Our government had to go along with whatever they wanted.

"We don't have a choice," Stephen confirmed. "As I've said, we do our best to cooperate with the Krinar Council in order to coexist with the Ks." Stephen's eyes swept the largely empty coffee shop before he added, "A division of Homeland Security here in the city got into a heap of trouble shortly after K-Day for interfering with one of their charl."

He'd glanced disapprovingly at me when he'd said the last part.

Jay took notice. "She's not one of their *charl*, Stephen. She's a human being, a U.S. citizen, and a damn fine journalist. What can you do to help her?"

Stephen shook his head. "I've just told you, I can't do anything."

"What about the FBI? Or hell, I don't know, the United Nations? Anyone? Come on, there has to be some covert anti-K organization out there that will help us, right? A charl safe house somewhere?"

"No. There's nothing. And it wouldn't help anyway. The Ks

have ways of tracking their charl. There's nowhere anyone would be able to hide her."

"You've got to be kidding me! You called me back and asked to meet with Amy just to tell her she's fucked? That she's registered as K property and there's nothing our government or any world organization can do about it?"

"No, I requested to meet with Amy because I wanted to ask her to stop writing x-club articles." Stephen's eyes shifted to me. "Regardless of Vair's decision to indulge you as his charl, your article *has* interfered. Whether you meant it to or not, your exposé popularized Vair's x-club, bringing it to the attention of innocent, naïve humans who otherwise wouldn't have known about it or gone looking for it. If you care about your country and your own race, you'll cease drawing attention to the 'Ecstasy-like' high attained from the sharing of blood and saliva between Ks and humans. You won't risk glamorizing what we know to be a dangerous and potentially fatal addiction to these aliens."

CHAPTER TWENTY-NINE

*J*ay fretted, ranted, and apologized at a mile a minute throughout the short cab ride back to our office. I barely heard him as I stared unseeingly out the window.

Once back at *The Herald*, I went through the motions of pretending to be working for the rest of the day.

I snapped out of my scared, confused, comatose stupor at 5:30 p.m., when I received the long-awaited but now-unwelcome text message from Vair inviting me to come back to his club that night. I texted back that I wasn't his property, stating in all caps that I would never in this fucking lifetime be his charl.

He didn't respond.

I waited ten minutes before shooting off another angry text telling him that I wasn't interested in being bitten and fucked to death as his sex-lab rat either.

No reply.

I wanted to call him out as a fraud and a liar, but it occurred to me that Vair had been telling me the truth for the most part —in *Vair-speak*—all along. And that only made me more upset.

So I sent another text saying that if he ever came within three hundred feet of me again, I'd appeal this bogus charl business at the highest level within the Krinar Council—even though rationally, I knew they wouldn't give a damn about my rights or about helping me.

I didn't hear from Vair all weekend.

I continued to send him angry texts. I barely slept, and I neurotically checked my phone for a reply from him.

At night, I lay awake in my bed, contemplating what satisfaction I might get out of charging back to his club and screaming at Vair to go to Krinar hell in person. But those fantasies somehow always took a wrong turn as they played out in my mind's eye, often culminating with me shackled to an animated glass wall or a Saint Andrew's cross, and screaming at Vair for other reasons entirely.

So I didn't go back to Vair's club that first weekend.

But Jay did. He went to see Shalee.

He said he intended to question her about the xenophile fatalities Stephen had told us about. But beyond that, he said that he wanted to understand how Krinar saliva worked in the human system as an aphrodisiac-slash-narcotic in order to determine, as he put it, if the most profoundly intense sexual experience of his life was about Shalee or just her spit.

When he stopped by my office on Monday morning to catch me up on how his visit to the club had gone, our editor and boss, Richard Gable, was just leaving, having delivered a rare "job well done" on the article I'd turned in that morning about the potential future perils of the Ks' forced vegan diet.

"Top shelf, Myers! I really do miss my bacon." He clapped Jay on the shoulder as they passed each other. "Afternoon, Jay."

Jay gave him a fake bright smile and returned, "Afternoon, Dick," just like he always did. And like every other time, Gable reminded him that Dick was his father's name, and that he went by Gable or Richard.

It was the most juvenile, stupid gag, but something in Jay's delivery each time kept it from getting old. I shook my head and smothered the smile breaking out on my face until we were alone and Jay had closed my office door.

He had texted me on Sunday night to check in and let me know that he was okay, saying that he was too tired to talk but would fill me in at work the next day. Judging by the satisfied, relaxed expression on his face and the bounce in his step, it seemed that he'd had a good visit to Vair's club.

I pushed thoughts of Vair and my own hurt feelings aside and asked, "So? How'd it go with Shalee?"

"Great. And before you ask, *Mom*, the answer is no, she didn't bite me again."

That was a relief. I had made Jay promise not to indulge in another K bite after what we'd learned from Stephen.

"But we did do other things." Jay's grin widened, and the most adorable flush crept up from his neck to his cheeks. "And I think... I think maybe the chemistry we have is about more than just spit."

After gushing about Shalee for ten minutes, he went on to relay what she'd told him about the fatalities that had happened at the x-clubs near K Centers. Shalee had explained that because so few Krinar and human pairings existed on Krina, little was known at the time of the invasion about how often or how much Ks and humans should indulge in blood and saliva sharing. And unfortunately, not enough research had been done since, prior to Vair's team arriving in NYC.

She'd told Jay that in the case of a love pairing between a Krinar and a human, the Krinar's concern for the charl's human frailty would naturally prevent them from overindulging. But in the case of these more casual x-club encounters, there was often less thought given to safety, because actions were driven by pure lust and judgment clouded by bite-induced delirium.

Also, the humans going to these clubs would sometimes hook up with multiple Ks per night, thus having too much blood taken, too frequently. This explained the need for an x-club enforcer like Tauce—a K terrifying enough to hopefully scare the most overindulging xenos from coming back, in order to save them from themselves.

Shalee had then said that the answer was more research and stricter regulations moving forward, confirming what Stephen had told us.

"Listen, baby girl, I know you're upset and you feel betrayed. And believe me, I was ready to punch Vair out over that archaic charl alien ownership shit when Stephen told us about it on Friday. But after talking to Shalee, I think maybe being on the charl list isn't as bad as it seems."

"Jay, he claimed me as his *property*."

"Yeah, to protect you from both his government and ours, *and* to let you have your journalism success, which you never would've had otherwise since both the Council and our government were planning to put the kibosh on your x-club piece."

"Are you listening to yourself? Like I give a damn about journalism success if it comes at the price of my freedom as a human being."

He rolled his eyes. "Right. But Amy, look around you. You're sitting in your office, you just wrote another K article for *The Herald*, and you're going to go home to your apartment tonight just like you've done for the past seven nights, not to mention the past month, with no interference and virtually no contact from Vair—other than the one time he made you go to his x-club."

These were all valid points that should've made me feel better. But for some reason, I felt even more deflated.

"He fixed my eyesight without even asking me."

"Oh, what a villain." Jay raised one brow at me. "Face it, you're not exactly being treated like a prisoner. Come to think of it..." He winced and sucked air through his teeth. "The guy left you alone for *a month*, even after he'd claimed you as his charl. *Yikes.*" He shook his head, giving me a phony pitying look. "If anything, maybe you should be concerned that he only did it to be nice and he's just not that into you."

I wasted no time calling Jay out for his obvious K-sympathizer matchmaking attempts as he succumbed to a fit of laughter. I told him I was happy for him about Shalee, but that he needed to get his lovesick ass out of my office before I pulled the big three-prong hole puncher on him.

And luckily for him, he did.

CHAPTER THIRTY

I was less angry about everything after my chat with Jay on Monday. By Wednesday, when I still hadn't heard from Vair, I realized that I was depressed.

By Friday night, with still no word from Vair and with Jay's time monopolized by Shalee, I realized that I was lonely—although it took drinking two glasses of red wine alone in my apartment to admit it to myself.

In my tipsy state, I thought about changing out of my ugly pajamas and catching a cab to Vair's club. But I put the wine bottle away and got out the chocolate ice cream instead. I spent the rest of the night composing and deleting numerous text messages to Vair.

Saturday came and went with still no contact. And Sunday marked two weeks since I had last seen Vair.

At that point, I began to fear that he might again go a month without seeing me. I even started to question whether Jay's teasing comment had been right and that perhaps Vair just wasn't that into me.

But then I reminded myself that he *could* see me... if he was watching.

So I decided to give him something to watch. After all, I'd gotten a text message from him inviting me back to his club after the last time I'd fingered myself in the living room.

I started with a little masturbation show in the kitchen to warm up—unsure if that constituted an "important room" where Vair would've set up surveillance. Emboldened by how empowered I felt afterward, I donned a new bra and panty set and pleasured myself in the bedroom.

The next morning, I was ecstatic to wake up to a text message from Vair: another video of us. Upon watching it, I was inspired to give a performance in the living room on top of the coffee table—dressed for work in my most prim blouse and pencil skirt.

By lunchtime on Monday, I was so aroused that I considered locking my door and giving Vair another show right there in my office. Fortunately, sanity prevailed and I went to grab a coffee and a salad at the deli downstairs instead.

It was close to quitting time and my fingers were flying over the keyboard when a tall, dark, sexy-as-hell Krinar strode into my office as if he owned *The Herald*.

He'd already shut my office door and was leaning casually against it as I struggled to breathe normally, wondering whether I'd gone totally mad and was simply imagining him there.

Dazed, I stood and walked out from behind my desk as I stared at him in disbelief.

"I missed you, Amy."

He looked huge standing in my tiny office, nearly blocking out the entire door as he took me in with those intense, all-consuming black-brown eyes.

"Did you miss me?"

My nipples responded before I found the voice to do so. My inner muscles followed suit.

"I—I'm at work, Vair." I said it as much for my own benefit as his.

He smiled. "I know. And I need to watch you take what you want. Now. While at your work." His eyes darkened along with his tone. "Bend over your desk for me."

A shiver coursed through me. And Lord help me, but I didn't hesitate for a second. I just turned around and did it, flattening my hands against the cool, hard laminate desktop as Vair jerked my pencil skirt up around my waist.

I couldn't think. I was already panting, my whole body hot as my sex came alive with need.

"Spread your legs, darling."

I did.

He made a noise of approval as his hand moved down over my bare ass to rub against the damp thong between my thighs.

"All the way." His other hand pressed gently against the small of my back, flattening me to the desk as he tugged my thong to the side and worked two fingers into me to the knuckles. I was so slippery wet they met no resistance.

Fuck, I had missed him.

"Very nice," he praised, sliding his fingers in and out, rotating and scissoring them.

With my cheek pressed to the cold surface of my desk, my half-lidded eyes faced the door to my office—*that wasn't locked.*

I felt an increased heat behind me and knew that he'd silently shed his clothes in that magical way he'd done before.

This was happening. He was going to fuck me in my office at *The New York Herald.*

And I was going to let him.

None of this was sane. None of it was safe.

Safety had long become overrated.

He removed his fingers, and I felt the smooth, blunt tip of his cock prodding against me where I was more than ready to accept him. I tilted my hips back, encouraging his entry.

"That's it, angel. You do it. I want to see you take me deep inside."

I gripped the sides of my desk and rocked back into him until the broad head of his cock slowly pushed inside.

"So perfect." He exhaled, and it was the most carnal sigh I'd ever heard. "Look at you stretching around me."

I bit my lip and stifled a moan as his fingers stole around the fabric of my bunched-up skirt to stroke between my split folds where we were joined.

"So slick for me." His thumb circled my clit. "Take all of me, darling."

This was crazy.

I'd gone completely mad.

I envisioned Vair staring down at my spread privates in the glaring daylight streaming through my office window. Watching me as I slowly impaled myself on his huge alien erection.

During office hours.

With my door unlocked.

I needed to get my head examined.

"More, love." His thumb pressed and rolled, toying with my swollen, throbbing flesh. "It's all for you."

I let out a soft grunt as I slid all the way back, stretching around the thickest part of his cock until I felt his balls pressed up against my wet center.

He groaned. "Such a good little human."

His patronizing endearment shouldn't have warmed my heart so much. Nor should it have made me clench and gush anew around him.

I was a goner.

A shameless K addict where Vair was concerned.

"Move on me."

It was an order.

I obeyed without question.

Going up onto my toes, then back down on my heels, I rocked back and forth on him. His fingers stroked and pinched my clit. His other hand caressed the backs of my thighs and ass.

"That's it. Faster, darling. Let me see you take what you want. Don't be afraid."

White-knuckling the sides of my desk, I let my body go, undulating back and forth, delighting in every rigid inch of him as his heavy cock dragged in and out of me.

I was already sweating. My cheap office desk had begun to make creaking noises under the strain of my movements. My computer screens were teetering and rattling atop the desk.

Still, I sped up at his command.

Knowing someone might hear. That we could get caught.

Because I couldn't stop.

"Harder." His fingers dug into the flesh of my ass cheek. "*Deeper.* I want to feel you come all over my cock." His voice was sounding less controlled. More urgent.

Then he began making a low, sustained growling sound deep in his chest. His fingers grew less gentle on my clit. His big palm mauled my ass in a bruising grip.

I knew he was restraining himself—eschewing his predator instinct to drive into me fast and hard for the sake of watching me take what I wanted.

And that just made me all the hotter for him as I sawed back and forth, my eager body swallowing every hard, thick inch.

"Fuck me like you'll never get enough, Amy," he snarled.

Something in my psyche broke at the harsh truth of those words, and I cried out as I suddenly flew apart, my movements graceless and jerky, my climax overtaking me.

His hand clamped over my mouth, and he drove his hips into me. His cock seemed to have swelled impossibly larger, and his strokes were rough and deep as my inner walls fluttered and squeezed around him, riding out the final waves of my ecstasy.

My legs were trembling from exertion, and my entire body felt like a wrung-out ragdoll as he pulled out and maneuvered me to my knees in front of him. His cock pushed past my panting lips into the back of my throat without preamble, and he spilled his hot seed as I gagged and swallowed reflexively around him.

His Krinar essence coated my throat and settled in my stomach, bringing with it the stark realization of what I'd just done and where.

But before complete and utter post-coitus remorse could set in, Vair groaned in pleasure and spoke the only words capable of eclipsing the horror of all else in that moment.

"*Fuck.* I love you, little human."

I had a history of having awkward, bad reactions to those

three words. And it had never once in my wildest imaginings occurred to me that I might hear them from Vair—a *Krinar*, a member of the ruling enemy alien species.

I was in a state of shock as Vair withdrew from my mouth, picked me up off the floor, and proceeded to gently straighten my clothing and hair for me.

He then sat me down atop the edge of my desk.

"Are you all right?"

I didn't respond, my mind too busy shutting out his revelation.

He captured my face between his hands and tipped it up to his. "Amy, I had your office soundproofed weeks ago. Zyrnase is standing watch outside your door. It's okay. No one saw or heard us."

I suppressed a nervous giggle at his revelation. It was both comforting and disturbing to know he'd taken the precaution —*and liberty*—of soundproofing my office.

And why not? He'd already taken the liberty of bugging it with all manner of high-tech surveillance equipment.

I shook my head. Swallowed. "We can't… we can't do this. Anymore."

The soft concern that had been in his eyes morphed into something a shade colder. Darker. "And why is that?"

I pulled his hands from my face. "It isn't right. This isn't normal. It's not healthy."

"And what *is* normal, Amy? What's healthy?" He stepped back, crossing his arms over his chest. "Can you define it for me, please? Because I'd love to hear you describe this 'normal' and 'healthy' relationship and explain why ours doesn't qualify."

"We don't have a… relationship. You're blackmailing me

into having sex with you. Everything between us is built on manipulation and coercion."

His eyes gleamed. "So you've hated every minute of it, then? You've endured every orgasm I've given you under duress?"

I looked away. "You know I haven't. It's complicated."

"You're avoiding my question. Tell me what healthy is. Describe how a normal relationship works."

"I don't have to."

"No. You don't know *how to*," he contended. "So you'd rather throw away what we have, even though you want it, because you don't think it's what you *should* want."

He was making my head spin. "I don't need you to psychoanalyze me," I snapped, looking back at him. "I'm not one of your x-club 'patients' or some xeno that's addicted to you."

But I was. I totally was.

And he loved me.

No, don't go there.

His mouth tightened. "What if I sent you terrifying emails daily, warning you of all the perils lurking around every corner of the universe? Would that make our relationship feel more *normal* to you? Would that be healthy? If I ended every email and phone communication to you with 'stay safe' or 'be careful,' would that make you feel loved?"

"You're blackmailing me," I repeated the obvious. "You can't build a relationship on a blackmail arrangement."

A hint of amusement lightened his gaze. "I thought ours was built on the foundation of being only children?"

"Vair, this isn't funny anymore."

"You're right." Annoyance flared in his mercurial dark eyes, along with another emotion I didn't want to acknowledge a

Krinar capable of: hurt. "The fact that you still believe my blackmail ploy—believe I'd actually ever consider going through with sharing private video footage of us with the public is far from amusing for me."

"Ploy?" My eyes narrowed. "Do you mean to tell me—"

"Amy, like I explained before, your parents programmed you to respond to fear, to threats of danger and intimidation." His raised voice was sharp and angry, belying the nonchalant shrug of his shoulders. "Of course I capitalized on that, knowing it was the most expeditious means of getting you to come back to my club."

My mouth dropped open. "Capitalized on? That's just a fancier way of saying you took advantage."

"Precisely." He pointed an accusing finger at me. "And guess what? You've loved it. Inwardly, you've rejoiced in the fact that *I* took full responsibility and bore all the guilt for our arrangement, allowing you to indulge in what you considered inappropriate fantasies. No matter what we did, you knew you could place the blame squarely on me, and that made it okay for you."

"That's not true!"

"Amy." He gave me a drill sergeant look.

Oh, fine. "Whatever. So maybe I was into *some* of it. It doesn't matter. It doesn't change the fact that we're still not compatible. Hell, our species can't even procreate. Shalee told Jay that human and Krinar couples aren't able to have babies."

Vair tilted his head, the corner of his mouth kicking up into a smile that made my pulse jump. "No. None have. *Yet.*" His warm, dark gaze fell to my breasts. "Interesting that you've given it such thought when you want nothing to do with me and my manipulation and coercion."

He leaned forward, invading my space and caging me in as he planted a hand on either side of my hips atop the desk.

"So now you object to us being together because Krinar and humans have not yet been proven compatible for procreation?" His voice was low and throaty, his eyes intimate as he asked, "Are you saying you want children with me?"

I felt my cheeks go red. "No, that's not what I'm saying."

"There are countless human couples incapable of procreation. Does that make them incompatible?"

"Of course not. Stop twisting things. I'm merely pointing out that we're not even the same species—that we literally come from two different worlds."

"Yes, and we're not the first Krinar and human to pair off, Amy. And we certainly won't be the last."

I placed a hand against his chest as his head dipped closer, his nose a hair away from mine. My voice emerged breathy as I threw out the last obstacle I could think of. "But what about my parents, Vair? I'll never be able to explain this—*you*—to them."

He cupped my face in his hands again, tipping it up. "I've already thought of that, darling." His nose nuzzled mine. "Let's tell them I'm still blackmailing you, hmm?" I felt his smile against my lips as his touched mine softly.

"You're so sick," I whispered, kissing him back. When I pulled away to catch my breath, I told him truthfully, "They're going to absolutely hate you."

He nodded. "Well, I'm prepared to blackmail them directly, too, if necessary. Do you think the threat of a Costa Rican human labor camp will make the idea of an eight-hundred-and-forty-seven-year-old Krinar sex club owner more palatable to them as a son-in-law?"

I released a hysterical giggle and shook my head, even as I

cringed internally at how bad the description of my E.T. lover truly did and would sound to my parents.

"You really don't know my mother." I bit my lip. "I'm afraid this is going to require multiple phony YouTube videos about how much Ks enjoy the taste of human brains."

"Oh, and I'm the sick one?" he said with a laugh.

I shrugged.

"Well, darling… for you, I think it can be arranged."

Part Three

THE EXPOSÉ

CHAPTER THIRTY-ONE

*W*as this really happening?

I pinched myself. Discreetly, of course, but Vair—who noticed absolutely freaking *everything* about me—saw it, and a satyr-like grin tugged at the corners of his full, dangerously sexy mouth.

"Yes, it's real, little human," he whispered wickedly. "And I promise not to eat *them*—only you, okay?"

A violent blush crept up my neck. "Hush," I hissed, grabbing his hand and squeezing it with all my puny human strength. "They'll overhear."

We were standing in front of my parents' house in Skaneateles, where Vair and I were about to have dinner with my family for the first time. If it hadn't been for the Krinar nanocytes in my system, I'd have thought the heart palpitations I was having were a premature heart attack.

But according to Vair, I couldn't have a heart attack anymore. Or get any other human disease, which apparently included getting older. Now that I was officially Vair's charl, with proper nanocytes and all, I had immunity to *everything*, death from aging included.

I still hadn't fully processed that, and I didn't know if I would anytime soon. It was enough that I'd been dating Vair—full-on, actual dating—for the past two months, ever since he'd showed up in my office and bent me over my desk, fucking my brains out until I'd agreed to give this madness a go.

Not that Vair regarded what we're doing as "dating." In his eyes, we were simply together. Forever. He wasn't my *boyfriend*. Oh, no. That would be too straightforward and egalitarian. He was my *cheren*—which, if I understood that Krinar term right, meant that he basically owned my ass.

But in a loving, cherishing, forever-responsible-for-me kind of way.

I hadn't processed that part of it either, nor was I in any hurry to do so. Vair *acted* like my boyfriend—albeit of the stalking, recording-my-every-move, ridiculously possessive variety—and that was good enough for me. I continued to work at *The Herald*, where I'd finally gotten a couple of meaty assignments, and the rest of the time we spent together, going out to dinner at the best restaurants in the city, visiting parks and museums, and hanging out with Jay and his Krinar girlfriend Shalee (*she* had no problems with that label). That is, when we weren't having unhealthy amounts of mind-blowing, very non-vanilla sex either at Vair's obscenely luxurious penthouse or at his kinky "research facility"—a.k.a. the x-club.

"What made you decide to become a human behaviorist?" I'd asked him a few weeks ago over breakfast, after I'd woken up still exhausted from observing an all-night x-club orgy (while being fucked by Vair out of sight of the orgy participants, naturally). "No offense, but I wouldn't have pegged you for a scientist."

"Oh?" His eyebrows had arched. "What would you have pegged me for?"

"Oh, I don't know…" If these had been Victorian times, I'd have labeled him a high-society rake, but that was too silly to vocalize. "A *real* sex club owner?"

His teeth had flashed white as he'd picked up a strawberry. "I *am* a real sex club owner; there's nothing fake about my club. And as you know"—those teeth had sunk seductively into the plump berry—"I thoroughly enjoy the research we do there."

Ignoring my body's reaction to that statement, as well as my primal urge to lick the strawberry juice off his delicious bottom lip, I'd determinedly pressed ahead. "I'm serious, Vair. What made you decide to go into that profession? The first time we met, you said you'd been bored on Krina. Were you just messing around with me? Playing a part of the playboy Krinar suffering from ennui?"

He'd chuckled at that, but then his expression had grown more serious. "No, darling. I've never pretended to be anything other than what I am with you. I *had been* bored on Krina. Nothing really held my interest for long, so for most of my life, I'd been a dabbler, going from one field to another without truly finding myself or making any major contribution. It wasn't until our Council had decided to come to Earth that I discovered the poorly explored field of human behavior, and it became a passion of mine. That is, until *you* became a passion of mine, little human, irrational behavior and all."

I'd thrown a berry at him then, but more out of awkwardness at hearing again about his feelings than out of any real anger at being called "irrational."

Because I *was*.

I was crazy irrational when it came to him.

For one thing, though Vair often told me that he loved me—or spouted off some variation of those words—I still hadn't mustered the courage to tell him how *I* felt. How even when we were in the middle of the kinkiest, dirtiest sex session, I was acutely aware of a growing undertone of tenderness between us, of a connection so deep it felt like it was embedded in my bone marrow. For whatever reason, I'd been keeping quiet about how I was starting to miss him when I was at work, even if I'd seen him that very morning, and how when we were apart, I checked my phone every minute, hoping to see a text from him.

A blush-inducing, horribly inappropriate text that would make me want to sink through the floor and orgasm at the same time.

It made me a coward, I was sure, but it had been so much easier when I'd regarded Vair as a villain. *When he'd been blackmailing me into doing what I wanted.*

And yes, I could admit that now. Unerringly, like the behaviorist that he was, Vair had found just the right approach to take with me. I had needed his implied threats to overcome the fears embedded in me by my parents, to fight my natural inclination to avoid all that was different and scary.

An inclination that I was still struggling with, to a small degree—hence my inability to admit to him how much I was beginning to need him.

How I was falling for him, despite my lingering fear of the unknown.

"You ready?" Vair asked, tugging me out of my parent-meeting-induced panicked musings. Grinning, he squeezed my hand back—but gently, so as not to crush my frail human bones. I must've still looked like I was about to throw up, though, because he raised my hand to his lips and dropped a gentle kiss on my knuckles. "It's going to be okay, darling, I promise. They'll love me. And if not, there are always those brain-eating videos on YouTube..."

I nodded, unconvinced, but it was too late.

Vair was already pressing on the doorbell.

CHAPTER THIRTY-TWO

*I*t was a disaster.

I'd known it would be, of course, but Vair had insisted on this meeting, and here I was, cringing into my plate of overcooked broccoli as Mom stared at me with accusing, red-rimmed eyes and Dad alternated between stuttering out awkward questions about how long we'd been dating and drinking too much wine.

Partially, it was my fault. I'd kind of sprung Vair on my parents. While I'd been open about the fact that I had a new boyfriend, it had only been last night that I'd finally admitted the truth to my parents.

At 9:38 p.m., when Mom had called to double-check what time we'd be coming today, I'd fessed up that Vair was a K.

The hysterics that had followed were the worst I'd witnessed yet, and that was saying something.

"He's going to kill you! Murder you in your sleep!" Mom had sobbed into the phone while Dad had spammed my inbox with links to all the negative articles about Ks—some of them my own. "He's going to crack your skull and drain you of blood and—"

"I won't, I promise," Vair had interrupted, taking the phone from me, and that had set off a round of shrieking that must've been heard all the way to Alabama.

I'd repossessed the phone at that point and spent the next two-plus hours soothing my parents, telling them all about how well Vair treated me and how he never, ever ate human brains, not even when he was really hungry. After I'd finally hung up, I'd kept my phone next to me because I knew my mom—and sure enough, she'd called me six more times throughout the night, crying and begging me to leave and go get help, and why, oh why wouldn't the FBI listen to her insistence that I'd been kidnapped and send a SWAT team to retrieve me?

So yeah, that had been a fun night.

And here we were now, in my parents' house, with my mom having served the blandest, most unappetizing meal I'd ever seen her make. I suspected it was her version of "fuck you, evil K." Maybe she was hoping that Vair would extrapolate the overboiled broccoli into a threat to overboil *him* if he ever hurt me?

I wasn't sure, but it was embarrassing either way.

"*Sorry,*" I mouthed to Vair when my mom went with my dad into the kitchen to get us a refill of water and wine—to wash down the unpalatable food. "I don't know why they did this."

I gestured helplessly at the table, where in addition to the overcooked broccoli and undercooked potatoes, half-squished, ancient-looking grapes stood in a bowl—apparently to be eaten for dessert.

Vair's dark eyes glinted with amusement. "Don't worry, darling. It'll take more than a bad meal to scare me off."

So he'd interpreted my mom's actions the same way I had, though he didn't know she was normally a good cook who'd gamely risen to the challenge of a plant-based diet.

Unless...

I narrowed my eyes at him. "Is my parents' house bugged?" I half-hissed, half-whispered, gripping the table as I leaned closer. "Have you been watching them, too?"

Is that how he knew this was a bad meal and not my mom's usual dinner fare?

The amusement in his gaze deepened. "What do you think?"

Ugh. Of course. I felt a flare of outrage on my parents' behalf, but I didn't have a chance to express it because my mom returned, carrying two glasses of water—which she plopped on the table in front of us so hard that some liquid sloshed over the rim.

Dad was on her heels, carrying an open bottle of wine and a tray with a charred-looking brownie.

So there *was* dessert other than the unappetizing grapes.

"Thanks, Mom," I said, picking up my water to take a sip. Belatedly, it occurred to me that she might've spit in Vair's glass —or put something bad in his food, in general—but I shoved the thought aside.

Even if she had done something so awful, it wasn't like he'd get sick from it.

"So, Vair..." Dad said after downing another glass of wine. "What are your intentions toward our daughter?"

I closed my eyes and prayed for one of Vair's wall/floor-dissolving tricks, so I could sink into the hole and disappear.

"Well," Vair said, completely calmly, "I'm in love with your daughter, Mr. Myers, so I'm hoping for a long-term relationship with her."

I opened my lids a sliver and verified it.

Yep. Not even a hint of discomfort or embarrassment on that perfectly formed face of his, nor any of his usual mockery.

He looked sincere. *Earnest.* Like a Boy Scout hoping to win his Scoutmaster's approval.

And my dad was lapping it up, nodding like he was in total agreement.

My eyes opened wider as Mom spoke to Vair for the first time, her voice only slightly higher pitched than usual. "How would something like that work, exactly? You are a different *species.*" She emphasized the last word, making it sound like something dirty.

"Yes, we are, but that doesn't matter," Vair said, giving her a carefully modulated smile. One that aimed to soothe and disarm. "I'm sure you'll remember a time in human history when people felt the same way about unions between different races."

My mom's freckled cheeks flushed. Despite living in a ninety-eight-percent-white area, she prided herself on being "blind" to race. "That's n-not..." she stuttered. "I mean, that's not the same *at all.*"

"Why?" Vair said, his tone gentle. "If I love your daughter and she loves me, what's wrong with us being together?"

Mom stared at him, speechless for once, and I knew I was wearing the same expression—a dumbfounded, "deer in the headlights" look of illogical fear confronting irrefutable logic. My heart thudded dully in my chest, and my hand bunched into a fist under the table as his words sank in deep, bypassing the layers of bullshit I'd used as my defenses.

A Krinar and a human, in love. What was wrong with it, indeed?

Why was I fighting this so hard?

Why was I so scared to admit how I feel?

For a few long moments, no one said anything, the silence stretching until it felt like a string on the verge of breaking.

Then my dad cleared his throat. "Um… wine, anyone?"

"Don't mind if I do," Vair said easily, as if we were all friends here, and as Mom shakily extended her empty wine glass, holding it next to Vair's, I stared at my Krinar, knowing—*no, feeling*—the truth.

We might not be the same species, but he handled my parents like a boss.

———

It was late by the time we got home, but I felt wired instead of tired, all but buzzing with nervous energy.

"We did it. Can you believe we did it?" I babbled as Vair led me into his penthouse. I hadn't been able to shut up the entire ride home. "And oh my God, the expression on Mom's face when you invited them to New York for Thanksgiving… I bet they thought you were going to say 'Krina.' And then when Dad tasted that awful brownie and literally spit it out… Do you think Mom *actually* swapped the salt and the sugar, like she claimed she did by accident? As in, the full amount? I mean, it sure tasted like that, but that's extreme, even for her. And then—"

"Amy." Vair's dark eyes held a vaguely predatory expression as he stopped me by pressing a gentle finger to my lips. "Hush, darling."

My eyes opened wide as he followed that with his clothing-dissolving trick—with my clothes and his—and my throat went dry as I stared at the masculine perfection laid bare before me.

Would I ever get used to him?

Was it possible to get used to someone so gorgeous?

He was already hard, his magnificent cock curving up to his navel, every muscle on his large body chiseled with inhuman precision. But it was the look on his face that stole my breath—a mixture of dark lust and unabashed tenderness, of hunger and sheer adoration.

Leaning in, he framed my face with his large palms, and my insides clenched in anticipation as his lips brushed across mine... once, twice, and then again. His breath was warm and tasted faintly of wine, his tongue soft and slick as he delved into my mouth, tasting me, teasing me. My hands curved around his solid wrists, and my heart hammered in my ribcage as a hot flush spread over my skin and an empty ache bloomed low in my core.

I needed him to fuck me.

Now.

First, though, I needed to tell him something important—something that had weighed on me the entire ride home, making my nerves jingle and my mouth run non-stop.

Something I should've told him long ago but had been too chicken to admit.

Breathing shallowly, I broke the kiss and pulled away. "Vair..." Despite my resolve, my voice shook as I stared up at him, still holding his wrists as though I could possibly restrain him. "Vair, I..."

He held my gaze, the tenderness in his eyes intensifying. "Yes, darling?"

He knew. Of course he knew.

From the very beginning, he'd understood me—even better than I'd understood myself.

"I love you," I said, my voice steadying as my nervousness evaporated, replaced by a surge of pure, true feeling. "I love everything about you, Vair, and I want us to make a real go of this—no matter what my parents or anyone else thinks."

"Do you now?" he murmured, a slow, warm smile curving his sensuous lips, and as he reached for me again, bending his head to claim me with a voracious kiss, I knew that this was it.

In a New York City x-club, I'd found my other half.

A Krinar I loved with all my heart.

EPILOGUE

Six Years Later

"*A*re you ready?" Vair asked, squeezing my hand, and I nodded as I took a deep breath and did a quick self-check.

Was I about to throw up? *No.*

Faint? *Unlikely.*

Squeal like a teenager meeting her rock star idol? *Quite possibly.*

It couldn't be helped, though. In a minute, we were about to enter a virtual meeting with the Krinar-human couple whose tumultuous love story had recently riveted the population of two planets.

Korum and Mia.

The most powerful K on the Council and the human girl he'd *married.*

"They'll love you," Vair assured me. "Your manuscript blew them away, and they know there's no one who'd do a better job with their story."

I gulped, trying to settle my wayward pulse—which insisted on hammering like a woodpecker in my throat.

I could do this. I could absolutely, definitely do this. So what if they were higher profile than any celebrities? Or that Korum had been the driving force behind the Ks' invasion of Earth?

Vair believed in me—enough to use all the goodwill his research had generated with the Krinar Council to get me this meeting—and I was no longer a newbie journalist. Over the past six years, I'd interviewed other highly placed Krinar, as well as human government officials and members of the Resistance. My articles, short stories, and exposés were widely acknowledged to be well researched and insightful, and my first nonfiction novel—the unusual love story of Emily Ross and her cheren, Zaron—was about to be published.

I was a freaking pro, and I had no reason to be nervous.

Other than the fact that this was the biggest journalistic coup ever.

Okay, then. "Let's do this," I said firmly, and as Vair grinned at me, the world turned into a blur.

Fighting dizziness, I closed my eyes, and when I opened them, I was no longer in Vair's New York City penthouse.

"Amy Myers and Vair, I presume?" a tall, intimidatingly gorgeous Krinar with peculiar golden eyes said, staring at me from across a long, floating table.

My nerves settled as I felt myself slide into my journalistic persona. With a practiced glance, I took in the petite human girl at his side and the ivory-colored sunlit room we were virtually sitting in.

A room in Korum's house on Krina.

"That's right," I answered smoothly, inclining my head at the couple in a gesture of respect. I knew better than to attempt a handshake with a male K. Vair would be tempted to kill him on the spot. "And you must be Korum and Mia?"

"That's us," the girl said, beaming at me. Her eyes were startlingly blue against the backdrop of her dark, wildly curly hair, and her smile was utterly radiant in her delicately featured face. "We're so pleased to meet you, Amy. And Vair, of course."

A heavy arm slid around my waist, and I looked up to see Vair incline his head as he drawled, "A pleasure, to be sure."

I barely stopped myself from rolling my eyes. *Ks and their ridiculous possessiveness.* Korum was holding Mia anchored to his side as if she might otherwise run away, so of course Vair had to stake a similar claim on me. Never mind that this was supposed to be a serious interview, or that both Ks rationally knew that neither had an interest in the other's charl. Or that we were all here virtually, and our actual bodies were on different planets.

Their territorial instincts didn't give two hoots about rationality or reason.

"So, Korum," I said, focusing on the task at hand, "how about we start at the very beginning? How did you and Mia first meet?"

He looked at her, and I saw his starkly beautiful features soften. Not a lot, but just enough to convey what anyone who'd watched a recording of their lavish wedding already knew.

He'd blast apart entire galaxies for her.

"Do you want to do the honors, my sweet?" he asked softly, and she smiled up at him, her small face glowing.

"If you insist." Still smiling, she turned to me. "It's kind of a long story. I'm not sure it'll all fit into one book."

"If it doesn't, then I'll make it into two or three books," I assured her. "Whatever is needed."

And as the human girl launched into her story, I jotted down, *"The air was crisp and clear as Mia walked briskly down a winding path in Central Park..."*

SWEPT AWAY

CHAPTER ONE

Greece, Third Century BC, 2293 Years Before the Krinar Invasion

*H*er heart pounding, Delia watched the naked god emerge from the sea. Water droplets glistened on his bronzed skin, and his powerful muscles flexed as he strode out of the surf, impervious to the violent waves crashing onto the shore. It was as if the storm meant nothing to him—as if the sea itself was his domain.

Was he Poseidon? Delia had never believed the gods were flesh and blood, like in the stories, but she knew the stranger couldn't be a mortal man. The storm was raging, the wind howling outside her rocky shelter, yet the strongest waves couldn't seem to budge him from his path. Ignoring the battering of the deadly surf, he walked out onto the dry strip of beach below her cliff and stopped, raising his hand to push back the black hair plastered wetly to his forehead.

As he did so, he tilted his head back, and Delia saw his face. Her breath caught in her throat, and whatever doubts she had about his origins disappeared.

The stranger was inhumanly beautiful. Even with the clouds darkening the morning sky, she could see the flawless symmetry of his features. His jaw was strong, his lips sensuously curved, and his cheekbones high and noble. It was as if an artist's steady hand had molded his face, leaving no room for nature to add its imperfections.

With piercing dark eyes, straight black eyebrows, and a warrior's broad-shouldered build, the stranger made the most handsome men in Delia's village look like lepers.

A crack of thunder startled her, making her jump in her small, cramped cave. The man outside, however, remained calm, turning to look at the angry sea with what seemed to be interest rather than worry. Delia followed his gaze and saw something silvery shimmering far out in the water.

A ship? Several ships, perhaps? The object was certainly big enough—maybe even too big, given how visible it was from far away. Is that where the god-like man came from? That mysterious silvery something?

Thunder boomed again, and with a flash of lightning, the skies opened, sheets of rain coming down with savage force. Delia shrank deeper into her narrow cave, but it was too small to shelter her completely, and cold drops pelted her skin. Below her, the sea churned harder, the waves growing taller with each moment, and she fought the urge to scream at the stranger, to warn him to get to higher ground. She could see the swells rising in the distance; the waves would be taller than two men when they reached the shore, and the narrow strip of land where the man was standing would be completely swallowed up by the sea.

In fact, she realized with growing dread, her tiny cave at the top of the cliff might not be safe either. When she'd taken shelter here an hour ago, she hadn't counted on the storm becoming so violent. If the waves approaching the shore turned out to be as tall as she feared, they could reach the top of the cliff. She'd never witnessed the sea rising that high, but the old fishermen had told stories about surging waters, and she couldn't take the risk that they were true.

Coming to a decision, Delia scrambled out of the cave onto the rocky ledge below. Instantly, the rain soaked her dress, and a gust of wind nearly pushed her off the ledge.

Gasping, she managed to turn around. Bracing herself against the wind, she began to climb, determined to get away from the fury of the sea. She knew the stranger was somewhere below her, but she didn't dare look down. The rain was blinding. Even with lightning flashing every few seconds, she couldn't see farther than an arm's length in front of her, and her bare feet kept slipping on the wet rocks, her soaked dress tangling around her legs as she climbed with growing desperation.

Just a little more, she told herself. Another reach, another push, and she'd be at the top, on flat ground. With lightning striking everywhere, it was far from safe—Delia had hidden in the cave for a reason—but it was a smaller risk than drowning at this point. Squinting against the rain, she reached for the top outcropping, but instead of cold rock, her fingers encountered something warm—something that curled around her palm with unbelievable strength.

A man's hand.

Gasping, Delia opened her eyes wider, and through the blur of stinging rain, saw the stranger from the beach looking down at her.

The god had somehow made it up the cliff and was holding her hand.

CHAPTER TWO

The human girl seemed so shocked to see Arus above her that she froze, stopping her climb for a moment. Below her, a giant wave crashed into the cliff, spraying them both with salt water. There was an even bigger wave behind it, so Arus bent lower and grabbed the girl's other arm with his free hand.

"The water is going to reach here," he explained in her language, pulling her up as he rose to his feet. The wave was still cresting, so he swung the girl up into his arms and leapt back a dozen feet, holding her securely against his chest. A moment later, the wave hit the top of the cliff and spilled over, the water swirling around his ankles before receding back into the sea. Had the girl still been hanging over the cliff, it would've washed her away, possibly causing her to drown. Arus wasn't certain of that last outcome, but from what he'd seen of her kind, it was entirely likely.

For all their Krinar-like appearance, humans were weak and clumsy, unable to cope with the most basic challenges of their planet.

The girl began to struggle, and Arus realized he was still holding her against his chest. He loosened his grip enough to make sure she could breathe but didn't set her down. Instead, he studied her, noting her large brown eyes and smooth olive-toned complexion. She was young; he guessed her age to be somewhere in the late teens or early twenties. With her thick dark hair and slender build, she could almost pass for a Krinar female—except her features were too irregular to have been designed in a lab. Her face was shaped like a heart, with a forehead that was a shade too wide and a mouth that was too delicate for true beauty. Still, she was pretty in a unique way.

Pretty enough that his cock stirred, oblivious to the cold water pouring from the sky.

As if sensing the direction of his thoughts, the girl redoubled her efforts to get free. "Please, let me go." Her voice held a note of fear, and her small hands pushed at his chest, her palms sliding on his wet skin.

To his shock, Arus felt heat streaking down his spine at her touch, and his breathing picked up.

He was getting turned on by a wet, scared human girl.

Before he could decide what to do about that, he saw another wave cresting over the cliff. The worst of the storm surge had yet to come, which meant his first priority was getting the girl to safety.

"We have to get away from this beach," he told her, turning away from the sea. She continued to struggle, but he ignored it, holding her tightly as he walked toward the hills in the distance.

He knew there was a village to the west—likely the girl's village—so he headed east, where he would be less likely to run into more humans.

He was supposed to observe the Earth's residents, not interact with them.

Still, Arus wasn't sorry he'd saved the girl. The more he thought about it, the more convinced he became that she would've drowned on her own. And that would've been a shame, because she was pleasant to hold.

So pleasant, in fact, that he couldn't help imagining how it would feel if he held her underneath him, his cock buried in her slick, warm flesh.

"Where are you taking me?" The girl sounded panicked now. "Please, I have to get home."

"Don't worry. I won't hurt you." Arus glanced down at his captive. Her rapid pulse was visible at the base of her throat, and his arousal grew as he imagined the coppery taste of her blood on his tongue. He had tried drinking human blood once before, and the experience had been sublime. He had a feeling that with this girl, it would be even better.

It seemed that his decision was already made.

"Where are you taking me?" the girl asked again, her voice shaking. She didn't seem the least bit soothed by Arus's reassurance.

"I'm taking you someplace you'll be warm and safe." Surely she would appreciate that. He could feel her shivering; the rough rag that served as her dress was soaked and had to be chilling her. "You shouldn't be out in this storm," he added when jagged lightning cut across the sky for the third time in as many seconds.

"I'll be fine if you let me go." Pushing at his chest again, the girl tried to twist out of his hold. "Please, let me down."

Arus sighed and picked up his pace, ignoring her puny struggles. Once he got her warm and dry, he'll work on calming her down.

He didn't want her frightened in his bed.

CHAPTER THREE

*D*elia had never been so frightened in her life. The god—and she was now sure he was a god—was carrying her without any sign of tiring, his arms like iron bands around her back and knees. Neither rain nor wind seemed to slow him down; holding her against his chest, he was walking faster than a mortal man could run.

"Please, let me down," she begged again, pushing at his broad chest. It was useless, like trying to move a mountain. "Please, I'll sacrifice a goat in your honor if you let me go."

That seemed to get his attention. "A goat?" He looked down at her as he kept walking. "Why would I want that?"

Delia's breath hitched at the intensity of his gaze. "Because you're a god?" Despite her certainty, her words came out as a question, and she silently berated herself for sounding foolish. "I mean, because you're a god and deserve to be respected," she said in a firmer tone.

There, that was better. Surely he would accept one goat. Her family couldn't spare more—even one would leave them without enough cheese for trading.

To her surprise, the stranger laughed, the sound deep and genuinely amused. "A god?" His dark eyes gleamed as another bolt of lightning split the sky above them. "You think I'm a god?"

Delia blinked the rain out of her eyes. "Are you saying you're not?"

He laughed again, the sound blending with a boom of thunder, and she felt his pace accelerate from a walk to a run. He was moving so fast the ground looked like a blur under his feet. Delia began to feel nauseated but didn't dare close her eyes.

She had to see where he was taking her.

After a few minutes, she realized he was heading for the hills to the east of her village. There was a forest there. Maybe he hoped to find shelter under the trees? She knew trees were dangerous during lightning storms, but maybe they weren't dangerous for him.

Maybe he was as impervious to Zeus's fury as he was to the waves in the sea.

What did he intend with her? Delia's stomach churned, and she knew it was as much from her anxiety as her captor's running speed. The god had said she would be warm and safe, but he was taking her away from her village—away from her family and people who could help her. Delia's sisters had to be worried already. Eugenia, the oldest, had noticed the darkening sky this morning and told her not to go searching for mussels, but Delia had been determined to gather extra food for their dinner tonight. With five daughters to feed, her family was always struggling, and Delia tried to help as much as she could.

Well, as much as she could without marrying the blacksmith, who'd begun courting her after his wife's death last month.

"You should accept Phanias," Delia's mother had told her two weeks ago. "I know you don't like the man, but he's a good provider."

He was also old, fat, and had beaten his last wife, but Delia hadn't bothered pointing that out. Her mother didn't care about such minor things. Her only concern was having enough food on the table, and she believed that Delia—the prettiest of her grown daughters—was the key to achieving that goal. Delia had been trying to delay the inevitable, but she knew it was only a matter of time before her father gave in to her mother's urgings and made Delia accept Phanias's offer.

"Here we are," the god said, startling her out of her thoughts, and Delia saw that they were already at the forest. Stopping under a thick tree, he lowered her to her feet. "We should be far enough from the storm surge now."

He was still holding her, his large hands gripping her waist, and Delia's breathing turned uneven as she tilted her head back to meet his dark gaze. She was one of the tallest women in her village, but the stranger was much taller. With both of them standing, the top of her head only came up to his chin, and his naked body was powerfully muscled.

To her amazement, Delia realized fear wasn't the only thing she was feeling. There was a strange melting sensation in her core, a pooling of heat that made her pulse throb and her insides ache in an odd way.

"Why did you bring me here?" She tried to keep her voice steady as she pushed at his chest again. His flesh was hard under her fingers, his skin smooth and warm to the touch. Even through her soaked dress, she could feel the heat of his palms where he gripped her, and the unfamiliar ache within her intensified. "What do you want from me?"

To her relief, the god released her and stepped back. "Right now, I want us both to get dry and warm." His voice sounded strained, as if he were in pain. Before Delia could wonder about that, her gaze landed on his lower body, and her breath stuttered in shock.

The stranger was fully aroused, his erection hard and massive as it curved up toward his flat, ridged stomach.

Gasping, Delia took a step back, but he was already turning away from her. Extending one powerful arm in front of him, he said something in a foreign language, and she saw that he was wearing a silvery band around his wrist. She opened her mouth to ask him about that, but before she could utter a word, she heard a low humming noise—almost like a buzzing of a thousand tiny insects.

Startled, Delia looked up at the tree, but the buzzing wasn't coming from there. The sound was emanating from somewhere in front of the stranger.

"Don't be afraid," he said, turning to face her again, and her eyes widened as she saw the air behind him begin to shimmer. The shimmer intensified, brightening with each second, and then she saw a transparent bubble rising behind him—a structure that looked like a mushroom cap made out of water.

"It's a tool I have, not magic," he said, watching her, but Delia knew he had to be lying. Her knees began to shake, and she backed away instinctively, afraid the bubble would swallow her as it grew. The wet bark of the tree pressed against her back, stopping her, and she turned to run, determined to get away from the god with such frightening powers.

Before she could take more than two steps, his steely fingers closed around her arm, turning her around. "Don't be afraid," he repeated, holding her, and she saw that the bubble behind him was no longer moving. It was now taller than him and wide enough to fit five people.

"W-what is that?" Her teeth chattered, and she had no idea if it was from shock or the cold rain and wind. "H-how did you—"

"Shh, it's all right. Let's go inside and get you warm." Wrapping one muscular arm around her shoulders, he pulled her against his side and shepherded her toward the magical structure. "It won't hurt you."

Delia tried to dig in her heels, but it was futile. She could no more resist his strength than she could fight a rip current. Within a moment, he had her standing in front of the water-like wall—a part of which disintegrated as they approached, creating a sizable opening.

Delia froze with pure terror, but he was already leading her through the opening. As soon as they stepped inside, she realized there was no more rain or wind.

They were shielded by the bubble the god had created.

CHAPTER FOUR

$\mathcal{T}$he human girl was shaking so hard Arus thought she might pass out. He hated terrifying her like this, but he didn't know any other way to get her out of the storm quickly. Her skin felt chilled as he held her pressed against his side, and he had no doubt the poor thing was cold.

Cold and scared of technology she couldn't possibly understand.

Loosening his grip on her, Arus let her twist out of his embrace. It probably didn't help that he was naked and hard, he thought wryly. He'd heard her gasp when her eyes landed on his erection earlier, and he had no doubt the evidence of his desire added to her nervousness. He had to calm her down, but first, he needed to make sure her health wouldn't suffer from this storm.

His computer was on his left wrist, so Arus lifted his arm and commanded, "Set the temperature to human comfort level."

He spoke in Krinar, and he could see the girl turning pale as the nanomachines went to work again, speeding up the air molecules around them to create warmth. He wished he could explain about force-field technology and microwaves, but her people knew so little about science that it would take him months to teach her just the basics.

"I'm not going to hurt you," he repeated instead, speaking her language. She didn't look the least bit reassured, her eyes wide and panicky as she stared at him, and he realized there was nothing he could say to calm her down.

He'd have to come up with another way to soothe her.

Stepping toward the girl, Arus picked her up and sat down on the ground, holding her on his lap. She stiffened immediately, her hands pushing at him again, but he kept his grip gentle and nonthreatening, hoping she'd settle down when she saw he meant her no harm.

"Everything is fine. You have nothing to fear," he told her softly, stroking her hair as she kept trying to wriggle out of his hold. The feel of her ass moving on his lap was arousing him further, which wasn't helping matters. Thankfully, after a couple of minutes, she seemed to exhaust herself and her struggles eased, letting him settle her more comfortably against him.

"I'm Arus," he said when she stilled completely and stared up at him, her chest heaving with rapid breathing. "What's your name?"

"Ares?" She tensed, her eyes growing wide again. "You're the god of war?"

"No. Ar-us, not Ar-es." He repeated his name slower, letting her hear the difference. "I'm not the god of war, I promise you."

Her slender throat moved as she swallowed. "What kind of god are you, then?"

"I'm not a god," Arus said patiently. "I'm just a visitor from far away. Where I live, everybody can do what I do."

She stared at him, and Arus knew she didn't believe him. Rather than waste energy trying to convince her, he asked again, "What's your name?"

The girl licked her lips in a nervous gesture. "I'm Delia."

"Delia." Good. They were making progress. "Are you from nearby, Delia?"

She nodded, still looking wary. "My village is to the east."

"Right, I thought so." Arus kept his tone casual despite his growing hunger. He couldn't see much of her body under her shapeless dress, but he could feel its soft, slender curves, and his gaze kept drifting down to the throbbing pulse at the base of her throat. Now that they were out of the rain, he could smell her delicate feminine scent, and his mouth watered as he imagined tasting her all over. With effort, he wrenched his thoughts away from sex. "What made you come out in the storm today?" he asked, forcing himself to carry on the conversation that seemed to be calming her.

"I wanted to gather some mussels." The girl—Delia—shifted on his lap, and he knew she had to feel his erection pressing into her ass. It didn't seem to frighten her as much as his technology, and Arus realized he'd done the right thing by using his embrace to calm her. The best way to demonstrate his nonviolent intent was to hold her and let her get used to his touch, so she'd stop fearing it.

So she'd focus on him as a man, rather than a stranger with magical powers.

"Are you hungry?" he asked, resuming stroking her hair. Even damp from the rain, it felt thick and silky to the touch. "Is that why you had to go out in this weather?"

She blinked up at him. "No, I just always gather mussels in the morning. My family needs the extra food."

"I see." He'd already guessed that she was poor. Even by human standards, her roughly made clothes were quite primitive. "So your family sent you out in this weather?"

"No, my sister warned me against going, but I thought the storm wouldn't be this bad."

Of course. Arus had forgotten that her people didn't have a way to track the storm and measure its strength. All they had to go on was the weather at the present moment and whatever experience their elderly had gathered over their short lifespans.

"Well, you're safe now," he told the girl, whose shaking was finally subsiding. Outside, the storm raged on, but inside their shelter, the temperature was comfortably warm. "Nothing can hurt you here."

She looked up at the transparent bubble over their heads, and he realized how odd the force-shield walls had to appear to her. When she met his gaze again, he wasn't the least bit surprised to hear her ask, "What are you? Where do you come from, if not Mount Olympus?"

"I come from another world, a planet similar to this one," Arus said, though he knew the girl wouldn't understand. "It's very far from here."

"Another world?" He felt a tremor go through her. "Like Hades?"

"No, not like Hades." Arus stroked her back in a calming motion. "It's beautiful where I live. Very green and bright."

She gave him a puzzled look. "Why are you here then?"

"Because I wanted to see your planet," Arus said, watching her lips. For some reason, that imperfect, delicate mouth of hers kept drawing his attention. "Your people fascinate me."

"We do?" Her tongue came out to wet her lips, the gesture unconsciously seductive, and Arus felt his hunger intensify. Her body was now soft and pliant as he held her, and there was more curiosity than fear in her brown gaze.

Curiosity and a glimmer of feminine heat.

The realization that she wanted him—and the intoxicating scent of her growing arousal—made his groin tighten. The balmy air inside their shelter suddenly felt steaming hot, and his skin prickled as her hands shifted on his chest, her palms splaying on his skin without any attempt to push him away.

She licked her lips again, her eyes darkening, and Arus could no longer control himself.

Sliding his hand into her hair, he lowered his head and claimed that tempting mouth with a kiss.

CHAPTER FIVE

Caught in the god's powerful embrace, Delia felt like she'd been swept up by the storm. When Arus had first picked her up, she'd been too anxious to focus on his naked body, but as her fear abated, the unfamiliar ache between her thighs returned—and with it, an intense awareness of him as an attractive man.

A man who wanted her, judging by the large erection pressing against her bottom.

Delia was a virgin, but she wasn't ignorant about the mechanics of sex. She'd watched many animals mate, and her mother had told her it was the same for humans. Delia also knew she shouldn't mate with anyone but her husband. It was a rule she had always intended to follow—except it now seemed that her husband was likely to be Phanias. She couldn't imagine so much as kissing the old blacksmith, and the idea of this exotic, powerful stranger taking her virginity was more than a little appealing.

So appealing, in fact, that when Arus lowered his head to kiss her, she pushed her fear of him aside and let herself simply feel.

His lips were surprisingly soft as they touched her own, and his breath was warm and faintly sweet, like he'd recently eaten a piece of fruit. His tongue probed at the seam of her lips, and she parted them instinctively. He immediately took advantage, his tongue sweeping into her mouth as his hand tightened in her hair, and the ache inside her core intensified, transforming into a peculiar pulsing tension. Her breasts felt full and sensitive, her nipples peaking as if from being rubbed, and a liquid warmth gathered between her thighs as he deepened the kiss, all but devouring her with his tongue.

He tasted both sweet and slightly salty, as if some sea water lingered on his lips. Delia's head fell back, giving in to the pressure of his mouth, and she moaned, her hands sliding up to grip his strong shoulders. The heat inside her grew as he shifted underneath her, his arms tightening around her body. His erection was like an iron rod under her bottom, and the knowledge that he desired her so much both thrilled and terrified her.

She'd heard the first time always hurt, and she wasn't looking forward to the pain.

Still, even that worry wasn't enough to cool the fire under her skin. Everything within her craved Arus's touch. The need for him consumed her, making her feel like a stranger in her own body. For the first time, Delia understood why Helen of Troy risked everything for Paris.

If this was passion, no wonder wars were fought over it.

Before Delia had a chance to dwell on that, Arus lowered her to the ground, stretching her out on the still-damp grass.

She managed to tear her mouth away from him long enough to gulp in a much-needed breath, and then he was on top of her, his large body blocking out her view of the storm raging outside. She still didn't understand how a transparent wall could protect them from rain and lightning, but as he resumed kissing her, she lost all inclination to care.

Whatever magic powers the god possessed paled next to the desire he evoked in her.

His hands were now traveling over her body, big, strong, and determined. There was skill and experience in his touch. He didn't grab at her breasts like the boy who'd kissed her when she was sixteen; instead, Arus kneaded her small mounds through her dress, his thumb flicking back and forth over her hardened nipples as he held himself up on his elbows. At the same time, his knee parted her legs, wedging between them, and she felt his thigh press against her sex, putting pressure on a spot that made her feel hot and dizzy. The pulsing ache within her intensified, and she gasped into his mouth, her hands clutching at his sides as the tension in her core coiled tighter and tighter.

"Yes, that's it," he whispered, moving his lips to Delia's ear. "Come for me, darling." His thigh moved rhythmically between her legs, rubbing against her sex through the rough material of her dress, and the tension inside her worsened. She could feel the heat of his breath on her neck, and her heartbeat thundered in her ears, her vision dimming as a throbbing pressure built inside her. It felt like she was dying, like something within her was about to explode. Frightened, she cried out the god's name —and then the explosion was upon her.

Every bit of pressure that built up seemed to release at the same time, sending intense pleasure blasting out from her core.

Her inner muscles spasmed repeatedly, and her toes curled. Gasping, Delia lifted her hips, seeking more of the sensations, but the pleasure was already ebbing, leaving her dazed and breathless.

Before she could understand what had happened, Arus rolled off her, stood up, and pulled her to her feet. She stood, swaying on unsteady legs, as he pulled her dress over her head and dropped it on the ground, leaving her naked—and starkly aware of the large, aroused male standing in front of her.

"Wait," she whispered, but he was already bearing her down to the ground and covering her with his powerful body. There were no barriers between them now, and Delia's earlier fear returned as she felt the insistent hardness of his erection against her leg. Her heartbeat spiking, she wedged her hands between them, her palms pushing at his chest.

"Don't be afraid," he murmured, holding himself up on one elbow. He slid his free hand down her body in a soothing caress, and she saw that his eyes were as dark as a midnight sky, his beautiful features tightly drawn. "I won't hurt you," he promised roughly, spreading her thighs open with his knees.

Delia opened her mouth to tell him she was a virgin, but he was already touching her sex, his fingers unerringly finding the spot that made her so tense before. It was even more sensitive now, and she could feel a strange, warm slickness inside her. Embarrassed, she tried to move away before he could feel her wetness, but his fingers were already there, parting her folds and pushing into her body.

It was just the tips of his two fingers, but Delia flinched away, the stretching sensation both unfamiliar and painful. Instantly, Arus stopped, looking down at her.

"What is it?" He sounded worried.

"I—" Delia felt her face heat up with a flush. "I haven't done this before."

His eyes widened, and for a brief moment, she thought he would release her. However, in the next second, his jaw tightened, and she saw a muscle pulsing near his ear. "Never?" he asked hoarsely, and Delia shook her head, too embarrassed to say it again.

He stared at her, his gaze oddly intent, and she realized that his hand was still on her sex, his fingers poised at the entrance to her body. "So you're all mine." There was a darkly possessive note in his voice. "No man has ever touched you."

Delia bit her lip. "Not—" She gasped as he pushed one finger into her. "Not like this."

His nostrils flared, and then he was kissing her again, his mouth consuming her with savage hunger as his finger pressed deeper into her. The sensation was foreign, but not painful, and the now-familiar tension returned as his thumb found the sensitive spot from before. The slickness inside her eased the path for his finger, and after a moment, Delia forgot all about her initial discomfort, her hips rocking to the movements of his hand.

Maybe she got lucky, and her first time wouldn't hurt at all.

CHAPTER SIX

*D*elia's pussy was so tight around his finger Arus knew he was going to end up hurting her. The only way to avoid that would be to stop and leave her alone, but that was beyond his capabilities. The lust riding him was dark and visceral, more potent than anything he'd ever experienced.

He wanted to possess this human girl, to claim her in every way possible.

The primitive desire stunned him, but he couldn't analyze it at the moment. His skin was burning, and his cock was so hard it hurt. He needed to be inside her, to feel her tight, wet flesh rippling around him. Her mouth was warm and sweet as he devoured her with his kiss, and the scent of her drove him insane.

He had to fuck her. Now.

Calling on every bit of his remaining self-control, Arus used his thumb to bring her to another orgasm, wanting her to be as wet and ready as possible. She cried out, her inner muscles contracting around his finger, and he used the opportunity to press a second finger into her narrow channel, preparing her for his possession. She stiffened under him, flinching despite her wetness, and he knew there was no way to avoid causing her some pain.

Raising his head, he pulled his hand away, grabbed his cock, and aligned it with her pussy. "I'm sorry," he whispered, catching her pleasure-dazed gaze, and before she could respond, he began to push in.

Delia cried out, pushing at his chest, but Arus persisted, knowing he had to breach her hymen. Her inner moisture helped, but she was still incredibly tight, her body tensing to resist his penetration. He lowered his head, raining kisses over her face and whispering that it was going to be all right, that the pain would ease soon, but he could see his reassurances weren't helping. She let out a pained cry as he pressed deeper, and despite his balls getting ready to explode, he paused as he felt the wetness on her cheeks.

He wanted her, but he hated causing her pain.

"Do you want me to stop?" he forced himself to ask, even though everything within him rebelled at the notion. His cock was only halfway inside her, and if he was already hurting her this much . . .

Delia stilled, staring up at him with tear-filled brown eyes, and he saw that she was breathing erratically, her chest heaving as her delicate hands pressed against his chest, as if trying to hold him at bay.

"Do you want me to stop?" Arus repeated, ignoring the pounding of blood in his temples. Despite the primal need gnawing at his insides, he was not a savage. He'd lived over two hundred years without fucking this girl, and he could survive it if she made him wait.

He hoped so, at least.

To his tremendous relief, she moved her head in a small, uncertain shake. "No," she whispered, blinking rapidly. "It just—"

Arus didn't have a chance to hear what she had to say because the last remaining thread of his restraint snapped. Leaning down, he took her lips in a deep, carnal kiss and pushed forward in one merciless stroke, tearing through the thin membrane blocking his way.

Tight, wet heat engulfed him, her flesh squeezing him like a fist, and Arus's spine bowed as sharp, stunning pleasure rocketed through him, sending his heartbeat spiking. She was beyond delicious, beyond perfect. It was as if her slim body had been made just for him. He felt lost in her, consumed by the sensations, but before he could get completely carried away, he tasted something salty on his lips.

Her tears.

They stopped him cold.

Raising his head to gaze down at her, Arus forced himself to hold still and not thrust. She was shaking, her face streaked with tears, and he knew he had to give her time to get used to him, to adjust to the invasion of her body. He managed to control himself for a few brief moments—and then the metallic scent of her virgin's blood reached his nostrils.

A dark, ancient hunger roared to life within him, mingling with his lust and intensifying it. The pull of predatory instinct was impossible to resist. Groaning, Arus lowered his face to her neck and felt her pulse beating under his lips. Delia was breathing fast, still trying to cope with the pain of her lost virginity, but her body was no longer the only thing Arus needed.

Opening his mouth, he sliced the sharp edges of his teeth across her tender skin.

Her blood spurted onto his tongue. Hot, rich, and coppery, it was an aphrodisiac a thousand times stronger than the synthetic versions on Krina. Genetic modification had ensured his people were no longer reliant on blood to survive, but the craving for the resulting high had never gone away. Arus could hear Delia crying out, feel her nails digging into his skin, and he realized distantly that the pacifying chemical in his saliva was working on her—that she was feeling some of the mind-bending pleasure that held him in its grip.

That was his last coherent thought. Everything afterwards was a blur of violent ecstasy, of her taste and scent and feel. Arus took the girl relentlessly, without restraint, and she met his savage thrusts with equal hunger, her slender limbs wrapped around him as he fucked her for hours on end. The bliss rushing through his veins left him unable to think or reason; all he knew was that he had to have her, over and over again.

When he finally rolled off her limp body, spent and sated, the sky above their shelter was dark and clear. He could see the stars, and he knew the storm had passed.

It was safe to let her go now, except he didn't want to.

Arus wanted to keep Delia for the rest of his life.

CHAPTER SEVEN

*D*elia woke up gradually, the images from her dream lingering in her mind as she slowly returned to consciousness. Her eyes still closed, she smiled, thinking how she'd never had such a sublime dream before. Even now, her sex throbbed pleasantly from the memory of the god's possession— of his powerful body driving into her as she lost herself in the heated rapture of his embrace.

There had been pain too, she recalled, but it had been over with quickly. She'd felt torn in half when Arus had first entered her, but then he had done something—touched her neck in a way that had initially stung—and the pain had dissolved, replaced by unimaginable ecstasy.

By a sexual pleasure so intense just the thought of it made her insides clench.

Still smiling, Delia rolled over, reluctant to wake up fully. It was incredible how vivid her dream had been. The storm, the bubble-like shelter made of transparent walls, even the god's unusual name—she'd never been able to remember so many details from her other dreams.

This dream had felt real. So real, in fact, that she could still smell the clean male scent of Arus's skin and feel his hand stroking her hair.

Wait a minute. There *was* a hand stroking her hair.

Delia bolted upright, her eyes flying open, and she saw him: the god she'd just been dreaming about.

Except it hadn't been a dream—it couldn't have been, because she wasn't in her family's ramshackle hut.

She was on a strange bed in a room with ivory walls, and she was naked in front of Arus, who was sitting next to her dressed in an odd-looking white outfit.

Gasping, Delia grabbed for the nearest piece of cloth—a sheet that felt incredibly soft as she wrapped it around herself. Her heart racing, she jumped off the bed and gaped at the god, who was regarding her with an unreadable expression on his beautiful face.

"Where am I?" Delia's voice shook as she cast a frantic glance around the room. "What is this place?"

Everything around her was ivory-colored, and there were no windows or doors. And the bed— No, surely her eyes were deceiving her.

The bed, which was just a flat white board, was floating in mid-air.

"You're on my ship," Arus said, getting off the board to walk toward her. His dark eyes gleamed as he stopped in front of her, causing her to crane her neck to look up at him. "I brought you here so I could make sure you weren't sore after last night."

Delia must've looked as uncomprehending as she felt, because he explained, "We have healing technology here."

"Oh." Overwhelmed, Delia stared up at him. Now that he'd pointed it out, she realized there wasn't even the slightest soreness between her legs. Details from last night continued to return to her, and she remembered how painful the initial breaching of her maidenhead had been—and how he'd kept thrusting into her afterwards for what must've been hours.

By all rights, she should've been *very* sore.

"You healed me?"

"I did." Raising his hand, Arus cupped her jaw with his large palm, his thumb stroking gently over her cheek. "I didn't want you to be in pain."

"Oh." Delia exhaled, everything inside her reacting to that warm, comforting touch. She didn't know what to do, how to respond to his peculiar kindness, so finally she just said, "Thank you."

Arus's chiseled lips curved in a smile. "You're welcome, darling. Now, are you hungry?"

Delia's stomach chose that moment to rumble, and he laughed. "Sounds like you are."

———

He fed her food that tasted like ambrosia—a mixture of some unfamiliar fruits, vegetables, and nuts, with a sauce that made Delia's taste buds weep with pleasure. He got the food directly from one of the walls. It had parted at his command, delivering the bounty they were feasting on while sitting at a floating table —which had also come out of a wall.

"What kind of ship is this?" Delia asked when she was full. She didn't understand Arus's magic, but it didn't terrify her quite as much anymore. It was clear to her that he didn't intend her any harm—and that he had to have come from Mount Olympus, despite his earlier protestations.

"It's a ship that carries us between distant worlds," Arus said, and his answer solidified her conviction. "The stars you see are not just little lights in the sky; they're suns, like the one giving Earth heat and light. Those suns have planets like Earth orbiting around them, and I come from one of those planets." He paused, waiting for her questions, but Delia had no idea where to begin.

All she got from his explanation was that his ship had carried him here from the stars—which meant that Mount Olympus was a place in the sky, rather than the mountain of legend.

Arus sighed, looking at her. "You don't understand, do you?" A rueful smile tugged at the corner of his beautiful mouth. "I guess I should've expected that. I wish I could convince you that none of this is supernatural, that we're just a more advanced civilization, but you'd have to learn a great deal before that would make sense to you. So for now, if it helps you to think of me as a god, you may do so."

Delia smiled, oddly reassured by his words. "You *are* a god. What else could you possibly be?"

"I'm a Krinar," he said, and she saw his face assume a more serious expression. "Delia," he said quietly, "there's something I'd like to ask you."

She blinked. "What is it?"

"I have to leave soon. To go home to Krina."

Her chest squeezed painfully at his words. "Of course," she managed to say. "You said it's beautiful there, and you have to return."

Arus nodded. "I do—and I would like you to come with me."

Before she could do more than gape at him, he said, "I know I'm still a stranger to you, and that everything about this"—he swept his hand out in a wide arc—"must seem foreign and frightening. But I promise I won't hurt you, and I'll take care of you. You'll be safe with me."

Delia couldn't believe her ears. "You want me to come with you? To the world where you live?"

"Yes, to Krina—or Mount Olympus, or whatever you want to call it." Arus reached across the floating table and took her hand. "It *is* a beautiful place, and if you come with me, I can promise you a life beyond anything you can imagine."

Delia had to be still dreaming. "Why?" she said in disbelief. "Why would you take me with you?"

Arus rose to his feet and pulled her up with him, his gaze filling with carnal heat as he stepped around the table. "Because our time together wasn't nearly enough for me," he said, drawing her against his hard, aroused body. "Because I had you, and I want more—so much more. I want you to be mine, so I can have you every day and every night for a long, long time."

Delia's pulse was rabbit fast, and a million questions crowded her mind as Arus gazed down at her, his erection pushing against her belly. His blunt declaration was far from tender words of love, and there were so many things she didn't know about him and the world he wanted to take her to. But he was giving her a choice, and that fact alone helped quell her fear.

She could stay and live an ordinary life—most likely as the blacksmith's wife—or she could follow this gorgeous stranger to a mysterious place in the sky.

"What about my family?" she asked as the thought occurred to her. "They need the mussels and I—"

"I'll leave them your weight in gold before we go," Arus said. "They won't lack for anything ever again."

"But—"

"Come with me, Delia." Arus's eyes glittered as his arms tightened around her back. "Your family will be fine, I promise. Come with me, and let me show you the wonders of my world."

She stared at his magnificent features, remembering how he'd saved her from the storm—how he'd sheltered her, fed her, healed her, and given her more pleasure than she'd ever thought possible. He was right: her family would be fine without her—better off, in fact. Even without the gold, she was an extra mouth to feed. And if Arus truly gave them that much wealth, her sisters would have their pick of suitors instead of being forced to marry out of desperation.

It was that last thought that solidified her decision. Delia had no idea what would happen to her if she came with him, what his world was like or how they could travel to the stars, but at that moment, caught in her god's embrace, she knew she wanted to find out.

It was unthinkable, insane, deliriously frightening, but Delia took a leap into the unknown and said, "Yes, Arus. I'll come with you."

SNEAK PEEKS

Thank you for reading these Krinar stories! We hope you enjoyed all three romances and would consider leaving a review.

Want to read more sizzling hot romance? Check out **Just Like Animals**, a steamy standalone in Hettie Ivers's *Werelock Evolution* series, and **Mia & Korum,** Anna Zaires's Krinar trilogy that started it all. To be notified of new releases, sign up for our newsletters at hettieivers.com and annazaires.com!

Want more Krinar hotness? Check out **The Krinar World stories**, Krinar romances written by other amazing authors.

Love the dark side of romance? Grab these twisted sizzlers by Anna Zaires:

- *The Twist Me Trilogy* – an epic kidnapping romance featuring Nora & Julian
- *The Capture Me Trilogy* – Lucas & Yulia's enemies-to-lovers captive romance
- *Tormentor Mine* – Peter & Sara's tale of love, obsession, and revenge

Prefer action and sci-fi? Grab these collaborations with Dima Zales, Anna's hubby:

- *The Girl Who Sees* – the thrilling tale of Sasha Urban, a stage illusionist who discovers unexpected secret powers
- *Mind Dimensions* – the action-packed urban fantasy adventures of Darren, who can stop time and read minds
- *Upgrade* – the mind-blowing technothriller featuring venture capitalist Mike Cohen, whose Brainocyte technology will forever change the world
- *The Last Humans* – the futuristic sci-fi/dystopian story of Theo, who lives in a world where nothing is as it seems
- *The Sorcery Code* – the epic fantasy adventures of sorcerer Blaise and his creation, the beautiful and powerful Gala

Love audiobooks? All Anna Zaires and Dima Zales titles are in audio. Visit annazaires.com to learn more!

And now please turn the page for a little taste of Anna Zaires's *Close Liaisons* and *Twist Me.*

EXCERPT FROM CLOSE LIAISONS

Author's Note: *Close Liaisons* is the first book in the Krinar Chronicles trilogy. All three books are now available.

———

A dark and edgy romance that will appeal to fans of erotic and turbulent relationships...

In the near future, the Krinar rule the Earth. An advanced race from another galaxy, they are still a mystery to us—and we are completely at their mercy.

Shy and innocent, Mia Stalis is a college student in New York City who has led a very normal life. Like most people, she's never had any interactions with the invaders—until one fateful day in the park changes everything. Having caught Korum's eye, she must now contend with a powerful, dangerously seductive Krinar who wants to possess her and will stop at nothing to make her his own.

How far would you go to regain your freedom? How much would you sacrifice to help your people? What choice will you make when you begin to fall for your enemy?

————

Breathe, Mia, breathe. Somewhere in the back of her mind, a small rational voice kept repeating those words. That same oddly objective part of her noted his symmetric face structure, with golden skin stretched tightly over high cheekbones and a firm jaw. Pictures and videos of Ks that she'd seen had hardly done them justice. Standing no more than thirty feet away, the creature was simply stunning.

As she continued staring at him, still frozen in place, he straightened and began walking toward her. Or rather stalking toward her, she thought stupidly, as his every movement reminded her of a jungle cat sinuously approaching a gazelle. All the while, his eyes never left hers. As he approached, she could make out individual yellow flecks in his light golden eyes and the thick long lashes surrounding them.

She watched in horrified disbelief as he sat down on her bench, less than two feet away from her, and smiled, showing white even teeth. No fangs, she noted with some functioning part of her brain. Not even a hint of them. That used to be another myth about them, like their supposed abhorrence of the sun.

"What's your name?" The creature practically purred the question at her. His voice was low and smooth, completely unaccented. His nostrils flared slightly, as though inhaling her scent.

"Um..." Mia swallowed nervously. "M-Mia."

"Mia," he repeated slowly, seemingly savoring her name. "Mia what?"

"Mia Stalis." Oh crap, why did he want to know her name? Why was he here, talking to her? In general, what was he doing in Central Park, so far away from any of the K Centers? *Breathe, Mia, breathe.*

"Relax, Mia Stalis." His smile got wider, exposing a dimple in his left cheek. A dimple? Ks had dimples? "Have you never encountered one of us before?"

"No, I haven't," Mia exhaled sharply, realizing that she was holding her breath. She was proud that her voice didn't sound as shaky as she felt. Should she ask? Did she want to know?

She gathered her courage. "What, um—" Another swallow. "What do you want from me?"

"For now, conversation." He looked like he was about to laugh at her, those gold eyes crinkling slightly at the corners.

Strangely, that pissed her off enough to take the edge off her fear. If there was anything Mia hated, it was being laughed at. With her short, skinny stature and a general lack of social skills that came from an awkward teenage phase involving every girl's nightmare of braces, frizzy hair, and glasses, Mia had more than enough experience being the butt of someone's joke.

She lifted her chin belligerently. "Okay, then, what is *your* name?"

"It's Korum."

"Just Korum?"

"We don't really have last names, not the way you do. My

full name is much longer, but you wouldn't be able to pronounce it if I told you."

Okay, that was interesting. She now remembered reading something like that in *The New York Times*. So far, so good. Her legs had nearly stopped shaking, and her breathing was returning to normal. Maybe, just maybe, she would get out of this alive. This conversation business seemed safe enough, although the way he kept staring at her with those unblinking yellowish eyes was unnerving. She decided to keep him talking.

"What are you doing here, Korum?"

"I just told you, making conversation with you, Mia." His voice again held a hint of laughter.

Frustrated, Mia blew out her breath. "I meant, what are you doing here in Central Park? In New York City in general?"

He smiled again, cocking his head slightly to the side. "Maybe I'm hoping to meet a pretty curly-haired girl."

Okay, enough was enough. He was clearly toying with her. Now that she could think a little again, she realized that they were in the middle of Central Park, in full view of about a gazillion spectators. She surreptitiously glanced around to confirm that. Yep, sure enough, although people were obviously steering clear of her bench and its otherworldly occupant, there were a number of brave souls staring their way from farther up the path. A couple were even cautiously filming them with their wristwatch cameras. If the K tried anything with her, it would be on YouTube in the blink of an eye, and he had to know it. Of course, he may or may not care about that.

Still, going on the assumption that since she'd never come across any videos of K assaults on college students in the middle of Central Park, she was relatively safe, Mia cautiously reached for her laptop and lifted it to stuff it back into her backpack.

"Let me help you with that, Mia—"

And before she could blink, she felt him take her heavy laptop from her suddenly boneless fingers, gently brushing against her knuckles in the process. A sensation similar to a mild electric shock shot through Mia at his touch, leaving her nerve endings tingling in its wake.

Reaching for her backpack, he carefully put away the laptop in a smooth, sinuous motion. "There you go, all better now."

Oh God, he had touched her. Maybe her theory about the safety of public locations was bogus. She felt her breathing speeding up again, and her heart rate was probably well into the anaerobic zone at this point.

"I have to go now... Bye!"

How she managed to squeeze out those words without hyperventilating, she would never know. Grabbing the strap of the backpack he'd just put down, she jumped to her feet, noting somewhere in the back of her mind that her earlier paralysis seemed to be gone.

"Bye, Mia. I will see you later." His softly mocking voice carried in the clear spring air as she took off, nearly running in her haste to get away.

————

All three books in the Krinar Chronicles trilogy are now available. Visit annazaires.com/book/mia-korum/ to get your copy. If you'd like to find out more, please visit my website at www.annazaires.com.

EXCERPT FROM TWIST ME

Author's Note: *Twist Me* is a dark erotic trilogy about Nora and Julian Esguerra. All three books are now available.

————

Kidnapped. Taken to a private island.

I never thought this could happen to me. I never imagined one chance meeting on the eve of my eighteenth birthday could change my life so completely.

Now I belong to him. To Julian. To a man who is as ruthless as he is beautiful—a man whose touch makes me burn. A man whose tenderness I find more devastating than his cruelty.

My captor is an enigma. I don't know who he is or why he took me. There is a darkness inside him—a darkness that scares me even as it draws me in.

My name is Nora Leston, and this is my story.

———————

It's evening now. With every minute that passes, I'm starting to get more and more anxious at the thought of seeing my captor again.

The novel that I've been reading can no longer hold my interest. I put it down and walk in circles around the room.

I am dressed in the clothes Beth had given me earlier. It's not what I would've chosen to wear, but it's better than a bathrobe. A sexy pair of white lacy panties and a matching bra for underwear. A pretty blue sundress that buttons in the front. Everything fits me suspiciously well. Has he been stalking me for a while? Learning everything about me, including my clothing size?

The thought makes me sick.

I am trying not to think about what's to come, but it's impossible. I don't know why I'm so sure he'll come to me tonight. It's possible he has an entire harem of women stashed away on this island, and he visits each one only once a week, like sultans used to do.

Yet somehow I know he'll be here soon. Last night had simply whetted his appetite. I know he's not done with me, not by a long shot.

Finally, the door opens.

He walks in like he owns the place. Which, of course, he does.

I am again struck by his masculine beauty. He could've been a model or a movie star, with a face like his. If there was any fairness in the world, he would've been short or had some other imperfection to offset that face.

But he doesn't. His body is tall and muscular, perfectly proportioned. I remember what it feels like to have him inside me, and I feel an unwelcome jolt of arousal.

He's again wearing jeans and a T-shirt. A gray one this time. He seems to favor simple clothing, and he's smart to do so. His looks don't need any enhancement.

He smiles at me. It's his fallen angel smile—dark and seductive at the same time. "Hello, Nora."

I don't know what to say to him, so I blurt out the first thing that pops into my head. "How long are you going to keep me here?"

He cocks his head slightly to the side. "Here in the room? Or on the island?"

"Both."

"Beth will show you around tomorrow, take you swimming if you'd like," he says, approaching me. "You won't be locked in, unless you do something foolish."

"Such as?" I ask, my heart pounding in my chest as he stops next to me and lifts his hand to stroke my hair.

"Trying to harm Beth or yourself." His voice is soft, his gaze hypnotic as he looks down at me. The way he's touching my hair is oddly relaxing.

I blink, trying to break his spell. "And what about on the island? How long will you keep me here?"

His hand caresses my face, curves around my cheek. I catch myself leaning into his touch, like a cat getting petted, and I immediately stiffen.

His lips curl into a knowing smile. The bastard knows the effect he has on me. "A long time, I hope," he says.

For some reason, I'm not surprised. He wouldn't have bothered bringing me all the way here if he just wanted to fuck me a few times. I'm terrified, but I'm not surprised.

I gather my courage and ask the next logical question. "Why did you kidnap me?"

The smile leaves his face. He doesn't answer, just looks at me with an inscrutable blue gaze.

I begin to shake. "Are you going to kill me?"

"No, Nora, I won't kill you."

His denial reassures me, although he could obviously be lying.

"Are you going to sell me?" I can barely get the words out. "Like to be a prostitute or something?"

"No," he says softly. "Never. You're mine and mine alone."

I feel a tiny bit calmer, but there is one more thing I have to know. "Are you going to hurt me?"

For a moment, he doesn't answer again. Something dark briefly flashes in his eyes. "Probably," he says quietly.

And then he leans down and kisses me, his warm lips soft and gentle on mine.

For a second, I stand there frozen, unresponsive. I believe him. I know he's telling the truth when he says he'll hurt me. There's something in him that scares me—that has scared me from the very beginning.

He's nothing like the boys I've gone on dates with. He's capable of anything.

And I'm completely at his mercy.

I think about trying to fight him again. That would be the normal thing to do in my situation. The brave thing to do.

And yet I don't do it.

I can feel the darkness inside him. There's something wrong with him. His outer beauty hides something monstrous underneath.

I don't want to unleash that darkness. I don't know what will happen if I do.

So I stand still in his embrace and let him kiss me. And when he picks me up again and takes me to bed, I don't try to resist in any way.

Instead, I close my eyes and give in to the sensations.

———

All three books in the *Twist Me* trilogy are now available at annazaires.com/book-series/twist-me/. Please visit my website at www.annazaires.com to learn more and to sign up for my new release email list.

ABOUT THE AUTHOR

Anna Zaires is a *New York Times, USA Today,* and #1 international bestselling author of sci-fi romance and contemporary dark erotic romance. She fell in love with books at the age of five, when her grandmother taught her to read. Since then, she has always lived partially in a fantasy world where the only limits were those of her imagination. Currently residing in Florida, Anna is happily married to Dima Zales (a science fiction and fantasy author) and closely collaborates with him on all their works.

To learn more, please visit www.annazaires.com.

Printed in Great Britain
by Amazon

25728561R00334